**Linda Grant** was born in Liverpool and now lives in London. *The Cast Iron Shore* won the David Higham First Novel Prize. *When I Lived in Modern Times* won the Orange Prize for Fiction. *Still Here* was longlisted for the Man Booker Prize. Linda Grant is also the author of *Sexing the Millennium*; *Remind Me Who I am Again*; *The People on the Street*, which won the Lettre Ulysses Prize for Literary Reportage; and *The Thoughtful Dresser*. Her most recent novel, *The Clothes on Their Backs*, won *The South Bank Show* Literature Award and was shortlisted for the Man Booker Prize 2008.

'A fascinating and poignant Chinese box of a novel, in which places and times hold each other's secrets, nothing stays still, and even the most important moments appear transitory. Linda Grant uncovers the tragedy inherent in chronology itself, and thus demonstrates, as only a novelist can, the treacherous falsity of dreams and ideology. This is a work of great tenderness and regret' Howard Jacobson, author of the Man Booker winner *The Finkler Question*

'As well as being a vivid pageant of late twentieth-century southern English life as seen by an outsider, Stephen's story is a careful study of transformation . . . *We Had It So Good* is a gripping family saga, stylishly told . . . Grant [writes] with her usual insight and subtlety and comes close to creating the perfect novel: one that never stops working to fill the reader's mind with good and difficult things, and which takes you to beautiful and often frightening places' Melissa Katsoulis, *The Times*

'Grant is a lucid, stimulating writer and this is a deep reflection on the life span of the baby boomer . . . Grant really is gifted: her ‹ t, sensible and constantly thought-‹ *y Times*

'Grant's best novel so far . . . This is a serious and thoughtful novel that asks questions Grant has asked before, but does so in a way that perfectly matches form and content. That perfect match doesn't make for an easeful or complacent work; on the contrary, it shows depth and feeling that both disturb and reassure' Lesley McDowell, *Financial Times*

'The material is handled with tremendous brio, wit, warmth and sympathy. It is a book you'll live in – and linger over its beautiful ending with a tear in your eye' A. N. Wilson, *Reader's Digest*

'Grant writes with pose and wisdom about human frailty' Catherine Humble, *Daily Telegraph*

'Linda Grant writes beautifully and depicts perfectly how we struggle to come to terms with the mediocrity of our lives as age takes the gloss off our impossibly rose-coloured dreams' Angela McGee, *Sunday Express*

'Grant's vivid narration sets us right inside the minds of her characters . . . Grant is building up an important fictional oeuvre that offers a fresh and perceptive commentary on our times' Rachel Hore, *Independent on Sunday*

'A carefully written, perceptive tale that takes in how we live in our own times, and how we adapt as they change around us' Clare Longrigg, *Psychologies*

'A rich and many-layered novel . . . Grant is never afraid to confront big ideas in her books, and this is no exception . . . skilful . . . That Grant can so vividly encapsulate the lives and times of her characters in less than 350 pages is testimony to her skill as a writer and perceptive observer of human behaviour . . . Above all *We Had It So Good* is a portrait of a marriage and a family, and the compromises and bittersweet truths that come with age' Catherine Heaney, *Irish Times*

# WE HAD IT
# SO GOOD

ALSO BY LINDA GRANT

*Fiction*
The Cast Iron Shore
When I Lived in Modern Times
Still Here
The Clothes on Their Backs

*Non-fiction*
Sexing the Millennium: A Political History
of the Sexual Revolution
Remind Me Who I Am, Again
The People on the Street: A Writer's View of Israel
The Thoughtful Dresser

# WE HAD IT SO GOOD

# LINDA GRANT

virago

VIRAGO

First published in Great Britain in 2011 by Virago Press
This paperback edition published in 2012 by Virago Press
Reprinted 2012

A CIP catalogue record for this book
is available from the British Library.

ISBN 978-1-84408-639-9

Typeset in Goudy by M Rules
Printed and bound in Great Britain by
Clays Ltd, St Ives plc

Papers used by Virago are from well-managed forests
and other responsible sources.

MIX
Paper from
responsible sources
FSC
www.fsc.org  FSC® C104740

Virago Press
An imprint of
Little, Brown Book Group
100 Victoria Embankment
London EC4Y 0DY

An Hachette UK Company
www.hachette.co.uk

www.virago.co.uk

To Nigel Pike

'He had like many another been born in full sunlight and lived to see night fall.'

Evelyn Waugh, *Men at Arms*

# Sunshine

Aged nine, Stephen standing outside the fur-storage depot where his father works, his sturdy legs in shorts planted on Californian ground. Feet wide apart, shoulders up, arms behind his back, his neck sticking out from the collar of a checked shirt to which a narrow bow-tie has been clipped, and his round Charlie Brown head dusted with the dark shadow of a crew-cut. All-American boy.

'That day,' he told his children, 'was the most exciting day of my life. That's when I put on Marilyn Monroe's fur stole. And got thumped on the head by my old man when he saw what I was doing.'

The cold-storage warehouse took care of the fur coats of the movie stars. Stephen struggled to express memories he could find no words for, of walking along the lines of minks and sables, ocelots and ermines, allowed to carefully stroke their satin pelts, insert his own small arm into their dangling sleeves and feel the silken linings. His scrubbed hand was permitted briefly to enter the great surprise of a velvet pocket.

'This coat belongs to Miss Bacall,' his father told him, in his immigrant accent, 'this one to Miss Hayworth. The animal was a living thing, a beautiful creature that once was. And only a beautiful woman deserves to wear a coat like this.'

If Marianne and her brother Max, even as children, cynically thought the world of their forefathers was unreal, made up by their father as a bedtime story, Stephen in his time had been far more credulous. For years he had believed that his father was on actual speaking terms with film stars, that he went to work every day with Deborah Kerr and Audrey Hepburn and Ava Gardner. Only after he made the momentous first visit to the cold-storage company, driving home with his father through Los Angeles suburbs, did he learn that the actresses never called to pick up or deposit their own furs: they had assistants to bring in the coats, the heat of the stars' bodies still trapped in the linings, redolent of their sweat and perfume, the Joy, the No. 5, L'Heure Bleu.

The brutal heavy-set warehousemen regarded the coats as skin, animal pelts, weighty objects to be moved about in freezing conditions. They were all short, tough types, with large forearms and thinning hair. It was a shock, after the feminine world of home, his mother, his two sisters – their hairspray hanging in the air long after they had stood up from the mirror, and face powder leaving scented trails scattered through the house; motes of lily-of-the-valley and lilac whitened the rugs.

Inside the warehouse Stephen listened to his father's explanations about why a fur needed to be kept under special conditions. The cool air and the darkness stopped the skins drying out, the hairs discolouring and held back the infestation of insects, which could eat away at the garment. The duties of the employees included not just hanging the coats but ensuring that they were not too close together, to prevent crushing. There was regular spraying of the unit with strong chemicals to control pests and rodents. Under no circumstances was a fur to be stored in a plastic bag, which could build up humidity and mould. The sight of a plastic bag in a cold-storage facility was the way, he said, you could detect an outfit run by a crook.

After the lecture, Stephen ran down the racks of furs which hung like heavy headless bodies in the darkness. Doubling back, he came to a rail of stoles that had just arrived for treatment and storage. His father was on the other side of the room smoking the stump of a cigar, his knee raised, his foot resting on a wooden crate, a small, skinny man – with the endurance, his wife said, of an ox – who arrived in America all by himself aged twelve and who barely grew afterwards, as if the soil of home in Europe had given him all the nutrients he needed. She was a head taller than him in her nylons, and her hair rose even higher, blue-black and held up with a butterfly comb.

The garment that lay draped around the hanger was slipping off, and before it reached the floor Stephen raised his arms to catch it. The fur body fell, weirdly, he thought, both heavy and light, and with a fragrance of hot pearls. The hairs brushed his face and tickled him. 'I had to try that thing on,' he told his children. 'I don't know what came over me, but you know all kids love fancy dress and maybe it was just Hallowe'en come early.'

The weight of the pale mink bore down on his thin arms. He came walking out towards a mirror so he could see what kind of being he had been transformed into.

His father turned and saw his only son draped and twirling on his toes in Marilyn Monroe's champagne-mink stole. Stephen thought he was taking the opportunity to try out transformation. He was exercising his birthright, the American capacity to be reborn.

A hard whack came from behind and he heard his father utter imprecations in his native language, in which there were few vowels and many syllables that seemed to get stuck in the speaker's throat, choking him.

*

At home, he was a momma's boy. He watched his mother take a series of unconnected items from various storage places in the kitchen and, by magic, turn flour, sugar, water, butter into a cake, which contained elements of all of them but, through an alchemical process, now resembled something completely different. He would climb onto a high stool and explore inside the recesses of the cupboards, finding bitter black baking chocolate, boxes of dry graham crackers, tiny glass bottles of vanilla essence. Alone, all these things were disgusting; in his mother's marvellous hands, bound together by strong voodoo, they turned into delicious treats. His older sisters did not care for desserts. They wore too much makeup and were rumoured to lead a wild life on the periphery of the neighbourhood.

In the kitchen Stephen failed to develop an interest in baking, as his father had feared – now the butt of daily jokes about his sissy boy, the *feygele*. Instead, baking had ignited a curiosity about the inner mysteries of the ingredients themselves, their hidden lives. One night Stephen's father brought home a child's chemistry set for him. Working late in his bedroom (the only member of his family not to have to share a room, the privileged little prince), he completed every experiment by two a.m., and awoke the next morning parched for more knowledge. At school he learned about chemical compounds and molecules. The very air you breathed consisted of oxygen, and when you combined it with a couple of measures of hydrogen, it was water. Things changed their forms because of events invisible to the naked eye, as if God was in the kitchen, with his crazy wooden spoon. The universe was spinning and expanding; great gaseous clouds were worlds. Years later he would be moved to sudden tears, sitting in the college library, by the beauty of physics, which was not even his major. He sensed the divine. God was in the sub-particle.

Observing his son propel his way through high school, like one of the rockets that the space programme was shooting up in the direction of the moon, with the best grades in chemistry, biology, physics and math, his father wondered from which side of the family the brains had come. He had had a grandfather back home who, by all accounts, had been a learned man, a bearded wonder, but he only remembered his herring breath. His wife was singular for her beauty, not her thoughts. Where did this amazing mind come from?

Yet he distrusted intellectuals. Si Newman still thought like a manual worker, moved by the herd mentality of the crowd. His son could not hammer a nail straight, or take apart and put back together a small appliance. He was skinny like his father, taller but weak, without the upper-body strength that the old man believed was crucial for personal survival. What maketh a man? Biceps, triceps and pectoral muscles. He didn't know, or could never remember, these doctors' terms but he felt them under his flaking skin. Strong quads were also helpful. Furs could weigh as much as lumber. Sealskin: that was a very heavy pelt, thankfully now out of fashion.

He badly wanted to have a son with a college education, the mark of tremendous respect, but he did not understand how a sissy could survive in America. You saw the film stars, the actors, in their beautiful suits and handmade shoes but they were a little class of tinpot gods. Some element of masculinity was missing in them (apart from John Wayne). Women couldn't see it – they responded to their sex appeal, but sex appeal wasn't everything.

Stephen's father believed his son needed basic survival instincts. Some things operated as a dark shadow in the recesses of his mind, primeval hunches. The weak, he believed, were prey for the carrion eaters. His own parents, he said, had been turned back from Ellis Island, diseased with tuberculosis, the chalk cross on their backs crucifying them. Simon Newman had refused to get back on board the ship; he would make his own way in life, and he had done so. He never saw his mother and father again, or spoke of them. Stephen grew up knowing all of this. He had not been protected from the terrible past, but the point, he learned, was that it *was* the past. He was in America now and, unlike either of his parents, American-born.

It was, his father told him, a different country in those days. Si had been found on the street and taken in by a childless couple and things generally went on from there. He had perfected the orphan shtick, moving from comfortable home to comfortable home, taking what he wanted, travelling like a hobo across the country until he arrived in Los Angeles and there was nowhere further to go. Stephen was in awe of his father.

They lived on the rim of the Pacific Ocean, which curled around half the globe, an unending potential for self-sufficiency in the face of hostile nature. The more Si considered its vast wetness, the more he saw it was the solution, the way to make a man of his son: the sea!

'You want me to go to *sea*?' said Stephen, stunned.

The ocean was a familiar quantity. You drove to the beach with your mother and father on holiday weekends and there it was, cold, wet, semi-dangerous. You unwrapped beach food and ate, and after a couple of hours of mandatory rest, during which your mother and sisters read a movie magazine and your father brooded silently on the horizon, his white legs sticking out of polka-dot navy blue shorts, you were permitted to splash around in the waves.

But his mother had a cousin in the maritime union, down in San Diego. This side of the family were the Cubans. The men wore gold signet rings and combed their hair back in oiled quiffs, like Elvis; the women all wore shoes with unfeasibly high heels and showed off a red-lacquered big toe.

'But I want to go to college and study chemistry,' said Stephen.

'So who says you can't do both?'

With a maritime-union ticket in his wallet, he shipped out every summer from the age of seventeen, starting out on the West Coast, making cruise-ship runs to Hawaii and up to Alaska. In

1965, he crossed America for the first time, saw New York for the first time, went down to the union hall, to the open outcry.

The hiring boss shouted, 'SS *United States*, seven cabin-class bell-boys!' and he ran and slammed down his union card on the table.

'Who's your rabbi?' the man with the wedge-shaped teeth said, picking up the card.

'Enrique Salvídar.'

'How do you know him?'

'He's my mother's cousin.'

'College kid?'

'Yes, sir.'

This was the first of his four-day hops to Europe, on the fastest cruise ship in the world – to Southampton, then Bremerhaven in Germany, down to Le Havre in France, looping back to Southampton and returning home. One year, on another ship, he got all the way to Italy. You could do three or four of these in a summer and not have to borrow a cent to pay for your education.

As for bringing him to manhood, on shore leave in Naples the purser offered to show him certain spots in the city. A month later he recollected a teenage prostitute lying in bed, looking at the wondrous contents of an American pigskin wallet, and he remembered where he had left his UCLA library card. When he had first enrolled in college, his father had held it reverently in his scarred hand. 'With this card,' he had told Stephen, 'a *whole world* of knowledge will open up to you.'

In 1968 he graduated and, with the thirst for travel awakened by too-brief shore leaves, decided to apply for a Rhodes scholarship, which, he explained patiently several times to his disbelieving parents, was postgraduate studies at Oxford University and came with everything you needed to live outside America, including a pre-paid ticket on the ship he already knew, the SS *United States*. Their son, a prince at Oxford.

But his father thought his boy was in one respect a dope. His was the ignorance of the people with letters after their name and pictures of themselves in black robes receiving scrolls (that very photograph, gold-framed, hung on the wall next to the cabinet containing china teacups with flowers painted on them, never used). On the sly he cashed in Stephen's ticket and handed him the whole amount in dollar bills in an envelope. 'Go over as a seaman earning a seaman's pay,' he said, 'and arrive at Oxford University like a lord.'

What could you do? His father was a man of the Old World – not the old world *he* was going to, but a place more primitive, atavistic in its inclinations, a peasant land. His father thought like a peasant. The furs he schlepped around all day were not so much for him the product of a master furrier's expertise but the excess from the meat the caveman bludgeoned with a bone. Stephen loved his father. He respected him for being a hard worker and a good provider. His parents seemed to have a good marriage; they enjoyed dancing and sometimes he had caught them in a kiss, sitting together in the car, parked outside their building. Years later, when he was married himself, he suspected that the marriage had always been glued together by sex. That his father saw a beautiful Latina woman with her black hair in a heavy roll above her forehead and powdered cheeks, while she saw in him a man confident, despite his scrawny size, in his masculinity, who had worked his way across America alone.

Stephen kissed his parents goodbye, kissed his sisters, smelt the riotous cheap scent coming off their necks. He was twenty-two and certain that he was the next Einstein.

Off the ship sailed, backing out from Manhattan, the Statue of Liberty receding, Ellis Island receding behind him, and in that high-tide moment, it was all over: all was done with America.

# All at Sea

There he stands, high on the promenade deck in various shades of grey, the grey sea and grey sky behind him. A grey figure has a big grey arm around Stephen's narrow grey shoulders. He is laughing with his grey lips. Nearly twenty-five years go past before this big grey boy suddenly swims into shockingly familiar vivid focus, in colour: stunning evidence, to Stephen's two children, that not everything your parents told you was a series of evasive lies. Even if those lies were related with honourable intentions by adults trying to protect not just the innocence of their kids but their own privacy. To which those kids had only recently understood they were entitled.

The ship was sumptuous. In the first-class ballroom, walls of pale gold leaf shone against etched-glass panels of underwater life. There were dining rooms, movie theatres, a kids' playroom, cocktail bars, theatres and libraries. If you peeled off the side of the ship at sunset, you would see an uncurtained city, cells of light, each stateroom and cabin rising up above the turbines until they reached the twin funnels, patriotically painted red, white and blue, exhaling the ship's breath with a throaty cry.

His own tiny cabin was deep below the surface. Heating pipes ran above his head so he could not have sat up to read even if he had wanted to. At night he was so exhausted he sometimes lay down fully clothed and fell asleep, and in his dreams he heard the water outside rushing hard against the steel.

The uniform he remembered vividly: a white Prince Edward jacket and maroon pants with a stripe running down the side. The duties were to be on the go. To answer the call of the bell.

'In the middle of the deck,' he told Max and Marianne, 'there was a little room, where we all sat, the bellboys, the cabin stewards and stewardesses. You had a board called an enunciator with numbers on it, and when the light went on, up you got. Basically, I was an errand runner. If a passenger wanted a drink in his stateroom, the drink got mixed in the cocktail bar, and I had to run up there to get it and deliver it. I brought them their dry-cleaning, picked up their shoes to shine and took messages to other passengers. Of course, it was absolutely against the rules to mix with them but quite a few were families with young daughters our own age and they were looking for shipboard romance. We college kids were tacitly understood to supply that, so at night you got changed, went up to the passenger decks and tried to find girls.'

He is busy all day long, running through gangways in his bell-boy's suit, stained with coffee spills and his own underarm sweat. He lies at night in the ship's inner stomach, as if he were Jonah swallowed up by the great leviathan while the glamour and romance of the last ocean-going transatlantic cruise liners glitters unseen above his slumbering head. He has witnessed with his own eyes in first class the white tablecloths, the silverware radiating in pairs of multiplying forks and knives and three kinds of spoon. Soup sways in bowls, jellies shiver, decorated with green leaves of candied angelica. The women's arms and shoulders are creamily bared under the lights and he notices, ascending the stairs above him, a host of men's patent-leather shoes like the black keys of a piano, tapping in time.

Movie stars and statesmen sailed to Europe on this ship, but in tourist class he ran into another Rhodes scholar en route to Oxford. His new friend was a big, blond Southern boy with a veneer of East Coast sophistication, a Georgetown graduate who just had to turn to a girl and smile and she was all goose-bumps. You couldn't imitate what he did – it was nothing to do with what he said to a girl, the pick-up phrases. Stephen had tried that and it never worked. The secret was probably hormonal. The boy radiated a chemical appeal, a cocktail of this and that secreted by his skin.

The second night out he picked up a girl in the novelty shop buying little shreds of Japanese paper that you floated in a glass of plain tap water and overnight turned into flowers. She was in first class with all its wondrous amenities, travelling with her parents, and he talked her into inviting him to dinner in the first-class dining room. It wasn't the girl he was interested in, he confided to Stephen, but how they travelled up there. He was absorbing how others lived; he was learning how to move confidently among the rich, studying their habits. Later, they climbed down into the bowels of the ship, to Stephen's cabin, carrying a selection of little cakes called *petits fours* wrapped in a white linen napkin.

They bit into the marzipan shapes. The girl was enwrapped in that big arm. They talked about the war, which they were as anxious as each other to duck out of, the girl equally emphatic about its criminality. They discussed Oxford University, a place that seemed as unreal as a riverside hamlet in *Huckleberry Finn*, an old story from the past but which was the boys' immediate future: they would be there in two days' time, among the English. Despite the war, to be a Rhodes scholar was to be an emissary of

America. Whatever you thought of your country, you were a walking flag – they all agreed on that.

The next day the ship landed at Southampton, Stephen slipping away from the crew. It was a serious offence to jump ship – the government could send agents to come and get you – but his rabbi would take care of it. College kids jumped ship all the time.

'And so,' he told Marianne and Max, 'I became the first American in history ever to re-enter Europe as a wetback.'

'How do you know you were the first?' Marianne said.

'This lady is going to become a lawyer,' he told her mother. 'We always needed a lawyer in the family.' There were no men of probity and judgment in either the Newman or the Salvídar families. Even he, Stephen, had turned out to be a moral failure in his own estimation.

He arrives by train in Oxford, all spires assembled. Walks with his bag to his college and is taken to a room that looks to him like an exhibit from the Smithsonian. He is introduced to a man whom he finally understands to be his personal servant. He cannot understand a word he says. From the window he sees another old guy pushing along an iron contraption, which he later learns is to keep the surface of the grass level. Why? What is the point? Everything is a bright green blur, his eyes used to the monochromatic seascape of grey water, grey sky. After a few hours of visual adjustment, he can detect various shapes, one of which moves into focus on the lawn: a large tree with copper-coloured leaves, a permanent feature of the view when he opens the drapes each morning. His name for it: 'that tree out there'. He can identify one type of tree only, the palm, an example of which grew in his parents' yard, an elderly specimen planted in the twenties.

The tree outside his room was hundreds of years old. The garden was full of stuff with names, both Latin and English, which you were supposed to recognise and he didn't. He had no idea that the qualification for being British was the naming of vegetation, of trees, flowers and types of landscape. What was the difference between a rill and a brook? Did anyone know? And why did it matter? Trees, in his opinion, came in two sizes, large and small. The smaller ones, he learned, were called shrubs or bushes. Same difference.

Further out, the river had three names: Thames, Cherwell, Isis. You took a boat on it and propelled the thing along with a pole. Couldn't you move quicker with a motor? And where was everyone going on these boats? What was the purpose of these aimless journeys, fingers drifting through the water, except to move girls in floral dresses around?

Stephen felt that he had come from a country so brand new that if you peeled off the layers of the present you would only find more present. Here, the continuous uncovering of the past, history's insistence on not getting out of the way, was depressing. It reminded you that soon you would be bones under the ground. One day you might be a fossil unearthed and on display in the Pitt Rivers museum.

These matters were discussed with his shipboard companion a few days after they arrived, meeting up again in a pub recommended by the college porter, a place of overpowering musty quaintness down a narrow alley that opened up to a kind of medieval yard, with wooden tables and benches, seen by impossibly ancient houses, which looked like their jutting windows would fall out on the heads of the drinkers below. This was what the *petits fours* on board the SS *United States* had been preparing them for: really small things. They were much too big for Oxford, for staircases they could take two steps at a time, ceilings too low, rooms too cramped, and professors who lacked a certain zest. At his first meeting with his thesis adviser, Stephen came away with the desire to drink a glass of water, to wash away the taste of dust in his mouth. In the pub they tried a glass of ale and did not like it. Stephen smoked incessantly the supply of American ciga-rettes, his beloved Camels, that he had brought to fortify him in the old land. He felt himself to be in motion, swaying from side to side between Europe and America, but his buddy was studying international relations and international girls. Already, after only a few days in England, he felt competent to speak knowledgeably of the differences between them.

Stephen, a late developer sexually, had had steady girlfriends throughout college; his tendency was towards monogamy because he found casual sex too awkward and time-consuming to organise. He had grown up among women and liked to live with women, without complications. Apart from the girls in Naples, he had never had a one-night stand; it wasn't in his nature. He was, he would later say, differently wired. That was him.

At Oxford, unless you studied the same discipline or were in the same college or a member of the various university societies or played sports, you didn't interact. The shipboard companions went on to form their own inner circles, reverting to the luke-warm status of acquaintances, bound only by the shared memory of a voyage already half forgotten and no longer important as the life of the university unfolded. For a term they still stopped and spoke for a few minutes when they passed each other on the street. Then the words were reduced to a distant wave, the wave to a smile, the smile to a nod, and they were strangers.

Twenty-five years later, watching the TV news, Stephen shouted, '*I know him*! That's Bill Clinton. We came over on the SS *United States* together – except he didn't have a father who made him work his passage. He had a real cabin, like I should have had, and now the bastard's going to become president.'

The children stared at the screen.

'Okay,' said Marianne, sceptically.

'Listen, I'm telling you. He and a girl from first class came down to the crew's quarters and we all squeezed in and ate *petits fours* together on my bunk.'

For the two terms of Clinton's presidency, Max would drily preface any mention of him with the words, 'Bill Clinton, with whom my father, you know, once shared *petits fours* on a cruise ship.'

The stories your parents tell you have many ellipses, Marianne explained to her younger brother. You cannot rely on them for the truth. Parents, by definition, are liars.

# The Froggy Day

When, the morning after Stephen first slept with Andrea, he decided to make the solemn red-headed girl laugh by telling her about the time he tried on Marilyn Monroe's champagne mink, she countered with the story of the froggy day.

Once upon a time there was a froggy day.

'What the hell is a froggy day?' he said.

'Don't you have fog in Los Angeles?'

'Not much – smog, not fog. There's fog in San Francisco.'

'So you don't know about froggy days.'

'Nothing at all. What frogs?'

'There are no real frogs.'

'I don't understand.'

'Well, listen and I'll tell you.'

'Okay.'

Andrea's mother picked her up from her bed in her night-clothes and held her against the window to show her an all-white world, featureless and cold. Her father laid his hand on his daughter's red curls, called her Mademoiselle Ginger Nut and went down the stairs to eat his breakfast. After he left for work, putting on his trilby with the interesting green and bronze feather in the band, her mother stood in the scullery and washed the porridge pot. The day before, clothes had been laundered and pressed through rollers, then pinned with wooden pegs to dry on the pulley in the kitchen's warmth. Andrea, now dressed in corduroy trousers and a spotted blouse with a Peter Pan collar under an emerald green jersey knitted by her mother, a brown velvet ribbon pinned by a kirby-grip to her hair, did not look up.

Before breakfast, held by the protective arm of her mother at the window, her father tousling her hair, sounds outside had seemed muffled. The usual garden birds, the sparrows, the black-birds, the winter robins, had gone silent. The bare branches of the cherry tree had vanished; the fence was invisible. All she had seen was the single bird standing on the lawn, balancing on a repellent foot, black against the fog's whiteness.

The house was at the end of a cul-de-sac, and beyond its garden, after the termination of the school playing-fields, London finally ended. They were already in the lower reaches of Hertfordshire. 'Over there, sweetie, is the north,' said Andrea's mother, pointing a square-nailed finger to the horizon. 'No more London.' The north. Darkness, land of crows. And she has no idea at all what London is, except it is a thing like parents, and your house, and your face in the mirror.

After breakfast Andrea climbed the high stairs to find her bunny rabbit, which was missing. 'The fog's clearing,' her mother called up to her. Andrea, who was agile, could crawl up first onto the ottoman, then onto the window-seat, standing unsteadily in her brown sandals on the velveteen cushions. Her mother was right, as mothers had to be. What colossal eruptions, should a mother be wrong.

Outside the window, everything had reappeared in its own form. A tree was a tree. The fence reared up. And behind it, the school playing-field was mistily present; on it, an entire army of horrible birds had gathered, opened their mouths and made a huge, raucous, disturbing noise as if they were trying to tear down the house with their heavy beaks.

She had thought, as far as it is possible to think at two and a half, that she was safe, high in the house balanced on the blue cushions of the window-seat, but the angry bird on the lawn, with its disgusting scaly legs and primeval feet, would soon be followed by the whole troupe, hopping into the house by the open back door, into the kitchen, taking the stairs in ungainly jumps, their wings steadying them, and into her bedroom where a real bed had recently replaced her fenced and guarded cot. They would peck out her eyes and eat her tongue.

'Crows,' her mother said, 'just crows,' as an arm came from behind to steady her on the velvet cushion and stroke her hair because the child was not aware that for nearly a minute she had been screaming.

Rocked back and forth in her mother's arms, she was taken downstairs into the warm kitchen and given a Rich Tea biscuit almost the size of her head, which dissolved into soggy crumbs around her mouth. (A chocolate biscuit would result in an entire chocolate child, smeared in her hair and on her naked toes.)

'We forgot Nunny,' her mother said, and picked up the damp beige rabbit, which was lying on the floor under the table. 'He's all clean now.'

Andrea watched her take Nunny and hang him up by the ears from the pulley. She dropped her biscuit.

Upstairs she was found hiding under her bed with the dust-balls. In the afternoon, she was taken to the doctor who prescribed a bottle of tonic: coloured water for nervous patients. Small glass animals stood in awkward attitudes on the surgery mantelpiece, warmed by a coal fire. On the bus coming home she fell asleep and dreamed of glass crows advancing across the golf links. 'She screamed the bus down,' her mother said. 'I don't know what's wrong with her. She's seems afraid of everything.'

Next morning the weather is back to normal. At the end of the week, snow, which brings its own peculiarities.

Two years later they moved to Cornwall with its mild climate, where she hoped there would be no crows, fog or executed rabbits.

'That's a very neurotic story,' Stephen said.

'Don't you like it?'

'I don't know. What happened next? Did you grow up being frightened of your own shadow?'

'No. We left London and went to Cornwall because my dad inherited some money and he did what he'd always wanted, left the wine trade and bought a hotel.'

The family had gone there with such high hopes. '"So long, Piccadilly, farewell, Leicester Square,"' they sang, as they drove west. Andrea was too young to understand what they were saying goodbye to, or what 'goodbye' really meant. They were starting a new life, but what *was* a life? She thought deeply about things. She was always turning them over in her mind, so the question of why her doll Elizabeth had thick cold plastic skin and hers was warm and responded to the touch with indentations made her retreat to the cupboard under the stairs where the electricity meter lay in the darkness, ticking, to pull Elizabeth's head off and find out what was inside. Nothing. A hollow into which you could pour water.

The various chambers of the hotel, its television room, card room, dining room, the reception desk with its leather-bound registration book, the maids' cupboards, the garage of the chauffeur, who picked up arriving guests from the station in the old Daimler: it was a vast, impersonal domain for a little girl.

The family's cramped flat was in the worst rooms. No one bothered to clean or make the beds, the air smelt of overnight sweat, soiled underclothes scattered across the floor. The kitchen, in which joints of beef swimming in fat and tepid gravy were unhygienically prepared by a chef who behaved like a warlord – in control, as her father came to understand *he* was not – of the entire battery of sharp knives, and the mallets used for tenderising meat.

The parents she had known in High Barnet, before her father's dogged pursuit of the inheritance from his aunt Mabel in Winchester had come off, became distant, harried creatures, forced to wear smiles that they tore from their faces once they had left the public stage. Her playtime was spent alone, ascending and descending in the Edwardian caged lift, the concertina doors opening and closing, the stairs with their faded rose carpets falling away or rising until you reached the top floor and could go no further. She climbed up an iron ladder in her plimsolled feet and came out onto the fake Gothic battlements where the estuary was an outstretched palm and the ships of the world, with Soviet, French, Taiwanese flags, sailed into harbour to load up with china clay and take it back across the oceans. The English Channel, rippled and ridged beneath watery clouds. The salt tang of the sea. The car ferry clanking back and forth a few yards from shore to shore to the village on the other side. And the foot ferry, and at midnight, the night ferryman with his black cheroot, a burning coal in the darkness.

Growing up in the hotel, Andrea understands that no one is going to pay her any attention, or not the kind her parents would permit. Her role is to stay out of the way in the family rooms, go to the kitchen if she needs food, ask one of the chambermaids when she is ready to go to bed. If she wants, she can go into the residents' lounge and climb the mountain of an armchair and watch television, if she is incredibly quiet and good and the guests do not complain about her presence.

She is not allowed to reach into the major's trouser pocket at his request to fish out a sixpence. She must not enter any guest's room with or without their permission, unless in the company of a maid. She cannot hide behind the bar and jump out to surprise people sipping sherry. She must at all costs avoid the blood-thirsty chef, who is rumoured to boil children for soup and serve their flesh in slices. She *can* permit the weekly visiting manicurist to paint her little fingernails shell pink. She *can* play in the chained ornamental gardens with their shrubs and begonia beds as long as no one is being served with a cream tea. She *must* listen attentively as her parents complain about the gruelling hours and the incompetent staff and the ungrateful, infrequent guests.

It is inevitable that the hotel will fail. By the sixties no one wants these Enid Blyton holidays any more. They don't want rock pools, shrimping nets, buckets and spades, long walks along the cliffs, rented rowing-boats, cardigans to protect their arms from the shivering cold. They want sun, swimming pools, the smell of suntan oil. They don't want to dress for dinner or listen to a palm-court orchestra playing mouldy show tunes from before the war. They want jukeboxes and jiving. The kind of guests that the hotel is supposed to attract are starting to summer in Tuscany and Provence. They don't want consommé or shrimp cocktail, they want *boeuf en daube* and risotto. The kind of guests who think shrimp cocktail is sophisticated can't afford to stay in this hotel and don't have a dinner jacket or cocktail handbag so would not be permitted to enter the dining room.

'People have got too much money for their own good,' Andrea's father said, 'or not enough for ours.'

Once, Andrea overheard her mother say to the housekeeper, 'If I had my time over again, I wouldn't have had children. I'd have been fancy free. We should never have left London. Frank wanted to get out, not me. I still miss the shops.' But her mother, seeing her standing by the door, said, 'Don't listen to me, Andy

Pandy. I wouldn't give you up for anything. Come and give me a kiss.'

Listening to this story, Stephen thought of the house in Los Angeles where he had grown up, the wayward sisters, his mother's arms steaming as she hung out the washing, the sweat on her brow, his father thwacking the side of his head when he tried on Marilyn Monroe's champagne-mink stole, and he turned away from Andrea and smiled: because it was all happiness, all of it, even being sent to sea. He had grown up *awash* with love. He wished he had paid more attention to his sisters, to their inexpensive glamour, their cheerfulness, their wild excesses. They were both married now, one already divorced, and he had nephews and nieces he had barely seen or paid attention to. They were coming up, in America, with everything to hope for and all their wishes were sure to be granted.

Andrea remembered her father trembling by the boarded-up window. He held his head in his hands and cried. Her mother said, 'Now, Frank, don't weep, it isn't manly.' Julia looked dishevelled; it had been some days since she last wore lipstick. 'Show some backbone, Frank.'

She stood for a moment, contempt on her face. 'Husbands are useless, Andy Pandy. Never get married – they just tie you down. Keep your options open.'

Frank looked up. 'Get out,' he said to his daughter. 'Go away and leave us.'

'You bloody coward, Frank,' said Julia. 'You don't want her to see you like this. Well, don't *behave* like this. You're a damned disgrace.' And she belted him round the face with a beer towel from the bar.

'What a story!' Stephen said. 'What happened to them?

'They went to the Lake District to be a live-in couple for an elderly housekeeper.'

'And did you go along?'

'No. They didn't have any accommodation to offer me. I stayed with friends from school until I came here, and now I stay with Grace in the vacs, except now we have this house we're not going home any more.'

'And the hotel? What happened to that?'

'It's boarded up. No one wants it. They don't have the money, I suppose, to take it on.'

'Why don't they tear it down and build houses or apartments?'

'I don't know.'

'They could take a stick of dynamite. They could throw hand grenades at it.'

'Some people think it's romantic, a decaying ruin.'

'Then they should think more about the future. The past is bullshit, believe me. That's what's wrong with this whole damned place.'

'Oxford?'

'No, Europe.'

And yet they still wanted to go on sleeping with each other. The reasons had nothing to do with the past, with life stories, champagne minks or executed soft toys.

# Pity the Poor Immigrant

Stephen's first year as a Rhodes scholar was spent industriously toiling in the Dyson Perrins lab over his research area: peptides. To synthesise a molecule is a daunting thing, but if it were possible to make full-size biological proteins, the pharmaceutical applications were awesome. Stephen was one small but critical cog in the grand endeavour to make synthetic analogues of insulin; the pharmaceutical industry was breathing down their necks – the market could be measured in billions of dollars. So there you were in your white coat, pursuing a doctorate, and the world was waiting, all those diabetics out there were relying on you, reading the articles in the popular science magazines, or *Reader's Digest*, or the newspaper reports of these ground-breaking miracles, because that was how the future was made in those days: in the lab. Scientists were above the common herd of men. They had done away with the need for the old God and Stephen felt himself to be, at the very least, a minor deity in the new scheme of things.

Outside Dyson Perrins, Oxford was not what he had expected. It was not a university as UCLA was: a campus, a student newspaper, classes, cafeterias, the administration, sit-ins and demonstrations against the war, a huge student body, most of whom you never saw. Oxford was a private members' club. It was something to which you gained admission and entered a world he did not understand. There was no membership fee, the government actually paid you to go there, and no one had to work their way through college. His own career as a merchant seaman, shipping out every vacation, was regarded with bewilderment. These guys had *never* had a job.

There were dinners in hall, gowns, the dons sitting at their high table (like a wedding back home) and common rooms for students graded in some way he didn't understand. There were student societies that involved their members wearing tuxedos and top hats. Meanwhile, out on the grass, the freaks were smoking joints, and from the windows of a seventeenth-century bedroom with oak carvings came the unremitting sound, amplified by professional equipment, of Pink Floyd battering the gillyflowers.

But Stephen Newman was likeable, and he was from California, and he had a comprehensive record collection of West Coast music dating back to the early sixties. Of the early stuff he had Jan and Dean, the Surfaris, the Beach Boys – all their albums – then the Chantays, the Byrds, Buffalo Springfield, Quicksilver Messenger Service, Creedence Clearwater Revival ('Susie Q') and the Grateful Dead. Of course, the Dead. His hair was thick and black and curly and had the potential to grow into a mighty bush. He was invited to sit out there on the grass with the freaks; he became friends with the college dealer (*his flashing eyes, his floating hair*) and ensured himself a regular stash, which alleviated the boredom of life at Oxford, the *ennui* experienced by a man who was used to going to sea and mixing with the common merchant seamen and observing the potentates who travelled in first class.

He badly missed ports, entrances and exits. Oxford lay in a stagnant marsh by a sluggish river that only got interesting when it had gathered speed and moved out of meadows towards the industrial build-up of the city.

He was also homesick for sunshine, blue skies, for everything he thought of as America, which included Coca-Cola machines and jelly doughnuts. Stupid things to miss, he thought. You could get them here, after a fashion, but they tasted nothing like the same.

Men. Celibate, bored, stoned men. There were no women in his college or any of the men's colleges. There were colleges for the chicks, but they were guarded by gate rules. In one of them, he was told, when a lady had a gentleman visitor she had to move the bed out into the hall.

He spent all day in Dyson Perrins, which women seldom entered, and when they did, they were ferocious brainboxes in staid tweed skirts and lace-up leather shoes. He had a few moves – you couldn't get out of high school in Los Angeles without them – but there was nothing here that resembled dating. You asked the English if they wanted something and they said no. You couldn't take this refusal at face value because it was merely the appetiser. You asked again, maybe two more times, before the answer came: 'Are you sure?' or, if food were offered, 'If you think there's enough.' This tedious game had to be played out in every social situation, including, he assumed, sex. If it took three tries to get a girl to share a pack of potato chips with you, what would you need to do to get her into bed?

At the end of his first year, the summer of 1969, Stephen moved out of college with John Baines, another Rhodes scholar, to Jericho, a neighbourhood of small Victorian houses, built for dolls, they both thought, but at least they had finally left the

Middle Ages behind and accelerated into the architectural future by several centuries to the nineteenth.

They were cottages for artisans and were coming to be admired as charming, but theirs was a doss, with mattresses on the floor and an ashtray full of roaches. The deck, amp and speakers of the stereo were the only items that resembled furniture. The squalor depressed him. The cabin of the ship where he could not even sit upright to read was more romantic than this Lilliputian dwelling, and at least above it life was in ceaseless motion, people coming and going. His idea of a class system was defined by dollars, the rich and the not rich, which was clearly observable on a ship and in Los Angeles, but in Oxford class was something that could only be understood in the long centuries it took to roll the lawns perfectly flat.

It was difficult to keep the house clean, and the kitchen's antique fittings were grimed with dirt going back to the Roman conquest. The gas stove was filthy and unhygienic; damp seeped in from the river. Stephen developed colds and was prey to viruses. It was at Oxford that he first developed a condition called bronchitis, when a cold went to your chest and you wheezed and coughed up green phlegm. He would have bronchitis with every cold until he finally gave up smoking in his thirties. In the meantime he dosed himself with a pharmacopoeia of drugs. He was sick and miserable.

And then two girls moved in next door. What a stroke of luck. What a life-saver. They had taken the house for their third year and were not returning to their parents' homes for the summer, waiting it out, like him, in quiet, deserted Oxford, a city now without thronging bicycles, replaced by American and French tourists with cameras that swung from their chests like bulky breastplates.

He had seen these girls before. Even if you hung out all day in Dyson Perrins they were still one of the sights of the city, drifting arm in arm along the High, trailing behind them the smoke from their roll-up cigarettes and the pungent scent of heavily perfumed Oriental oils dabbed on their arms and throats. Their eyes were rimmed with black, like film stars' of the silent era, and their lips stained purple with paint applied from a matt black tube. Each wore matching green stockings but the blonde with her hair shorn like a lamb was outfitted in skirts with rips in them, exposing a slash of cerise petticoat, while the redhead was a Pre-Raphaelite painting: a tangle of tawny hair and an ankle-length green velvet robe.

Soon, all over Oxford girls appeared in ripped skirts and shocking pink petticoats, and cascades of hennaed hair fell across the pages of books in the Bodleian Library.

But beyond the involuntary turn of his head at a sight so bizarre, even in California, Stephen had paid no attention for he was not part of a crowd which asked who people were and where they had come from. He assumed that everyone, like him, came from nowhere and was a nobody. They were just two weird girls, part of the ongoing pageant of Oxford life: for you could find at Oxford men in cricket whites self-consciously carrying teddy-bears, girls with monocles and cigarette holders, guys with Old Etonian accents wearing donkey jackets (a serge fabric with plastic patches on the shoulders, usually seen on hod-carriers). Who cared?

The girls were part of that parade, and now they were next door, moving about behind the party walls, their voices inaudible. They rode bicycles and hauled the heavy machines into their tiny hall. In the evenings, Stephen could hear the sound of bath taps and imagined them sliding, naked, into the tub; this picture sustained him for many nights alone on his mattress, though usually he thought about his last girlfriend but one, Polly. He remembered the time they had driven down to the Mexican border and stared across it to unknown lands. He had been that close to asking her to marry him, but had come to his senses. It must have been her French perfume that had half crazed him.

He was sitting in the garden under a tree smoking a joint. Next door the two girls were having a dolls' tea party with cups and saucers and finger sandwiches laid out on the weedy grass. He heard cries of raucous laughter and the lower murmurings of another voice and a tabby cat mewing on the fence, an empire, he thought, of fleas and other sneeze-making contaminants. He was allergic to cat fur and pollen and spent as little time in the garden as he could, especially during hay-fever season, but the warmth of the day, the need to feel the sun on his face after the endless English spring of low cloud and moderate temperatures – the relentless *averageness* of English life – compelled him out of doors.

A joint towards late afternoon relaxed him, and he had begun to take an intellectual interest in the hallucinogens, LSD, and peyote, which you could still buy legally at a horticultural shop on the Banbury road. Once he'd got to the bottom of them he would probably take a trip, but he liked to be sure, to know exactly what he was ingesting, the chemical properties, the toxicity.

The mild summer sun made him drowsy. Along the street someone was playing the Doors and, closer, the girls' voices rose and fell, bees moved with determination towards the lavender bush, and a worm unheeded made its way across the obstacle of his bare foot.

A head appeared above the fence. 'Hey, man, do you have a stash? Can you bring it over?'

It wasn't a girl but a guy with blond curls, blond mutton-chop whiskers, an Afghan waistcoat and, yet to be revealed, pink bell-bottoms and suede desert boots.

Stephen stood up unsteadily and walked to the fence.

'Hello, I'm Ivan. I'm just visiting the girls.'

He could see them in the garden with their cups and saucers, teapot, jug of milk, a tray. The two girls lounged around on the grass. The redhead, in the long green velvet dress, lay back with her head on the lap of the blonde.

'Stephen. Hi.'

'I'm Balliol. Grace and Andrea are St Anne's.'

'Wadham. I'm a Rhodes scholar.'

'Do you know Clinton of Univ?'

'We met on the ship coming over.'

'Excellent, so we might as well have been formally introduced. What have you got in your stash?'

'Just grass. I don't like hash – it's too strong for me. There are a lot of side effects they don't tell you about, especially if it's opiated.'

'Grass is more than acceptable. Can you climb over?'

'Sure.'

He put a leg over the rickety fence and tried to vault across to the other side. The redhead stood up. 'I'll give you a hand,' she said. He didn't know if she was Grace or Andrea.

'No, I'm okay.' The fence swayed beneath him.

'It might come down altogether,' said the blonde.

'You're a bit betwixt and between,' Ivan said.

'In fact, I'd say you were stuck,' said the blonde.

Stephen crashed down into a patch of nettles.

'Oh dear,' said the redhead. 'I think vinegar is good for stings. I'll go and get some.'

'No,' the blonde said. 'My mother always says dock leaves. Dock leaves grow near nettles – they're nature's remedy.' She handed him a large coarse green leaf. 'Rub that on your hands.'

Stephen thought about the patent paper he had read on ibuprofen. It was supposed to knock pain on the head like a mallet – he couldn't wait to try it.

'You probably won't be able to skin up with those fingers,' Ivan said. 'Should I do it?'

'Good idea.' He handed him the bag of grass from his jeans pocket. 'What are your names again?' he asked the girls.

'I am Grace,' said the blonde.

'And I am Andrea,' said the redhead.

'I'm surprised you didn't know that already,' said Ivan. 'The girls are famous.'

'Famous for what?'

'We are the zeitgeist,' Grace replied haughtily.

'The what?'

'The spirit of the age,' Andrea said, and smiled slowly, revealing very crooked un-American teeth. She was the easier of the two to deal with. More relaxed. The other girl was so tightly strung she twanged and snapped.

A shaft of sunlight passed across Grace's face. Blue eyes blazed coldly. No one in Stephen's family was blue-eyed. His own were the colour of stirred mud. She was so beautiful he felt wiped out by it. Her beauty wasn't human. And she had the most stupendous breasts he had ever seen. He blinked several times to imprint them indelibly on his pupils. He wanted them packed away somewhere in his mind for later. The other girl had large breasts, too, but this one was the raving beauty.

'What business do you have being American?' she said.

He looked at Andrea, hoping she would help him out, but she was silent, her green eyes taking him in, the bee-stung lips slightly parted over the bad teeth, and an expression he and many others had misunderstood as spiritual.

'To state the obvious, I was born there.'

'Yes, on stolen land.' Grace poured herself another cup of tea and picked up a finger of cucumber sandwich. 'Yum. Just the right amount of salt. Are you hungry? There's plenty.'

'Stolen from who?'

'The Red Indians.'

'Honey, we don't call them Red Indians. That's just in Hollywood.'

'It doesn't matter what they're called, you're squatting on their land. That's a fact. You really should have a sandwich – they're excellent. And there's a cake of some description in the kitchen. We'll get it in a minute. Andrea, what kind of cake do we have?'

'I think it's ginger.'

'Shop-bought today, I'm afraid. Andrea makes a very good cake but no time this morning – we overslept. We like a nice piece of cake, don't we?'

'Well, you do, Grace. I can take it or leave it. I'm fat enough already.'

'That's her, selfless. Makes a cake she won't even eat. I'm not selfless. Obviously.'

'I like baking. I like things you do with your hands, though not dressmaking. That's Grace's talent, not mine. She makes all our clothes. But, Grace, you should eat *more* cake. You're so thin.'

'Never mind cakes and dresses. He still hasn't owned up to being what he is, a squatter on stolen land.'

'Oh, do stop it, Grace,' said Ivan. 'She's only teasing. Have you read much Merleau-Ponty and his work on perception, Stephen?'

'No. I never heard of him.'

'What do they teach you in American universities? How to make money and then how to make more money?'

'Don't goad, Grace. It's ill-mannered.'

'What exactly have you got against America? Apart from the war, anything else?'

'I hate it.'

'Have you ever been there?'

'Of course not. Why would I do that?'

'To ground your opinion in objective reality.'

'Sorry, we don't do empiricism at Oxford.'

He had fallen in with humanities people and he found them just as he had suspected: full of bullshit. It was all about the war, he supposed, which he didn't support – no one he knew did, apart from his parents, of course, who were right behind it, particularly his mother – but the war was not America. America, he thought, was his father stepping off a ramshackle ship onto the dry land of Ellis Island, a boy alone, and now with a son at Oxford University.

'My old man came to America from Europe. Everyone he left behind was murdered. My mom is from Cuba. I look around Oxford and I don't see too many black or brown faces, apart from the overseas students from India and Africa.'

But instead of surrendering, Grace carried on enumerating America's crimes.

Man, he thought, she could wear a person down. Dope did not appear to mellow her. Yes, that was true about Oxford, she said, and why the whole place needed blowing up along with every other political institution of English life. She had run through the town trying to save guys from the flames.

'What guys? You burn *people* here?'

'I mean Guy Fawkes. We burn him in effigy on Bonfire Night because he tried to blow up Parliament.'

'When was this?' Stephen did not pay much attention to the local news but he was certain he would have heard if someone had tried to take out the government.

'It was 1605,' said Andrea, helpfully.

'For crying out loud, you still remember *that*? That was before the fucking *Mayflower*.'

'Of course we should remember him. We should name a national holiday after him, our greatest revolutionary.'

'Oh, do shut up, Grace. You do go on sometimes. Leave him alone.'

Ivan put his hand to her lips and closed them. He has some nerve, Stephen thought. But she did nothing.

The afternoon wore on. Andrea went into the kitchen and brought out the cake, which they ate very quickly because they were suddenly ravenous – apart from Grace, who cut a wafer-thin slice. They talked and then fell silent. Stephen understood almost nothing of the conversation. Andrea spoke of R.D. Laing and his theories of madness and sanity. Grace and Ivan studied politics, philosophy and economics, Andrea read politics, philosophy and psychology. They knew things he didn't, and the things he knew, they did not have the training to understand.

English afternoons drew to a close with a slight smattering of rain, he observed, as if the day had exhausted itself before it was even over. In California the light held up for as long as it was able, then shut down fast, at the horizon.

Church bells, of which Oxford had many, chimed seven.

'Let's go and have something to eat,' Ivan said.

They got into his van. 'Where are we going?' said Grace.

'There's a good pub in Wiltshire I've always wanted to try. And we could go and take a look at the White Horse at Uffington afterwards.'

They drove west along what seemed to Stephen like narrow green alleys. Darkening flowers nodded in the hedgerows. The Downs rose up on either side of them like a bosom.

They stopped at a village and ordered food from a menu chalked up on a blackboard at the bar. Stephen had no idea what to have: there were no steaks or hamburgers or macaroni cheese.

'Maybe you should order for me,' said Stephen to Ivan.

When his food came, it was some kind of pie. Stephen dug in his fork and pulled out a piece of what seemed to be the breast of a very small chicken. Tiny breastbones lay half concealed by gravy.

'What is this?'

'It's pigeon pie.'

'Pigeons? Those birds?'

'Yes.'

'Don't they live on the streets?'

'Not these. They nest in the woods.'

They started talking about revolution. Grace was of the party that wanted to blow everything up and start all over again, while Ivan favoured an alternative society that would co-exist with capitalism, and replace it when capitalism had collapsed of its own internal contradictions. Andrea said that capitalism was more than an economic system: it was a means of manipulating desire.

'Do you know about Wilhelm Reich and the orgone box?' said Ivan.

'No idea.'

'There is a primordial cosmic energy in the universe called orgone, which comes about through having an orgasm.'

'No, there isn't,' Stephen said.

'Let me finish. You have people go inside this box and screw, and they produce this orgone with their orgasm. Then people who are mentally or even physically ill go into the box and the energy from the orgasm cures them. Now, orgone is blue and you can see it because it's the colour of the sky, and it's also responsible for gravity. Red corpuscles, plant chlorophyll, gonadal cells, protozoa and cancer cells are all charged with orgone.'

'Where's the data?'

'I don't know, I'm just telling you the theory. If we all fuck enough, we'll release enormous amounts of orgone, and capitalism will disappear of its own accord because capitalism is simply a manifestation of sexual repression.'

Stephen looked at Ivan. You have to be smart to get into Balliol, he thought. That's a top school. 'You're just kidding around, aren't you? Did you make this guy up?'

'Of course I didn't.'

Ivan had mustard in his mutton-chop whiskers. Grace leaned over to him, stuck out her tongue and licked it away.

What is going down here? Stephen thought. Where am I and who are these people? Outside the leaded windows of the pub, night had fallen. He was miles from Oxford and his solitary mattress and John Baines and the Dyson Perrins lab. The sky was full of intermittent stars and a large moon.

They got back into the van.

'Roll another joint, man,' said Ivan. 'We need to be wasted to see this.'

They were profoundly stoned. The moon acquired satellite planets and the lanes were full of goblins. Andrea began to speak of a book called Lord of the Rings, which everyone but Stephen had read. Apart from the essential works of high school, Huckleberry Finn, The Grapes of Wrath and some Jack London, Stephen had only read two novels, Catcher in the Rye and Catch-22. 'I'm waiting for another novel with the word "catch" in the title,' he said.

Grace had put on a cloak: he had never seen a garment like it before, apart from movies about the olden days with Errol Flynn when people wrote with feathers. Andrea shivered in her green velvet dress – he wondered whether to put an arm around her.

The van stopped. They got out on the edge of a steep escarpment.

An outline in white lay below them, but Stephen could barely make it out in the darkness.

Andrea came and stood next to him. 'What do you think?'

'I don't know. I can't see anything.'

'You're not really enjoying yourself, are you?'

'I wouldn't say that.'

'Look, Ivan and Grace are making orgone.'

A few feet way he could see a moving shape on the ground.

'Is that why we schlepped all the way out here? So they could fuck on a hill?'

'Probably.'

'Why are you and I here?'

'Ivan likes company. He needs an audience.'

'Your friend Grace is very ballsy, and I don't mean that in a good way.'

'She wouldn't mind you saying that – she'd take it as a compliment.'

'Are you cold?'

'A bit.'

He put his arm round her. She laid her head on his shoulder and he smelt her skin. Next he kissed her, because it seemed like the expected thing to do.

# Mister Button

Undressed, her skin was ivory, with a tuft of coppery hair. His clothes were rags on the floor covering her mouldy green dress.

'That was quick,' he said. 'I'm really sorry. And now your sheets are all wet.' He rolled her away from the seeping patch. 'For crying out loud! What's this?'

She looked down. 'Oh, it's true, then. You do bleed a little.'

He was stunned. 'I don't know what to say.'

'You don't have to say anything.'

'I had no idea, how old are you?'

'Twenty. It's late, isn't it?'

'Why me? Why did you decide on me of all people?'

'I suppose because you were so unimpressed with us. And didn't want to know why I wear this and Grace wears that or who we are and where we come from and do we know Giles or Peter or Claire. You just tagged along. And you were very funny on that fence.'

She had never met an American: she thought they must all be like him, with black hair and beaky noses, and an upfront way of talking. She supposed there must be endless depths of complication, hidden under a straightforward surface. It would be interesting to find out. 'And why me?' she went on.

'Well, I guess because you were there.'

He realised it was a disappointing answer: her smile had faded. But having made love to her, or rather abruptly combusted inside her, he began to like the *idea* of her. He liked her red hair and the bumps of her ivory body underneath her long velvet dress, though the dress itself he couldn't stand. He knew it was polite, after you had made love to someone, to properly introduce yourself, to give a little bit of Stephen and to receive a little bit of Andrea in return. Once these presents had been exchanged, you could decide how much more you wanted. Or if you should get out of bed fast and run.

So he told her all about Marilyn Monroe's champagne mink and growing up in LA, and she told him about the froggy day, the hotel, her parents' disappearance, as she smoked her little roll-up cigarette. Stephen found the tale so bizarre she might as well have been describing Hottentots. Parents were there to *love you*: that was the purpose of their whole existence. (You fall for what you do not know, he figured out eventually. But you do fall: the loss of balance is the point.)

But he also wanted to know about the blonde, the dragon-lady – what was her story?

'That's a big question. You have to begin by understanding that Grace made me. I am her creation.'

'How could she have made you? That's crazy.' He recoiled from her in the bed.

She felt his withdrawal and knew she had to get him back. 'No, it's true. We met on my first day. We had rooms in college next door to each other. I was a country hick with hay in my ears in a Crimplene miniskirt from a jumble sale in Truro, and Grace showed me how to dress and what films to say I'd seen, even when I hadn't.'

'You shouldn't be ashamed of where you come from and who you are.'

'It wasn't shame, exactly.'

'But why would you listen to *her*?'

'Well, because I didn't know anything, nothing at all. I could easily have been one of those first-term suicides – there's always a few. People come up, they've worked so hard to get here, and then they arrive and they don't know anyone and they don't fit in and it's all far too much so they top themselves. Someone threw himself off the tower at Magdalen last year. But I don't think I'd have done it that way. I would have just got terribly depressed and swallowed a lot of aspirin. But, anyway, there was Grace, and she took me in hand. She always said I had something, potential. And she had a plan.'

'What was that?'

'She was able to take me home in the vacs to stay. It wasn't a problem because I didn't have a home any more, not anywhere to go back to, so the idea was that I would always be there.'

'Why?'

Stephen had only known loving, irritating, aggravating parents. He was the sun that came up every morning in their eastern horizon and rose higher and higher. He believed that he (and, in a lesser way, his sisters) were the sole purpose of his parents' existence.

'So I could stand between her and her father. I am the *obstacle*, you see.'

He considered this proposition. Only one idea attached itself to it, something he had read about but by no means understood. 'You mean he messed around with her?'

She thought for a moment. 'Yes. He did. He messed around with her head. I don't expect you to understand. No one does, really, and that is Grace's misfortune.'

'What exactly did he do?'

But she remained silent, and they lay there looking at the walls of her bedroom, which she had covered with postcards of faces, portraits, of kings and queens, society beauties, statesmen and artists.

It was the summer the astronauts walked on the moon. There was nothing more glamorous than an astronaut, not even the film stars with their minks. Stephen wished he'd gone into astrophysics or any science that would investigate the stars. What was matter, anyway? Sometimes he saw people as swirling dense clouds of proteins, walking along the street in coloured formations, and wished he could shrink them down to a size that could be examined through a microscope. He'd like to take Andrea to the lab and irradiate her with light, see her bones.

A month after the moonwalk, Ivan got tickets for the Isle of Wight rock festival. The short ferry ride over was the first time Stephen had been on a boat since he had arrived in England. You could see the point of departure and the point of arrival, a journey of no more than a few minutes, and he thought of this Toytown life he was leading, in his miniature house, and the green alleys you drove down to reach somewhere else.

Next, as far as the eye could see, hippies. Chicks who took their tops off and walked around bare-breasted, guys in bell-bottoms, naked dirty children, and an overpowering stench of shit, boiling brown rice, peeled oranges, joss sticks and patchouli oil.

On the stage, Bob Dylan was a tiny figure in a white suit.

After several hours Ivan reappeared from a mission to score some hash, his eyes like spinning tops, and without Grace. He waved his arm in the direction of the stage. 'She's back there somewhere,' he said.

'How did that happen?' Stephen asked jealously.

'I don't know. She said she ran into someone she knew who was with the crew. He was going to take her through.'

'How could she know anyone? Who does she know?' Stephen couldn't bear the idea of her chatting to Bob Dylan. The idea infuriated him. If anyone was going to meet Dylan it should have been him: they could have talked about so much stuff, such as the meanings of certain lyrics he had been thinking about for years, and hitchhiking across America, and being American. Dylan would have said, 'Man, you should come see me some time in New York. I'm living in the Village now. Drop by for coffee. When do you get back to the States?'

It was a long time before she turned up again, sitting outside the tent, rolling a joint with her long pale fingers. Everyone else was filthy; Grace was not.

'Did you meet Dylan?' Stephen asked.

'Yes, as a matter of fact, I did.'

'And?' said Ivan.

'Well, he was okay, but I spent more time with Leonard Cohen.'

And because Grace did not usually lie they had to believe her, though she refused to say another word about the encounter. It had either gone very well or very badly, Ivan pointed out. You could drive yourself mad wondering which it was so it was best just to take her at her word. There was no alternative.

'Do you know what her father did to her?' Stephen asked him.

'Yes, of course.'

'And was it really bad?'

Ivan was uncharacteristically silent. Eventually, he said, 'Reich may not have fully understood the negative effects of orgone.'

'Reich? Do you really believe in that?'

'Look, man, the sixties are a carnival of ideas. We throw a lot of stuff into the air and some of it flies. Most of the rest falls back to earth, burns out. The decade that's coming is the one when we catch hold of all the airbound concepts. We take them by the tail and see where they carry us. Reich, I haven't entirely made my mind up about yet, but Andrea is right in one respect. Capitalism is about stimulating desire, and we have to subvert it by creating a desire counter-culture. The pot-heads need to beat the bread heads.'

'What has this got to do with Grace?'

'I'm thinking that if you put orgone into the hands of the wrong people, like Grace's dad, you might have a problem. We have to take all the orgone in the universe away from the Man.'

'How are we going to do that?'

'I don't see why it should be a problem. They'll all be dead soon, and then we'll take over.'

Andrea returned from the periphery bearing bowls of unidentifiable food that they ate with relish because they were perpetually hungry.

Andrea moved into Stephen's room, bringing with her a trunk of the weird clothes made by Grace and her glass phials of patchouli oil, which he surreptitiously poured down the sink.

She insisted he begin a dream diary. Every morning he had to write down as many dreams as he could remember. They were mainly a rehash of the mundane events of the previous day. 'Perhaps I don't have a subconscious,' he suggested, but Andrea said that if he did not, then it would be by far the most interesting thing about him. Besides, a boy who tried on a mink stole could hardly be said not to possess repressed desires.

In Oxford people floated and drifted and spoke slowly. The word for this was 'languid', Andrea said. No one was languid in LA: it was a city too vast not to be permanently paying attention. In his teens he had watched the surfers and hadn't got what they were after, in and out of the shore, always returning to land, their backs to the horizon. He had shipped out, he had reached somewhere, and these tiny repetitive voyages on the margins of beach bored him. Now he revolved in a gyre.

Arriving at Oxford in jeans, sneakers, T-shirts and a Second World War-era army-surplus khaki jacket he'd bought in Manhattan in 1966 – which was still going strong by the time the war in Iraq started in 2003 (if slightly threadbare) because it had been made to repel Nazi bullets – Stephen experimented under Andrea's guidance, first with a paisley scarf knotted round his neck and then an embroidered Afghan waistcoat, which stank of goats. If he went back in time to his Oxford days, he sometimes thought, he would not be able to stand the smell. No one washed enough – there were no showers, only huge cast-iron bathtubs, with leaking, tarnished chrome taps and a rubber hose attachment if you wanted to wash your hair.

Ivan obtained some acid. The girls said, no, they wouldn't do it. Grace was entering a Marxist phase, which Ivan had already worked through at boarding-school, and she sat in the garden, her back against the fence, reading Trotsky. She was not interested in altered consciousness; Andrea was, but had powerful instincts of self-preservation having seen her father's calamitous mental collapse at the time of his bankruptcy. She knew there was no safety net, no home to go to or private sanatorium if things turned weird. She would be in the public asylum, forgotten by everyone.

Sitting on the back step with Ivan, waiting to peek, Stephen grew increasingly astounded by a dandelion. *This*, he realised, should have been his field of study all along. It was a massive proclamation of the sun, its vast gaseous starry being, and all the laws of geometry! Everything you needed to know about the physical world was right there in one common flower that grew between the cracks of Oxford pavements, ignored, and then transmuted itself overnight into a ball of cloudy white tendrils. The study of the dandelion was the path to the Nobel, so obvious, yet he was, as far as he knew, the first person to study it.

Unless, he thought, in a queasy pang of paranoia, John Baines was secretly racing towards Stockholm.

An hour later he understood his error. Milk was a whole white floating universe and, forget dandelions, *milk* was the answer. It came to him that he now knew his own dissertation could be summed up in a single short, elegant paragraph, which he wrote on Ivan's pale forearm, his own having too many black hairs to make a surface for a ballpoint pen. When he excitedly examined the arm the following day all he could see was a series of wavy lines.

Ivan looked at him as they walked through the Parks towards the river. Stephen's hair was a huge black Afro, standing upright round his head, and a round beard covered half his face. He was jabbering about milk. Ivan had a thought of uncompromising clarity as a swan moodily swam towards them, its small eyes sending downy messages into the reeds.

'I know how we could turn the whole world on,' he said to Stephen.

But Stephen was distracted by a rabbit, which somersaulted over a toadstool and, turning into a small boat, was boarded by a duckling with a green face and very blue eyes.

'Could you actually make acid?' Ivan said. 'Would you know how?'

'I guess so. I'd need to find the paper – it's probably in the library.'

Stephen tore out the pages and took them back to his fume-hood at Dyson Perrins. Within a week he had obtained his first sample, and a month later Ivan, who appeared to know every freak and pot-head at Oxford, had established a distribution network, selling it at a pound a tab. Once a week he would take the train to London and return with a shoulder-bag, made of a piece of Turkish carpet, filled with money.

'Who are you selling it to?' Stephen asked.

'Just people I know. And people they know. Word gets around.'

He had created a kind of advertising flyer, which consisted of photographs of girls' breasts with smiley faces where their nipples should have been. Andrea and Grace had posed for the pictures – their tits were admired all over Oxford and far beyond. He named the tabs Mister Button.

Mister Button bought Stephen a second-hand car, a red two-door, open-top Triumph Herald, only six years old.

When he looks back, this is the high-water mark, he and Andrea tearing through Oxford, their hair flying, his paisley scarf whipping in the breeze, her hand on his knee and all the old things of that old city vanishing as they got out of town, driving on and on until they reached the outskirts of London and turned, abashed, not yet ready to penetrate the metropolis.

Mister Button kept them in cheesecloth shirts, loon pants, LPs, and a monthly dinner at the Elizabeth with a bottle of Burgundy, until a don dropped his fountain pen on the floor at the lab one lunchtime when Stephen was sitting outside on the grass, thinking about how to persuade Andrea to let him come up her ass. The Parker pen rolled into Stephen's fumehood and was followed by two brown lace-up brogues until it came to rest beneath the table on which Stephen had left, propped against a condensing coil, the torn-out pages from the library.

'I have to go see the proctors,' Stephen told Ivan. 'Am I in trouble?'

'Do you know what they're charging you with?'

'Defacing a library book.'

'Oh, man.'

'Is that serious?'

'Shit.'

'It's just a damned book,' he said, unable to take the proceedings seriously. 'I'll pay for another.'

He was made to dress up in subfusc. Black suit borrowed from a friend of Ivan's – he and Ivan were nothing like the same size and shape – white shirt, white bow-tie and his academic gown. He looked like a crow, standing in front of the mirror.

'Do you not understand, Mr Newman,' said the proctor, flanked by bulldogs in bowler hats, 'that the Radcliffe Science Library is a copyright library? We do not offer a selection of volumes chosen for the taste and amusement of our students. We receive one copy of every book published. This is not *a* book that you have defaced. This is *the* book.'

'What – is it the Bible or something?'

'If it were the Bible it would be *the* Bible.'

'Oh, come on. This is ridiculous.'

Then they sent him down.

With the loss of his student status came the loss of his Rhodes scholarship and, like the fountain pen rolling across the floor of Dyson Perrins, the consequences went on and on, hitting no obstacles to stop their progress. A letter arrived from his father. His dad wasn't all that good with English, his writing childlike. He had learned to read and write but not fully absorbed where you made a big and where you made a small letter or how to spell.

DeAR Sun

Hope this finds you fine and in GooD HealtH. Your MOTHER sends her Loving WiSHeS. This came For YOU in the mail for the GOVERMENT. I know it IS important SO I sent this REAL quick.

Yor Loving FatheR

For the first time in his life he started to have vivid, sweat-soaked dreams. He dreamed of being sewn alive into an army uniform, his head shaved and, like cattle, loaded up with other shaved men and shipped out to Indochina to shoot and kill small yellowy people with conical hats for absolutely no reason. Stephen knew he was going home to America to die; he couldn't see himself surviving longer than the minute or two it would take him to descend the steps of a military troop carrier, and some sniper in the trees taking aim and then shouting, '*Got one!*' He'd make Nguyen's day and his parents would erect a dust-gathering shrine to him in their best room and his body would lie in the mortuary for years while they argued about whether he should lie in the Jewish or the Catholic cemetery – but, no, they'd burn him in an oven and scatter his sooty ashes in the Pacific Ocean. It would be all over with him, Stephen Newman, son of America. But nobody of his generation, he believed, was born to die, except by accident. Life was extraordinary, the only acceptable condition. *Life is my birthright.*

So fuck Mister Button, who had brought him to this. Fuck Ivan, fuck Grace. But not sweet Andrea, who had told him she loved him, and would do anything for him (apart from that thing).

Andrea with her terrible teeth and green fingernails, her little roll-up cigarettes, her clouds of red hair and large eyes, her plump thighs beneath her velvet dresses and her wet tongue. Who had no one but him in the world, apart from the dragon girl, and who was surprisingly ruthless when she found something she wanted.

# The Island

'One of the ways my father went on controlling me was by putting money into my bank account. There was no pattern to it. He never tried to contact me to say the money was there, though I don't know how he would because he didn't have an address, but I would go and cash a cheque and the cashier would say, "Do you want to transfer that to a savings account?" And I would say, "Why?" And they would write down my balance on a piece of paper and push it towards me and I'd see that he'd put a thousand pounds in.

'So this gave me a lot of freedom to travel, but I see now that it meant I always had this safety net – I didn't need to worry about getting a job or starting a career. And I could live very cheaply. I became good at that because I never knew when the next sum would be deposited and I never wrote to him to ask him to put it in on a more regular basis. It was like winning the lottery every few months. He must have had some plan in his head precisely *because* there was no regularity to the payments. He was stringing me along for some devious purpose of his own that I've never been able to fathom. If he wanted me to be okay, he'd have paid it in on some kind of system but he didn't. It was just about power, his power over me.

'I don't know what my mother thought about – she didn't really speak. My mother was the most silent person I have ever known. If she had opinions, I have no idea what they were. She didn't vote, she didn't listen to the radio or watch television, she just turned brown. I watched her becoming dun-coloured, like the earth, and of course my father wasn't attracted to her any more. Why would he be?

'She wore brown trousers and an old brown jersey and gardening boots and often she didn't bother changing for dinner, because when the days were long she'd go straight back down to her flowerbeds. The flowers were her children, not me. She wasn't cold, she wasn't distant, and she wasn't unloving. When I was little I remember her being very warm and even playful – we would sit on the grass and sing songs. Which songs? You know, I think they were from the music halls. "The Boy I Love Is Up In The Gallery" and "After The Ball Was Over". She liked that one because she'd been at balls before she met my father. She wasn't a countrywoman at all – that was him, the scholarship boy from the hop fields. She'd been presented at Court. But I don't know the details. I saw my grandparents occasionally, they came down for the weekend, but they were snobs. They didn't like my father – they thought she'd married beneath her. My grandfather was in the Diplomatic Service. My mother spent part of her childhood in Rome but it didn't seem to have had any effect on her, unless that was where she first saw fabulous gardens.

'I do know she always expected to have a large family. She wanted a house in the country where she could bring up all her children, and what she got was an Edwardian villa on the outskirts of Sevenoaks and miscarriages . . . and instead of lavishing her attention on the one child she did have, it was as if she gave up on the whole idea of being a mother and devoted all that fecundity to the garden, where she *could* make things grow and live. To be honest, I think she more or less forgot about me, especially when I reached my early teens, because I suspect she was one of those women who only really like babies, and have more and more because they lose interest when the baby starts to turn into an active non-dependent child. And I accept that I can't have been the easiest of daughters.

'But I don't want to talk about my mother.

'Let's get back to the question of money. These deposits my father kept putting into my account allowed me to go to Cuba after Oxford, which was a complete eye-opener because it was the first time I was exposed to a Latin culture, and they *loved* me. They completely got me. There was absolutely none of this Protestant bullshit, this Puritanism that infests the northern soul. There, they just know how to live and they live out on the streets. Everything was outdoors and in colour. People drank, people ate, they made music, it was *fabulous*. I had this little room above a café, very simple, and I was reading a lot of Marx and Lenin, and thinking you could only have successful Communism in warm countries, hot countries. These very grey-granite left-wing ideas have to be mitigated by a strong pleasure principle. The Soviet Union was the last place a revolution was ever going to work.

'Of all the places I would love to go back to it's Cuba because you can live very cheaply there, and one thing it did for me was that eventually I stopped reading Marx and Lenin. When I was at Oxford it was Ivan who was the anarchist, not me – I thought those ideas were really woolly – but in Cuba I didn't become an anarchist, I just dropped all ideology. I lost interest in it.

'What happened to me in Cuba was that I fell in love. We moved in together – it was so crazy, this little place we had, and we spent all our time in bed. He was teaching me Spanish and

I was teaching him English and we were each learning all the sex-words before the words you could use with anyone but a lover. God, I was so happy. I would watch the shadows on the walls thrown by the heavy old mahogany furniture, the shadows that looked like hunchbacked women crossing the room. The dust motes in the sunbeams. The torn ivory lace of the curtains. The meals he cooked me of beans and rice. The strong morning coffee. The rum in the evening. The taste of his skin with the cheap, horrible perfume he used. Him playing his guitar, badly, sitting on the edge of the bed. His toothbrush drying on the cracked sink. The ceaseless sound of people in the street.

'When I look back, that's how I see myself. I'm twenty-two and I'm in that room and no one has the address. However hard they look, they'll never find me. I painted the walls browny-red, the colour of an old lipstick, and the room seemed to hum and vibrate with the heat of it. We went out sometimes on the back of a motorbike he borrowed, out to the sea, to the Atlantic coast. You could see ships on the horizon, their black funnels clear against the blue sky, which was always salted with clouds. That's what he said – "A sky without clouds is like a steak without salt." I told him in England we had a roof of clouds, but he had no idea what I meant. He just laughed.

'He could be very mean and moody. He'd go off and not tell me why or where. I said, "Why don't you just admit you have another girlfriend?" But he shook his head. So I thought maybe he was a government spy, he was spying on me, but then they arrested him. They took him away and told me I had to pack up and come to the airport right away.

'He must be over sixty now. Maybe he's a fat old Cuban living in Florida with his fat wife and Republican children. Or maybe he got out of gaol and went back to his old life before he met me and he's a broken-down old man who still remembers some

English to speak to the tourists because he had an English girl once.

'No. I won't tell you his name. I feel that if I release it with my breath, I'll lose it. I can't explain why. I just know that he's all I've got, me, him, that room. The red walls. The shadows. The curtain. It's more real to me than your fucking two-million-pound house, or however much you say it's worth at your dinner-party conversations.'

# Brown Rice, Brown Sugar, Brown Days

This is my wedding day, Andrea thought. Sooner than I expected.

They gathered outside the register office with John Baines and Ivan as witnesses. Grace wouldn't attend. It was a point of principle, she said.

Stephen thought Andrea looked very pretty in an orange silk maxi-dress. They walked together along Little Clarendon Street, past the head shops, and he thought he had never seen her so happy. She means this, he understood. He would go along with the deception if it meant so much to her. Chicks, even liberated chicks, had ideas about marriage that were hard to overcome. They were always waiting for someone to come and rescue them, the person they called The One. He understood this was a marriage of convenience, an immigration wedding to keep him out of the army, and if she thought it was more than that, he would collude with her. Why should I hurt her? he thought. She's just a kid, a sweet kid. She had saved him from a certain fate in Arlington cemetery.

He hasn't told me he loves me, Andrea thought. I suppose

because he doesn't. Yet he had bought her a ring, a gold one. 'No point in not doing the thing right, kiddo,' he said. So it was not entirely a charade.

He turned to look at her as they stood in front of the registrar. Christ, he thought. What am I doing? Where am I? Sweat ran down the back of his neck. And then the moment passed. The wedding party went to the Radcliffe Hotel. Ivan had snapped a rosebud from its stem in a passing garden on the way to the register office and given it to Andrea to hold.

At the Radcliffe they ordered drinks – 'And the flower would like a glass of water, please,' Ivan said.

'Well,' said John Baines, who would go on to a full professorship at Cornell, according to a Google search thirty years later. 'Next you need to learn all the words of "God Save the Queen".'

'No way,' Stephen said. 'I'm an American.'

Grace turned up. She was dressed, mockingly, all in white.

'How are the love birds?' she said, sitting down.

'Very happy,' Stephen said, to annoy her.

'I'm sorting out somewhere for us all to live in London,' said Ivan. The undergraduates had finished finals and their Oxford years were drawing to an end.

'Not me,' said Grace. 'I'm going to Cuba.'

'Are you now, babe?'

'You didn't tell me,' said Andrea. 'Why didn't you tell me?'

Grace looked coldly past her through the window.

Excellent, thought Stephen. We'll never see *her* again.


Grace and Andrea said goodbye at the railway station. Andrea held her, Grace stood stiff as a board, receiving the embrace. She was leaving everything behind, her trunks of clothes, her books, her pictures. Ivan promised he would look after them for her, but she said there was no need: she was never coming back. 'Fuck this fucking country,' she said.

Stephen envied her the palm trees and the flat blue skies and the waves slapping against the shores of the island. Cuba was his mother's home, her native land, though she had come to America when she was fourteen years old and thought of herself proudly as an American. In front of the television she had sat in anguish through the Bay of Pigs fiasco. 'Those poor dead boys,' she said. 'Good-looking young men who are never going to open their eyes again.' And her blue eye-shadow formed blue tears that dropped from her chin onto the spotless white collar of her dress.

Of Castro she said, 'That beard! A man with a beard has something to hide. A moustache is very nice – it gives you something to look at on a face – but a beard is just a nest for germs.' Stephen had not sent her any photos of himself with his beard.

The train trudged along the track with Grace inside it. Ivan said, 'Poor girl.'

But Andrea replied, 'Don't be silly. Grace will do great things. That's what she's made for.'

Stephen took the drastic step of cabling California, which produced a number of letters: two from his sisters, wanting to know the girl's name and was she pretty, was she rich and was her father a lord; one from his rabbi, Cousin Enrique, enquiring what he could do to get him out of it, money if necessary; and one from his mother saying she had wept for two days until her eyes were so red and sore her eyelashes had fallen out from rubbing. His father was silent. A month later a parcel arrived containing a rabbit-fur jacket with Andrea's new initials, AN, embroidered in the silk lining.

Stephen held out the jacket like a gentleman, as he had seen his father do for his mother, and she slipped her arms into it. The satin lining slid over her skin. 'Now I know how you felt when you tried on the mink stole,' she said.

'You don't know what I felt.'

But she just smiled. In the rabbit jacket she could do anything, be anyone. Her red hair fell down over the collar. In the mirror she saw a whole new person. Stephen, his reflection standing behind her, looked for the first time like a man who had suddenly, and without warning, fallen in love.

'I'll dress you from now on, kiddo,' he said. 'Throw out that green robe. I hate it.'

'No. Grace made it for me.'

'Try on my jeans – you'd look great in blue jeans.'

But she was too fat for them.

'You don't have any hips at all,' she said. 'You're like a rake.'

'I'm not supposed to have hips, but you are. Come on, we'll buy you some new jeans.'

She had telephoned her parents to tell them she had got married. The phone rang in the hall and her mother answered, in her professional voice. Andrea transmitted the happy news.

'You've fallen out of bed the right side,' Julia said. 'A rich Yank. You're set up for life. I've no idea what's going to happen to us when Ada dies. She *has* mentioned there might be a little something in the will, but you never know, do you? We could easily be on the street. Stick with the Yank, that's my advice. I nearly had a Yank during the war. My mistake. I could be living— Where was it? Boston, I think. But he got sent away, and that was the last I heard of him. That's what the war was like, full of what-might-have-beens. Stick with your Yank. He'll see you right, and if he doesn't, you can always be a rich divorcee. That's the life.'

'Can you put Dad on?'

She heard his steps advance hesitantly over the carpet, a slippered shuffle.

'I'm useless,' he said, before she could tell him her news. 'I can't offer anyone anything. Better not count on me. Talk to your mother again. Here she is.'

A bell rang in the background. 'No rest for the wicked,' her mother said.

A few days later a card decorated with a silver horseshoe arrived in the post and, inside it, a ten-shilling note. It was so sad and paltry, Stephen thought. The girl was on her own, apart from Grace, who was gone, so she only had him. He accepted the responsibility. It was off the radar of his moral code not to – and, anyway, who wanted the hassle of finding another chick, when there was one already?

A week later they drove to London, Andrea sweating in her rabbit jacket, Stephen behind the wheel of the red Triumph, approaching the orbital system, Hanger Lane, Acton, Hammersmith, Shepherd's Bush, Notting Hill, Bayswater, Marble Arch, swinging north up Baker Street and circumnavigating the white palaces of Regent's Park, through Camden Town and north again to Chalk Farm where the newly-weds had a room in a squat just south of Belsize Park, which Ivan had organised.

'Don't think of it as a squat,' he said. 'It's more of an urban commune based on the principles of Proudhon.'

Stephen had no idea who Proudhon was, so Ivan wrote down the three principles of their new life on an index card, which he could carry around in his pocket for easy reference.

(a) Property is theft
(b) Property is impossible
(c) Property is despotism

No one had lived there since the war and its ownership was in dispute. Ivan and his school-friend Julian, who had been studying Taoism in Devon until he caught dysentery from drinking unsanitary water collected in a water butt, had broken in through the rotten rear windows and moved in their mattresses.

Those windows, cracked and grimy, were now shaded with striped Indian bedspreads and bare light bulbs dimmed with Chinese paper lanterns. Electricity came and went, periodically stolen by hot-wiring the supply to adjacent properties. Eleven young people were inhabiting the squat, each with varying talents and competing visions. Ivan's round face and button eyes, his cherubic puffs of blond hair, belied his ingenious ability to commandeer goods and services from the tremendous waste of the wealthy neighbourhood. People threw things away, Ivan went and got them. He had what the rest of the house lacked, scuttling energy, disappearing for hours at a time, leading some critics of the regime to speculate that he might have crossed over to the other side, the dark side, and got a job. But if he had, he was not sharing his wages. Stephen liked Ivan more and more. He made everything happen.

Stephen and Andrea lay in bed smoking joints under the wedding-cake mouldings of the high ceilings. Once, there had been a chandelier. Mice huddled behind a derelict chest of drawers no one dared open, which smelt of mould and pre-war newspapers, with the inky, smudged faces of old murderers and their shadowed victims.

To both of them, the chaos of London was bewildering. It was a hideous city: its massed red-brick houses with their postage-stamp front gardens and net curtains were full of peering, furtive faces, as if behind those windows were dismal, uninteresting secrets. London's railway lines were overgrown with wild flowers and saplings on the embankments, the bridges graffitied. All the pubs closed in the middle of the afternoon and woke, dozily blinking, in the early evening; they smelt of sodden beer mats and stale sandwiches. The lumbering double-decker buses deadlocked in the narrow streets, the dirty newspaper pages blown on a hot wind – the whole *mess* of London intimidated them.

But Andrea was more resourceful – they could have done with a girl like her at sea, in more ways than one, Stephen thought admiringly.

After a few days, with an A–Z and a tube map, she went down to the Savoy Hotel, located the staff entrance and got herself a job as a chambermaid. She knew hotels, how they functioned. She understood that they were a hive and that a hive always fed its drones. Her hair tied back, her body dampened under a white-and-blue-checked maid's uniform and apron, black lace-up shoes on her feet, she passed anonymously through the rooms, seeing the unmade beds, the stained sheets, the half-written letters on the desk, the condom in the wastepaper-basket, the clothes in the wardrobes, the indentations made by the feet that inhabited the shoes left out each night for polishing. Every chamber in the hotel surrendered to her key.

Andrea brought home from work soap, needles, thread, small bottles of shampoo. The hotel staff ate together in the basement: she secreted slices of bread and butter in a paper napkin in her pockets, ends of ham, sometimes a Scotch egg and tomatoes. The couple consumed them in secret. She kept the rabbit jacket well hidden when she wasn't wearing it. Stephen loved to see her walking quickly across the room, naked apart from the fur, which reached just below her waist and the auburn triangle above her lovely white thighs and dimpled knees. He liked the little extra flesh on her. He couldn't stand gaunt women. One day he would have enough money to buy her a bottle of perfume so the jacket would be scented like the coats of the film stars.

He wrote his father a thank-you letter, and enclosed a photograph of Andrea sitting by the window, the light of London on those veiled eyes and parted lips.

*

In the house Julian cooked, and was investigating the principles of macrobiotic eating. A row broke out in the kitchen when one of the girls stole (or, rather, liberated from their capitalist oppressors in a corner shop) a packet of chocolate biscuits. A house meeting was convened to discuss their presence in the kitchen. Julian wanted them thrown out: the sugar in them was poison. Ivan thought they should be fairly distributed, while Elaine believed that they should be given as a prize to the commune member who was considered to have made the greatest contribution to the general well-being and maintenance of the collective, thus introducing the notion of meritocracy, which was howled down.

Stephen sidelined the debate by going out to the shop and buying his own packet of chocolate biscuits, which he ate at night, in bed with Andrea. He did not mention this act of bourgeois individualism. He wanted Andrea to lick the melting chocolate from his fingers.

When Ivan was on a prolonged absence of several days the squatters painted a mural across the stuccoed surface of the house depicting an idyllic land of large-breasted chicks harvesting marijuana leaves from an endless garden while the face of Karl Marx beamed down from a bearded sun. 'We're not bloody Marxists,' Ivan said, when he returned. 'We're anarchists.'

'This must be Marx in his anarchist phase,' said Stephen, pointing to the marijuana plantation. He had enjoyed painting his beard.

'I've decided we're going to share everything,' Ivan said, 'even clothes. Every night we'll take off whatever we're wearing and put it in the clothes stash, then next morning people can just come and take whatever they like. It will be amazing.'

'I don't want to wear your smelly jeans.'

'And no one's wearing my fur jacket,' said Andrea.

The girls in the house set up the clothes stash but the boys refused to take part. Andrea noticed they did not like the idea of someone else's shirt or shoes touching their own skin, which was curious, a sign, she thought, of their fear of intimacy. While Stephen slept she slit the outside seams of his jeans from the hem to the knee, cut triangles from the green velvet dress and sewed them in. His Levi's had turned into flares. In the morning he awoke and stumbled into his trousers. He looked down and saw his feet disappearing below the flapping fabric. Was there something a little faggoty about wearing parts of a girl's dress in your pants? Men with long hair were often taken for girls or pansies, but not him, not with his beard and his black Afro. In the end he decided he liked the altered jeans. Something of his wife, his old lady, was next to his skin. She belonged to him. The thought was agreeable.

'We were poor for so long,' Stephen told his children, 'but, man, it was a great kind of poor to be. We didn't miss money, not at all. You could always get what you needed, and you didn't really need much. The summers were wonderful. We used to walk down through Regent's Park and go to the art museums because the pictures were free and there were parties all the time, and happenings. You don't seem to have those any more. A happening was an anarchist kind of thing. That was it – it just happened, despite all the reasons why it shouldn't. I liked the anarchists. The other stuff, the Marxist bullshit, I could take it or leave it.'

Under Ivan's energetic direction the squatters did what they could to reverse the dereliction of the house; they painted the walls and covered up the mouse-holes. They restored the toilets to working order and paid a chimney sweep to unblock the fireplaces. Andrea planted sunflower seeds and vegetables in the garden, and they grew. They had a crop of tiny finger-shaped carrots and sour white onions. The sunflowers reared up, waving overgrown heads and dense, pollen-heavy hearts around which

radiated hectic yellow petals, held up on thick, hairy stems.
Stephen was amazed at his wife's numerous gifts.

When Andrea had first gone to Kent to stay with Grace in
the holidays, after the failure of the hotel, she had strayed out
beneath the wisteria bower and down an *Alice in Wonderland*
path that twisted back upon itself and took you into a maze
of box hedge, and instead of getting lost she found her way out
of there, down to the scented roses and stood watching Grace's
mother, who silently handed her a hoe and nodded at the green
heads of weeds that needed to be amputated. This is how she
learned to garden, a skill Grace had refused to acquire, but
Andrea, Stephen slowly observed, was a homemaker, a fixer-up
of things untidy or even derelict. She made things better; she
would make him better, if he gave her half a chance.

Andrea taught Stephen how to grow all kinds of things and
built him a simple lean-to shelter to cover the traces of his marijuana crop. He had thoroughly digested the 1964 landmark
paper of Mechoulam, Gaoni and Edery which isolated $\Delta^9$-
tetrahydrocannabinol as the main psychoactive substance in
dope, and asked his wife to advise on how to maximise growing
conditions to produce Grade A grass. This was for the private
consumption of the house.

The acid factory at Oxford had been covered in the underground press and its closure by the university authorities, the
fascist pigs, had led to a sudden supply shortage of high-grade
hallucinogens. The lesson was that quality drugs, produced by
ethical manufacturers, non-bread-heads, not out to serve the
interests of the Man, gave quality trips with no unwanted side-
effects involving demonic visitations, extreme paranoia and
lengthy stays in psychiatric wards.

'You know a lot about drugs, Stephen,' Andrea said one night.
'You know more than anyone else. Why don't you write a book
about it?'

'I can barely write a letter,' he said.

'Well, you could write something.'

'What could I write?'

Ivan came in from his secret travels. 'Andrea thinks I should write a book about drugs,' Stephen said.

'Funny you should say that because one of the underground mags is looking for someone to write about drugs. They want someone who knows what's safe to take and what isn't, what the effects are, that kind of thing.'

'Wow,' he said. 'I could do that. Thanks.'

So Stephen Newman was famously, for a few months in 1971, 'Doc California', explaining the chemical make-up of various legal and illegal substances. Why dexedrine made you hustle and why hash made you want to sit still. His column featured grainy photographs of drugs currently available and came with a disclaimer that the author did not, of course, endorse the purchase or taking of these drugs. His mug-shot at the top, photocopied, reduced him to contrasty black-and-white, and his eyes to burning coals of intense, staring knowledge.

Winter arrived. Their room, with views across London to the cloud-shrouded revolving restaurant of the Post Office Tower, the city borne down under the weight of brown skies, was heated by a two-bar electric fire when the power was on. Stephen knew nothing at all about cold. The ice tormented him. The chill was in their bones. The damp was in their internal organs. He feared waking to find a frozen drop of semen at the end of his penis. Would it hurt? Would it damage his precious cock? The last thing they did at night before they put their bodies gingerly down on the frosty sheets was to lay their clothes out on the floor around the electric fire. Waking in the morning, hugging each other to exchange the heat of their bodies, they watched their breath freeze in the icy air and dared each other to jump up and run a few feet across the icy floorboards to flick the switch to turn it on, then come back to bed and wait for their jeans, dress, T-shirts and shoes to warm a little, to take the intense cold off the fibres before they could wear them.

The communal meals, the ritual nightly eating of brown rice seasoned with tamari sauce, the half-cooked soybean croquettes, which induced sudden attacks of flatulence, had been turned by Julian into a strict macrobiotic experiment based on the principles of *yin* and *yang*. Which Stephen said were simply acids and alkalines.

Macrobiotics, said Julian, made you placid: an army could never go to war on a macrobiotic diet (but you could fart your enemies into submission, Stephen thought). 'In Tibet,' he said . . . In Tibet he would be happy. Julian's skin was even whiter than Andrea's and his watery eyes peered out from beneath a fringe of poker-straight yellow hair. He did not make a move without studying the tarot cards, whose old figures sat complacently looking back at him with their determined outcomes. With trembling fingers he dealt and redealt the deck, searching for an acceptable future but always drawing such figures as the Hanged Man.

'I really can't stand that stuff,' Stephen said to Ivan. 'Why does he do it?'

'Poor Julian.'

'What's his problem?'

'I think he's queer. He sucked me at school – everyone sucked everyone else, there wasn't much on offer at boarding-school – but he was the one who liked it. We never refer to it now.'

There were a few pansies on board ship. You knew how to deal with them or you got someone else to do it for you.

'There's nothing wrong with being a faggot,' said Stephen. 'I mean, they can't help it, can they? As long as they stick to their own kind.'

'Yes, but he's starting to bring them home.'

'Here?'

'He goes out at night to Hampstead Heath and asks them to come back for a cup of tea and a bite to eat. They're not our type at all.'

'What type are they?'

'Well, they look like builders. Or lorry drivers.'

'And he makes them soybean croquettes?'

'Exactly. Then they start getting nasty. They want a fry-up or at least a bacon sandwich, and he starts lecturing them about *yin* and *yang*.'

One day Julian disappeared, his stuff emptied from his room, vanishing into a dying era without trace. (Decades later, Stephen Googled him and came up with nothing. He assumed that he really had gone to Tibet, and almost certainly died there of some illness to which his Western system had no immunity, or else he worked his way across to San Francisco, taken part in the great carnival of human flesh in the late seventies and died of that instead.)

A different type took his place: Les, a feral boy, who had grown up in poverty with too little calcium in his diet. His fingernails peeled and his teeth were tiny, sharp and pointed like a cat's. He made a living begging on the bridge that led over the Thames to the South Bank. 'I am hungry,' his sign said. And he looked hungry. Ivan brought him home, but later regretted it.

In turn Les introduced Scotch Dave to the commune. He wore the regulation jeans, T-shirt, beads and bells, and his hair and beard were a matted brown tangle.

Andrea was the thing that hadn't yet been invented: a cash machine. She was a lassie with a pay packet and a fur coat. Winter was cold: he had his eye on that bunny.

'I need money,' Scotch Dave said to her, in the kitchen. 'I need it quick. Come on. Don't waste my time.'

She opened her purse and handed him the change. He looked at the coins in his hand, picked out the brown pennies and threw them in her face. 'You don't insult me,' he said. 'Next time you'll give me a note.'

'The problem was,' Stephen told Max and Marianne, 'the experiment was constantly being subverted by people who didn't have a higher consciousness, just an eye for a free space and a free meal.'

The children didn't believe in the squat. In 2004 the house in Chalk Farm would go on the market for two and a half million pounds, bought by a couple who worked for Goldman Sachs. Max said, 'These are just stories they tell us to make us think that once upon a time they were interesting. I mean, can you really see Mum in a squat? Or Dad with his food fads eating anything without a nutrition label?'

'They had to have been young once,' said Marianne. 'Grace says they were.' But they had not seen Grace for years; she was a legend.

Ivan confirmed that everything they had told the children about the squat was true, but nothing Uncle Ivan said was credible. Everyone knew that people who work in advertising are professional liars.

# Moving In

Ralph had been having a kip on the camp-bed in his office. These after-lunch naps were his sole pleasure now, when he could return for twenty minutes to a dream world in which images better than the cinema, for often he was part of the action, were lit with flattering clarity. They were about boys. In real life he would not have dared even to look too closely at a boy. And these boys were nothing like the one who stood on the step, with a black unattractive beard and the slightly chubby ginger-haired girl next to him. The boys in his dreams were clean-shaven, short-haired and wore simple white singlets. They smelt of soap. He believed he could smell the soap in his dreams, though he understood this was not possible.

'We've come about the rooms,' Stephen said. 'We sent you a letter.'

'Hippies – good. You won't need the bathroom much.'

'Don't be ridiculous. We wash.'

They climbed the stairs to the top of the house. The first room was almost entirely taken up by a double bed – they had to sidle their way around it to reach the wardrobe.

'And here's your lounge. All this furniture was made during the war, top quality. Government issue. It'll last a lifetime. And you've got a view. You can see the Post Office Tower over there. I should charge extra for that.'

'We could see it where we were before,' Andrea said.

'How much?' said Stephen.

'Eight pound a week, but that's all in. There's a television room downstairs for use of all the tenants and a hotplate out in the hall where you can make a bit of dinner if you know how to juggle the pans about. The bathroom's on the floor below.'

They walked down to his office, a cupboard on the second floor where he kept his rent books and his camp-bed. They were made to sign a contract expressly forbidding many activities, such as playing musical instruments. 'But apart from all that,' Ralph said, 'it's Liberty Hall. You can come and go as you please – you've got your own front-door key. I can also give you a ten-per-cent discount on anything you buy at my shop.'

'What do you sell?'

'Haberdashery. Tea towels, linens, nighties, ladies' corsets. Come and have a look – it's just on Upper Street. I used to be in show business, but you get more pleasure out of selling a woman a reasonably priced girdle. At least you receive some appreciation.'

'What did you do when you were in show business?' Andrea asked.

'I had a conjuring act. One time I had a chance of a spot at the Palladium, but it didn't quite come off.'

'You should show us some tricks some time. Can you saw a lady in half?'

'I know how it's done. I can draw you a diagram. But the fittings are very expensive.'

Looking out of the window of their flat Stephen saw the roofs, the chimneys, the birds alighting on fences, the leaves browning and burnishing in the mild autumn sun, the pungent burning of bonfires, evenings drawing in and inside their room, a fireplace where Andrea toasted bread on a long fork and they ate it with slices of strong yellow cheese. They had been in London for a year. She had been promoted to trainee receptionist at the Savoy and was taking part-time courses at the Tavistock Clinic, learning how to be what Stephen called a shrink.

Ralph's shop was halfway along Upper Street, with the corsets in the window, pink, boned like fish, with suspenders hanging off them. Everything in the neighbourhood was fly-blown, old, decayed, dusty, unkempt and, apart from the houses, very small. The air in north London smelt of grease, blown on the wind from the chip shop. If, in a pub, you asked for ice, they would lift the lid of a leather-covered barrel and with tongs remove a single cube, too sluggish even to slip around, melting in a puddle of oily water. This would be plopped ceremoniously into the glass, where it vanished on impact.

'Oh, stop moaning,' said Andrea. 'In the hotel we reused the water left in the guests' glasses to make ice.'

She mocked his standards of hygiene, the minutes he spent brushing his teeth and drawing lengths of string between them, as he had been taught by the family dentist back home. He was, she said, an unduly clean person.

'Don't do that,' he replied. 'Don't analyse me.'

The tenants of the house were a mixture of elderly widowers and spinsters, who shuffled up- and downstairs with their shopping in string bags, and a few new arrivals in London. The old people died and their coffins were carried off down the narrow stairs by men with black ribbons tied round their hats to a pauper's grave somewhere in Essex. Stephen did not understand how a life could be lived and end so forlornly, without the press of relations, of uncles and cousins and sisters, and crowded rooms and raised voices. He had never spoken to them. They did not answer when he said a polite hello. He did not understand that his Afro hair and messy beard frightened them.

On the floor below, Martin also had two rooms, in the second of which he kept his stock, which consisted of cardboard boxes containing complicated machines that had to be plugged in and, after emitting thunderous noises and great wafts of hot steam, produced a cup of coffee with a head of white foam sitting on top of it, like a pint of beer. It was called cappuccino and it originated in Italy.

'You see, on the Continent,' he said, 'they wouldn't dream of drinking that instant muck. On the Continent, coffee is a rite, almost a religion. Now, you might object that we're a tea-drinking nation, that we don't like coffee. You're an American, Steve, you appreciate what I'm trying to do. A cuppa is all very well, but when you introduce coffee to a country you're bringing sophistication. Coffee is more of a delicacy than tea, like caviar but affordable.'

Stephen's parents drank nothing but coffee, semi-transparent stuff brewed in an electric percolator. This cappuccino was a fancy-schmancy beverage. It took half an hour for the machine to get its act together to produce a single shot, and then you had to start all over again, emptying the grounds, washing out the filter, not to mention adroit handling of the steam arm, which needed to be manoeuvred at a particular angle. At first he couldn't see it catching on.

But Martin, who wore brown, wide-lapelled suits and orange kipper ties that covered half his chest, his trouser flares flapping, resolutely went out every morning with a briefcase full of brochures and worked his way through the cafés of the West End, retiring towards the end of the afternoon to Soho, his spiritual home. On Old Compton Street there was a café where such a machine was already installed, and they served slices of cream gâteau with cherries steeped in liqueur. By six he would walk up to the French pub to drink gin and bitters and discuss coffee with Gaston, the moustachioed publican who had served General de Gaulle during the war. The romance of the Continent. Martin had dropped out of a language degree at the University of Birmingham after he had gone to Rome for a week one summer. When he returned, his brain was fried with the unfeasible vision that London would one day be a city where people sat out on the pavement in the sunshine, drinking coffee, watching a passing parade of their neighbours stroll arm in arm along the boulevards.

'I like Martin,' Stephen said. 'At least he has some initiative.' He reminded him of Clinton of Univ, both with big dreams and ambitions. Stephen was drawn in, became convinced that Britain would eventually become a coffee-drinking nation. The stuff tasted too good for it not to, but Andrea said what did that have to do with anything? The English, she believed, enjoyed things that tasted awful, hence the national cuisine. The first principle was to boil a vegetable until all taste and texture had been beaten out of it by the water's ferocious energy. Better still were foods that tasted of nothing at all. There was the huge popularity of packets of powder, which, when hot water was added, turned into a simulacrum of mashed potato, without lumps or any discernible flavour. Her parents had used it in the hotel.

'British food,' Stephen said, 'is a substitute for central heating.'

Martin did a moonlight flit, leaving behind his coffee machines, which no one wanted. Ralph tried to sell them in all the cafés along Upper Street but discovered, as Martin had done, that no one was interested. Eventually the bin men took most of them away, their chrome still bright beneath the cellophane wrappers, but Stephen and Andrea kept one, which they didn't use until finally they had a kitchen large enough to accommodate it. The highlight of their dinner parties in the eighties was the coffee they made in their restaurant-size Gaggia.

# Marx

'The seventies in London are really hard to describe,' Stephen would say to his children. 'I was there and yet I can't pin it down. It was a very amorphous era, with no discernible edges or outlines. I couldn't really tell you what it stood for. All I can do is describe how *we* lived, but others were going through very different times. You'd had this tremendous burst of energy and excitement in the sixties, the clothes, the music, the politics, and afterwards everything became less or even more of what it had been. When I say more, I'm thinking of that soulless overblown rock music, heavy metal, glam rock, prog rock. They messed and messed around with it until it was just a bunch of wigs and outfits. I mean, Kiss!

'There was this time in Britain in the early seventies when they turned the power off for a few hours every day and you just had to literally sit there in the dark. We were lucky that the house had fireplaces in every room and we could go and scavenge wood, old boxes, anything you could burn to keep ourselves warm. We always had terrible colds, our noses running in the winter, and in my case it always went to my chest because of the damp and the fact that I still smoked thirty cigarettes a day. And it wasn't just here. In America there were lines of cars waiting to get gas because it was rationed. Can you imagine Americans with rationing?

'Britain was in hock. We were failing and going cap in hand every five minutes to the IMF for loans and it still didn't make any difference. It was like you woke up from the sixties and asked yourself, *What changed?* And the answer was, not that much. Of course Nixon resigned, that was great, the war ended, but here in London, it was . . . nebulous. Like an English summer. That's the best thing I can do. I'm not a words guy. So I can't think of anything good that came out of that decade, yet for us, me and your mother, those were good times.'

'After the squat, commune, whatever you want to call it, we found a bedsit a couple of blocks away from where we are now, and then a few months later we got the flat in this house. We moved to Islington in 1972, when it was a run-down, working-class section, and we've been here ever since, with everything coming up all around us. Now you have to be as rich as Croesus to buy here because it's an easy commute to the City. We're probably the poorest middle-class people in the neighbourhood and we can only afford it because we started so long ago. Everyone else is in hedge funds or works for Lehman's and Goldman Sachs. People we thought were the devil when we were their age.

'We were freewheeling for a couple of years after we came to London. Your mother was working at the hotel and I was scraping a living doing a little bit of freelance science journalism. It started with a column in an alternative newspaper and then I began picking up pieces from some proper magazines, I believe the first one was about a subject no one was talking about in those days, the use of medical marijuana to ease the symptoms of multiple sclerosis, and this led to some actual reporting on the pharmaceutical industry. Soon I was writing a lot for *New Scientist* and hoping they might give me a job. We could eat, let's put it that way, and if you could eat you didn't have too many other hassles.

'I remember one night we went to a party in Hampstead. What we had no idea about when we were living in the squat was that Ivan's parents owned a house just up the road and he used to retreat back there when he'd had enough. It was why he always looked and smelt cleaner than the rest of us, and he was filching stuff from there when we ran out of what we needed. Ivan was always a very pragmatic anarchist. His father was a barrister and he'd checked out the legal position about squatting, written letters to the council and the police, and all this was going on in the background without us really knowing. It was actually Ivan's old man who was the true anarchist, a really crazy character who always made a rule of only defending clients he was certain were guilty because he liked to get one over on the law. So he usually lost his cases but it didn't matter because his wife, Ivan's mother, had money.

'After the squat was taken over by this Scottish guy everyone was scared of, Ivan moved back home for a while, which was fine by us, because he was always having great parties. The one I remember very clearly, because of what happened the following day, had an Arabian-nights theme and you had to come in fancy dress. I was a sultan with a turban round my head and robes made of curtains. Your mother made everything – she cut me out a scimitar from cardboard and painted it silver. She wore a red gown and a gauzy veil that fell over her face and, dressed like that, we went by tube to the party.

'In the garden they'd covered the whole of the grass with a marquee and right in the middle of it was a long table full of food and in the centre of that a whole roast boar with an apple in its mouth. Which, now I come to think of it, wasn't so Arab, but even so, it was just a magical evening. There were these flowers which didn't look much but had a sweet perfume to them and apparently they only give off a scent at night. I don't know the name – your mother does for sure. But I still remember that party in the garden, and the smell of the flowers and the spice smell of dope, a swinging censor with joss sticks, and the smell of the pig, which was being carved up, and thinking, How does it get better than this? But also believing wholeheartedly that it *would* get better because surely the rest of your life was going to be parties, more parties, that would surprise and delight you. London was a big place and all over it there must be these kinds of events happening and you would go on and on turning up at nine and ringing a bell and being invited into a magical world.

'I remember thinking, London is *okay*. It's really okay if it's like this, that others live this way, with this stylish ease. Style in a different way from how they mean it now. Inside, the house was full of books, endless shelves of haphazard volumes – you could have been blindfolded and pull one down and find something that interested you. The furniture was old and shabby, armchairs with torn chintz covers with flower patterns, and up one wall there was a line of empty cans from other countries with Arabic writing all over them and pictures of what they'd once had inside. Tomatoes, henna, okra. Well, we stayed up all night and ate bacon and eggs in the kitchen around six a.m. having had *no* sleep. There was dancing, and your mother and I bopped under the moon among the scent of those night flowers, and even then we can't have been too tired because when we left, we took a wrong turn and we ended up on the edge of Hampstead Heath.

'To me it looked like open country, we'd got to the end of London altogether, but she said, no, it was a kind of park. "Let's walk across it", she said and so we did. We walked clear across the Heath in the early-morning sun and we came to a hill, which we climbed, and there was London, spread out in front of us. Wow! You could see everything – St Paul's Cathedral, the Post Office Tower. It was only the river you could not see but it was there. That's why we went back the day of the big eclipse, decades later, and sat on the same spot where we had lain down, the morning after that party. And looked up at the sun through the special glasses, then saw the lights of London come on automatically as the city thought it was dusk at midday. But we saw it with our own eyes. It only happens twice a century.

'And on we went until we reached some high walls and this was Highgate cemetery where Karl Marx is buried. So I wanted to see that, for sure, even though I wasn't a doctrinaire left-winger – he was still an important man – and we climbed up and over the walls, falling down among the weeds and the nettles, completely filthy and our fancy-dress robes torn, and we wandered around for ever through the graves, the dew still on the grass. The cemetery in the early-morning light was so eerie and beautiful, the ivy clinging to the walls. There was a little section with the graves of children and babies, and your mother burst into tears when she saw a teddy-shaped gravestone, a little boy who only lived a few days.

'After a while we found this big bombastic statue of Marx, just his head on a kind of plinth. There is only one thing to do when you're in front of the father of Communism and no one else is around. We rolled a joint, of course, and then we fell asleep. The sun was rising higher and higher in the sky. It must have been around eight thirty and shadows had started appearing. It was utterly peaceful. No one was about, just the two of us, and though we were in a burial ground, still it felt to me like we were two kids in the Garden of Eden, the first and only people alive, and we had no troubles, just hope and happiness. Your mother woke up and touched me, I touched her back. What can I say? That, we both believe, is how you were conceived, Marianne. On a sweet summer morning in the grass below Karl Marx's monument.

'Quite a few people we know are buried just across from him in the journalists' section and I have been to funerals there, especially during the Aids time when a lot of people our age died. And others were killed by their enemies – that's where they buried Farzad Bazoft, the journalist who was murdered by Saddam Hussein. I've stood in a suit by the coffin of some poor dead soul and looked across the path to Karl Marx and remembered that morning so long ago in the seventies, which now seems lost in a mist that came down from history, obscuring it. And even though I'm mourning, I always remember that it was there we started something – *you*, Marianne.

'Eventually we found our way out and walked across another park and we were in Highgate village. It was Saturday, and we fell asleep on the top deck, the front seat, woke up in the West End and had to double back home to Islington.

'So, these are my memories of the seventies, just things we did together. And the people are long lost. You walk along the street or you're on the tube coming home from work and someone your own age, or older, some tired-looking person, is sitting there reading a novel or a newspaper or just staring into space, and you think, Did I know you once? Were we at the same parties? Did I sit on the floor eating a bowl of brown rice with veggies in our squat and you were there, rolling a joint on an album cover? Did you turn out just like us? Middle-aged people whose kids are older now than we were then?

'I keep thinking of all the people I've known in London, all these years of living here. They pass through your life and you have got old and they must have got old, but if you saw them you'd cry, because you'd understand for the first time how old *you* are, and that it's all long gone and we didn't treasure it. We thought there was no way it would not last for ever, together with our hair. Isn't it weird that hair of all things turns out to be so important? I look in the mirror and I do not know myself. So I look away. This wasn't supposed to happen. I'm the kid from California who was born in sunshine and I've spent almost all my life in one cloudy day after another.'

# The Gift

For twelve hours they have been driving across Missouri and Kansas and Andrea is beginning to hallucinate whole towns, with traffic jams and zebra crossings and Gothic church spires and the melodic trill of ice-cream vans. She is suspended in enduring flatness. The van doesn't seem to be moving, making no progress at all across the unfolded map she holds on her knee, while Stephen is clenched over the wheel behind his sunglasses, locked into a robotic mode of driving. She wonders if his body has been sucked out by aliens and replaced by a husk, capable of doing one thing only: hanging on to the steering wheel, keeping his foot on the gas pedal and occasionally overtaking a slower vehicle.

Earlier on in the journey there had been baffling signs – 'Ped Xing!' 'Deer Xing!' – but that was days ago. There have been no peds or deer since. She thinks the signs were as long ago as Indiana. Square white churches, red barns, silos, strange buildings whose agricultural purpose she can't work out. Tiny towns marked with water towers – they look like a few Lego bricks thrown down on an empty table. Other places are just a marker, abandoned of habitation, devoured by the vast prairie. The sky is immense and filled with milky galaxies; the moon appears as a spherical orb, not a flat disc, its back in shadow. Andrea feels that she and her family are dots, pinpricks, their planet too insignificant to be observed from the stars with the naked eye. No wonder Americans think big, *are* big (horrifyingly obese) if they need to assert themselves in this vast, empty landscape.

The children sleeping in the back, Stephen catatonic at the wheel, make her feel she is the only sentient being in the cosmos. Only her own mind thinks and imagines. They pass other vehicles, cars, trucks, vans, but the occupants are remote, aloof, solitary. Everyone drives alone, she realises; even when there is someone beside you in the passenger seat, the road itself is your all-absorbing companion. She cannot drive, is unable to help out her husband. Partly this is because of her eyesight. She has an astigmatism and has always been too vain to wear spectacles, but she has finally given in at Stephen's insistence and now has a pair of gold-rimmed glasses. But even corrected, the deformed lenses in her eyes make the exterior world a little flat: she cannot make good judgements about spaces and finds it difficult to change lanes. She has failed her test four times.

She remains someone who is mostly comfortable on foot, but America is totally different from home. The car is your clothing. You cannot go about naked. All the family meals are eaten at truck stops, where she feels herself to be a tiny, diminished figure standing waiting for Stephen to zip up as he closes the door of the restroom, handing the key back, her sheltering in the shadow of the giant wheel of a Mack truck with a scarlet nose jutting out, and a far-flung community on the CB radio in which cops are 'Smokeys' and female hitchhikers are 'beaver', and accredited female hitchhikers who can't be messed around with are 'angel beaver'.

The truck stops have the same menus whichever state you're in. She always has a chef's salad and Stephen always has a burger with fries and the children eat off their parents' plates, according to what they fancy, because it is too exhausting to interrogate the many choices available.

But Stephen reassures her that soon they will reach the mountains; the landscape *will* change, he promises. She will see the Rockies, which are almost as good as the Himalayas.

The kids are suspiciously well behaved, sleeping a great deal as if drugged. Stephen has not told Andrea that he is indeed drugging them, slipping small amounts of sedative, crushed, into their food. It would have been impossible to do America the way he wanted, flying to New York and then driving in a rented van from coast to coast, without their compliance, even involuntary. Max is a happy child; he can take anything and is easy to cajole or distract with a story. Marianne is the difficult one, cranky and demanding. She passed through the terrible twos repetitively asking *why* of everything she came in contact with. Why are there corners? He does not have an answer, him the Rhodes scholar.

The back of the van has been laid out with wall-to-wall mattresses that the kids can bounce around on, and if they stand on boxes they can see out of the window, except, as Andrea points out, there's nothing *to* see: everything is the same same same.

'Look! The mountains!' Stephen cries, when they finally reach the Rockies. And the children stare, unable to understand what it is they're supposed to be looking at. They feel vague and placid; Marianne holds her brother's hand and sucks his other thumb, which she is not allowed to do to her own thumb. Max sees his sister as a strange swirl of colour. His thumb sends waves of pleasure up his arm and down into his body, and he gets a little erection. This is all he will remember from the great trip across America. He is only two and still working on the interesting mechanical difficulties of fastening shoes, which come with more than one option, such as the lace and the buckle.

The whole family finds Utah curious. The Great Salt Lake looks to Marianne like snow, which she has seen over the course of a couple of London days, and Max closes his eyes against its dazzling whiteness. It reminds the adults of the moon. Then they cross the penultimate state line into Nevada, spend a night in Reno, drive on, and finally Stephen is home.

The border is Lake Tahoe. Beyond that, the promised land, the land of milk and honey, which God, he believes, must have made a covenant to grant to people like his father, the travellers who go on moving until they run out of land to cross and find themselves on the rim of the world, the mountains finally behind them. The beach is where a person can be happy, and the sea our original home. This is always the destination: the sand, the scrubby grasses that grow in it, the birds gliding in the thermals.

All the money they have saved by sleeping in the van is to be splashed out on a hotel in San Francisco. Now here, Andrea thinks, she could live. She loves all the ups and the downs and, in particular, the afternoon fogs coming in from the sea. The place is atmospheric. Stephen shows her the neighbourhood of Victorians, which survived the 1906 earthquake; everything is so charming and everyone seems so middle class, which is not what they are at all because, he explains to her, middle class means something different and there is no word in the language for what the people are who live in these Carpenter Gothic houses.

On the other side of the bay they find Sausalito, where blond couples are rollerskating about the streets, and she cannot help but notice how incredibly healthy everyone looks, all lightly tanned without being bronzed, and sitting out of doors in cafés eating large sandwiches with what looks like bushy clumps of thin grass poking out of the sides. She can see her children growing up here lean and fit, with American accents. Her chief anxiety is how she would resume her work, because her consent to this exploratory trip, this month-long visit to the US to size up the opportunities for Stephen's career, had been based on his reassurance that she could not find a better place in the world to pursue her new profession than America.

There had been days when Stephen was walking towards the tube, navigating the windy roundabout at Highbury Corner on a tepid summer morning of intermittent weak showers, when he was engulfed with crushing nostalgia. For the parents he had not seen in nine years, for the balmy Los Angeles weather with its lack of extremities, for the ocean he'd taken for granted, for the suburban home lounging on its lot with the palm tree growing out front, and his bedroom with its childhood chemistry set and college textbooks, his mom in the kitchen baking chocolate cake and his father pulling up in his automobile after work, the smell of the pelts on his skin, going straight into the bathroom to wash, and *The Ed Sullivan Show* and the passionate rows that sometimes broke out between husband and wife in which each would revert to their native language in their helplessness to fully express themselves, and his big sisters who smelt of woman. The two girls, as he still thought of them, both taking after their mother with Latina looks, high-breasted, with slender ankles, the early shadow of a double chin. Taking hours in the bathroom, reading movie magazines, ignoring their little brother, the pest . . . He often felt he could not tell them apart; they morphed into each other. But one had a mole on the side of her chin, from which she plucked dark hairs with tweezers, despite their mother saying she had read in *Reader's Digest* you could get cancer that way. And the other when she laughed had a tendency to start hiccuping. So she kept to an enigmatic smile.

And then, with the memory of Carole and Rita overwhelming him with nostalgia, reminding him to write more often on blue airmail paper, he would open his eyes: here he was, in London, under those interminable brown skies that lowered with rain.

He was doing okay in London. He had a good job, a staff reporter on *New Scientist*; he had a family. But Stephen Newman was not born under blue skies only to do 'okay'.

'I want to go home,' he said one night, when they lay in bed and the children were rocking their way to Dreamland. It was 1978. President Carter had declared an amnesty: the draft-dodgers were free to return to America without retribution.

'This *is* home,' she said.

'This? It's just a rented flat.'

'But what difference does that make? Look, all our things are here, our pictures, the children's toys.'

They had the whole floor of the house now. Every time someone moved out, they went to Ralph and asked him for the room.

Stephen said, 'We'll get new things, kiddo, better things, much better – you'll see.'

'But I don't understand what we're going to do in America. I can't envisage our life there.'

'Look, I can find a job, no problem, probably back in the research field, a university job, I bet. As for you, whatever you want! Whatever you're doing here. Whatever makes you happy. That's the whole *point* of the country. It's where people come to make a fresh start. We'll all be American. Our kids will be American.'

'I don't want to be American. That's your shtick, not mine.'

He always smiled when she used such words, which came out of her mouth daintily in what was to his ears her cut-glass accent, as if the shtick was presented on a doily resting on a porcelain cakestand.

'Hold my shtick,' he said, cupping her breasts. 'We'll talk about this tomorrow.'

Their sex life together was still very good. He was clumsy, but when that happened, she thought of something else.

'But what exactly do you have here?' he began again, the next evening, when he got home from work. 'Your parents who write to you once in a blue moon? Crazy Grace? Our friends? We'll make *new* friends. We can do anything we want, but I never, ever said I would stay here. We got married because you were prepared to do me a favour and save me from the draft, and we made a real marriage out of it. Thank you. But I really do have to go home.

'And the other thing,' he said. He had reached his clinching argument. 'You've spent all this time training to be a psychotherapist, and if there's one country in the world where they're crying out to hand over half their pay cheques to shrinks, it's America. The Jews are neurotic.'

There was a theory that psychoanalysis was a Jewish science; many of her tutors and mentors at the clinic in Hampstead where she went to lectures were Jewish. She had had to submit to being analysed herself for several years; the crows had been thoroughly excavated, and the hanging rabbit and her parents' abandonment.

Her years of therapy, paid for by part-time reception work in hotels, had allowed her to make her peace with her parents. She had taken the train to Keswick and spoken to them about how they had failed her. The confrontation resulted in no recognition on their part; they acknowledged nothing; she had never thought they would. Hope was not the same as reason. But she felt the weight of a coal truck lifted from her back as she walked away from the small, stifling house.

Her mother had dusted ornaments the whole time she was talking and looked round occasionally to correct some small detail in her daughter's account of each incident. Her father was drunk.

They had turned themselves into walls and doors. The doors had been carefully locked. She knew she had to proceed on her own from now on; the hotel and all its horrors were metaphors more than memories. There was no alternative.

Stephen said that, over in Europe, it was inevitable that all the Jews were screwed up: they lived shadow lives, neither one thing nor another. Once you got out of there, all that kind of thing should have just stopped more or less automatically. Emigration was the cure for European ills. And yet it turned out that when they got to the land of plenty, all they wanted to do was go back down into the darkness. There would be more than enough work for her, dealing with their neuroses.

Here, in London, psychotherapy was still a new career. The talking cure – not cure, which sounded like the clients (not patients, the therapists did not dare call them that) *were* sick – the talking therapies were there to help people through life's crises and the usual ineffable sadness of merely living. The English wept in private, frightened to reveal themselves in case of the sudden appearance of the straitjacket and the chemical cosh. Andrea had seen her father do so. It was a shame culture. Therapy was American self-indulgence; she had heard it said over and over again when she was introduced to someone at a party and they asked what she did.

'Aren't your clients, or whatever you call them, just spoilt children crying to their mummies when they're sad? If you ask me, they lack backbone.'

She was finding it more difficult than she had anticipated to build a list, and still more therapists were being trained, coming up behind her. That bloody English stiff upper lip, the stoicism, the determination to break down in secret. This, in the end, was what decided her to, as Stephen put it, 'just go take a look!'

But Californians seem at ease, so shallow and content, she cannot guess what traumas they might conceal behind their lightly smiling faces.

They drive along the coast road, south to Los Angeles. The scenery is spectacular and everything is incredibly *clean*. Andrea does not know what to make of the absence of dirt and disorder. 'You could eat your dinner off the floor,' she says, as they go into a convenience store.

Stephen turned and looked at her. 'Why the hell would anyone want to do that?'

'It's just an expression.'

'Well, don't use it, okay? Not in America.'

The coast is incredibly beautiful – she's dazzled by the ocean light, the change in climate and vegetation, the absence of afternoon fogs, the sun as if it were always noon, the high spot in the sky. Now she feels alive. She channels the great physical freedom of America and understands, for the first time, how claustrophobic her husband must feel in little England, with its narrow city streets not made for cars to pass each other. She covers one of his hands on the steering wheel and squeezes it. *It's going to be okay*, they both think, because, frankly, how can it not be?

They spend the night on a campsite and the children paddle in a fast-running river, their parents' arms protectively around them. At night they light a fire and fall asleep in their sleeping-bags under the stars. In the showers the next morning Andrea sees reflected in the mirror standing behind her two extremely fresh-faced women of no age she can determine, because none of the markers is present, dressed in shapeless linen trousers, with shaggy colourless hair, examining her critically as she applies her lipstick and mascara. She feels she has broken a cardinal rule of camping, that she is an artificial creature who has sullied nature's purity. In America she feels she wears too much makeup, even though she doesn't think she wears much at all, but her clothes are all wrong. They are, she has heard a waitress at a truck stop say, *fancy*. But she'll learn, she supposes. It's not as if, normally, Stephen could ever be dragged under canvas for the pleasure of it and if she has to dress down, in jeans and the plaid shirts everyone seems to be wearing, she'll do it.

Then they reach Los Angeles. A gigantic neon clown stands on the street advertising a liquor store. 'Home!' cries her husband. 'I *loved* that clown when I was a kid and we couldn't go in there because my folks never bought any liquor.'

Now they are in the city the skies suddenly turn alien, wide and flat blue, and nothing ascends into them. Stephen's neighbourhood is a *low* place, with houses that look to Andrea to be impossibly generous and expansive, lounging on their lots with yards and wrap-round porches and swing-sets and screens to keep out insects. She can't believe that these are lower-middle-class homes, built for people who work with their hands.

And the roads are ruled ribbons, going on and on. All intersections take place at sharp angles. No one is on the street: everyone is driving, or hurriedly getting out of a car onto the baking asphalt of a parking lot and purposefully moving indoors. The appearance of all this, to Andrea, is something brand new, but its novelty is entirely kitsch, like the neon clown. LA seems to her to be relentlessly, aggressively banal. 'Where are the shops?' she asks.

'In the mall,' says Stephen.

Her instant anxious impression is that LA is far too vapid to require psychotherapists. What traumas lie beneath? Everyone is happy. Everyone is lightly smiling, urging her to have a nice day, the first time she has heard this expression. It was a void statement. How could a supermarket checkout girl know what lay in store for you? Maybe you'd just had a cancer diagnosis, or lost all your money, or were on your way to a funeral. Yet the desire for others to be happy was slotted into a brief commercial transaction. Was unhappiness a rebellion against that great wall of social bliss?

The old neighbourhood, the street where his high school still stands, and the memories of it almost entirely forgotten during his years in Europe – everything looks unfamiliar to Stephen, as if he had shot like a rocket through outer space to a parallel planet in which he sees the mirror image of what he has known, back to front. The modest homes and apartment buildings look as strange as if he were observing it all through the distorted vision of an acid trip.

The palm tree is gone. It got some kind of disease, he finds out later, and was chopped down. Its gaping absence in the front yard is an insult to him.

And through the front door are his parents. To his surprise, he bursts into tears, unable to tell and certainly not caring whether these are tears of joy or tears of sorrow at what the passage of time has done to them. But they erupt all the same. He hadn't understood how much he had missed his mom and dad, or the extent to which he had taken for granted their undying, uncritical love.

His father is considerably smaller than he recollects, and not a lot left of his once black hair. His mother looks unbalanced in the chest area, because (and no one in the family had told him this, on the principle that there was no point in worrying him, unless the worst should happen, which, thank God, it didn't) she had breast cancer three years ago and has had a mastectomy. Her own hair has changed colour altogether. From the jet black roll that she pinned back from her forehead, revealing her brown, kind eyes and her plump melting chin, she is now honey blonde with what she calls platinum highlights.

'Mom,' Stephen cries, shocked, bewildered, uncomprehending. 'Your *hair*!'

'I know, Stevie, I know. But it went grey and it's too expensive to keep colouring the roots. What do you think? Does it suit me? What do you say?'

It doesn't suit her at all, but he runs into her arms, into her navy blue crêpe dress she bought last week at JC Penney for his homecoming, and once he has pressed himself against her, he understands that there has been a mutilation.

'My bosom,' she says. 'It's not all there any more. Don't worry, I'm okay now.'

'Oh, Mom,' says Stephen, and bursts into tears again, full of shame and disgust with himself for having been so far away when all these calamities were overwhelming her, oblivious, receiving the placid letters from home and reading them too quickly, taking for granted their misspelled contents and clichéd sentiments about how much they missed him, and the little news of life in the neighbourhood, high-school friends he had almost forgotten who had done good in their professions, had babies, bought a house. She had said nothing. He squeezed the breath out of her and smelt her gardenia perfume.

'So this is Andrea,' says his father. 'And, look, here are our beautiful grandchildren.'

Andrea has no idea his parents would be so *foreign*. His dad is a little gnome-like Jew, very short and stocky, with a guttural accent, nothing at all like the rather cold, stern Jews at the Tavistock Clinic who listened to Schoenberg in their offices and read Thomas Mann in the original language, acolytes of Melanie Klein. Si Newman has the fleshy nose and large, drooping eyes she has only seen in photographs of Polish men queuing up to be taken to an extermination camp. The Jewy face. And his mother Ximena is a garish dyed blonde with far too much frosted-pink lipstick and too many gold necklaces. The two people standing there are cartoons of what she thinks of as normal human beings.

The kids won't let go of Andrea. Marianne is holding on tightly to her hand while she stares down her new grandfather and Max has his arms round her leg. Any minute he's going to wet himself. He has always been shy about asking for the toilet, and there will be a pool of urine on the carpet.

The sight of these parents takes her back to her father in his brief heyday, standing at the bar of the hotel in his claret-coloured cravat, and cavalry twill trousers. She can hear in her head her father say of a Jewish couple from Leeds, who arrived at the hotel in a Humber Hawk, the wife with a mink stole and a pearl necklace with a diamond clasp, the fat son in shorts and a bow-tie carrying not one but two hula hoops, in different colours, and spinning a yo-yo: 'It's always the wrong people who have all the money.'

But Si Newman, who has never come across snobbery, whose only understanding of anti-Semitism is blond Polish boys with sticks torn from growing trees chasing you down the street, is out to woo his daughter-in-law. His son has come home with a wife, and a man must have a wife to *be* a man. It is the natural condition. Wives are kept sweet with gifts and promises and sometimes lies. This is the received wisdom of his co-workers at the fur-storage warehouse, and the ones who raise their hands to hit a woman are trash. The simple, obvious differences between the sexes must be preserved and honoured. Your son brings home a girl, and because you have had no say in whether he should marry this girl, the deed already being done, she is to be treated as family, a condition that everyone, including Stephen, understands to be a lifelong prison from which there is no escape or parole.

Her photograph from the time in the squat, just down from Oxford, in the rabbit jacket by the cold light of the north-facing window, had reminded him of an old star from the early silent era, before women shingled their hair. The women had such innocence, their faces not obviously painted apart from the lines of kohl drawn round their eyes. Of course, she is a few years older now, and a mother, and she has a self-assurance he has seen before, in the assistants who came to pick up the stars' coats. This, he thinks, is a *capable* girl. It's a shame about her crooked teeth.

'You liked the coney jacket?' he says. 'You still have it?'

'Of course I have it.'

'Well, I got you something to go with it.' And he hands her a gift-wrapped box. Inside the box, beneath its decorative wrappings, is another box.

'You bought me a box,' she says. She understands that this feeble joke is merely the self-defence of someone who has no defences, apart from her husband, who has gone into the bedroom with his mother.

'This is what's known as a hat-box. You never seen one?'

'I've never *had* one.'

Long ago her mother had had hat-boxes. The hats had vanished and been replaced by an assortment of lipsticks and old letters, and their preserved ration books from the war.

Inside this box is a mink hat.

'Is that a kitty cat?' asks Marianne, who is just coming out of her drugged stupor.

Si places the hat on Andrea's head and adjusts the angle, lightly touching her hair.

'Jesus,' says Stephen, returning from the bedroom, his arm around his mother's waist and his face still damp with tears. 'What the hell's that?'

'A mink hat.'

'Wow.'

'It will keep her warm in the winter in London,' says his father. 'The fogs are very cold, I guess.'

''Well, that's my big surprise,' says Stephen, 'because we're moving back here, to America.' He feels exultant as he says the words, and his mother raises her hands as if offering a prayer to the God she has neglected, but who all the same has rewarded her.

What happened next taxes Andrea to the limit of her understanding of her new life: they move out into the garden, which Stephen and his parents called the yard, for a barbecue, a meal she has never heard of. You can have a picnic in the garden, sandwiches, cold roast-chicken legs, cake, but to go outside to cook is just outlandish.

Si Newman has laid coals and placed giant steaks on a metal grille, bloody haunches of animals marbled with white fat, and at the last minute throws on hot dogs for the kids. There is potato salad, green salad, corn-on-the cob in its green husk, also grilled on the fire, and potato wedges. Andrea has no idea how you might approach eating a corncob, which resists being cut into slices with her knife and fork. She watches as her husband picks the thing up in two hands and drives his white, even, American teeth into the kernels, mowing them down, butter dripping onto his chin, and tossing the empty husk over his shoulder.

'Go on,' he says, to encourage her. 'Try it.'

She looks up: the sky is blue, not a cloud to be seen. The abundance of food amazes her – there is *so much* of it. The steaks drip off the grille, there isn't enough room for them, and Stephen grabs the fork from his father and moves them about the coals, a cigarette between his lips, his face fiery from the heat, sweating, happy, having kicked off his shoes and turning before her eyes into one of her own children while she remains seated on a lawn chair, experimenting with the taste of Thousand Island dressing. No, there is no salad cream, a condiment no one in America has heard of. They offer her mayo from a Hellman's jar – she loves it. Can't stand the yellow mustard in the squeezy bottle.

Dessert is emerald green jelly ('Jell-O,' Stephen corrects her. 'You might as well learn the right words for things') in which white marshmallows are suspended. The kids are in seventh heaven. Her own mother used to make a jelly dessert, emptying in a tin of fruit cocktail, little cubes of fruit with the cherry the prized delicacy, but marshmallows are so exotic that she has never been able to work out exactly what you're supposed to do with them.

The children love the meal; Stephen adores the meal. Home is where the stomach lies, she thinks. She won't be getting him to eat brown rice again, or lentils, or nutritious soups made of cheap ingredients.

This is how we're going to live from now on, she thinks. Out of doors. Maybe she can plan a garden, but none of the evergreen bushes on the grass is recognisable to her. Since she has been in America she has seen no roses.

The mink hat has to be kept in its box because Max has already mistaken it for a potty and tried to pee in it. Stephen pulled him away only just in time by the arms.

They lie that night in the single bed in his old room.

'Tomorrow we'll take the kids to the beach,' says Stephen. 'And then the next day I thought you'd like to see the studios.' The feeling of exultancy has not left him since he entered his old home and made the announcement that he was returning to America. He's on a better high than he ever got from the one time Ivan obtained some cocaine and he experienced the icy rush of clarity and optimism, followed by a come-down so intense he wanted to scratch off his own skin. It's all come good, he thinks. You really can get what you want, as well as what you need.

But as for his wife lying next to him, he really has no idea what she is thinking. She goes away like this – she is always disappearing but always coming back. Some people, he has come to understand, have shallow roots in the past. She had remade her family inside their own life together and he appreciates that it must be difficult to see for the first time, to *understand*, that he had another life, one that had come before her and still exists; she's bound to feel threatened and uncertain. And his parents, he consents in his mind, are not really what she's used to. They are not what anyone in England is used to: they are an idiosyncratic pair, that was for sure. But wonderful. The ache of love fulfilled and satisfied. *I have everything.*

'Are you okay?' he says, stroking her hair, and wanting to touch the place in the nape of her neck that is a privileged spot on her body, the zone of a strange, non-sexual pleasure that causes her face to relax and melt into formlessness.

But still the silence.

'You don't like the mink hat. That's it.'

'It's not just the hat.'

So it is the hat. 'It's just a hat. It's not like you're ever going to wear it.'

'But he thinks I'm the sort of person who would wear a mink hat.'

'He doesn't know you. He bought you a mink hat because he thinks that's what women like. My mother has one. My God, when he brought home that hat!'

'Well, she would have one.'

'What do you mean?'

'That's what she would wear.'

'Exactly. All moms wear mink hats if they can get one.'

'Not in my world.'

'*Your* world? You don't have a world, not as far as moms go.'

'That's a hateful thing to say.'

'Well, it's true.'

'You've never met my parents.'

'And why is that?'

'You know why.'

'That's my point.'

His Mickey Mouse alarm clock ticks on the nightstand and Andrea lies in the dark, illuminated only by the hands of the clock, loathing herself, loathing the hat and loathing his father for giving it to her.

The initial shock of the new family she has been bolted on to has only partly subsided during the barbecue. Her in-laws had talked non-stop about their son, about his childhood, about his first chemistry set, about his graduation, about his time in the merchant navy, about how they had come all the way to New York to see him off on the SS *United States* when he had set out for the old world, a Rhodes scholar. She sees it is possible to grow up awash with family love, even from parents who are vulgar and uneducated. She has warmed up a little to Stephen's mother, who has tales to tell of her childhood in Havana and, most important of all, Marianne spent the whole meal sitting on Ximena's knee, as good as gold, waiting until the last mouthful of Jell-O salad to wriggle down and run free on the grass – a luxury, Stephen reminds her, that they do not have at home in Islington where the garden is shared with all their neighbours, some of whom you would not want to leave alone with a small child.

She remembers how she had read R. D. Laing when she was a student. All madness derived from the family; the mad are sane and the sane mad. But if this illogical warmth, this exuberance, this atavistic understanding of what you should cling to in life and what you should let go is madness, then she is all for it. She does not understand Si and Ximena at all. The Newmans touch each other constantly – they are tactile people. Stephen's mother sits for a few moments between courses, holding Andrea's hand for no reason she can understand other than a natural affection Andrea herself has had to teach herself how to feel. To live is simple and obvious, is the point that is being made.

Still, the nausea of revulsion. She persuades herself that her persistent knot of anxiety is probably down to the long flight across the Atlantic and the van trip, and worrying about the kids. Because she needs to snap out of this snobbishness right now. This is where they are going to live. It has all been decided. She has given her consent to becoming an American, even if it involves a mink hat. The one thing she is not giving up is her husband, for whom she has fought. *She*, not he, insisted that they were going to make a real, not fake, marriage. *She* gave birth to two children. Always she has been bedevilled by those crows and their many meanings in her life, but she won't put up with them spoiling this. She loves her husband and nothing will possess her to inflict a broken home on her children. Stephen is a fantastic father: he even irons their little clothes when he gets home from work; there is no way he will abandon them.

In the future, when she sees clients whose marriages are faltering and are wondering whether they should leave or stay, she will remark, despite the rule of non-directional counselling she must abide by: 'Marriages last because the people in them want to be married.'

So what choice does she have?

'It'll seem different in the morning,' she says. 'I'll be fine.'

'Good. I'm going to sleep. This is all nothing. It's just a damned hat.'

He closes his eyes and the road rears up in front of him.

All across America he had been noticing cripples. Boys his own age, with long hair, earrings, bandannas, jeans, in wheelchairs or on crutches, missing an arm or a leg or two legs or two arms. He had seen, for the first time, a fleshy stump in shorts. He had noticed an eye dragged permanently open, with no eyelid, which must have been burned away. A missing nose. Scorch marks across the neck and chin. The maimed children of America. In Denver he saw a boy in a chair screaming at his parents in the street as they pushed him across an intersection; the poor mom and dad were in jail along with their kid. He thought of his parents like this, wheeling him around for the rest of his life, wheeling him to the bar where he would have sat and drunk and wept. He'd known cripples, but they were poor bastards who were born that way and came up living in their own world on which he could gain no purchase, nor wanted to. Or they had had an accident (there was always some fool who really did jump off the roof for a dare). And in the neighbourhood there were those who had come back from the Second World War no longer in one piece, people his parents' age whom you could never imagine young and who stayed at home in a permanent twilight on military pensions.

Shocked and frightened to see what has happened to his own generation, that his decision to stay on in England to avoid the draft was well founded, he lies thinking of those crippled men. For while he has often imagined his own death in combat, he has never given any thought to the war damaging him for life. That could have been me, been me, been me. He has no idea who he would be if he had no legs. Where, for example, would he have found a woman, unless she was some poor creature who would take a partial man because she could never get a whole one?

For several days Stephen is behind the wheel again, as the family takes in the sights of Los Angeles and eats at the Brown Derby restaurant, a diner in the shape of a hat, where they spot Farrah Fawcett with her hair in the Flick, a sight so charming and innocent, Stephen thinks, so absolutely American: a buttered corncob kind of girl. But, alone, he drives the van to the campus to see his old professor, who had guided him through the process of applying for his Rhodes scholarship. They had always liked each other and he had written to Professor Whaley to confess that he had been sent down, and what exactly for, a difficult letter to compose. The response had been cool but without any tone of moral outrage, and at the outset of this journey across America he had hoped that this misdemeanour would be long forgotten.

'A research job?' Professor Whaley laughed. 'With only a bachelor's degree we could just about offer you a position as a lab technician.'

'*What?*'

'I'm so sorry but what did you think? You've been out of your field for nearly a decade. You really don't have any qualification for getting back into science. You were doing your research back in the solution phase. We've been automating peptide synthesis. Of course, if you want to come back and start your doctorate again, I'll take you on as a student, but someone who graduated this summer is more up to date than you are.'

'That's not true. I read up.'

'No, Mr Newman, it's not the same thing at all. Here's what has been happening just here in our department.'

And Stephen is totally fazed. He has no idea what Professor Whaley is talking about – he can only just keep up. 'But what am I to do?' he cries.

'Well, we always need science journalists. Have you thought about trying *Popular Science*? Though, of course, you'd need to relocate to New York.'

Is this how Professor Whaley thinks of him? A guy who writes dumbed-down articles for *Popular Science*, which marvels over new inventions such as Velcro? He understands that his old professor is punishing him: he feels personally let down that his kid, his *protégé*, has turned out to be one of those hippies whose eyes have never been on the prize.

'Are you sure there's no other opening, no avenue I could go down? What about the commercial sector?'

'You could try something like General Foods.'

Develop new breakfast cereals and potato chips? He would rather die.

'So, you said in your letter that you got married,' says Professor Whaley, changing the subject.

'Yes, I have. And two kids.'

'Is your wife a scientist?'

'No. She's a shrink.'

'Ah, the voodoo science.'

This is it. Professor Whaley has made it clear what he thinks of him, the defector, the second-rate phoney. The verdict is agonising because Stephen's self-image is so bound up with his being the blue-eyed boy, the Rhodes scholar with everything ahead of him, and now he is caught, trapped in a tight corner from which he can see no obvious escape.

He walks out to the van under blue skies and past palm trees, the Pacific only a mile or two away lapping the shores of the continent. I'm a nobody, he thinks.

Behind the wheel of the van he finds himself not heading home but striking south towards San Diego. This wasn't his intention, but he needs half an hour to clear his head, to take in what he has just heard. Half an hour is not enough, though, for the cataclysm that has occurred. With his eyes ahead of him, it seems entirely possible to keep on driving south until you run out of road, but that's a long, long way in the future – you can reach near the end of the world before the road dies. Crossing America, he was intent on a destination, going home, but now he is just a hand on the wheel and a foot on the gas.

When things like this happen to him, when he got sent down from Oxford because they found his acid-making factory, he experiences a heavy numbness. Andrea is always asking how he feels and the answer is, he feels nothing. He is encased in a thick membrane of indifference. That's what envelops him now as he drives on. Fog.

The signs to San Diego remind him of his uncle Enrique, and of the merchant seaman's document he has carried always in his wallet, proud of its possession, that once he was a sailor and still is, with the papers to prove it. The key to life is in the oceans. He could do it: he could just take himself to the hiring hall, leave the van at the dockside and Andrea, Marianne and Max at his parents' place to console themselves any way they can and find their own way home. He could be clear across the Pacific, sailing down past the coastline of Patagonia. Anything is possible.

Brooding on these thoughts, at Carlsbad he picks up a lone hitchhiker who is working her way down the coast to Mexico. Standing at the roadside with her rucksack, her long hair swinging round her face, her tight jeans and cut-off top, she awakes in Stephen memories of long ago, of his forgotten college girlfriends who all looked much like she does. There is a type, this Californian kind of girl who dresses simply and is fresh and natural and does not have too many complicated European ideas in her head. She looks about twenty, more than a decade younger than him, and on an impulse he does not want to think too hard about, he pulls over and picks her up.

Susie is not Californian: she's a girl from the real north country, way up in Canada, up and over the high line, Alberta, a place where you look out and you see endless nothing, and the longer you stare, the more you start hallucinating. But it's not even where she is originally from: she was born in a cold, cold town in Ontario where nothing worthwhile has ever happened or will, and her dad moved the family out west to find work in the oil fields. So here she is, running away to find the Aztecs and eat peyote buttons and learn to fly like the guy in the Carlos Castaneda book.

'You know that's not possible?' Stephen says. Back in college, a few of his customers had read the same book, *The Teachings of Don Juan*, and figured that if a Yaqui shaman could fly under the influence of mescaline, it ought to be possible to take off from the window of their college. All this had produced was broken legs and broken necks but adherents of the guru claimed that this was due to the lack of a higher consciousness in Oxford undergraduates, the purity of whose minds were corroded by Western precepts like the Enlightenment.

'I heard people did,' says Susie. 'Someone flew right across the Grand Canyon. A lot of people saw it.'

'It's just an urban legend. No one can fly unless you're a bird. No ingested chemical can overcome gravity.'

'Okay, Dad.'

'What do you mean? I'm not your dad.'

'You *sound* like my dad.'

'I'm not old enough to be anyone's . . .' But he is. Not only does he have kids of his own but technically, just about, if he'd started really early, if he had been precociously sexual and found someone willing to do it with him (though he wasn't and no one would) this girl could be his daughter. Which was absurd because he was not that old, just thirty-two.

The scenery of the southern coast is utterly beguiling. This is where someone like him could live, with the ocean ever present and a few strange plants whose names he doesn't need to know growing by the roadside. Everything is big and meaningful and Susie, leaning her head out of the window, points up to the sky, to a bird she thinks she's seen there. 'Is that an eagle?'

'I don't know. I don't know what an eagle looks like.'

'Do you mind if I sing a little?' she says, turning to him. Hey! She has dimples.

'Do you have a good voice?'

'I sang in the church choir.'

'Okay, give it a try, I'll listen. But no hymns. I'm not into that stuff. What else can you sing?'

'Are you okay with Leonard Cohen?'

'Of course. I grew up on him.'

'He's super-cool for an old guy.' And, opening her mouth, she begins to sing in a lovely voice of Marianne, to whom the speaker is saying goodbye.

'That's my daughter's name. She's Marianne, also. A friend of ours named her for that song – that is, she and my wife cooked up the name. I had no say at all but I'm glad that's what they chose.'

Stephen remembers Grace standing by the bed in the hospital, as he might have thought the bad fairy would have hovered over the cradles of newborn infants in fairytales had he been brought up in European darkness, where lives were fated and doomed from the outset. But he merely thought that Grace cast an unwelcome shadow over the sleeping head of his baby girl, whose startling blue eyes and dark head-down marked her out as a human being with visible characteristics. Grace had lit a cigarette. The smoke wreathed around the newborn's head, drawn into her lungs by the two tiny points of her adorable nostrils. 'I think she's Marianne, like in the Leonard Cohen song. So long, Marianne, because I'll always be saying goodbye to her.'

The girl next to him scratches her flat belly. 'I got a bite,' she says. 'I slept in the forest somewhere and it was full of bugs.'

'You slept in the forest all by yourself?'

'Yes.'

'You weren't frightened?'

'No, I grew up in the wilderness – it doesn't scare me.'

'What will happen when you get to Mexico? Do you know people there?'

'No, but I'll be okay. I'll find the people with the peyote and they'll take care of me.'

'People can be nasty. You should watch out.'

'I never really met any who were, not in my home town.'

'You're too innocent. You really should reconsider this whole thing. Are you in school? Don't you have studies?'

'I was, but I didn't find it interesting. I don't think I could survive if I didn't have this trip. I know it's going to be amazing. I just have to get to Mexico. I read up all about it. It's the place I should be, I'm sure of that.'

'Here's San Diego,' says Stephen. 'I can't take you any further.

I'll pull over somewhere you shouldn't find it too hard to get a ride. If you get in any trucks, just tell them you're angel beaver.'

'I know that already.'

'Good.'

He pulls over and she leans across and puts her arms round him. 'Here's a hug for you,' she says. He lightly kisses her cheek, and on the same impulse that caused him to pick her up, he suddenly asks (and the words come out of his mouth before he's thought them), 'Listen, can you do me a favour?'

'What do you want?'

'A kiss, that's all.'

'You want me to kiss you?'

'Yes, and that's it, I promise. I won't touch you anyplace.'

'Sure.'

She smells not too clean from her long road trip and her hair is dirty close up, but she kisses like she means it, which is all he really wants, with his tongue in her mouth and hers in his. His hand moves automatically towards her breast but he stops himself. 'You can if you want,' she says. 'I don't care.' So he feels her breasts. Over her shoulder he can see the mattresses in the back where his kids have slept their way across America. Can he do this? Does he even want to? Oh, Susie. Oh, Susie Sue.

# Hamster Years

In the house in Canonbury there were rooms that Marianne was not permitted to enter. It was a house that was all stairs and corridors, doors with numbers on them, and some of the doors were always locked and others were not. Behind certain doors she could hear cats. In your childhood, places seem more vast. With age they contract, but the house in Canonbury went on expanding, even after Marianne eventually left home.

A closed door would open suddenly to reveal an empty room, the carpet decorated with a faded ivy pattern, and where the cats had lived there were stiff, ammonia-smelling patches. Cold ceramic plates of gas fires stood in the fireplaces. Workmen came and removed them. False ceilings of Styrofoam squares were taken out to reveal ornamental ceiling roses and decorative cornices. Weeks later, the rooms were high, light and painted white or dragée-coloured pastels. One afternoon her father took her by the hand and opened a door that led to a place she had only seen from the window of her bedroom: the garden. The house just went on growing as Marianne grew.

A single door was always closed to her. Behind a sign that said

'Do Not Enter, Silence', she could hear low voices, often weep-ing. One visitor to the closed room arrived in a chauffeur-driven car and the driver waited for her outside, smoking on the street.

Marianne dismissed these arrivals and departures. Her mother had a great many friends who came and went at exact intervals but she was always there, from when Marianne awoke in the morning, was given her breakfast, walked to school, picked up again for lunch, returned to school and then there her mummy was, waiting yet again at the gates with the other mummies. And only in the school holidays did she understand the vast extent of her mother's social network and how implacably she was prepared to ignore her daughter when these idle gossips were present, behind that closed door with its unfriendly signs.

(There is no point in a little brother.)

When they returned from America, back to the top-floor flat in Canonbury. Stephen went haywire for a few weeks. Every evening after the kids had gone to bed he lit a joint and put on his Beach Boys, Lovin' Spoonful and Jefferson Airplane records, leaving Andrea to do the housework and look after the chil-dren. It was the point in the marriage when Andrea, looking back, could see that the whole thing might have gone under. He turned away from her in bed as if her flesh was repugnant to him; he averted his face when she was changing into her clothes, stripped down to her bra and pants. The children were patches of fog moving across the floor. He was going to leave her; she didn't know he had already failed.

'All I do is work a job,' he said. 'I recycle press releases. I might as well invent a better breakfast cereal.'

'Yes, but there are jobs and jobs,' she said stubbornly. She was going to save her marriage. She had got what she wanted – they had not moved permanently to America – but she knew he thought she had entrapped him somehow. He must stay trapped, happily trapped.

She found an advertisement in the *Guardian* for researchers to work on BBC science documentaries for the Open University. The programmes would not just be in the chemistry or pharmaceutical field, he would be able to cover the whole spectrum. A science degree and a background in science journalism was required; he had both. Enquiries revealed that a researcher became a producer. He might even be sent on location to film primates. That would be fun, he consented, reading the advertisement. 'I'll go for it,' he said.

And it turned out it was fun. It brought out in him the latent polymath who had sat in the science library, reading about the glories of particle physics, or watched the space capsules hurtle towards the moon, or synthesised his own LSD.

Stephen thought of the voyage over on the SS *United States*, of the cabin-boy who ran along the gangways in his Prince Edward jacket, carrying coffee and dry-cleaning for the gilded passengers. Of the first-class staterooms, and his own tiny cabin below the water-line, too small even to sit up and read in bed. It was a process of emigration, he now understood. He had waved goodbye to the Statue of Liberty, and Manhattan had receded behind him. Goodbye. Goodbye.

The only person he ever told about the girl in the van was Ivan. 'She was so pretty until you got up close, and then she smelt of not having washed much lately. That's what I chiefly remember about the whole thing, that she didn't have a good smell, and afterwards all I could think about was that maybe she had some disease. I don't even mean the clap – herpes would have been bad enough. Imagine if I gave Andrea herpes. It would have killed me. Yet I still wonder what happened to her. I wanted to give her money, just to make sure she had somewhere to sleep, but giving her money would have looked really insensitive.'

'It was nothing,' Ivan said. 'Absolutely nothing. Don't give it another thought.'

Ivan was in Gibson Square on the other side of Upper Street. It was permanently, obstinately wealthy. The square lived on opulently, despite the petrol-fumed dusty main road it lay alongside, where coffee was a beige, sweetened drink served from a metal urn.

What Stephen liked about Ivan was that he had no principles, just ideas flitting about his mind from moment to moment. He was like a kid chasing soap bubbles. How could you despise him for that? The idea of now was to eat tremendously expensive meals on the company expense account and go out with actresses.

'The orgone thing was correct in a certain sense,' Ivan said. 'We're a mass of desires. Andrea was the person who convinced me of that. We're doomed to be irrational so any political system based on reason has to fail. You can accuse me of selling out, but I only make people aware of the things that make them happy.'

'Candy bars?'

'Yes. Why not?'

'Fish fingers?'

'Very useful if you have kids. The portion size is right for them. Don't you feed your kids fish fingers?'

'Yes, we do, but . . .'

'There isn't a but, Stephen. You saw them advertised. You bought them. No?'

Stephen had no idea how they came to buy fish fingers for the children. He just knew they were in the kitchen, waiting to be heated up and served with ketchup. He had no idea why they always bought the same brand and not random ones. He calculated the mathematical possibilities of always buying random products: it was far more likely than buying the same ones every week, yet they didn't. There must have been something they liked about Bird's Eye, yet there was nothing special about it. What was going on? The problem troubled and baffled him. He felt that there must lie in the unexplored territory Andrea called his subconscious all kinds of irrational pathways, a maze of knots. Neural pathways would have to be relaid.

And Ivan just sat there and smiled, sitting at his matt black ash dining-table, laying out a line of coke. He was still the same boy who had driven through the night to see the white horse carved in the hillside. He was like his old man, the barrister, Stephen thought, who took the bus to chambers, put on his wig and the rest of the legal fancy dress, then came home and read a book about the whirling dervishes.

'Have you heard anything from Grace?' Ivan asked.

'Andrea has. She's travelling in Latin America.'

'Cuba didn't work out?'

'I don't know what happened there. I just know she's in Nicaragua at the moment.'

'Poor Grace.'

The coke took hold of them and they stared exultantly out of the window to the square, which inexplicably had filled with sunshine, though Stephen thought that on his side of Upper Street there were border guards who did not grant it permission to enter.

In 1981 Ralph, turning sixty, was tired of the responsibility of the sitting tenants, some of whom had already been there when his father bought the house during the war for five hundred pounds, cash. He had been the custodian of the property after his parents died; they wanted him to bring up his family in it and he'd let them down. There had been a fiancée for a couple of months but that was as far as it had ever got. He would have liked to move to Finchley, but that was just a pipe-dream. If he could sell the house to Stephen and Andrea they might tolerate him in a couple of rooms, which was all he needed; he could close down the underwear shop and live on the interest from the house sale. He could practise his conjuring tricks all day long and take long, pleasurable naps. It was enough. He'd never wanted more, except what he couldn't have, what he understood would always thwart him, forbidden longings that he subsumed in magic, which was also all about concealment.

'We *should* buy it,' Andrea said.

'Why?'

'It's a good house. The area is coming up – it will be harder to buy if we wait.'

Stephen could not work out why he was resisting. His father had owned his own home; it was a point of pride with him that he had put down a deposit on a house as soon as his first child was born, though he had never quite made it to that middle-class accessory of Californian life, the pool in the yard. But that was LA. Everyone owned their own home in California; you were a dolt if you did not. This was London, a place that people like him came to temporarily.

Andrea said, 'We can't live like students for ever. Ivan has bought a flat.'

'Ivan's parents are rich. We can't make the deposit.'

'Well, we'll just have to find a way.'

'We'll still be living with Ralph and all the old folks. We can't get rid of them.'

'For now, Stevie. Just for now.'

What does the past matter? Stephen thought, when he cut his hair short to open a building-society account and put down their names for a mortgage. They were already expanding through the house. He saw the family as an enclosed square with four sides, mother, father, daughter and son. He felt he walked on air, like the cartoons where the tom cat runs like crazy until he comes to the edge of a cliff and keeps on running, is halfway across the ravine before he glances down and realises he is without support. The trick, Stephen now understood, was to keep looking straight ahead in order to stay airborne, and this had always come easily to him.

At work he was approached to apply for an internally advertised post as producer on a new science strand on BBC2. It was a fantastic job: you travelled the world making glorious documentaries; you met and interviewed everyone you might want to meet. Carl Djerassi, who had synthesised artificial oestrogen to make the contraceptive pill and launched the sexual revolution, the man who launched millions of free fucks! Linus Pauling and his theory of the molecular clock, which pinned down when humans and chimpanzees had first diverged as species, and so much more – there was nothing this man's teeming mind had not thought of, and then some. *And* he had campaigned against the Bomb! Under Pauling's influence, Stephen first began ingesting large quantities of vitamin C as a way of warding off the common cold. He was convinced of Pauling's correctness, though the system failed every time to prevent his bronchi congesting. He did not cease to collapse with a wheezy chest until he finally gave up smoking at the age of thirty-seven.

Stephen took the tube to White City each day and had his own office with his name on the door and a team of production assistants. This BBC, it was like working for an exclusive club where everyone was doing something interesting, and when you sat down to lunch in the canteen you might as well have been at an Oxford high table, where your colleagues talked of poetry, history, plays, music. He was once more a member of an institution. He felt comfortable there; he enjoyed office politics. The building circled around like a concrete doughnut, ugly, functional and beloved. His first assignment was a series about the origins of the universe, which involved commissioning animations of the Big Bang. Soon he and Andrea had enough for a deposit and a

crippling mortgage, so they bought the house from Ralph, guar-
anteeing him a lifetime tenancy of two rooms.

Nothing would now remove Andrea from this place – it would
take a crowbar to get her out, Stephen realised. She was finally
home. He was as far from home as ever, but looking at her climb-
ing ladders, painting hallways in her jeans, how could he not feel
grateful for what was his, this feeling of love for someone who
drives you nuts and you don't understand but who brings you
soup when you're sick, and touches your shoulder when she
passes you in the kitchen for no reason at all, except that your
bodies have exchanged themselves over and over again? You're
the same person. That's marriage, that's how his parents got
through it, and he would too. He was happy to give it his very
best shot. He adored her. Why wouldn't he? She was his wife and
the mother of his kids.

Ralph first showed the children simple card tricks, then moved
on to feats of close-up magic with pieces of cord. Both watched
his hands carefully. Max still believed in magic, in fairies, goblins, elves, witches, wizards, unicorns, flying chairs and wishing
chairs. He was too young to understand that the nature of the
tricks was deception, and when Marianne explained this, he
believed that all she had done was illuminate the principles
behind magic, which remained deep and significant and beautiful. For if you took ordinary things in the house that were
stupendous – like flipping a switch on the wall and the objects in
a room and the persons in it were suddenly obliterated – they,
too, had an explanation. It wasn't an illusion.

Ralph had trouble not touching Max, he wanted to kiss his
peachy cheek. He could cup his hand over the boy's when he
showed him how to conceal a card, but that was as far as it could
go. The business with boys was a locked door in his head, which
only found its expression in sleep and the moments after waking.

Most of the sitting tenants of the house had eventually left in their final boxes: only he and one old lady on the top floor remained, and him in his two rooms with his mother's furniture, her double bed, her china ornaments, her lace antimacassars. Andrea and Stephen's dinner guests, bearing wine, flowers, chocolates, a silver twist of hash, Ivan with a folded paper of powder, arrived, rang the bell and, entering, would sometimes see the old man emerging from the bathroom, buttoning his flies and ask, 'Who is that ghost in the hall?'

'It's Ralph. He was here before we were and when we bought the place we agreed to give him a sitting tenancy. We can't get rid of him, it's the law, but he's absolutely harmless and Max likes him.'

The years of growing up in the failed hotel had taught Andrea how to manage a household. Money was terribly tight at first. They economised on all luxuries and took their summer break in her home town, another place that was coming up. The hotel still lay empty but the fishermen's cottages were being turned into holiday homes. Stephen learned to like it there: the port, the pilot boat, the Customs house, the dredgers, the Russian sailors walking through the tiny streets, the up and down paths straightening out to become the old rope walk, which led to the opening mouth of the estuary and then the sea. He enjoyed the stubborn ugliness of the tugs towing the ships in and out of the deep-water harbour.

The children played on the beach; he and Andrea sat on the sand reading the newspapers, the raucous cries of *Watch me, Daddy*, the water-wings attached to his son's shoulders (the little rubber angel), the melting ice-creams dripping onto the news-paper and onto the face of the prime minister, the smell of the sea, and the ships sailing out under their flags to unknown ports. That could be me, Stephen thought. Still, he sat on the beach while Andrea unpacked a picnic lunch.

She bit into an apple and felt a hard, unfamiliar crunch in her mouth. She spat the contents out into her hand. A blackish lump lay on the palm.

'What's that?' said Stephen.

'A filling, I think.'

'You know what? If ever I make real money I'm going to get your teeth fixed.'

'Fixed in what way?'

'There are all kinds of things they can do. In America we have veneers.'

'What are they?'

'They'd give you a row of straight white teeth, like mine. At least the kids don't seem to have inherited your British teeth. I hope not – they go to the dentist enough.'

'You don't like my teeth?' In all the years they had been married he had never mentioned them. She was in her thirties: what other imperfections did he find in her body? She struggled with her weight, slimming down with difficulty after Marianne was born and gaining it all back after Max, then making the Everest climb to the unreachable summit of nine stone. A stubborn ten pounds would not leave her thighs and stomach, yet he told her he liked her body: he wanted something to grab hold of. Her breasts drooped; he said he didn't care. And all this time she had overlooked her teeth, which were suddenly defective and needed 'fixing', as if they were a leaky roof or unstable foundations.

'The point is, you don't like your teeth. You smile without opening your mouth.'

'Do I?'

'Of course you do.'

'I never realised.'

She looked across his shoulder to the sea. A shaft of sunshine illuminated her face like the old days, in the squat, when the light from London had lent her that spiritual expression, the old movie-star look he had fallen in love with.

There were little lines round her eyes. He did not care. What was going on in her mind? He had to know – she could still surprise him.

'You're lost in some thought. Tell me what it is.'

'I was thinking about what Freud said about teeth, how across all cultures everyone has the same dreams involving the same four themes: flying, falling, being naked and losing our teeth. Some cultures believe that dreaming of losing a tooth portends the loss of a family member but Freud thought it symbolised fear of castration.'

'I've never dreamed about my teeth.'

'How would you know? You say you can hardly remember your dreams.'

'True.'

'I think dreaming of our teeth is to do with the fear of growing old.'

'We'll never grow old,' said Stephen, watching his children building a sandcastle with their plastic buckets and spades.

On summer weekends in London Andrea landscaped the long garden with fruit trees and wisteria trellises. The house and garden were all flamboyant display, while work was a secret pact between therapist and patient. Did she ever really cure anyone? No. She just made them less dependent on her, more equal to surviving with equanimity life's sorrows and unpleasant surprises. After several years she came to realise that the problems were always the same. The patients presented themselves at her consulting rooms and opened up their hearts, exposing their torments, and nothing was surprising any more.

A patient told her husband she was leaving him. He told her he would kill himself if she went through with it. Still she left him. She took a new job in London. He told her that when she left Norwich he would kill himself. She moved to London. She told him she was divorcing him; he said if she served the papers he would kill himself. She served the papers. He invited her to the house to sign them and have a drink for old times' sake. When she arrived she found him lying on the bed, dead, with a plastic bag tied round his head and a note beside him saying that he couldn't live without her.

As a story went, it had an unexpected twist. Most people who threatened suicide were all talk, those who wanted to end their lives did so quietly and with resolute determination. But what was predictable were the intense feelings of guilt in the woman who believed she had murdered her husband or, at least, had given him tacit permission to kill himself. Andrea's task was that of the defence lawyer, who gets their client off a charge. She was teaching her clients (particularly the women) that they were not responsible for the actions of other people. Women, she observed, had centres that were constantly leeching away from them to others. They had no sense that they deserved to put themselves first and foremost.

She thought of Grace often, and they kept in touch by letter and Grace's occasional visits to London from wherever it was that she was travelling. Grace put no one but herself first. Perhaps it was an unhealthy extreme, her life, the way she lived, but Andrea admired her. She had mastered the art of absolute freedom. This is what I do, Andrea thought. I teach women to be free, even if they are, like me, in a marriage with children. You can still be a feminist when you're married.

She and Stephen laid down a stone-flagged patio where they sat on summer evenings when he came home from work. Stephen, holding a glass of wine, would gaze up and up past all the windows to what they owned, or what the building society owned. Birds sang in the branches of the pear tree. His children looked out from their bedrooms and waved to him. Inside, Andrea was spraying herself with scent and stepping into a white linen dress, fitted at the waist. Her hair was not exactly the same red that he remembered. Neither was he the same man in the mirror.

Stephen in 1986, at forty, reverting to the jeans, the leather jackets, the denim shirts in which he had arrived at Oxford before his make-over by Andrea, had lost both the beard and now the upper reaches of his hairline. He owned three suits and several ties. His Prince Edward jacket from the SS *United States* still hung in the wardrobe but the buttons and the holes they were supposed to fit into were separated by a wide gap across his chest. Even the sleeves were too tight. The kids used it for fancy dress.

Looking back at this time in his life, Stephen can't think of much to say about it. It was the period of growth followed by satisfactory consolidation.

The children brought home head lice, and friends who announced, 'My dad says there's no point getting an education cos there's no jobs.' Ivan had raised the question of whether they had put anything aside for school fees.

'Didn't we think kids would do best if they were allowed to run wild?' said Stephen. 'Didn't we say no one ever grew because they were being measured? Didn't we say that property was theft?'

'All of that may be true, but not in Islington.'

So Marianne was sent up the hill, to the school where serious girls wore shit-brown uniforms and formed unfriendly cliques, of which she became an enthusiastic member, and then a bossy leader.

From the outset, from when they bought the house from Ralph and were no longer confined to a few rooms, and held the key to the garden door, there had been the issue of a pet. Marianne wanted a dog.

'No dog,' Stephen said. 'Absolutely no dog. A dog is *verboten*. You want to see me get nasty? You want to see me get Nazi?'

'Why not? Give me five reasons,' said Andrea.

'I'll write them down for you.'

1. They're stupid.
2. They're dependent.
3. They lead a pointless existence.
4. They're stupid.
5. They're stupid.

No amount of begging moved him. It was the line that could not be crossed. Dogs terrified him: they barked, they bit, they gave you rabies, which was a horrible disease – he'd made a programme about it. You drowned in your own saliva. How terrible was that?

What about a cat? Cats did not bound at you with their slathering fangs when the doorbell was rung, wet fur around their unpleasant blackish lips, but when you were sitting on someone's sofa drinking coffee they jumped on your lap and buried their claws in your thighs, digging through your jeans. Cats were sly and nasty. They kept themselves to themselves except when they wanted something. And they made him sneeze.

Marianne said that if you took a small photo of a cat and blew it up really, really large you'd get a lion! Stephen studied other people's cats. Ivan had one, a black-and-white thing that came with all kinds of accessories his new live-in girlfriend, probably-wife-to-be, Simone had bought for it. Cats found the places on the floor where shafts of sunlight fell through the windows and made it their spot. Carlos Castaneda's shaman had said everyone had their spot on the surface of the earth; you just had to discover it. Cats made it their business to do that without even having read the book, which was impressive. There used to be an underground comic strip called *Fat Freddie's Cat*, which made him laugh. The cat would take revenge on its owner by shitting in his headphones, and generally led an anarchic existence, which Stephen respected more than the slavish devotion of the dog.

On the downside, cats appeared to have absolutely no sense of humour. If cats could speak they would never have developed jokes. If you told a cat a joke, a joke about cats, and they could understand your language, they would stare at you with their cold, unpleasant gaze. You'd have to explain it to them, like a problem in mathematics. Cats were Egyptian. They came from the land of the pharaohs and the Pyramids, from a time of many cruel gods. They existed without humour or real affection.

He consented to a cat on a trial basis. The cat lasted three or four days before Stephen understood that when it stared at him with its large, seemingly intelligent eyes what it saw was a five feet ten inches tall can-opener. The smell of its food sickened him, open in a bowl by the door, the cat picking away at the fishy morsels. The cat's fur proved nearly lethal, causing his eyes to close up and his breath almost to fail in his chest, and he made Andrea ring Ivan to drive him to hospital.

They moved down several notches in size to a hamster, which lived in a cage quietly in the kitchen, being generally no trouble, not living too long, and teaching the kids important lessons about the inevitable cycle of life and death. When Max left home Stephen found himself voluntarily looking after their fourth hamster, Cuddles, not wanting it to die, with no excuse to replace it with another. He liked the little guy in there, who looked at him with bright, specky eyes, and demanded nothing. It ate grains, peacefully, and emitted tiny inoffensive droppings. One day, obliged to answer the phone while he was cleaning out the cage on a Saturday morning, he left the gate open and Cuddles escaped from his confinement. Stephen searched the house for him. Later that afternoon, Andrea did the laundry. Cuddles had made a nest among the sheets and duvet covers and she scooped him up inside a pillowcase, without noticing. He emerged from the machine forty minutes later, damp and dead. Stephen wept for ten minutes, feeling like an accomplice in a murder.

These hamster years were how he thought of the eighties and nineties, the blur of middle age and child-rearing.

He was British now. He had taken out citizenship to avoid the boredom of waiting in long lines when he arrived home at Heathrow Customs and Immigration, and he and Andrea had both joined the Labour Party. Sometimes he even went to meetings. Twenty years later he was damned if he could remember what it was about Margaret Thatcher that had made him so angry. Was it merely her hats, her handbags, her hair and her appalling teeth? For he could no longer really recall what her policies had been, apart from her demonic urge to destroy the coal miners whom he sentimentally supported because he saw them on TV, the wives, plain and indomitable, standing at the doors of their modest houses in the driving rain as the defeated men left for work or, more likely, the dole queue.

He looked at the government and thought they were stuffed shirts, pompous upper-class windbags. America had a president worse, if anything, than Nixon: an actor, a total fake. But what had Thatcher and Reagan stood for exactly? It was possible to live in London in a middle-class bubble inside which everyone said the same things, thought the same things, ate the same meals, travelled the same tube line, read the same newspapers and books, watched the same TV programmes and films and used the same grammatical constructions in their sentences. You agreed with everyone else because you believed that you could not know anyone who was so badly wrong about anything fundamental. The real variables, Andrea said, were in their inner lives, that inside they all suffered and managed as best they could to manage that suffering. 'I don't,' Stephen said.

# Max's Room

Watching Ralph's hands, Max entered a world in which communication could be entirely visual. The card was secreted in a sleeve or displaced between two fingers. It was possible to train his own eye to look where he was supposed not to look in order to understand where the deception lay, but eventually Ralph showed him how the tricks were done and handed over his expensive magic books.

In his bedroom Max practised for hours in silence. When his sister entered he did not look up. When his mother told him he should brush his teeth and come to bed, he did not look up. When, in the kitchen after dinner, his father turned on the radio, he did not register the sound. When lightning illuminated the garden he turned his head to watch the rain pounding the pavement. When, a few moments later, a thunderclap seemed to smash into the side of the house, he moved uneasily in his chair.

Stephen rose from the kitchen table and stood behind his son. He emptied the apples from a paper bag and blew it up, then clapped his hands against it a few inches from Max's ear. Max looked puzzled, as if aroused very gently from sleep, unsure whether he was in the land of waking or dreaming, then went back to drawing pictures in his mashed potato.

'He can't hear,' said Marianne, who was waiting to be allowed to get down so she could watch her permitted hour of television. 'He looks at the shapes we make with our mouths and that's how he knows what we're saying.'

'Since when?' Stephen said, feeling a sac of poison moving in his stomach.

Marianne considered the question. 'Since I was three.'

'Don't be silly. It's a long time since you were three,' Andrea said.

'I might be exaggerating.'

Max was eight years old, Marianne eleven. Under their noses, their son had gone deaf without them noticing.

Privately, Stephen had thought Max was slow, his own son a dimwit. He had said nothing to Andrea, fearing that she would assault him for being an intellectual snob. So what if their son was not an intellectual, would not follow his father into science, or either of them to Oxford? Mental health counted, that is what she would say.

Privately, Andrea had thought that Max had withdrawn into silence as a weapon against what he sensed were fractures in his parents' marriage. She did not tell Stephen this, because to do so would be to admit that there was an underlying trouble, and that this potential destabilisation was her. That for five months she had been nearly having an affair. There had been no infidelity, except that when Stephen was away filming she rang him up, they had coffee, or lunch, and agreed that nothing would happen, both of them being married, and exhausted each other with conversation about the merits of their agreement not to take anything further until they had wrung dry this putative relationship, talked it out.

And she thought afterwards, Better to have got it over with, had a one-night stand, or it would have been in the afternoon, when all their children were at school and spouses otherwise occupied. They could have gone to bed and satisfied each other's curiosity. They hadn't. So there was nothing to tell Stephen, and he would have understood far better if she had said she *had* slept with him than if she offered an account of their vacillation, their minute examination of their choices, the talk talk talk. They were both therapists. And Stephen would have said angrily, 'So why didn't you just get on with it?' and he would have been right, because she could not let it go.

The thought of him, the hairs raised on the back of his arms, his blue eyes, the sudden sight of him waiting for her in the café reading his book, his fingers marking something important with a pen, his interesting mind. His body. She had only ever seen one grown man naked – it was too absurd.

And all this time Max was going deaf. And she was deaf to his suffering. She did not believe she was being punished for practising adultery in her heart, she did not believe in God or karma, so she punished herself. She refused to have her teeth fixed. She would not waste the money.

These feelings of guilt are so intense inside all of us, she thought, that they seem almost biological. She and Stephen were a couple, one of whom dealt in reason and the other in the irrational, yet there was nothing you could do about these shocking emotions, your neuroses, except learn to make your peace with them. That was all she could offer her patients. She could make the pain subside a little, no cures, just an acceptance of sadness.

What is inside us is primeval, she thought. There was never any enlightenment, just the banality of peace of mind achieved by accepting the utter ridiculousness of the unconscious. It was a crazy place down there. Let it be. And so she accepted that because she had nearly, but not actually, had an affair, she could not justify spending the money on porcelain veneers, having been so preoccupied that she had failed to notice her son's hearing gently fading away. She did not tell her husband this; she merely said that she was happy with her teeth the way they were and she would rather do up the house than her face.

Max lived on for some weeks in the vault of his silence. He was utterly absorbed in his book of magic tricks. Ralph told him he needed to practise in front of a mirror so he locked himself into the bathroom, climbed onto a stool and watched the cards, lengths of string and small balls perform feats of illusion under his control. It built in him a sense of invincible power. Soon he would be ready to stun his parents and their friends with a performance. Until he was ready he stuck with his audience of one, Ralph, his head resting against the lace antimacassar, nodding, sometimes even crying for no reason. No reason.

One day he was taken from home to the hospital, his best magic book packed in a small suitcase. They sent him to sleep. His hearing had subsided slowly – he had not remembered missing it: he enjoyed the stillness, the peace. He woke suddenly, oppressed by noise. A child was crying in the next bed – he put his hands over his ears to cut off the din. Papers rustled, nurses walked heavily across the lino, a glass of water made a noise, your own hands did. Looking back as an adult, he wished they had allowed him to stay deaf, not inserted the grommet in his ear; he would have enjoyed learning sign language, and would have been good at it, being manually dextrous. Performing his magic act, he preferred not to hear the audience, uninterested in their applause. It was their faces he watched, the look of astonishment, the brain reeling from the impossibility of what it had just seen. He loved watching jaws drop.

The restoration of his hearing after his temporary deafness, Andrea realised, had done nothing to reverse a tendency in his personality to quietness, secrecy, withdrawal and a discomfort with social interaction. Of all the family members, he was the one who expressed no opinions. His school work was completed and handed in on time, but he wasn't listening: he had fallen out of the habit. It didn't interest him to hear what others said, what information they imparted. It could all be obtained from books. He had few friends, finding their company unnecessary. He kept them at bay with his command of illusion. He lived in a solitary world of distant admiration and respect. It was all he wanted.

# Transitory Gardens

'The white girl, the white girl. Here comes the white girl.' She was always standing outside my house in the snow or in the sticky heat, wearing a red Santa hat come rain or shine. I don't know where she slept at night – a whole family was living on a heating shaft so I guess she was on the street, like everyone else, or maybe in a shelter. The city was full of beggars holding out paper cups with a dime or two in them, or even pennies. It was cruel to give a homeless person just cents. But up in Harlem and maybe other places as well, on wasteland, some of the more energetic homeless people made gardens, with fruit and flowers, and after a while I found myself going there every afternoon to see how they were getting on.

'There was something very Zen about those gardens. It was a short cycle of life and death, no more than a summer or two at most, because they were planting in ground that torn-down buildings had once stood on, and something would be built there again, but there was always a transitory moment when the earth breathed and these homeless people came along and dug. I believe it was because they had a longing for permanence, for a connection to one spot. I found it really moving, what they did. Everything about the enterprise was so uncertain. I used to watch my mother in the garden at home in Kent, pruning the roses and removing any suckers. She had a long-range plan: she wanted to make a landscape that would survive and be documented. My father said you build a house for that, but my mother saw the creation of a permanent garden as an act that defied God. At least, I think that was what she meant, it's my interpretation, because to defy God meant that the garden would have an underlying form that couldn't easily be erased by the seasons. Adam was the first gardener – I know that because we had a poster in the hall that my mother bought and had framed. It said, "When Adam delved and Eve span, who was then the gentleman?" And there was a drawing of a naked Adam with his hoe. My father never noticed that it was a slogan about class – he rushed past it every day on his way to the station and rushed past it again when he came home at night. But for my mother, gardening was some weird holy ritual, a pact with the Deity and a contest with him.

'The street people who made the gardens in Harlem were the urban poor, and the poorest of the poor. If they needed materials they had to go hunting in the trash, and the only water they had came from the sky. So I was drawn to go and hang out with them, and help where I could with the carrying and the planting.

'I met a guy called Howard who was lounging in a broken armchair in a tomato patch in a gap on the street where he'd pushed away the rubble of a torn-down brownstone, and he was sitting back eating one of his juicy tomatoes, like a king on his throne. In front of him he'd dug a hole and lined it with plastic garbage bags, and when you looked down into the hole, there were six fat goldfish. God knows where he got them.

'Another woman called Maisie, who was originally from Detroit, grew huge sunflowers just for the hell of it. She could have sold them on the street but she wouldn't. She just wanted to see those sunflowers reach up with their massive yellow heads. It was a totally piss-off gesture. Someone else gathered rocks and painted them with the flag of their home country, which I couldn't recognise – I don't like flags, and faces like masks. That was not so much a garden as a sculpture park. These people were so incredibly limited. They had no money, everything was found, and everything would either be stolen eventually – they'd go to sleep in a cardboard shelter on the lot and in the night someone would come and cut down the flowers and take the vegetables – or the winter would inevitably arrive and the earth would disappear under the snow, and the gardens would disappear too. Sometimes they'd return in the spring – they'd come looking for shoots, for some sign that there was a recovery, but mostly the gardens were temporary.

'I went to work as a cocktail waitress for a while. It was all I could get because I didn't have a work permit and it was the sort of place that wasn't very picky about who they hired. My feet would be swollen from standing all night and the straps of my shoes cut into my instep. I had to keep my fingernails and toenails neat and painted, and present them every evening for inspection, as if I was a fucking horse.

'But at that stage I wasn't ready to leave New York. If I had ever been able to sell my origami dresses everything would have been all right, but Americans are so anti-intellectual. It's all the bottom line – you can see their fingers moving, like they're counting their money without even being aware of what they're doing. They're sick people. I mean the white people – African-Americans are very much more human than the rest of us. They understand things without them being explained. I showed them my origami dresses and they took them. One woman tied the cloth round her head and made a huge hat – she had absolutely no inhibitions. But when I went to see the buyers on Fifth Avenue they looked at the dresses as if they'd been dropped down from outer space. And there *was* something lunar about them, you know. They were just very out there, and in New York, which was the one place where they *should* have been understood, they weren't, because the buyers were too stupid.

'I felt like I'd discovered the laws of relativity, and everyone carried on with the old science, the antique explanations. It was just a dress, but it was the final boundaries of what cloth could *be*. That was what I did and no one cared. They looked at the folds and tucks and said, "Well, that's fine for you, but I'd be all thumbs."

'I walked up and down Fifth Avenue and Madison Avenue and then down to the Village and to Soho and those dresses didn't sell. All they were was pieces of cloth and a set of instructions about what to do with them, how you could make at least fourteen kinds of dress, and the rest was left to your own imagination. The possibilities were limitless. I was trying to sell a total individuality because even when you'd made the dress you could add a belt or pull up the skirt to a different length. The idea was from China, from Mao, who made these suits for everyone to wear so you would eliminate the tiresomeness of all that choice, but I twisted it, so that you just had one piece of cloth and a thousand and one ways of making it your own. But when I went into the stores, they just looked at my samples and said, "Where's the *design*? This is just a piece of fabric."

'There was one woman I started arguing with. I said, "It's a concept," and she called me a flake. I'd never heard that expression. I had no idea what it meant. It could have been a good thing, I had no idea, but I found out later that it wasn't.

'Do you ever have the feeling you want to fly? You're with someone and you want to unfold wings behind your back, and they spread out, heavy and white, and the air rushes and folds and bears you up, and you just take off. And they're sitting there, stunned, because you've done something no one can do, and for a few moments you hover and you're gone. I always wanted wings. When I was a child, at home in Kent, and I could hear my father's footsteps walking past my bedroom in the hall on the way to his study, I used to wish I could fly out of the window and over the valley. I could see some oak trees in the distance and I thought I'd beat my wings really hard until I reached them, and nest with the eagles.

'So in the afternoons I'd be helping the homeless people make their gardens. Howard used to drive the rats away with his slingshot. He had plans to make a birdbath out of a pail of water balanced on a pole if he could fix it firmly enough in the ground. The birds lived very fragile lives and it was hard for them to find food and water – the skinny cats would chase them for food. We found half-eaten birds on the ground among the tomatoes. Then at night I'd dress up in my cocktail-waitress costume and I'd go downtown and take orders for drinks from out-of-state businessmen. The management turned a blind eye if you wanted to go further with them – it was much better money than the tips, but too distasteful. A few of them did it – they suggested that certain men were interested in me, men who liked dominatrixes, and enjoyed being tied up. They offered to show me the knots, and it was tempting – I'd have loved to have some man on his knees – but inside I suppose I'm just a middle-class white girl, because when one night this guy approached me, I ran.

'I only lasted there a few weeks. The other women all had far greater stamina than me. I couldn't take the hours on my feet – I kept sitting down at empty tables, which was absolutely forbidden, and eventually I was fired.

'I had the Harlem apartment as an eight-month sublet from someone I met in Paris who was part of the whole early project of gentrifying Harlem. The neighbours hated me. They were rich black yuppies, dentists and lawyers and professors from Columbia, and they didn't want white people in Harlem. "Go back to the East Village," they said. "You don't belong here."

They were so conventional. They would have *loved* Islington. They would have died and gone to heaven if they could have seen your house, all this dead-salmon Georgian paint. By the time the sublet was coming to an end, I hadn't made many friends in New York, and all of them were from somewhere else, recent arrivals like me, people who came there because we were so absolutely sure that we'd make it, and we didn't. Some of them wound up selling jewellery from a blanket on the street – it was that bad. I mean, these were people who had expected they were going to be hanging out with Andy Warhol and Robert Mapplethorpe. They were only one jump up from the homeless. A girl I knew became a junkie, and then I heard she died of Aids. She was an artist, but whatever it was she did, no one cared. She was living in a rat-hole – my place in Harlem was a palace compared to hers, even though it backed onto the crack house.

'America threw us out. It picked us up, like you pick up a frog and hold it by one of its legs and fling it as far as it can go, and sent us hurtling back across the ocean. Nothing good happened to me in New York, except the gardens, and they vanished. They are buried under hotels and offices now. The seeds and roots are sleeping. I suppose the people who made them are dead, too. They weren't well – they would have had it hard surviving the winter. This was before Mayor Giuliani cleaned up the streets, and when he came along they vanished back into America, if they were still alive, if life still held them.

'It had been a long time since my father had put any money in my account. I kept on checking but there was nothing there. I suppose he must have given up on me finally, thinking that years had gone by and still I hadn't come home so he wasn't able to have any control over me other than by stopping the supply.

'I wound up selling my blood. I didn't want them to deport me so I sold my blood to buy my plane ticket and I went to Barcelona, when it was still cheap and you could live an open-air life on the Ramblas. I met a guy and he took me to Ibiza. He had a house there with stables where he bred Arabians, but his main business was a club he owned in town, a discothèque, he called it, where rich Eurotrash came to party. I stayed all the time at the house, which was inland, and very peaceful. I would sit on the roof sunbathing and look out across the hills and valleys. The sky was flat blue with a few clouds, like a sprinkling of salt, and I thought of my old Cuban boyfriend. Juan bought me a horse and I learned to ride, and I spent more and more time with the horses. He was mean, but the horses were always very nice to me.

'If I could go back anywhere, apart from Cuba, it would be to Ibiza, to the house with the horses. We usually spoke to each other in Spanish but he'd picked up this English expression, I have no idea where. "Mind your manners." And he used it relentlessly on me. He was always telling me that I was rude to his friends. I said, "Well, you know, I just say what I think and if other people can't handle it, that's their problem."

'"People don't like you," he said.

'"Who doesn't like me?"

'"No one. My friends ask me, 'Why are you with her? She's a crazy bitch.'"

'"Well," I said, "*you* like me because you're always showing me off."

'"You spend too much time in the sun," he said. "English women should not sunbathe. Your skin is wrinkling. You lie up there on the roof all afternoon and you are turning into an old lady."

'I found his hair dye under the sink in the bathroom and I dyed one of his pure-white Arabians with it. He was furious, but I thought it was the most hilarious thing. "The poor horse", he kept saying, "the poor horse". But what's the problem? The dye washes out eventually. The shop was out of his particular shade of dye and he came back from town empty-handed. His roots were already showing. "Old man!" I taunted him. I wasn't in love with him, the way I'd loved my Cuban boyfriend, but we had a wonderful life, I'll give him that. The house was fabulous, I had the horses to ride every day. And very good sex. I can't fault him on that.

'It was in Ibiza that I had my second and third abortions. I don't know why you're surprised. The last thing I would do is bring children into this hateful world. If I hadn't been able to get the terminations I'd have strangled them as they came out of me. I'd have killed them with my bare hands.

'This was around the time that the Berlin Wall came down. I kept wondering what Fidel thought, and made Juan go to the port to buy all the papers because we didn't have a TV. I made him buy me a radio. I wanted to know what was happening, and couldn't work out what was going to come next. Now everything was an unknown quantity and I was still very curious. Before certain things had been beaten out of me. I didn't expect that I would be so thwarted. I never thought I'd find myself on my knees.

'I wish I'd stayed in Ibiza. It was a big mistake to leave. Juan would have looked after me – he would never have allowed these things to happen. I was happy there, back in the eighties, before life turned so strange. I could have married Juan and raised horses and gone to Barcelona every couple of months, which would have been enough. It was Juan who pointed out that I was a country girl at heart. "You belong among the peasants," he told me, "except you don't think like them, which is a tragedy for you."

'I can no longer remember why I left him, and sometimes, at night just before I fall asleep, a memory comes to me that I didn't leave but that he asked me to go because of some absurd crime I'd committed, which caused him to lose face. But if that's true, I really don't remember it.

'I should have stayed out of the sun. I'm always having to have lesions biopsied. So far no cancerous cells. I assume I'm fine – I have no symptoms.'

# Mounds

Stephen dreamed of his mother's meatloaf with gravy and creamed potatoes. He rebelled against his wife's healthy nutrition plan and her new mantra of only eating when you are hungry and stopping when you are full. He was the rationalist, not her, yet he found her regime joyless. Eating connected him back to his mother's kitchen, to her cake-baking, to his first experiments with the principles of chemistry, and how ingredients like butter, sugar, eggs and flour lost all resemblance to their original selves when combined. But he still enjoyed eating the results of the experiments.

No: food was more than fuel in ways he was not particularly interested in examining. In the BBC canteen at lunchtime, he chose the lasagne, the fish and chips, the quiches, and experimented with English desserts, like jam roly-poly and trifle. He learned to like custard and what the British called biscuits. The only thing he drew the line at was Christmas pudding and mince pies, for what was the point of a dessert made of dried fruit? Had the British never heard of pecans, chocolate? He had inherited his father's wiry frame, thickening now around the middle but with no tendencies to be a fat man, so why should he not eat what he wanted? He *liked* to eat. What else were his pleasures, when the only drugs were the joints he and Ivan lit at weekends and the occasional line of coke Ivan brought over for his birthday? Apart from that, all he had left was food. He no longer smoked cigarettes, and sex was irregular – neither of them had the energy.

Periodic cravings washed over him with the longing and yearning he had once felt as a hormone-assaulted single man at Oxford, staring at the girls in the next-door garden with their spectacular breasts. He wept at the thought of lemon chiffon pie with a scoop of vanilla ice-cream on the side – maybe two scoops. He drooled over the recollection of fudge brownies, fudge sundaes, apple cobbler, chess pie. Sometimes he ate two chocolate bars on the journey home from work and put his key in the door feeling guilty and nauseous. He badly missed a candy from his youth called Mounds, which was unavailable in Europe. Its name summed it up: a pile of sweetened coconut enrobed in chocolate. The British had something similar – they called it a Bounty bar – but it wasn't the same in a way he couldn't put his finger on. Perhaps it was as simple as the colour of the packaging and its associations. Nor did it have, as its sister confection, the Almond Joy, which was identical to Mounds but with an added nut.

Whenever he went to America to see his parents, he took an extra bag with him to fill with Mounds, Almond Joys, Peppermint Patties, Clark bars and Peanut Butter Cups. His favourite candies did not have caramel in them, which he couldn't stand. Snickers would be an ideal bar were it not for the thin layer of light brown goo holding in place the peanuts. Caramel, he worked out, was primarily used as engineering, to make things adhere to the base ingredient, usually a fondant or nougat, while chocolate held the whole thing together and kept it from sticking to your hands. He suggested to the commissioning editors a fun science programme on the construction of famous confectionary bars, but was knocked back by the BBC's ban on using brand names, which rendered the idea pointless.

He was forced to buy a small refrigerator for his study to keep his American candies, as he called them, from deteriorating before he had worked through them all. Chocolate, he observed, developed in the heat a whitish mould-like substance, called bloom, which he found unappetising though he knew it was harmless. A sub-section of research argued whether the bloom was caused by phase separation or polymorphic transformation. This was how he could have earned a living in the commercial sector: analysing chocolate deterioration. It no longer seemed as shameful as it had when he had sat in Professor Whaley's office at UCLA. You settled for less, he thought. That was what life was, perennially settling for less.

And you fought these absurd little domestic wars, such as with your wife, who would not permit sugar of any kind in the kitchen: it wasn't needed as she did no baking and expected guests to take their tea and coffee without it. All meals ended with fruit, selected according to the season. Winters were an endless bore of apples and pears until the short, tepid summers of strawberries or raspberries, served with yogurt. On special occasions they were allowed a sorbet. In the end, arguments over sugar had become his protests.

Andrea had been plump when he met her. He liked that, he liked a *zaftig* woman, short and squeezy. Now she was lean. She was a jogger, pounding the streets of Islington where there were no parks and no fresh air. She did three circuits of Highbury Fields, thinking through her patients' problems as she went; Stephen did nothing. At home at his parents' house in LA, no one followed any sports – physical activity outside work was for jocks – and in England he had never learned to watch soccer, let alone cricket or tennis. Andrea bought him a set of what he insisted on calling dumbbells, suggesting he might lift them for twenty minutes before breakfast three days a week. They gathered dust under the bed.

Stephen no longer had any real idea what his wife's hair colour was; white lines occasionally appeared at the roots, which he was too polite to mention. Was it his imagination or was she growing blonder, with what he called yellow streaky pieces? He'd gone to bed with a plump redhead on a mattress on the floor in a room scented by joss sticks and patchouli and woken up in an Islington mansion next to a firm, toned body and a sleek, ever-lightening bob of hair. In the mirror, he saw his own wiry black hair grazed with grey, and a widow's peak developing as it receded from the temples, leaving pink, mottled skin. Scared of the new health hazard, skin cancer, he started to wear a hat: an American baseball cap from Gap, the only kind of hat he was prepared to wear, with its name and logo on the front. His old clothes still hung in the wardrobe. He was not prepared to get rid of them – they were who he really was: he could not forget the boy who had sailed across the Atlantic on the SS *United States* with high hopes.

When he went out to buy a pair of thirty-two-inch-waist jeans and they didn't fit him, he came home empty-handed. He was a thirty-two-inch waist. This was his measurement; it was a descriptor, like a birthmark. 'But self-evidently you're size thirty-four,' said Andrea.

'No, I'm not,' he said stubbornly.

'You should cut out chocolate. Then you'd be back in your size thirty-twos.'

'Never happen,' he replied, in a sulk.

To Andrea, her husband's refusal to abandon the childishness of what she called his sweeties was obviously a symptom of unresolved issues he refused to confront. He had, from the start, declared himself not a candidate for therapy. He accepted and indulged her career as a way of making money out of other people's neuroses, but if he possessed a subconscious, and he unwillingly accepted that he must do since she insisted he did, (and he was prepared, for the sake of a quiet life and respect for her and her career, to agree), it was and would remain concreted over. The world, in his opinion, had too many wonders to investigate to waste time exploring imaginary ones. He had purchased one of the first Apple Mac computers and one of the first modems on the market. Like an intruder, he could enter university departments, where he experienced the eerie sensation of walking through the halls late at night when all the faculty had gone home and the place was silent, but you could read the notices on the boards, the names of the professors, the courses they taught and their research interests. These were the first websites. He joined user groups and chatted about biotechnology. Andrea caught him on the Internet, a half-eaten Mounds bar on the desk next to him, 'talking' to a woman at MIT.

What did this compulsion to eat chocolate mean, she wondered, and why the candy bars of his childhood? Something infantile had not been fully outgrown. He had always been a breast man, and before that a mommy's boy. There was something not entirely adult about her husband, she thought. He retained a boyishness he should have long abandoned. It was her theory that in all marriages there is one person who is the grown-up and the other who is the child, and she knew which role she fulfilled in this particular partnership. He still had the eagerness, the curiosity, the straightforward humour of the boy she had first met in the garden and had decided was the one to whom she would lose her virginity. This was what she still loved about him, that he was not depressed or sour or bitter or angry, like many men who sat before her in the patient's chair. She was very tired of listening to male rage and male misogyny.

For she had a husband who would come home from work and tell her to stop what she was doing, turn off the cooker, lay down her book, because he had just been commissioned to make the most *fabulous* programme, a whole history of the discovery of DNA, and he would get to interview Watson and Crick. He would be buoyed up for days with excitement.

But as for his candy bars, Stephen said that all he had was a sweet tooth and there were more important things for her to worry about, like what exactly was wrong with their daughter, who kept them up late into the night, in their shared bed, talking and arguing, each blaming the other for her distressing condition, which to Andrea was absurd since it was obvious that Stephen himself was the problem. Until, exhausted, they turned out the light and Stephen lay in the darkness, his eyes wide open, wondering if it was true and this was what he had done to her, to Marianne.

# Portrait/Landscape

For many years Marianne had waited for Grace to come and rescue her. Grace had white blonde hair and her mouth was the colour of a postbox or a telephone box. When she opened it, her eyebrows moved up and down. People's faces were always in close-up. Marianne could see, by a power of magnification, their pimples, open pores, the hairs in their nostrils. Many people had a monstrous appearance because of this heightened perception of hers. Grace's skin was porcelain, and you had to concentrate hard to see her eyelashes when she had just got out of bed and hadn't put the black on them.

She wore a green embroidered kimono with nothing under it and Marianne came across her in the hall, sitting on an old carved wooden chest, smoking a cigarette, her legs apart and a patch of blonde hair between her thighs, growing down the sides of them.

Her reddened smoking stubs were all over the house. She left them in saucers, in the earth of plants, extinguished in the dregs of coffee cups or abandoned, up-ended, with a column of tottering grey ash.

In the mornings she did bending exercises in her bra and pants, old grey garments compared with Andrea's lace underwear. She reached up to scratch her head and a dead insect fell from her hair. Marianne watched in horror and anxiety. Grace picked it up between her fingers and examined it. 'I don't know what it is,' she said to Marianne. 'What do you think?'

'It's not a spider. It's not a fly.'

'Something that belongs in a warm climate. That's why it was attracted to me. It was building a nest as close as it could get to an island.'

'What are you *talking* about?'

But Grace closed her lips. She flicked the insect away with a finger. It skittered across the room. Marianne followed it with her eyes. Later she would find a matchbox and put the insect into it. It would be her souvenir of the fabulous Grace who came and went without warning.

But she forgot, and the insect was removed by the vacuum cleaner, into a dusty hot world.

She comes and goes, Marianne thought. And one day she will take *me*. But the visits grew more infrequent.

'You're my godmother,' she said, the last time she saw her. 'You're supposed to bring me a *present*!'

'Who told you that?'

'Everyone knows that godmothers bring presents.'

'No, I mean who said I was your godmother?'

'Mummy did.'

'How ridiculous.'

'But you were there when I was born. You named me.'

'Yes, that's true. I was.'

'What was I like?'

'When?'

'When I'd just been born, of course.'

'Small, slimy and red.'

'Oh! So you didn't like me.'

'All babies are small, slimy and red. I suppose your brother was too.'

'Let's not talk about him. He's got his own godmother – no, not a godmother, a godfather, Uncle Ivan. Do you know Uncle Ivan?'

'Of course. I've known him longer than I've known your father.'

'He brings Max fantastic presents.'

'He's rich, that's why.'

'Well, it's just not fair that he has a rich godfather and I have a poor godmother. I *should* have a present.'

'What do you want? What's missing from your life?'

'Lots of things.'

'Well, write a list and I'll think about it.'

'All right.'

'Or I'll take you to an island where the sun always shines and there's singing, and people are happy, apart from the secret police.'

'I don't know what secret police are.'

'You wait.'

'I'd like to go to the island. Can we go soon?'

'Okay. In a year or two.'

'That's too long.'

'I'll get you something in the meantime. Where's that list?'

'I would like . . . a camera.'

'Why?'

'Then I could make everything stop. You look at someone and they're doing something interesting and you want to stop it so you can look at it, but they just go on moving.'

'I'll buy you a camera.'

But Grace forgot all about the promise and Ivan bought it for her instead, with a card on which was written, 'love from Godmother Grace'. For Stephen, overhearing the conversation through the partly open door of the bathroom, thought that

Marianne, at eight, was too young to have it broken to her with such cruelty that promises were just words.

Because of the camera, Marianne continued to believe that Grace would come for her one day and take her to the island, where everyone was happy and people burst out singing for absolutely no reason, which was not something you could say about London, a place where no one even whistled any more.

Marianne took photographs of her mother and father, her brother Max, Uncle Ivan and Uncle Ivan's new wife Simone, who had large pink lips and smelt strongly of something that made Marianne's eyes water. 'The closest we'll ever get again to opium,' Ivan said.

When the pictures came back as rectangular shiny prints, she laid them out on the bed and examined them carefully. There were expressions in people's faces she didn't understand, particularly her father's. She felt that his eyes and his mouth were pulling in two different directions, they belonged in different pictures, of separate people. Her mother didn't look the same in any photograph, but that was perhaps to do with the fact that she was always changing her hair and her cheeks expanded and contracted. Max stayed the same. Ivan and Simone arranged themselves in poses, which she had to ignore.

She had seen different cameras which had lenses that stuck out at the front, and when you looked through them, everything was really near. One day, perhaps, Grace would buy her one.

But Grace did not come back. When she asked her mother where she was, Andrea said, 'South East Asia, I think. Vietnam and Laos. Let's go and look at it on the globe, shall we?'

Marianne's finger spun the sphere. Round and round it went. Stephen showed her about why there was night and why there was day and, using her own body, why the moon waxed and waned.

When she was grown-up, aged thirteen and taking the bus

every day to school in Highgate in her shit-brown uniform, she would take pictures of people, and later she would walk part of the way home so she could photograph interesting events far from her own neighbourhood. She photographed a woman smacking a little boy in a sweet shop because he was naughty, and an old lady with a big bump on her back, and two young men walking along licking ice-cream cones, which made her laugh, and a man with a bunch of flowers, and a woman sitting on the pavement screaming, and a policeman whose head was buried under a heavy hat burnished with a silver badge. She never took any photos that did not have people in them.

One day she saw Ralph sitting on a bench in Highbury Fields. He always dresses very neatly, she thought. He always has a tie and a tweed jacket and lace-up shoes. Daddy almost never wears a tie, and his lace-up shoes aren't real shoes. They are white and you can't polish them with a brush and a cloth.

He doesn't see me. I'm invisible. She raised her camera to her eye. Ralph could be portrait or landscape, words she did not yet know, but she had to decide. A blackbird with its yellow eye hopped about his feet. The autumn leaves were blowing around in a light breeze. It had snowed here once – she had seen it; she had been taken out to make a snowman.

Ralph's hands lay in his lap. The blackbird pecked at something between his shoes. Marianne decided on her picture and took it. When it was developed she could see that he was smiling, a little bit. He's so peaceful, she thought. That's what death must be: it comes and visits you on a bench and leaves you with a smile and a blackbird that isn't afraid of you any more.

Ralph's rooms became Stephen's study. The house, as Andrea had hoped, was all theirs.

Marianne's room was the place where she spent hours looking at her pictures, eating food she had bought and hidden in her pockets on the way home from school.

# Anniversary Lunch

Grace is coming! Finally, after years of being a ghost, Grace is returning. Where from? No one knows, Postmarks indicate only that she has passed through a place. It was Indo-China, but lately there have been a number of letters from Paris.

These letters are unvaried in their content: amusing pen-portraits of the people she has met, just a paragraph long, sometimes a drawing of a face in the margins of the aerogram; several lines on her depression and anger, culminating in her desire to leave. Wherever she is, she doesn't like it, until she's long gone, and then she looks back with nostalgia: 'I was so happy in Saigon.' But when confronted with the evidence of her unhappiness, she sneers, 'What – are you an accountant of happiness now?'

The letters Andrea wrote back to her received a reply only occasionally, because Grace had usually moved on before she got them. Her capacity to survive on very little money since her father stopped making intermittent deposits to her bank account was one of her greatest accomplishments, Andrea thought. She lived like a saint, like Mother Teresa. Her diet consisted of the simplest food and she made all her own clothes, usually remodelling the discarded garments of others. She travelled by the cheapest means and found jobs when she reached her destination. She took English-language students, she worked occasionally in restaurants, she once directed the decoration of a house in Nice; momentously, she had a job as a set decorator on a film. Andrea had not seen it. She did not know if it had ever been released. The plot, explained to her, was unintelligible.

'My godmother is coming to see me,' Marianne boasted at school. She had grown a great deal both in height and weight since puberty, heavy round the shoulders with a large bust and her black hair scraped back in an unbecoming top-knot. Ivan had bought her a basic Pentax and Andrea found a cupboard in the house where she could establish a simple darkroom. A large photo of Ralph, finally at rest on the bench at Highbury Fields (in perfect focus, Marianne noticed with pleasure), hung framed in the entrance hall. The blackbird was caught too, pecking between his shoes. Stephen and Andrea thought it was gruesome, but how did anyone *know* he was dead? Marianne insisted. He was clearly just sleeping the long sleep.

Twenty years ago today, Stephen and Andrea had walked up Little Clarendon Street, Andrea with a flower in her hand, to the register office, with Ivan and John Baines. How many marriages conducted that day still stuck? It would be interesting to find out, Andrea thought. Theirs had been the least likely to survive, yet it had done.

She stood in the florist's surrounded by irises, roses, snapdragons, lilies, baby's breath, pinks. The flowers seemed to be crying, 'Choose me.' She wanted a centrepiece; she needed strong heads that wouldn't wilt. They were arranged along the wall in massed abundance, as if you could step through the vases into a garden. She looked up to see a slim, confident woman in her early forties surrounded by blossoms.

What happened to me? she asked herself. Where did this self-assurance come from?

She considered the possibilities. The career, the success (not great, she was not a household name, but she had a full client list). Marriage, certainly: the continuity of it, the accomplishment of surviving for two decades in the company of another person who often seemed like a complete stranger when she saw him typing at his computer, and then as familiar as a sock when he raised his bar of chocolate to his lips. The children: they change you; they redraw all the horizons.

Many of her clients were single women in their forties who had never managed, as one had said, 'to close the deal'. She tried to tell them that marriage was not one long blissed-out romantic movie, but she knew that she preferred marriage, however imperfect, to their microwave meals for one and single-supplement holidays. She felt like a hypocrite when she suggested that they mourn their loss of relationships, accept their single fate and move on. She herself could never live with it.

Thirteen people, not including the children who would join them for dessert, were to sit down for Saturday lunch at the oak dining-table to celebrate their twentieth anniversary. Even Grace was coming. She had consented to return to hateful London.

Marianne came home from school. 'Has Grace arrived yet?'

'You would know if Grace was here,' said her father, 'because there would be a contemptuous expression in the room.'

She arrived late the next morning, only an hour before the first guests, walked silently up the stairs as Andrea showed her the masterpiece: a whole house restored and redecorated.

'If I was living here I'd knock down all the walls and make huge rooms separated by Japanese screens,' Grace said, looking round. 'The light would be amazing. These Georgian houses are really poky.'

'That wouldn't have worked for children's bedtimes and my patients.'

'Children will sleep when they want to sleep.'

'Like you'd know,' said Stephen.

The sun drizzled through the french windows. Shelves of books reached to the ceiling. Arrayed in lines, the knives, forks and spoons were all shining in the summer noon, radiating out from the empty waiting plates like the place settings on the first-class decks of the transatlantic liner. Folded white linen napkins lay by each one. I have achieved a form of first-class living, Stephen thought. He had got used to his life. It had settled on him lightly, like a snowfall in the night.

Above them, the floors reached up and up to Max's room, where he was noiselessly practising his magic act for a performance he had been persuaded to give after lunch.

Marianne, at seventeen, had no show-off party piece, but she did not mind her fourteen-year-old brother being the star. When she returned home from the library at dessert time (she had observed three kinds of cake waiting in the kitchen), she would make adult conversation with Ivan and his wife Simone, the soap star, who played what Ivan called a gangster's moll, an idea that made him laugh so much he wiped the tears from his eyes when she was on screen. And yet she was in the newspapers all the time, often on the front page.

People are so incredibly stupid, Marianne thought. Looking at the passengers on the bus, *anyone* was more interesting than Simone, who kept her hair held back from her smooth wide forehead with a black velvet Alice band. Your eyes slid all over Simone's face, unable to get any purchase on it. The man across the aisle had such a hooked nose – it stood out like a gargoyle above his little mouth. Marianne could have stared at him all day. But Simone was kind and had a throaty laugh (identifiable by twenty million people) and did not take herself or her career seriously. 'It's just a ride,' she said, 'and rides never last very long, do they, darling?'

What am I doing here? thought Grace, sitting in front of her plate of prosciutto and melon. Who are these people? What do they have to be so smug about? Their opinions were second-hand and second-rate. No, third-rate. No one had had an interesting thought in their lives. Their mouths opened and closed like fish and only bubbles came out.

Everyone ate, they dabbed their lips with the white napkins; they spilt wine on the tablecloth; they knocked over salt and dropped meringue on the floor. The poached salmon was gone. The salads, the breads had all been finished. The centrepiece of peach-coloured rosebuds was wilting. The serving dishes contained the broken remains of what was left; a smear of mayonnaise marked the tablecloth; crumbs had fallen from the breadboard and the plates had been pushed away. A few petals lay among green beans with almonds.

'Look at this,' said Andrea, the table extending away from her towards her husband seated at the other end. 'If I picked this table up exactly as it is and took it to a gallery and said, "It's an installation called *Has Everybody had Enough?*" would anyone be taken in? Is it art?'

'If a dealer said it was art, then it would be art,' said Ivan.

'So art has no inherent properties of its own?' asked Stephen. 'That's what I always thought.'

'He's just being cynical,' said Amy, second wife of Nick, meeting the bumptious Ivan for only the third time and unsure whether she liked him or not. 'Art has been contaminated by advertising. Everything has. When Charles Saatchi entered the art market, art was finished. He has the soul of a salesman, a man who makes us want things we don't need. I'm sorry if that sounds like a cliché but it's true.'

'Going on holiday this year?' Ivan asked, winking at Stephen.

'Yes, next month.'

'And where are you going?'

'A *gîte* near Bordeaux. It's actually an old mill, not far from the village, and the millwheel is still working in the stream. It's amazing to get out of London to a simpler life, even if it's only for ten days.'

'And how did you book it?'

'There was a small ad in the back of the *Sunday Times* magazine.'

'An *advertisement*? So you are susceptible to advertising!'

'For heaven's sake, that's not the same thing at all.'

'Really? It's exactly the same thing. It's just that you are a snob. More than half of the advertising in the *Sunday Times* magazine comes from classifieds and you perceive them not to be advertising but individual things for discerning people like yourself.'

'Come off it, Ivan. You sell people toothpaste and washing-powder and bog roll,' said Grace. Grinning, smirking yuppies bobbed their heads up and down. This fucking country, she thought.

(Back in Harlem the transitory gardens would be re-emerging, the tomato seeds rushing up from below the earth, threatening the foundations of the buildings that had been raised on top of them. Under London there are fields and rivers. What is under this house? Suppressed rivers. Let them come, let them rise up and overwhelm fucking Islington.)

'And can you do without toothpaste and washing-powder and toilet paper? Is there anyone around this table who doesn't use any of these products? Or do you make your own soap and your own shampoo?'

'No, I don't make my own soap, but in the Third World they probably do,' said Amy, turning to Grace and nodding, incorrectly perceiving her as an ally. Grace ignored her.

'In the Third World, as you call it, they would far rather have a shampoo made by L'Oréal than wash their hair with bananas. Why do you think L'Oréal sells all over Africa?'

'Because you've forced them to believe L'Oréal is a superior product,' Amy said.

'That's because it is. Have you actually tried washing your hair with bananas?'

'Oh, do stop talking about bananas. The point is, how can a grown man earn a living persuading us to buy Bold rather than Persil?'

'Because they're different. It's all in the name. They may seem the same to you but few people use them interchangeably. In fact, I'm prepared to bet that you're brand loyal. You pick up the same packet of soap powder every time.'

'Yes, of course I do. I'm not going to agonise over which powder to buy. I don't want to have to think about it because they *are* all the same.'

'No, they are not. They have personalities, as the people round this table do. You've got your powerful, brash Bold, which will clean a car mechanic's overalls, you've got your Fairy, which is nice and soft, to wash baby things and delicates, and then there's your Persil – it's on Mum's side, the understanding brand, for kids' dirty T-shirts – and finally Ariel, which is "scientific".' He raised a finger on each hand to indicate quote marks, which everyone understood and laughed at, even Amy, who could see now that she had unwittingly set herself up as straight man for a well-worn comedy act.

'On the surface,' Ivan went on, 'it's a parity offering, but the formulations are completely different, and instead of boring you with formulations, we've given them brand identities, so you *know* what to choose.'

'And what's the difference with toilet paper?' asked Stephen. 'All that does is wipe your ass.'

'Aha! Now, toilet paper is a problem because there's only one consistent brand, which is Andrex, and the only way you can sell someone another product is if you offer them something Andrex doesn't, so you could make it quilted or with added aloe vera. Why would you do that? Well, you categorise by attitudes to the physical usage. The hurried three-sheeter, the hygienic six-sheeter, et cetera. You find all that out through focus groups. The point is that men never buy it so it's one of the most fascinating and most discussed problems in advertising, how you get a woman to buy a brand of toilet paper that suits every member of the family, including the little kid who's just toilet-trained and is starting out on the lifelong event of wiping his own arse. You see, no one ever talks about *how* they wipe their arse, it just doesn't come up in conversation. Do you fold or scrunch? At what stage during your piss or shit do you release the paper from the roll to have it ready, and should the sheet hang over the top of the roll or behind it? Arse-wiping is one of the most secretive acts a human being can perform, and yet we do it once a day if you're a bloke, more often if you're a woman, and absolutely no one wants to walk into a bathroom and find that it's run out of toilet tissue, as we call it in the trade. The lack of toilet paper takes us back to our animal selves, and that's before we even start to think of what colour the paper is. I suppose all of us prefer white and think pink and green and purple are naff. But if you really want to understand advertising, Amy, the holy grail is how you sell to men. They're the mystery because they believe they're above influence.'

'How so?'

'I'll give you an example. We pitched a few months ago for a new client, a private healthcare plan that felt its campaigns weren't reaching its target market – middle-aged men with disposable incomes. All our rivals did a study of public attitudes to private healthcare and to the NHS. How do you persuade someone who gets something for nothing to pay for it instead? It was *totally* the wrong tack. Our competitors kept on showing the client more of what they already had, shots of men being wheeled into surgery, doomy music and images of wifey and kids at home. The idea was that it would trigger in the breadwinner an anxiety about what was going to happen to his family while he was ill.

'But when we did *our* research we discovered that men cannot stand the idea of themselves being sick. It's like opening a tap and draining away our testosterone – the image of a man ill is the image of a man castrated. Now, women have stuff happening to their bodies the whole time – periods, contraception, cervical smears, mammograms, childbirth – and these are not perceived as illnesses, even when they involve pills and hospitals. So what we did was to create a campaign in which we showed the wife lying in a hospital bed in a nightie, surrounded by her family, which guilt-tripped the men – who, after all, were going to be the ones who would write the cheque – into thinking they weren't good providers if they left their loved ones in the hands of the NHS waiting lists.'

'I took out private health insurance,' said Stephen. 'I took it out when the ads still showed guys being wheeled into surgery.'

'That's because you're a hypochondriac,' Ivan said. 'We can't get enough of *you*.'

Grace lit a cigarette. She was the only person in the room who still smoked, apart from Ivan's after-dinner joints. 'I remember you when you were an anarchist at Balliol. I remember you when you had a full head of hair. And didn't talk bullshit.'

Poor Grace, Ivan thought. She had been such an exciting girl at nineteen. He had lost his virginity to her. He remembered his hand trembling on her breast because it was the first breast he had ever felt, and her coloured tights peeling off so he could feel the damp triangle of lace, and then she'd blown him. The very first time he'd had sex he'd been blown. She'd only been up a few weeks, yet she was already famous. He had stopped, gaping, at the sight of her on her bicycle in her outlandish clothes, lifting her arm to indicate a turn as she swerved left into the Broad, and he'd lifted his own: he'd saluted her. She'd smiled and carried on.

They were in his room in college in the middle of an autumn afternoon. He rolled a joint afterwards, and when they came out onto the street it had been raining, hard. The street was an archipelago of wet coppery leaves plastered to the pavement, gusted from the trees by high winds. He had taken her hand and she had let go of his immediately. 'I'm not your girlfriend,' she said.

'Shall we go and have some tea?' he asked her.

'You can, if you like. I'm meeting Andrea.' And this was the first he had heard of her best friend. A blow-job on a wet afternoon in the sixties, skin reeking of patchouli oil, and now a lunch of poached salmon and champagne in a room smelling of roses and the lighter Chanel perfumes, which all the women wore, and his own skin scented by the Dior Homme he'd bought at duty-free.

He was lucky to have started on her but he could not imagine what that body would look like now, beneath the manky bit of cloth she had wrapped round it. He was surprised, really surprised, at what had become of her. He blamed himself that he had done nothing to protect her. She could have come back to Belsize Park during the vacations. His own mother would have taken her in. But, after all, she was damaged goods, right from the start, and it was too late to fix her now. What a shame.

'That was just the influence of my father,' he said, 'who was then and still is an anarchist. I liked him too much to rebel against him. He really does think the law is an ass. As for the hair, what can I say? All of us are follically challenged. Look, this job is just an intellectual exercise, Grace. It's exactly the same as what we did in our tutorials. Take sanitary protection—'

'For Christ's sake, Ivan,' said Stephen. 'We're still eating lunch.'

'No, no, listen. You have this massively successful brand, Tampax. A woman goes into a chemist's once a month and buys a product, what we call an offer. This is not something she's going to do brand experimentation on. She starts with a brand and she sticks with it for the next thirty-five years, and when her period is due, she wants to walk over to the bathroom cabinet, get out the trusty blue box and know that for the rest of the day she's going to be comfortable and leak-free. Thirty-five years of using the same product for three to five days, every single month. And if she has daughters, she introduces the brand to them. Yet Tampax is declining in market share. Why? Because it's perceived as mumsy. It's the cardboard applicator – it's seen as being from an era when women didn't want to touch themselves "down there", as they used to call it. So Lillets, which is a simple tampon that you push in with your finger, is gaining on them.'

Marianne stood at the door of the dining room, listening and watching. She had identified Grace immediately and felt herself to be on her side in this argument: the earth was being raped for toilet paper.

Grace was not what she remembered. She had thought of her as a fairy queen in a crown, like the lovely Witch of the North in *The Wizard of Oz*. It was rubbish, she understood that, yet Grace, who had stood by her bed when she was born and named her, who came and went with no notice, who obeyed no rules except the ones she had invented, had been her secret inspiration. The gaunt, leathery woman with the hair now white rather than ash blonde had an interesting face, the most interesting in the room. Lines radiated around her mouth like a child's drawing of the sun. Her exposed breasts were brown and wrinkled. She's like a woman hobo, thought Marianne.

And she saw Grace turn, stare at her, take her cigarette from her red-painted lips and say, with an astonished drawl, 'God, what a fat lump.'

# Magic

Max came down the stairs with his conjuring paraphernalia, the sliding boxes, the silk handkerchiefs, the packs of cards, the cups and balls and the lengths of rope, to find Grace jammed against the wall of the hall outside the dining room and his father with a vein popping in his forehead, stabbing his finger in her face.

The face was a long white plank. His sister was sitting on the stairs, Ivan's arm around her, looking as if she had been punched, knocked down, winded: an expression Max knew from her first weeks at her school in Highgate when she came home and slammed the door of her room. He had not seen it for several years. She had learned to deflect the blows, which were always about her appearance. He could laugh her out of them by doing simple tricks. They did not talk much, but operated by telepathy, a system they had perfected during the time he was deaf. Someone had said she was fat. He knew who. That dreadful woman with the ugly face.

Max waited quietly but felt thwarted: he had planned a grand entrance into the dining room, which was blocked by his mother standing in the door trying to speak in her soft voice, drowned by his father's, which sounded to Max like metal scraping against metal.

'You come here, you accept our hospitality, you eat our food and sleep in our beds and you insult *children*. I'm sick to death of you. You're a monster – you couldn't give a shit for anyone but your own sick self. What is the matter with you? Can't you grow up? Is it because she's my kid? Is that your problem – that you think you can insult me through her?'

'Leave me to deal with this,' said Andrea, who tried to pull her husband away from Grace.

'No, I'll do it,' said Ivan. 'Come on, Grace. Let's go for a walk.'

Grace said nothing. She felt herself to be a bird that had stumbled by accident into an overheated house and crashed into mirrors and panes of glass and chandeliers. She scattered her droppings across pale carpets and in a straight line along a table of artfully prepared food, tasteless food. Andrea's cooking was always undersalted. Her wings were beating in the stifling air – people were raising slingshots and air-rifles to bring her down. She could fly this way and that, but she was unable to find the exit, the gap out of which you swooped upwards and out into the blue, beyond the clouds. In Mexico one time she had seen flights of pelicans, lumbering brown birds with heavy spooned bills that swept down onto the water to fill with brine and fish. Frigates glided above them in the thermals. That is me, she thought, that is me, one of the ones up there.

'We've got to go back into the dining room,' said Marianne. 'Max has been practising his show for weeks.'

'She needs to apologise to you first,' Stephen said.

'I don't care.'

Marianne knew she was a fat lump. She knew she was a secret, uncontrollable eater and that she was able to deal with the world only through the unpredictability of her observations, which unsettled people, and by staying behind the lens of her camera.

Years ago, Grace had told her that she never explained or apologised; it was the first time Marianne had heard this maxim. Her mother was all for ceaseless explanation and apologies meant to redress wrongs and move beyond pain. Marianne understood that an apology from Grace was worthless – she would never mean it, it was just words – and she herself had lived with a deaf brother: she knew how insignificant words could be.

'I'll go to my room,' said Grace.

'*Your* room?'

'Yes. The one I'm sleeping in, which you gave me to sleep in.'

'But I'm doing my show,' Max said.

'Everyone else is here,' said his father. 'There's plenty of people.'

'No, she has to stay.' He couldn't bear to lose a single member of the audience.

He went to Davenport's children's magic club and graduated from cups and balls to card tricks, using American decks that real conjurors used. He had learned that the great magicians taught themselves, through hours of patient practice, to shuffle the deck so that the cards would stay in the same order. But the elementary stages of magic were the lesson that each finger had its own role to play: the digits of his hand were little actors, each taking on a different role; unless they performed together, the trick could not work. He had been taught how to angle his arm from the shoulder to the tip of the furthest finger and where to place his eyes, because he had found out that where the eyes went the audience's eyes would follow. If you get the audience to focus on one hand, the other one could do what it wanted. What he *said* was the misdirection, 'Look, I'm not touching it!' but the trick was already done.

But the hardest lesson he had learned from watching videos over and over again was that the kind of magician he wanted to be was the kind who had a personality.

'You're looking for the moments when the audience is

relaxed,' Ralph had told him. 'If you can find that moment, you can do anything – you can produce an elephant. But *you* have got to relax them.'

'How do you do that?'

'You win them over. There's more to it than just the trick.'

Ralph had never achieved what Max already hoped to do, aged fourteen. Max observed that this was because he did not have the right mental condition to be a very good magician, which was mathematical logic. Max had his father's brain, but his father didn't realise it: his father only recognised mental attributes when they were measured by school grades. But Ralph had had a personality; it was the same one he used to sell a housewife a foundation garment or a flannel nightdress. Ralph had the capacity, when he turned it on, to be what Stephen called a schmoozer.

Max was so absorbed in the practice of magic, alone in his room with the door locked, that he rarely bothered masturbating. It seemed a waste of time to do that with his hands – and he was too afraid of injuring them. His highs and lows rocked between the sense of terror and shame if a trick went wrong and the exhilarating power of it working.

He had been promised that the dining-room table would be pushed back against the wall and two rows of chairs laid out. It hadn't happened. He had come down, on cue at two forty-five, and they were bickering. 'It's time for my show,' he said. 'Everyone has got to go back into the dining room.'

'You,' Stephen said to Grace. 'The only sound I want to hear from you is your fucking hands clapping.'

The guests rearranged the furniture to make an intimate little nightclub in the broad daylight of a summer Saturday afternoon. They sat down in chairs and waited for the children's entertainment. Max entered and smiled. It was an expression of vulpine cunning, the trickster's smile of fake sincerity.

He understood at once that this was his first failure. He had not pulled off what he was hoping for: he had failed to relax them – instead they were startled.

Ivan took up his position by the mantelpiece with his cine camera. The next day Stephen and Andrea would play the tape of the performance over and over again until they relinquished it to their son to study for his mistakes.

'He's doing what is logically impossible,' Stephen said. 'You know that it's impossible yet it's just happened, so it has to be based on lies, but it's more than that because the brain is colluding with the lying. It seems to be wired to *be* deceived – this has to be the reason. You don't seem to be able to be force yourself to look the way that's not intended.'

He had tried playing the video back in slow motion, then had taken it into work and played it back on a professional machine. He realised Ivan's own eye had followed the deceit: he had not filmed the place where the deception was happening. Max said nothing. He did not tell his father that a flash of light on a coin makes the viewer believe that it's in the place where it is not. His father was very stupid sometimes.

Stephen would drive himself crazy wondering how each trick was done, ticking off all the possibilities. One thing that would never occur to him was that Max had gone to Ivan and Simone's house three weeks earlier and proposed to Simone, the television soap actress, that she play the part of his stooge. And she had giggled and accepted. Of course she would. When he had asked someone to come forward and take a card and said, 'Lovely lady with the golden hair, what about you?' she had laughed and first shaken her head, then graciously agreed. They had practised the trick together twice a week until they had perfected it. And they had kept it a secret from Ivan. She didn't tell him until they were walking back home to Gibson Square across Upper Street, and Ivan said he wouldn't have thought the kid had it in him, he seemed like such a scared mouse, and they agreed they would not tell his parents.

Max understood implicitly that if anyone knew how his tricks were done, they would be crushed with disappointment. Even the most hard-boiled wanted it to be magic: no one likes to be deceived. Magic, he later said, was a hedge against cynicism. It gave you the sense of wonder that is to be found in God and science.

Off-stage, he was very good at staying silent, of vaguely evading questions about how David Blaine could take a watch from a passer-by on the street and seemingly pass it through the melting window of a shop-front, then point to it behind the re-formed glass, sitting in the display of merchandise. He knew the principles of how it was done. One only needed to think logically and you would soon exhaust all the possibilities. But all he would say was 'Yes, David Blaine is a very good street magician and he's meticulous with his preparation, but he has a very strong personality and a lot of his work depends on that.'

Andrea, watching the video, was stunned. She had seen her son put on a costume, another self, a little joking mannequin with a patter. He had paid Simone a compliment about her golden hair before stroking her velvet Alice band and producing a scarlet feather from it. He seemed to be wearing another person, and it was so obvious to her that this was not his true self that she felt frightened that he could admit a being so alien into his body. And after he had taken his bow he seemed to peel off the public boy and revert to the quiet child he had been most of his life. And the longer she watched, the more she realised that *he craved an audience*. He wanted and enjoyed the attention. Because she had not given him enough? That could be the only explanation.

She had taken him every week to magic club because she had thought that it would end his solitary life, that he would be with others and learn social skills, but all that had happened was that he had learned how to behave as if he knew how to socialise. Suppose they took the books and videos away from him, with the sets of cards and the cup and balls, and the boxes with the false backs? What would happen to him then? Would he implode back into silence?

Max returned to his room after the show feeling as if he had just had an orgasm. The applause in the dining room, the tricks, which had all worked, the compliance of Simone who had done exactly as he had told her and had beautifully acted the part – it all felt explosively climactic and he had to lie down on the bed, exhausted, before he could remove his clothes and put away the concealed cards and other pieces of his apparatus. He slept for a few minutes, and dreamed. He dreamed of Simone and her velvet hairband and the smell of her scent, and awoke wet.

It had been a glorious day. For his birthday he would ask for the vanishing-ketchup-bottle trick. It was the one he most wanted to do, to make a bulky object disappear. One day, when he was older, he would learn to disappear himself.

Behind the wall he heard his sister moving about heavily. She was in distress, he thought. He got out of bed and knocked on her door but she did not respond. He knocked again. It was like being him when he could not hear but she could hear. 'Marianne,' he said. 'I want to show you a trick.'

She opened the door. 'What trick?'

He was holding one of Grace's pieces of cloth. It was navy blue. He had gone into her room and taken it when she was downstairs in the kitchen.

'I'm going to make this vanish,' he said.

She knew he had never made anything so large disappear, so she sat patiently on the bed, her arms folded, watching.

'I need to open the window.'

'Go on.'

He pulled up the sash of the lower pane.
'Watch.'
He dropped the cloth out into the garden.
'See?' he said, closing the window. 'She's gone.'

# New Year's Eve

He experienced such dread at the idea of turning fifty. It was all so extraordinarily surprising that he should be older now than his father was when he, Stephen, had set off for England on the SS *United States*. So unwelcome and unbelievable that he turned down the party, the restaurant meal, the romantic weekend in Paris or Venice, even the gift to himself of a new car – he fancied a Saab. He wished to extract from himself, by violence if necessary, his *fiftyness*. He understood that he was more than halfway done with his life, unless he lived to be a hundred, but it was more likely to be eighty, and the next thirty years would pass in a flash. The final decade would be full of ill-health and dimming eyesight or hearing; he would be sitting in a chair watching TV instead of making TV.

At fifty Jimi Hendrix had been dead for twenty-two years, Jim Morrison for twenty, Elvis for only eight. It was romantic to die young, but not a fate Stephen had wished for himself. He wanted to stay young for ever. He had once heard his mother say, looking in the mirror at her lined face and the sagging jowls, 'But I'm only twenty-two!' There were photographs of his mother looking impossibly young, but dressed in the styles of wartime. Her youth did not count. His parents' generation had been adults all their lives: they had had the Depression and the war and responsibilities. They had been born into middle age.

How can I be fifty, he asked himself, when I only just began? The kid who has tried on Marilyn Monroe's champagne mink in the warehouse felt closer to him than the man in the mirror with the pepper-and-salt hair, the emerging widow's peak, the brown spots on the backs of his hands and the hairs that had started to grow from his nostrils. His feet hurt when he walked too far. He had developed a gastric intolerance to over-spiced foods. If he wasn't careful with his diet he was prone to constipation. When he looked into the mirror he was taken aback by the absence of his hippie beard and bush of Jewfro hair. He was twenty-three and sailing across the Atlantic on the SS *United States*, experiencing the romance of the sea, having already slept with a girl in Naples and left her by accident his UCLA library card. He was sharing the napkin of *petits fours* in his cabin with Bill Clinton, Clinton of Univ, currently President of the United States, and a girl whose name he could no longer remember. He had written to Clinton to offer his congratulations on his election, and reminding him of the passage over, but had received a form reply from one of his aides. He doubted that Clinton had ever seen the letter. It was one thing to be fifty and running America, a job *only* fitted for adults, another still to be the boy burning inside with ambition thwarted, and longings for things that could not be.

Andrea was tired of listening to his neuroses about turning fifty. What concerned him so deeply? Was he facing the menopause, as she would in a couple of years? No. It was just a word, a little F-word, it was meaningless, he should get over himself. But he was the first of his crowd to turn that corner – what did they know?

*

Christmas in Islington. Andrea lit candles and put them in the windows; she decorated a tree with lights and baubles; they ate food she would not have allowed into the house at other times of the year and the children walked past the churches and wondered what people were *doing* going in there, to those cold naves and marble altars with plastic Jesuses lying in wicker cribs.

On New Year's Eve there were parties all along the street – you ran from one to another. When they first began, the young adults came bringing their babies, then their children, who ran ceaselessly up and down the carpeted stairs all evening. The guests were neighbours; they were parents who had met at the school gates, and the infants had turned eventually into sullen teenagers, smoking cigarettes secretly in the garden until they went to university and returned in the vacations. Consenting to look in 'for a few minutes' at these obligatory neighbourhood gatherings, yet not managing to leave until late when they had filled up on free food and alcohol, and the boldest had scored some dope from Ivan, who was childless, glamorous, rich and brushed off the protests of their mothers and fathers.

You dressed up; you drank champagne; some of the hosts hired young people dressed in black to open the door and take the coats and serve the wine and canapés. At the far end of the garden a few of the men, and women shivering in evening gowns, ventured down to the fish pond to smoke a joint.

Fairy-lights hung from the black trees. A line of frost along the fence, and their feet sliding on the wet grass around the pond with its cold carp.

A summer house with Oriental cushions to recline on was lit with lanterns, and candles guided the path back to the house, every window ablaze with chandeliers, Christmas trees, fairy-lights and only at the top, where the au pair had a whole floor in what had been the Victorian maids' quarters, were the curtains drawn and dark. They had started in Highgate twenty-five years ago, going to parties, and now they were in tuxedos and the women in gowns. So he had been right: it had gone on being parties, but no one here was going to walk home in the dawn and make out on Marx's tomb.

Andrea was somewhere in the house, talking to her friends, absorbed in preventing herself from touching the tray of canapés that circulated through the house. And this was it: this was where it had all been leading to, this light-headed feeling of pleasure and too much champagne and the stars.

Sitting in the summer-house, stoned, nearly fifty, loosening his bow-tie, Stephen accepted the company of a woman who came and sat down next to him, a cashmere shawl around her white shoulders.

Mary Bright, tall, fashionably dressed, said, 'We've met before, a long time ago, at Oxford.'

She had once walked with her boyfriend down the Woodstock Road to Ivan's flat to score some acid, and Stephen had been sitting on the floor rolling a joint, the legendary chemist who made Mister Button.

'And did you take it?' he asked, unable to remember her but impressed by the glossiness of her appearance, the high heels, the short skirt revealing the slender legs, the waist belted in patent leather and the smooth face.

'Not me. I was far too nervous. I just wanted to meet you.'

'Meet *me*?'

'Yes. Because Mike said he was sure you were CIA.'

'Why would he think that?'

'Well, you know, he said what else would you be doing in Oxford?'

'But that's absurd. Bill Clinton was there at the same time. We were all Rhodes scholars, not spooks.'

'Yes, I realise that now, but we thought many more *absurd* things in those days, didn't we?'

'Very true.'

'Absurdity – it feels so retro now. We live in an age of utilitarian common sense.'

'We do?'

'It certainly feels that way. To me.'

'What were you studying?'

'Law.'

'And did you become a lawyer?'

'Yes, I did, and still am.'

'Did you marry Mike?'

'Yes, I did, as a matter of fact.'

'So is he here? I could set him straight.'

'God, no, we were divorced years ago.' He looked down at a hand full of silver rings, none on the relevant finger. 'I used to read you, you know, in that column you did in the underground paper. I don't even remember its name any more – it all seems so long ago. What do you do now?'

'I'm in television.'

'How did that happen?'

Someone came down to the summer-house with a bottle. 'Leave it here,' Stephen said.

He told her about the voyage over on the SS *United States*, and being sent down from Oxford and the squat in Chalk Farm – this story, this novel it seemed now to him. He laid it at her feet like a dog eagerly bringing in a bird from the garden.

'So we had you all wrong.'

'I don't know. I don't know how I was supposed to be. What about you?'

'I love the law – I'm argumentative. My practice is litigation, personal injury and clinical negligence. The more difficult the better. I'm considered what is called in the profession robust.'

'So I shouldn't get on the wrong side of you.'

'Inadvisable. How do you know the Pallants?'

'We live two doors down. Look, that's my house.'

'The lights are on. Who's home?'

'My son, I expect. He's a bit of loner. My daughter is in Yugoslavia, or whatever they call it now, taking pictures.'

'How frightening.'

'Yes.'

It was eighteen years since Susie in the van, with the musty smell, the dirty hair and the angelic face, the running away of both of them, but he had turned back, had not gone to San Diego. Of course he had not shipped out. His maritime-union ticket stayed in his wallet, a lifeline to the sea, but he had never used it since he'd jumped ship at Southampton. They were inching towards New Year: he would be wanted very soon in the house to listen to the clock chime, sing 'Auld Lang Syne' and kiss his wife. He was expected. He looked at his watch. 'Only ten minutes to go,' he said.

'Another year.'

'I'm gonna be fifty.'

'Are you?'

'I don't know what comes to an end, or if anything does. I don't know what to expect.'

'We'd better go into the house now,' she said. 'Your wife will be waiting for you.'

'Yes, she will. Perhaps you'll remember her. She was at Oxford too – she was often at Ivan's flat.'

'Did you marry that very melodramatic blonde?'

'God, no.'

'Then the plump carroty one.'

'That's her. Or was. She's neither plump nor a redhead now.'

'We all change. Here's my card. Give me a ring if you ever feel like lunch.' She took the card out of her evening bag and placed it in his breast pocket. They walked into the house, where

Andrea was waiting, holding a glass of champagne, looking at them walk in together, a handsome if ill-sorted couple.

Mary Bright. Mary Bitch. Andrea was forced to endure five months of her before Stephen finally sent her away.

'Do you have to be so fucking obvious?' she said. 'I had never thought of you as banal. A mid-life crisis? Spare me.'

But Stephen was enslaved to Mary Bright's little erotic secrets, such as her penchant for wearing stockings and a suspender belt under her tight bandage dresses, and the first shaved pussy he had ever seen. She was not so far from fifty herself, but had an entirely different mental attitude towards this queasy milestone. She was full of life, and she was out there in the world. She did not brood, as Andrea did, on who she was or where she had come from. Andrea described her as a carnivore. 'Well, so am I,' Stephen said.

'No you're not. You just wish you were.'

For years he tried to recollect their first meeting at Ivan's flat with the large windows and the expensive sound system until one day, in a box of photographs, he saw her. Andrea and Grace were posed by their bicycles in their radiant days of Pre-Raphaelite hair, coloured stockings, ripped cerise skirts, the velvet dress, looking to him now not like women, but plump-cheeked children. And there she was, Mary Bright, a passer-by pushing her bicycle, standing at the side of the frame while the photograph was taken, leaning against the wall of Oriel, looking straight at him, into the future, through the curtain of parted black hair.

There were so many beautiful girls like her at Oxford, seen on the street but never in the Dyson Perrins lab. They were inaccessible to him, the horny, lonely grad student who could only look. And he finally had her. She was his reward. He felt like someone who had been on a long diet who finally allows himself dessert.

The five months had nothing to do with Andrea, or their marriage, or the family, the house, his career. He had never had any intention of giving up the gains of thirty years to compensate for the loss of some strands of hair. Mary Bright was the loser, but surely, he said to her, she must have understood that from the outset, being strong, bold, independent and liberated. He had assumed she knew. How could she *not* know?

# Her First War

Everyone was waiting. Day after day, nothing advanced in the situation. The guests sat under the gilded dome of the Hotel Esplanade drinking coffee, eating strudel and waiting for the dinner hour when waiters wheeled metal trolleys across the carpeted floors and stood by the white-clothed tables flambéing cherries in liqueur. Blue flames rose from the sizzling pans illuminating bored faces. The diners walked back and forth restlessly. Was there any news? If there was news, no one would share it. News was a secret you kept to yourself. It was a commodity you did not give away.

Marianne could not afford to dine in the restaurant. She was not a guest at the hotel; nor was she interested in its sumptuous menu, the veal dressed with cream and brandy, the braised pork, the white wine soup, the goulash and the schnitzel. The staff were trying to keep up standards, but only five tables were taken out of fifty and the diners had no idea about etiquette and decorum: they clamoured for hamburgers and macaroni dishes, which the chef despised. The maestro at the piano kept his head down, smiling secretively. It was rumoured that he was a spy, though for whom it was not possible to determine.

Marianne's hotel was a more modest affair. Its guests were Croatian, Slovenian, Austrian and Italian commercial travellers, dealing in sunglasses, drill bits, coffee, wine, Mercedes parts (stolen), aluminium pipes, chocolate, nylon tracksuits, Swiss watches, light bulbs and fancy china. These guests were all men, though one or two had stationed mistresses in the city and brought them back to their rooms for entertainment. Only the young blonde desk clerk spoke to her in a way that did not involve a sexual invitation. But her English was not good and all she could offer was a poorly printed map of notable churches.

Marianne was in a rush; she had not expected to be delayed. No one had told her that war was five per cent fear and ninety-five per cent boredom. She was only twenty-two and she expected things to happen immediately: the world revolved around her – why shouldn't it be arranged according to her wishes? Sitting on the narrow hotel bed with its yolk-coloured counterpane, she looked out of the window to dark, drizzly streets. The evenings were still coming too quickly – it was a late spring. A small TV showed only Croatian and German programmes, a war was going on and she was out of the loop. She had already been waiting for two days.

She had walked round the city taking pictures of women in the markets, of the UN vehicles along the half-empty boulevards, a brass band marching with drums and bugles, a policeman eating an ice-cream cone (there was nothing funnier than men eating ice cream, particularly men in uniform: she took such pictures whenever she got the chance), but didn't she know there was a war on? And was she not separated from it by the futile impediment of a missing piece of laminated card?

Everyone went to the bar at the Esplanade, a place she had not yet entered. She felt intimidated by the old hands she had already seen at the UNPROFOR office, who all knew each other and were woven together by a web of connections going as far back as Vietnam. They were the same age as her mother and father, or that was how they seemed. No one had spoken to her. She was all by herself with her camera bag and her letters certifying that she was an accredited correspondent.

But the night was so long in Zagreb, lying on the single bed with only the Croats and Germans on the TV for company. You must do it, she told herself. You have to get up and go there, try and strike up a conversation. Entering the bar in her jeans, Timberland boots and the familiar lopsided stoop of the photographer, she was immediately recognisable as one of the band of brothers.

The band of brothers: 'I haven't seen you since Pristina.'

'No way. Surely we ran into each other at Mostar? Didn't we get totally wrecked on some plum brandy?'

'That wasn't me, that was Foxy.'

'Foxy? Are you sure?'

'Yeah, he told me all about it. He said you were sitting slumped against a wall unable to tie your shoelaces.'

'Well, then, it must have been Pristina. I did have some trouble with my boots in Mostar.'

'Don't worry, it's hard to keep it all straight. All these fucking Yugo towns look the same to me. Have a drink.'

Marianne entered, and sat at a table by the window, the waiter brought her a glass of wine. It felt no better to be waiting here than in the hotel room, except there were people to look at, such as the old woman in the black hat with the veil who was sitting alone in a corner writing a letter. She seemed to Marianne to have been sitting at the table for fifty years, with her doll's face and her two spots of rouge and her glass of brandy which she had not touched. She reminded Marianne of the old tenants she had lived with when she was a child. She could recollect all their faces, every one. But the woman did not look up, her cramped hand moved slowly across the sheet of paper.

In her boots and jeans, her dark hair loosened, her heavy bust and her impatient hands on the table, Marianne was sexually confusing. Men were initially put off by her. They did not know if they were attracted or not; this took some time to work out.

Pretty girl, thought Colin, who had a vocabulary designed for short, descriptive signalling sentences and designated all women as pretty/dogs. She was marginal but young enough to give her the benefit of the doubt.

Funny face, thought Tim. Her mouth looks like it was put on upside-down.

'Hello,' Colin said. 'Are you stuck too?'

'Yes, I am.'

'Come and have a drink with us.'

'Okay.' She picked up her glass and went over to the bar.

'First time in Zagreb?'

'Yes.'

'Enjoying yourself?'

'Not really. I can't get into Bosnia.'

'No one can, if your pass has expired or you haven't picked one up yet. We're all in the same boat.'

Every day Marianne went to the UNPROFOR office to get her press pass and every day she stood with the crowd of waiting journalists, and every day the official said there were no passes. This happened from time to time. Where were they? They were on a plane that had been diverted to Sarajevo; they had been sent to Belgrade by mistake; they were out of stock at the printers; they were lost; they were being deliberately withheld by the authorities to prevent any access to the worst of the atrocities. None of the explanations satisfied the journalists, who waved their expired passes in frustration or made ham-fisted attempts to alter the final date.

They could not get into Bosnia without the press pass. With it, things were rosier: they could be ambushed, their car stolen; shot, left for dead on the road; or occupying a room in the shelled structure of the Sarajevo Holiday Inn where there was no running water or electricity. They could take a cruise down Snipers' Alley. Without it, they were forced to sleep in sumptuous splendour beneath satin counterpanes, brush their teeth in marble bathrooms, drink coffee and eat cream gâteaux in the echoing public rooms and periodically check at the desk to find out which new journalists had arrived today. It was even possible to have a facial and a massage at the beauty spa on the first floor.

'So who are you?' said Colin.

'I'm Marianne Newman.'

'Who are you with?'

'I've got a commission from a magazine.'

'What magazine?'

'It's a women's magazine. They were the only ones who would give me press credentials. I've shot a lot in Britain, but this is my first war.'

The war had been going on for four years. Like a cumbersome tank, it had been making its slow but determined way eastwards from Croatia, treading familiar pathways, tracks worn over centuries, entering Bosnia and with its yellow eye on Kosovo and Macedonia. It was the kind of war that had been fought on European soil since the Middle Ages, admittedly with more sophisticated weapons and materiel, but sometimes neighbours grabbed what was to hand and hacked each other to death with agricultural implements. You could not walk a step on this soil without treading on the blood of ancestors who had died in primitive battles. European wars had absurd names, the War of Jenkins' Ear, the Hundred Years' War, the War of the Spanish Succession. This one was the War in the Former Yugoslavia.

It was a war both bloodthirsty and convenient. The militias

swept into town and made a base for themselves. They rounded up a few local girls and locked them up in the school or a small hotel. Every morning they took tabs of Ecstasy and went out for a day's slaughter; in the evening, thrumming with blood and surplus energy, they came back, got drunk and raped their captives. They wasted the surrounding countryside, laying land-mines, looting and burning. The first rule was to kill, there was no second rule to complicate matters, and everyone fed on everyone else's enthusiasm. But the civilians were not entirely innocent either: families who had been neighbours for a hundred years turned on each other and burned down their houses. When people spoke to each other, their principal feeling was distrust – you killed the family across the road to be on the safe side. In the cities where, at the beginning of the decade, the population had been renting videos and having home deliveries of pizza, medieval siege conditions were now prevalent.

And it was all reachable within a two-hour flight from London – the Italians could go home for the weekend. Its advan-tage was that there was more than enough war for everybody and it wasn't even an expensive destination.

Now a barrier stood between the media and the war. Each of the two men had heard that the press cards would be available tomorrow. Neither revealed this information to the other. They had obtained it from the same source: the hotel desk clerk, who had a web of connections throughout the city. The girl, they assumed, was too green to ask.

'If you do get your press card, how are you getting in?' said Colin.

'I've got a plane ticket to Split, then I'll rent a car.'

'What would you do if you were ambushed on the road and they wanted to take it off you?'

'I'm not giving them my car.'

'Quite right. That's the spirit,' said Tim.

'But what if they threatened to shoot you?' Colin said. 'What's your strategy then?'

'Give it to them?'

'Of course not. They'll take the car and leave you in the middle of nowhere – you'll die of exposure. You'd be an idiot to give away your car.'

'But you said they'd shoot me if I didn't give it to them.'

'That's the conundrum, yes.'

The bar filled up with a party of European politicians who ordered cocktails. Marianne observed that everyone was beautifully dressed. They did not wear jeans and boots and stone-coloured cotton jackets with multiple pockets, but Italian cashmere coats and cocktail dresses, and she was with two old men, sitting at the bar, who were trying to make a fool of her. But she would rather sit on her stool with her camera bag at her feet than engage in the light chatter about UN resolutions and peace conferences.

Her mother had asked her, 'What is the moral dimension of this project?' and Marianne replied, 'I don't know. I didn't realise there had to *be* a moral dimension. I just want to show people what I see.' (But they both hated and were afraid of war, her parents; they were of that generation.)

'So what would *you* do?' she said.

'Me? I wouldn't rent a car at all. I'd hitch a ride with one of the UN convoys.'

'Then I'll do that.'

'But if you're on one of the convoys, you haven't got the story. You're at their beck and call. You have to go where they're going. You might as well be an embed. Have you got a flak jacket?'

'Yes.'

'Does it have Mylar plates?'

'I don't know – I don't think so. It's very heavy. A friend of my dad's got it for me.'

'You should go home,' Colin said. 'It'll all be over by the summer anyway. Go back to your boyfriend.'

'No, no. She'll be all right,' Tim said. 'She's gutsy.'

She wasn't his type. But in all honesty, he conceded, in this line of work, anyone can be your type if you've got time on your hands.

They bought her dinner. Under the gilded dome of the empty dining room, eating ridiculous food and drinking sweet German wine, their faces lit by the glittering chandeliers, Marianne thought, I could take portraits of them, but how can I capture the way their eyes never focus? They're always darting from one side to the other in case they miss something. Everything happens at the periphery of their vision. They just don't stop and *look*.

The school she had gone to had taught her to fit in, to be a leader or be bullied. At school, girls were her friends because they were frightened of her – her eyes on their faces made them nervous. She seemed to stop dead and stare, locking on, they called it, trapping them in her headlights. But then she would say something outlandish that they didn't understand, such as, 'Do you know you look like a pelican?' to the self-styled most beautiful, vain girl in the school, which would *destroy* her and send her to the cloakroom in tears. Unattractive girls received compliments they would cherish for the rest of their lives: 'Leonardo da Vinci would have wanted to paint you.' At school she was a kind of heroine, with her heavy bust bouncing inside her bra, and the fat suddenly melting away over the course of a few months, proving that ugly ducklings could turn into some kind of swan.

She had lost weight by the simple, effective method taught to her by Ivan's wife Simone: she only ate half of whatever was on her plate. Half a bread roll, half a pat of butter, half a steak, half a potato. If she ate fifty per cent, she could be one hundred per cent what she wanted to be.

'You haven't eaten much,' Tim said. 'On a diet?'

'No. I'm not very hungry.'

'So what's your assignment?'

'The raped women.'

'That? It's yesterday's news,' Colin said. 'A few years back we were all trying to get to the bottom of the rape story. I saw through it. If all the Bosnian women had been raped by the Serb irregulars there should have been a whole crop of rape babies except no one could find any. There was no spike in the birthrate. So where were all these babies?'

'Just because they were raped didn't mean they got pregnant. A lot of them had stopped menstruating because of the shelling.'

'That's just a theory. Each side will tell you anything that serves their interests. The main thing to know about war is that you need to treat everyone as a liar. They'll show you pictures of men with their dicks and balls cut off and stuffed in their mouths and swear on their mother's life it was taken a week ago and they know the guy personally – they were at school with him, or he's their uncle or their brother or the mayor or what-have-you. That picture has been doing the rounds since the First World War. Who knows who the poor bastard was? I don't. The point is, there are always atrocities. You just have to peer through the fog of war and see if you can make out the shape of something, but even then, you can't always understand what it is.'

'But women were raped,' said Marianne, stubbornly.

'There's no real evidence.'

'No one's *found* it. That's not the same thing.'

'War is mostly lies, bullshit, and occasionally some glamour, but even that's dying out. The pictures I take no one wants to look at. They're just of depressed-looking people walking along a road with their belongings, and some teenager with an AK47 and a bottle of slivovitz in his pocket. You've turned up too late, far too late. It's all over.'

A waiter in a short white jacket wheeled a metal trolley to their table. It contained baba au rhum, apple strudel, Black Forest gâteau, crème brûlée, English trifle, and a spirit lamp and small pan to make crêpes flambéed with black cherries. He was the priest of the high craft of *pâtisserie*.

The men scorned sweet things: they thought they were womanly.

At the revolving doors of the hotel, Tim said, 'I'll walk you back, if you like.'

'No, I'm okay.'

Outside the streets were completely empty, the shops dark, the boulevards wet and black. 'It must be the dullest capital in Europe. There's no night life, or we could have gone for a drink.'

'I'm not looking for night life.'

'I suppose not. Listen, the cards will be in tomorrow. Get there first thing and you can be on the plane to Split by lunchtime.'

'Thank you for telling me.'

'Any chance of a kiss of gratitude?'

'No, not really.'

'Boyfriend at home?'

'I don't have a boyfriend, no.'

'You should have a boyfriend. You look like you need one.'

'What's that supposed to mean?'

'You seem like a new toy that's just been taken out of the box and no one's played with it yet.'

'You mean I'm a sex toy?'

'I just mean you look a bit untouched.'

'I suppose you prefer your women shop-soiled.'

'I do have a type, that's true. My type is a short little blonde girl with a big smile. You're nothing like that, but you're still attractive. Not sure you know it, though. You look like a girl who, deep inside, think she's a dog. You walk like a fat girl, to be honest, which is weird because you aren't fat. I think you used to be fat, didn't you?'

Usually getting under women's skin caused a reaction, of some sort. They cried or were angry. But the tall dark girl with the camera bag simply looked at him, like an X-ray machine, then turned away and walked down the street, slightly stooped to one side as the weight of the equipment bore her in one direction.

Lying in her room beneath the yolk-coloured counterpane Marianne had already forgotten about Tim and Colin. She was thinking about the raped women and what a woman who has been raped dozens of times by dozens of men might look like now, a few years later, what there would be in the eyes. She was trying to imagine people she had never met and working out how to frame the shot. Her mother had shown her the articles about the raped women of Bosnia; they had sat and read them together at the kitchen table. 'Oh, my God, those poor girls,' Andrea had said.

No one had taken them seriously at first. Andrea had a friend who had a friend in Dubrovnik, a Jungian analyst. She had treated a woman for six weeks, insisting that her lurid stories were sexual fantasies. Eventually the penny had dropped. 'We're not always right,' said Andrea. 'Sometimes we miss it by a mile.'

Marianne was not a virgin. She had had sex with two boys, both her own age, and it had hurt, quite badly, particularly the first time. She had never told anyone this. She feared she might have an unusual physiological condition that she could not cope with, not on top of having so recently been fat. Sex, she thought, is not for me. Or, I'll try again later, in a year or two. Maybe it will have worked itself out by then. She wished she could talk to her mother, but Andrea would not just sit and offer grown-up advice, like other mothers, usually, but not always, hitting the mark. She would devour Marianne's very soul with her analysis; she would become her mother's subject. Everything had an underlying meaning, according to her mother, and Marianne wanted to work out those meanings for herself, at a time of her own convenience.

For example, the interesting thing about Grace was that she seemed unable to live without a man, however pathetic, and Grace's men were poor specimens. Grace has never really been free – that generation is so hung up on sex, she thought. They can't bear the idea of being without it, and they're romantics, too. Which led to: No, sex isn't for me.

She knows she has entrapped herself at the wrong end of a lens, that she is looking without being seen, that she has not yet forged emotional connections. She knows her mother believes she has a fear of intimacy. Marianne thinks she doesn't. She simply has a curious and restless mind, and the world is so large and interesting that she has to move on into the centre of it.

But now, under the yellow counterpane, she thought of tomorrow and the plane to Split. Life is beginning! Grace's way, but with the necessary corrections.


Light rain in the mountains. The road is lonesome and no birds sing in the wet trees.

Other vehicles passed her on the road – UN trucks, private cars, a troop of Dutch soldiers eating chocolate, even buses transporting civilians from village to village. Marianne had taped 'TV' to the roof and sides of her four-by-four, the new universally accepted sign of the media. Its message, not always understood, was 'Don't shoot!'

An hour and a half from Split, she turned a bend and came to a primitive roadblock: a telephone pole resting on two oil drums. No one seemed to be around. The trees dripped rain from their branches; the sky was a grey hood. She had made up her mind that if she was hijacked on the road she would try to use her youth to deal with the situation: the militias were no older than she was, and she was used to dealing derisively and firmly with teenage boys. She did fear being raped – the fear was of the pain of penetration – but she did not think it would come to that. In her experience, people usually surrendered to her will. They were too intimidated not to.

She waited for a few minutes but no one came. She turned off the engine, got out of the car and walked towards the barrier, wondering if she was strong enough to move it with her arms or if she could kick the pole down with her booted foot.

Out of the trees came a flash of vivid pink, which she thought was an optical illusion or a tropical bird flown disastrously off course. The pink was a nylon bubble wig worn by a boy in a blue tracksuit, and with him another kid dressed in the usual army fatigues you could buy on market stalls anywhere in Eastern Europe. In their hands they proudly held Kalashnikovs – not very good Kalashnikovs, being Bulgarian imitations, and inclined to rust easily, jam or even break up in your hands as you were trying to shoot them.

Before they'd got their Kalashnikovs the two boys had practised on small animals with rusty Second World War revolvers or farm shotguns, working their way up from chickens to dogs, whose heads blew off and turned into splintery pulp. They had heard that killing children was pleasantly easy: they dropped to the ground without a sound, like killing mice with a catapult, leaving only the echo of the retort in the air.

The girl was ugly, which itself was no impediment to rape. They had friends who had raped grandmothers, but there was a bigger Christmas present sitting on the road and it wasn't worth wasting time dropping their jeans to humiliate her. Older boys might come along and take it from them if they weren't quick.

A torrid, drenching shame briefly heated Marianne's body, as she understood that the car keys were in the ignition, and her camera bag on the passenger seat. The boys pointed at the

Toyota and began a discussion. After a few exchanges, they directed their guns at her and she understood she was to sit down on the wet leaves at the side of the road.

The boys got inside the Toyota. They lit cigarettes, offering her the packet through the window, but Marianne associated smoking with Grace, the cigarette with the red-stained tip, taken from the lips, 'God, what a fat lump.' She let out a torrent of raging abuse, fixing them with her headlamp eyes, jabbing her fingers at them.

'You shut up,' said one of the boys, who had learned a little English from TV. 'Shut up, ugly girl.'

They opened the camera bag and estimated the worth of the equipment. They let out exultant cries. A golden goose had been left lying in the middle of the road and all they had to do was pick it up and walk away with it under their arms. War was easy. The only thing they dreaded was peace accords, politicians, generals and all the other ways adults could fuck it up for them.

The boy in the pink wig lifted the telephone pole from the oil drums and ran back to the car. And then they are gone and she is alone on the road, in the middle of the afternoon, and the rain coming and going and so she waits, waits for a couple of hours until a UN convoy comes along, on its way back to Split.

# The Doctor

The city of Split is a sparkling Adriatic seaside place, with beaches and nightlife and frequent ships crossing the water from Italy with their cargoes of contraband cigarettes, which are the basis of the economy that funds the fighting.

Even under white skies, Split is an attractive city. There are places where people are meant to promenade along the boulevards in light-coloured clothing, and this is one of them. It is the kind of town her father would adore, with docks and ships and sailors in their whites, and you can stand and look across the sea with your back to the war.

Marianne had been helped into the UN truck by an Englishman. 'What happened to you?' he said.

'I was hijacked. They took everything. I was hijacked by *boys*, teenage boys. It's so humiliating. One was wearing a pink bubble wig and I don't know why.'

'Cheer up. At least they didn't shoot you.'

'No, that's true. I'm still alive.'

'Why were you going into Bosnia?'

'To find women who have been raped. I'm a photographer.'

'But you can find them in Split or Zagreb. You don't have to go into the war zone.'

'I *wanted* to go into the war zone. It's my first war.'

'It's my third.'

'Are you a journalist?'

'No. I'm a doctor.'

He was aged about forty, a solid man with sandy hair, pale blue eyes and creases on the back of his hands. Marianne's eyes found a great deal to take in.

'You're looking at me,' he said.

'I know. That's what I do. Am I making you uncomfortable? Lots of people say that about me.'

'No, not really. I like being paid attention.'

'Because you're always paying attention to others?'

'Very perceptive. What are you going to do when we get to Split? Do you have any money?'

'Yes, my wallet was still in the back pocket of my jeans.'

'That's a strange thing. I thought only men carried their wallets in their back pockets.'

'I need to keep my hands free. I never carry a handbag.'

'No lipstick or comb?'

'No, never.'

'Very unusual.'

He told her his name was Janek. She said, 'That's not English, is it?'

'No. My father came from Poland during the Second World War to fight with the British and he didn't want to go back to the new workers' paradise so he stayed and married an English girl, my mother. I grew up in Surrey – which isn't very exotic, is it? – but with this strange name, and we went to a different church from everyone else.'

'My grandfather was born in Poland.'

'Where?'

'I don't know. He lives in America. I don't often see him.'

'My father's from the south, near Krakow. I've never been there. I think some time I should go. I never even met my grandparents, though they're long dead, of course.'

The convoy arrived on the outskirts of Split. The sun was parting the thin cloud and the sea turned blue.

'Come on, I'll help you find a hotel, clean and respectable.'

'Why does it have to be respectable?'

'I don't know. Perhaps it doesn't.'

Marianne had a headache. She did not know if the car-hire insurance covered theft by teenage militias, or what she was going to do now, since her first war had come to an ignominious aborted conclusion. She wondered if Janek could help her locate some raped women to talk to. If he could, she was prepared to stick with him if he would ask her out for a drink.

They found a three-star hotel near the beach, which had catered for tourists until the war and still hoped that it could again. It was a much nicer room than Zagreb. Beyond the curtains evening had fallen. The lights of the city had come on and illuminated the promenade and its palm trees. 'You can never go wrong where there's a palm tree,' her father had once said. It was how he judged all destinations. There were no palms in Bosnia.

'Will you meet me for dinner?' Janek asked her. 'I think I can help you find raped women.' Anything goes in a war zone, he told himself. And what's wrong with dinner? It's just a meal.

'Yes,' said Marianne. 'I'd like that.'

They went to a restaurant by the beach and ate seafood. He impaled a grilled prawn on his fork and looked at it, then put it down again. The sight of it depressed him. He could not afford to find out how it tasted. Perhaps the bread would be enough. These visits beyond the enclave seldom worked in the way he hoped, providing neither rest nor the refreshment of his spirit. You looked at good food and it repelled you.

'What's the matter?' she said.

'I come from another time and place.'

'What place?'

'Have you seen pictures of the Second World War?'

'Yes, of course.'

'That's where I came from, just this morning, a place that belongs in the history books, not now. I can come and go there at will. I can leave the past and sit here eating expensive seafood and drinking reasonable wine. It's impossible to reconcile. The paradox is getting worse every time I leave there.'

'Can you please describe what the past looks like?'

'Why?'

'That's the way I can understand it.'

'It's colourless, like mud, and smoke rising from the burning waste. Emaciated faces, refugees who have lost all their belongings and have nothing to do but endure the endless monotony, often barefoot and with old clothes they've scavenged from the dead. It's not monotonous for me, I have plenty to do. I treat skin diseases, lice, respiratory infections, which afflict the weakest, a great deal of tuberculosis, chronic diabetes. Urological complaints, because of the low quality of the drinking water, Caesarean deliveries, which are very complicated to conduct when there is no electricity. And, of course, many amputations among the children, who thought they could help their parents by going to collect wood from the forest where there are snipers and the horrible surprise of the landmines.'

'Where is this? Where did you come from this morning?'

'Srebrenica. It's close to the border with Serbia, an enclave. Everyone's trapped. Not me, of course. We're the special ones. We can get in and out under UN protection, the UN that does nothing to protect the people who actually need protecting. They make me sick.'

No one she knew talked of war this way. At home in Islington, they discussed it as if it were politics. Among her photographer friends it was a story, a photo-opportunity.

She watched him eat a piece of bread. He sprinkled on a few grains of salt – salt is necessary in the diet, he said, to explain to her what he was doing. She had laid down her knife and fork. He took a sip of wine. He felt like getting drunk, but not on this.

'Should we leave?' she said.

'Why? Why should you be deprived of your nice dinner after your unpleasant ordeal? You've done nothing wrong. Enjoy your meal.'

'I'm not hungry any more.'

'That's my fault. I've spoiled your appetite.'

'Yes, but I don't mind.' He liked the fact that she did not indulge in polite phrases and circumlocutions. He had heard enough of those to last a lifetime. 'Would you like to go for a walk along the beach?'

'It's cold. You'll freeze.'

'No, I won't. I'm hardy.'

The sand was black and the surf white.

'My wife dislikes the sea,' he said. 'She prefers rivers. We have a boat moored near Henley.'

'How long do you stay away from your family?'

'Three months out of twelve. I volunteer.'

'Why?'

'It's difficult to explain. I was brought up in the Church, the Polish Catholic Church, which is very intense. When I was a child I lived in a bedroom with Christ impaled on his cross above my bed and he bled wooden blood from his wounds.'

'I think that's gruesome.'

'Many people do, these days. Did you have a religious upbringing?'

'No. Nothing. My father's a scientist – he's totally opposed to the idea of gods and religions – and my mum's a shrink, so she has her own religion. She worships the great god Freud.'

'It sounds very bland to me. Ours was a rather muscular Christianity. I can't remember a time when I didn't go to sleep without saying my prayers and looking up to that wounded, dying body. So I became a doctor, to cure the sick. I'm not licensed to perform surgery at home, but here I'm forced to do amputations. Could I have saved Christ if I'd treated him? Could modern medicine have saved him? Of course – but then he wouldn't have died for our sins and our salvation. It's a paradox I can't explain, though I've thought about it often enough.'

'So you're doing God's work?'

'Yes, that's it. Someone has to.'

'Why doesn't God do his own work?'

'I don't know.'

Marianne walked about the city on her own, taking pictures. She took a picture of a child beggar squatting on the pavement in front of a cigar box into which passers-by sometimes dropped low-denomination notes. The child's mouth was stopped by a blue plastic dummy; she looked about three years old, and no mother or father came near her. The city thronged with refugees; many were begging and some were stealing. They walked about with a dazed expression on their faces, unsure where here was. Two teenage Muslim girls in soiled white headscarves applied lipstick to each other's mouths. Men with the faces of beasts walked painfully on swollen feet too large for their boots. In the cafés, the waiters attempted to maintain their meticulous pre-war standard. Waiters, Marianne observed, were the people most impervious to conflict: their rituals were too important to them to be relaxed, or if they were, it was only with shame and many embarrassed apologies. A stained napkin and a shred of tablecloth was sometimes all that survived of civilisation. Waiters were heroes. She took many pictures of them in the years to come.

On Monday Janek took her to the psychiatric hospital. She spent all morning talking to the doctors. It was as her mother had told her: they had treated the raped women for sexual disorders, rape fantasies, submerged desires.

A doctor said, 'An old woman came in and said she had been raped by seven men, young men. Of course we did not believe her. We thought she was a fascinating subject – to hear an old lady talking in such detailed graphic terms about things that usually belong in pornography. A whole team was looking after her, we were terribly excited, and then slowly we understood that it was no fantasy, that these things had happened. And we were helpless, we didn't know what to do. All our sophisticated training was no use. The sex had also been very painful for her because she was past the menopause and her husband was dead so the walls of her vagina had atrophied. She bled like a menstruating girl.'

'Did you not think to examine her?' said Janek. 'A physical examination would have shown the truth at once.'

'No, we didn't think of that. We assumed it was all a metaphor.'

'Is that the only reason sex is painful?' Marianne asked. 'The menopause?'

'No, no,' Janek said. 'There are many reasons, and some are very simple, like excessive washing with perfumed soap.'

They went to a ward where a woman in a coloured nylon headscarf sat in a chair by the window. The hem of her skirt reached down to her ankles. Her face had cracked in many places and she held her fingers to her mouth.

'She watches TV when we turn it on,' said the doctor. 'She is very quiet, no problems, but we don't know where her relatives are. We tried to trace them, with no success. She has two daughters but she hasn't seen them for over a year. They got stuck in a place where the fighting was very intense.'

Marianne thought that her mother would have sat down next to her and held her hand. They would have sat in silence, exploring the sense of touch. She had been robbed of her equipment: she had no mediating lens; she felt as if she was in the familiar recurring dream all of us have, of walking naked down the street, the dream whose meaning her mother had told her and she could never remember.

But what *should* I do? she thought. I came to bear witness. I can't even do that without a camera. Snails don't do well without their shells. That's what I feel like. She was raw and flayed in the old lady's presence.

'I can find you more women like this,' said Janek. 'There are plenty.'

'No,' said Marianne. 'I don't think so.'

'What do you want to do now?' he asked her, when they got outside.

'Buy a new camera.'

'Here? In Split?'

'They must sell them somewhere.'

'I suppose they must. Do you have money?'

'I've got a credit card.'

They took a taxi back into the city. The sense of the other place continued to oppress him but her young, odd face raised his spirits a little. She lifted her arm and her T-shirt revealed a slim brown band of skin above her jeans. She's not my type, he thought. She's no one's type.

'About the painful intercourse,' he said. 'Was this a personal question?'

She blushed a dark red. It blackened her face. 'Yes.'

'I'm sure that's the problem. I have some unscented soap I can give you. It will probably clear up very quickly.'

He waited in the shop while she bought a new camera and lenses. She seemed to him to have an unlimited supply of money, but it was a friend of the family, she said, who was secretly paying the bills when they came in; her parents had no idea. Janek didn't believe this, about the parents not knowing. He suspected some arrangement, a carefully contrived safety net in place; were she in trouble she would be hauled back straight away. As soon as the charge came up for the new camera they would be alerted to her current difficulties. That was how he would have behaved if his daughter had grown up and gone to Bosnia.

For half an hour he forgot about the past in the present, the land of 'never-again'. She told him about her parents and the house where she was born and had grown up and all the strange people who used to live there. The American father, the mother with the faded red, later blonde hair, the brother who had come back reluctantly from deafness. She had refused to follow her parents to Oxford, had done a photography course instead.

Her elbows on the table. Her black eyes. Her upside-down smile.

God forbids, he thought. Yet God allowed so much worse. She was right to have made that very basic point to which he could supply no intelligible answer.

# Her First Love

It was a *coup de foudre*, a blow to the side of the head as she photographed Janek holding the limp arm of an old man, trying to find a pulse. The other place was as he had told her: mudcoloured under a low brown sky.

He was physically exhausted, had gone without sleep for twenty-four hours and had lost his temper with the Dutch peacekeepers. 'There is no bloody peace to keep,' he shouted. 'What are you doing here? Being neutral is to close your eyes, to tie a blindfold round your head. It's perverse and dogmatic. Take off your helmet and *see*.'

Turning away, she felt the whack and staggered. Two days later, watching him remove shrapnel from a girl's body by the light of a torch she was holding, she resolved that she had to say something. She could not stay silent – she wasn't interested in unrequited love. The girl, bandaged, was taken away by her father, who was crying.

'You can put down the torch now,' Janek said.

Instead she shone it on his face for a moment. It was an unassuming face, the sandy hair receding from the hairline, the watery blue eyes with pupils suddenly contracted. What was it about this face that she adored? She did not know. She didn't understand it, but understanding was unnecessary. Her mother had taught her children to be in touch with their feelings and to trust them.

'Listen,' she said, 'we have to talk.'

'About what?'

'I know you will find me ridiculous, but I can't help it.'

'Why should I find you ridiculous?'

'Because I love you.'

'My God, this is a bolt from the blue. Marianne, I'm married.'

'I know that. I don't care.'

'You should care.'

'Why? Because it's a sin?'

'What do you know about sin?'

'Nothing. I don't believe in it, but you're a Catholic. Isn't sin what your religion is all about?'

'Of course not. It's about God's love.'

'I'm not interested in God's love. I want yours.'

'Are you always so bold in your affections?'

'Not at all. I don't have much experience with men. I have some, but not much.'

'So I'm your first love?'

'Yes, you are.'

'I'm flattered, but I really don't know what to say. I don't have a good answer for you, not the one you want.'

She was wearing a strange hat, of khaki cotton lined with rabbit fur, more like a hood than a hat, with flaps that came down over her ears and tied under her chin with two strings. She looked like a creature from a fairy story, an elf; she was unkempt and her fingernails were rimed with dirt. She stood in her heavy coat and boots and her fairytale hat with a child's face, a dark mole almost hidden by rabbit fur, peering out, asking him to go to bed with her. It was ridiculous. But she was so earnest and unafraid. She was at the beginning of life and he was in the middle of it, with all the fuss and complications.

'Look,' he said, 'I have work to do. The work is all that matters.'

She shook her head.

'What?' he said.

'It *must* happen,' she said. 'I want it so much.' She sat down on the edge of the makeshift operating table, still and stubborn, looking up at him full of impatience and yearning.

'I like you a lot,' he said, 'but . . .'

'Well, then.'

'No, Marianne. I'm afraid not. You'll meet someone.'

'I *have* met someone. It's all done.'

'Who?'

'You – you!'

He laughed. 'Why me? I'm old enough to be your father and I'm not exactly a film star.'

'I don't know. I'm not even interested in the question. My mother would be, but I'm not her. I don't understand why things need explanations when they are so obviously real. Do you ask why children are coming in here with their limbs blown off by landmines? Do you ask God and get an answer?'

'No. I don't receive an answer, but I do ask.'

'But you still operate on the children, don't you?'

'Of course.'

'You see? Everything's easy when you stop questioning it.'

She took off her fur hat and loosened her hair.

'Is this your seduction?' he said, laughing. 'Are you going to undress now?'

'No. I'm hot.'

It was true that he had never met anyone like her. She was certainly fearless and her pictures were beautifully composed – he barely recognised himself in them. His face had an intensity of purpose that he never saw when he looked in the mirror. She made him look like a holy man, a priest, delicately probing the abdomen of a small child with his instruments. He was astonished by what she showed him.

'Look, next week I'm going to Split. Come with me and we'll talk again there. I expect everything will seem different once we're back in the real world.'

'What isn't real about this? I thought you said this *was* the real world?'

'No, you've misunderstood. This is the place out of time. It's a place to visit from the real world.'

'But it's real for the people who live here.'

'No, it's not. What is real for them is what they can remember – renting videos and eating pizza. This is a bad dream.'

Split was developing signs of once again being a seaside resort. There was a certain levity in the streets, despite the refugees, the wards of injured in the hospitals, the UN vehicles, the journalists, the active life of war. You could eat ice cream and forget about blood.

She was still in her fur-lined hat and her Timberland boots; she had done nothing whatsoever to make herself an attractive and seductive proposition. She could be cross, blunt, impatient, she could talk too fast and with too much conviction; she would fall in love too foolishly for her own good and retire, hurt and then hardened. It was such a shame, he thought, and she was so young.

After lunch, walking along by the sea under cloud-speckled skies, she raised her camera and began to photograph him.

'What are you doing?' he said.

'I'm doing what I do.'

'Why do you have to separate yourself from the rest of the world with a piece of glass?'

'I don't know. It's the kind of question my mother would ask and I would just ignore her.'

'Maybe your mother's right.'

She laughed. 'My mother believes in helping the afflicted.'

'I was brought up to go to the parish priest and tell him everything, all my secrets. Now no one tells the priests anything, even though they do their work for nothing instead of charging by the hour. And what does your father do? I can't remember.'

'He works in television. He makes science documentaries.'

'Of course – so the two things come together in you, looking through a lens at the afflicted.'

'I never thought of that.'

'Put down your camera for once, Marianne.'

'Okay.'

They walked on, along the seashore, watching the large ships coming in and out of the harbour, connecting them to Brindisi and other normal places. Janek's mother had had a brother in the tank regiment who was killed in Italy during the Second World War. The photograph of him in a pair of rimless glasses and with a soft blond moustache had stood framed on the sideboard in their house in Surrey all the time he was growing up. Poor boy. He was only twenty-three. Later in life Janek had wondered if he had died a virgin.

I'm forty and I have never had an affair, he thought. What do you do when someone throws herself at you? How are you supposed to respond? I'm only human. But what's wrong with my marriage? This is having your cake and eating it, and what a strange cake. A cake with salt instead of sugar. And all day I try to prevent genocide with a stethoscope.

They ate dinner at the restaurant they had gone to on the first night in Split, a month ago. This time, Janek thought, the food tasted fine. The other place seemed distant; he experienced no guilt in wolfing down a large meal and drinking most of a bottle of fresh white wine. My appetites are returning, he thought. He tried to concentrate on the image of the field hospital but it kept evading him. She sat opposite him, still in her jeans and boots but with a white T-shirt. What glorious breasts, he thought. Suddenly he felt the urge to eat them too.

Returning to their hotel, he kissed her in the lift. It was an act without explanation. Why did I do that? he asked himself.

The hallways were white stucco, yellow in the low-wattage bulbs of the ceiling lights.

'I will always tell you the truth, Marianne,' he said. 'I'm married, I have children. I'll show you photographs, if you want. You have to understand that from the outset.'

But as so many of her school-friends' parents were divorced (her own an anomaly in staying together for so long, almost, she thought, *ludicrously* faithful), she regarded Janek's marriage as an easily alterable detail.

# The Internet

Stephen could not get out of his mind how lucky they had been: himself, Andrea, Ivan and all their other friends. The sun had risen on them and had stayed all this time on their faces. Their purpose was to fulfil the ultimate destiny of the human race.

He was fifty-five years old and for the first time he understood that nothing bad had ever happened to him. He lived in a house worth a fortune with his wife of thirty years. His children's lives had worked out: no one was on drugs or in prison; no one had died of Aids. Everyone he knew led a nice life, and on and on it was all supposed to go.

Then this. Out of the clear blue.

Only in the days after the catastrophe did he realise that all kinds of warning signs had been there all along. Not of the atrocity, but of his own misguided judgement about the permanence of the universal condition of his generation, to whom nothing bad was *supposed* to happen.

'We've had such a long run of good luck,' he said to Andrea. 'We thought it would go on all our lives. We were born in sunshine . . .'

'You were. Not me.'

'We all were.'

How could it be that he, Stephen Newman, of all people, should have turned into one of the grey men of the BBC, the stooped ghosts who lived on in a deluded fantasy of public-service broadcasting, who stood with begging bowls outside the commissioning editors' offices, wanting handouts to make extravagantly expensive programmes involving whole production crews being flown to the Galapagos Islands to film a documentary about Charles Darwin?

He knew that people like him, his grizzled head, his sad leather jacket, his Gap jeans, were figures of fun. He was by far the oldest person in his department: everyone else was hatched at twenty-two and rose and rose until they reached their late thirties and then they vanished. He had no idea where to. Independent production companies? Or did they just wither and die? Almost no one had clung on as long as he had, ducking and diving redundancy and the temptation to accept a big pay-out to leave the institution. That life, the life outside, was not for him. He was a company man and, as such, belonged in a museum.

Once he had been the object of satire for the conventions of his existence, for his Islington address and psychotherapist wife, for having once or twice been at dinner parties with the Blairs; now he was merely ridiculous. He was just clinging on. Was it cheaper to promote him to some non-job, like executive in charge of noticeboards and paperclips, and drive him out through boredom and shame than pay his expensive redundancy and final-salary pension?

I've been complacent, he thought. I truly believed this trip would go on and on. The commissions were drying up – he went for months with nothing to do, ashamed of drawing his salary but dependent on it. They had remortgaged to build a conservatory six years ago. Andrea had wanted it, and why not? He enjoyed sitting out there with a glass of wine, talking over their day, talking over the children's lives, their naïve errors, marvelling at their toughness and cynicism. At their ages, they agreed, they had been babies.

Last year colossal pressure had been brought to bear on him to leave. The advantages were sketched out over lunch with the controller. He could set up an office in Soho, pitch ideas to any channel he liked, pocket the money from overseas sales, instead of drawing a monthly pay cheque, but what guarantee was there that he would have any ideas commissioned? And deeper still was his anxiety about what lay outside the doughnut. He *liked* feeling himself to be a cog – it didn't diminish him: it was teams who won the Nobel; even the humblest researcher had a hand in every scientific breakthrough. Of course, the ideal was to be at the head of the team, the genius, but he was no genius. He would have been content to know that he was part of something bigger than himself, and this, he thought, was what his generation was all about.

'Our parents had the war. That was their big thing. We had ideals,' Ivan said, 'most of them cranky and failed, but we did dream, didn't we?'

'Have you noticed how acid is completely out of fashion?' said Stephen. 'My kids admit they smoked dope and their friends have done Ecstasy and amphetamines, but when I asked them about LSD they said it was an old-school drug. I've no idea why.'

'It's because no one wants to open the doors of perception any more. Acid was about revelation, about the vision of what lies beyond the rim of the knowable. It's a drug for revolutionaries and they have no interest in revolution. And the other thing is it just takes up so much bloody time – eight hours minimum and then a day or two to recover. I just don't think anyone has that kind of leisure. If I had to market it I'd aim the product exclusively at retirees.'

Stephen wished that he was not laughed at for clinging to an old-fashioned way of thinking. No one at work looked him in the eye. He was, as the expression went, merely meat in the room. It was brutal, the cocky assurance of glossy youth, a youth without optimism. They lacked what had sustained him for forty years: his belief in the future, retaining the quaint notion that there were technological fixes for everything. One of the things that had drawn him to the BBC was a funky little programme called *Tomorrow's World* in which they had introduced a gasping audience to Velcro and the Sony Walkman. But no one believed in tomorrow's world any more.

Now everything changes. He had a nephew in New York. He had no idea where the boy worked, not even a boy any more, a thirty-seven-year-old man he had never met who was in the restaurant business somewhere in Manhattan. His sister Carole, the boy's mother, was living in New England, over sixty now, divorced twice, riddled with arthritis, every joint in her hands and feet swollen and dysfunctional. She still wore too much makeup, still nostalgically sat down after dinner with a glass of wine to listen to Elvis on her thirty-year-old record player, went once a year for a three-day vacation in Vegas, but every day was an hour-long struggle to get out of bed, to fasten the tabs of her white shapeless shoes with fingers that didn't straighten out, and unsteadily stand on feet that could no longer support her weight. Was that what *he* had to look forward to?

On the phone it took several hours to get through to her: Anthony was fine, she had spoken to him, and all the family; no one had been affected, just shocked, then frightened and enraged.

And at the BBC, from people he had known for years, lunched and joked with in the canteen, and at home in Islington, from his charmed circle of friends, the Islington set, whose kids were now all grown-up yet still met for dinner and went on holiday together to Tuscany and Provence, he first heard the words that made him understand that everything he had taken for granted about himself, his adopted country, his own sense of reality in time and space had been just dead wrong. He could not have been so far out of kilter with what he imagined his own life had been.

'*America had it coming.*'

His mother was frail. He came from long-lived stock, it turned out, but at the age of eighty-three she was dying. He hoped to God that she would last a few more weeks so he did not have to try to return home for her funeral in this state of chaos and confusion. His father had hung a flag on the porch – everyone had, all the neighbours. His mother watched the news on TV from her hospital bed; she ordered a Stars and Stripes pin in red, white and blue rhinestones from a TV shopping site and got the nurses to attach it to her nightdress. They took a picture of her and it arrived in London a month later, the old Cuban lady, the white roots of her hair now relentlessly moving down the wave that partly hid her ravaged face. But still she had put on her red lipstick for the occasion. For sixty years she had worked through one tube after another, Max Factor every time, the makeup of movie stars.

And this dying woman in a hospital bed in Los Angeles, who jabbed her finger at the TV screen whenever Fidel Castro came on the news ('Why doesn't he shave off that horrible beard after all these years?'), for whom Che Guevara was not a poster but a common murderer – she, it turned out, was held responsible for every evil in the world and *had it coming*. His nephew and wife, and their kids in New York had it coming. His sister Carole in New England, with her arthritic hands that could barely cook a meal, and his sister Rita in Phoenix, running a little gift shop in the mall, the two once-glorious girls with their hairspray and face powder and poodle skirts and Frankie Avalon records, had it coming.

His father, long retired from the fur business, and fur itself denounced, out of fashion, had it coming.

Late at night, hunched over the Internet, Stephen found a world so shocking that he berated himself for his own ignorance that he had known nothing at all about it. He had genuinely believed that there were people like him, who took a liberal view of politics and were right; there were the fuddy-duddies who read the *Daily Telegraph* and still mourned the lost Empire; and there were the stupid people who took no interest in politics unless it involved their own taxes.

Apparently he had not been paying attention because inside the beige box, where in the early days of the Internet he had once guiltily chatted to girls at MIT, were a million cranks and conspiracy theorists, people driven nuts by rage and hatred.

They would say anything, anything at all, however insane, unkind or irrational.

The attack on America was an inside job, a controlled demolition (but *why?*). The Israelis were behind it: Muslims and Arabs were too dumb to fly a plane or think up such a convoluted plot. From nearly a quarter of a century of working at the BBC Stephen knew in his bones that cock-up was always the more likely explanation than conspiracy. Bureaucracies were too incompetent to plan and keep secret anything on such a scale, while cock-ups were depressingly frequent, nearly always attributable to someone in the chain of command not having received, or having received but sloppily read, the inter-departmental memo. Or spilling coffee over the relevant paragraph. Or leaving it on the tube. People were just not that good at keeping secrets or executing a plan to flawless perfection, not in his experience.

And washing through the Internet, common to the right, the

left and the centre ground, was this massive hang-up, which had been gathering like a vast, poisoned underground lake that had sprung out of the earth to flood any rational discourse. There was absolutely no crime, no evil, that did not have the Jews behind it. Everyone seemed to think the Jews had a secret and, whatever it was, it was definitely a guilty one. The Jews had something to hide.

What was it about the Jews, Stephen wondered, hunched over his computer, that seemed to drive everyone else completely crazy?

Am I a Jew? he asked himself. He had been circumcised, but that was common in America in the 1940s. No one in his family went to church or synagogue, not the uncles in San Diego, not his father. Religious faith was a superstition, one he had thought was dying out. How wrong could he have been about that? As far as he was concerned, the Middle East was a place of archaeology; his eyes had glazed over during any news from the region. The whole thing was too complex to apply his attention to, with no obvious right or wrong.

His identity was not that of either a Jew or a Cuban, but an American in exile. He had never expected his bones to lie in a damp English graveyard. He had told Andrea this often enough, and she merely nodded. It was a problem they would have to thrash out later, when retirement was eventually forced upon him. But she could go on and on, she said. She could see patients until she dropped, and what about the children? Did he want to be on the other side of the ocean to them?

Andrea had no interest in computers. She had never sent or received an email. She did not know what lay in the bowels of the Internet, and when he led her to the screen to show her the toxic waste that washed across it, she said, 'Well, who *are* these people?' And, of course, he didn't know.

'A bully is still a bully, even if he has a bloody nose,' he read.

'Well, isn't that true?' said Andrea.

'Christ, are you turning into Grace all of a sudden?'

Much common sense was talked about America, Andrea said. It needed saying. Of course it was appalling what had happened in New York, unforgivable, inexcusable, but no one was trying to forgive or excuse. They were simply stating the obvious: that America was no innocent victim in all this. 'That's a sophisticated argument,' Stephen said, 'but look at the filth that underlies it. Look at what it says here on the Internet.'

'Well, who are these people?' she said again.

'I told you, I don't know.'

'Exactly.'

You worry about your kids, Andrea thought. You will worry about them for as long as you live, perhaps unnecessarily, but are you really supposed to worry about your husband, who is not ill, not unemployed, not anything that should bring him to his knees except the ridiculous hours he spends hunched over the Internet, reading the ravings of lonely people in sad, squalid rooms? He seemed to be drawn to the sheer toxicity of it all – he smeared the poison into open wounds. But that was because he had too much time on his hands. She couldn't remember when he had last been away filming, mostly he went to work and came home again, with the same briefcase full of papers, nothing added, nothing taken away. How could he not be depressed?

She could go for months totally forgetting that her husband was American. He was to her now the hairs that had started to sprout from his nose, and the particular comforting shape of his empty shoes by the bed at night, his flossing, his toenail-cutting, his hypochondria, his dietary fads, the fading freckles on his back, the loose sac of skin behind his penis, the memories they shared of all the holidays they had taken together, and the way she could read his mind.

She had been incredibly lucky, she thought. He had given her everything she had wanted. It was preposterous to think that she, a girl of her generation, had only ever slept with one man but the edifice of their marriage was built on that fact. That he was an American was a meaningless description, like saying he had black hair. Sometimes Marianne asked him for the American expression for something, and he realised he could no longer remember: he had been here too long, more than half his life. *He* was responsible for nothing America had done, yet America's arrogance and hubris could not go unpunished. He had gone down to the embassy twice at election time to vote for Bill Clinton, Clinton of Univ, with whom he had once shared *petits fours* on the ship that had brought him to England and to her, so long ago. He owed it to Bill to vote for him, he said.

Yet all the accumulated rage against America had been gathering force during his presidency, Andrea pointed out. Surely he could see that.

'This is not rage,' he said. 'It's psychosis.'

'What would you know about psychosis?'

'Nothing. But isn't it?'

He had a point. There probably was a study to be written about political anger and the mental state of the bombers, but it was so outside her field of expertise, which dealt with everyday sadness, that she could offer no psychological explanation for this fury that was consuming everyone. What she knew came from letters from Grace, and Grace had always had penetrating insights into the state of the world. Grace had seen it coming. She hung out on the edges of the city. She had a little apartment in the Parisian *banlieue* where she lived with her Algerian boyfriend and he told her things that were so far beyond Stephen's horizons of knowledge that Andrea had not dared show him the letters.

Grace endured. She went on being Grace. How did she do it? Here they were, in middle age or whatever it was called these days, and Andrea on HRT had reverted to her former plumpness, sick and tired of the bathroom scales and kitchen scales, longing to *eat*, to drink a glass of fattening wine and eat fattening olives without feeling she was a failure for having no willpower. Grace was thin as a rake, her white blonde hair just white now and her face a maze of lines, sun-damaged, decorated with a defiant slash of red lipstick, the exact same shade she had always worn. The Algerian was a decade younger than her, the little sponger.

She had not forgiven Grace for what she had said to Marianne on the day of the anniversary lunch. Stephen had told her to get out of his house. Andrea had told her to apologise. Ivan had gone after Marianne when she had run into the garden, and told her, 'Don't take any notice of that old crone. One day she'll walk into a room and you'll be there, slim and lovely, and she'll be sick with jealousy. You'll have your revenge.'

Andrea said, 'Grace, you need therapy. You have spent your whole life running away from one horrifying encounter. You have distorted your whole personality around this scar.'

Grace sat in the kitchen drinking tea. 'I don't want to talk about it,' she said.

'I know you don't. And that's the problem. No, it's your tragedy.'

Grace said nothing.

It isn't going to work out, Andrea thought. She's come to nothing. I thought she was going to be amazing, and she isn't. There's nothing here to be impressed with, but I can't abandon her. Who else does she have?

Andrea remembered herself at nineteen, her first day at Oxford, standing outside her college room, too frightened to open the door, looking down at her feet in blue suede sandals and her legs in American Tan tights, with reinforced toes in a darker shade. Poor child, she thought. Poor kid. Lost and bewildered, and here was her daughter who, at twenty-eight, talked calmly of land-mines and dismembered children begging on the streets. Wherever she came back from there were no pictures of land-scapes, no peaceful water buffalo or paddy fields, just a series of unhappy faces. Marianne's photographs were the greatest chal-lenge of Andrea's life – nothing, not even the froggy day and her hanging rabbit, compared with the evidence that her own daughter should be in such close proximity to a baby's head blown off, rolling down a hillside, or a child's eyeball blasted into a gutter.

On the wall of Marianne's living room in her flat in Bethnal Green there was a single photograph, one of her own, depicting a medical team at a field hospital in Bosnia, taken in 1995, one of her earliest pictures. The doctor and nurses gather round the figure of an injured boy and the light is on their faces. The composition, Marianne explained, is exactly that of an Old Master. The medics just seemed to have arranged themselves into a classical pose and the light had shone through a dirty window onto them, illuminating the intense concentration of their work. It was an accidental shot, she insisted. It was *always* accidental. Life sometimes organises itself as art, and the pho-tographer is lucky enough to be there and press the shutter at the right moment, then wait until she sees what appears in the developing fluids, emerging like a ghost returning to life from the hazy greys.

Except now, she said, because of the new technology, digital photography, you knew at once what you had. It was a shame. Another instant experience. Robert Capa's pictures of the D-Day landings, the tremendous force of the water through which the men were wading, would not have been possible today: the film was damaged during the journey home; this was all that was salvageable; and almost no one at *Life* had thought they were even worth printing.

Andrea thought it was gruesome to have a picture of an oper‐ ation on the wall of a living room, over the mantelpiece where she would have placed a gilded mirror. In fact, the whole room seemed clinical to her. The camera equipment was neatly arranged on a table, and along the walls were filing cabinets of negatives, which her daughter was in the process of transferring digitally to her computer. The intense order of this room struck her as containing an element of Marianne that she did not understand. Everything was technical in some way, masculine, without untidiness or any decorative detail.

Only in the bedroom did a softer touch emerge, with candles by her bed, and a glass bottle of scent on the dresser. This, Andrea conceded, was a woman's room, and the room very defi‐ nitely of a woman who had a lover, though Andrea had failed to elicit any information about him, and had assumed, correctly, that he was married and that this bedroom was the place where he came to make love to her daughter.

It did not occur to her that the middle‐aged doctor in an open‐necked denim shirt with rubber gloves on his hands, prob‐ ing the abdomen of a boy injured by shrapnel, was that lover.

She felt a dismal failure both as a mother and as a therapist that her daughter told her nothing about her life, that her teenage bounce and gusto had been replaced by a reserve and secrecy, as if she was always tending to some inner flame. She wished Marianne would dress better; she wished she would attend to her looks. But Marianne had accepted plainness, when a more flattering wardrobe and even a slash of lipstick occasion‐ ally could have made her a beauty: a beauty with a discerning band of admirers. But perhaps the married man saw in her dark face what others failed to. Andrea assumed that he was in the same business as her, another photographer.

Andrea prayed for world peace, so her daughter would be reduced to taking photographs of fashion or anything whose shallowness was proof that beyond the frame lay nothing but normal human misery, not made worse by cluster bombs, shrapnel, landmines, white phosphorus, conscripted child soldiers and columns of fleeing refugees.

Her brother was a professional conjuror and going out with a deaf girl. They spoke to each other with their hands, conversations that excluded his mother and father. Their lives were enveloped in quietness, apart from the applause of the audience when he did his act. Was he happy? He said he was. He stood on stage like a little wooden marionette, puppet movements. His public presence tricked you – you couldn't take your eyes off his unusual face with its pointed eyebrows. He drew them on with eye pencil. 'It's all deception, Mum,' he said.

Max, she could not help observing, had grown into his life; he had filled it. Despite his weird job, not really a job at all, he was the member of the family best equipped to deal with the terrifying changes that worried all of them. He was a man of the moment, she thought. He rode the wave. He had neither hopes nor ambitions, did not wish to make the world a better place. 'I just live in it,' he said. And living in it did him well. He had bought his own flat, with only a little financial help from his parents.

She had never forgiven herself for not noticing the gradual loss of his hearing. It had made an affair out of the question; she would spend her whole life knowing the body of only one man. She accepted this. Max loved her, even if she didn't deserve it. Every year on her birthday he performed a special show with an audience of just one, delighting her with tricks he had devised involving flowers, which were difficult to work with. He kept away from his father – 'Too noisy,' he had once said.

I used to be so frightened of things, Andrea thought. Birds terrified me, crows in particular. But nothing she had ever feared in her life had come to pass. The bears with their sharp teeth had never found their way into her bed: her rabbit had guarded her. Back in the deep past our life together goes, and our children are the strangers.

The past is a narrative, a story. You try to tell them but they don't believe you. You might as well relate the tale of Tom Thumb. The facts disturb them: they run from the room jabbing their fingers down their throats when their mother and father reminisce about the afternoon in 1969 when they met and how quickly it all came together, in an hour, because that was how it was in those days, no dating, no hesitation.

*They make it all up, you know*, she once overheard Marianne tell her younger brother when they were teenagers. *They have to invent something to make themselves sound interesting, but do they seem interesting to you? Dad's a bore and Mum's a nag.*

'I'm a *bore?*' said Stephen. 'When did that happen?'

'Better a bore than a nag.'

Marianne thought her parents' generation were phoneys. They had been given everything and squandered it, they had '*eaten up* the planet'.

'We weren't phoney,' Stephen said. 'Our whole point was to live an authentic life, to challenge the bourgeois conventions of our parents' generation. We wanted to make it real.'

'And did you?' said Marianne.

# Evening Interior, Bloomsbury

'You asked me once why I didn't tell my mother. She was the *last* person I would have exposed myself to. As you know, she had three miscarriages before me and another two afterwards. She spent all her time trying to get pregnant and failing, failing, failing, and if her fifteen-year-old daughter had come to her and said, "Help me," she would have made me have the baby and brought it up herself.

'You think that's a cruel assessment? It's quite true. She would have pretended it was hers, and the kid would have grown up thinking I was its sister and I'd have been even more fucked up than I am already, except that I would never have got away from home because she would have kept me there as an unpaid nurse-maid. I don't mean to say that my mother is a terrible person – she isn't – but she's a thwarted earth-mother, and that's why she's spent her whole life in the garden.

'So I got the train to Victoria and I turned up at my father's flat, round the corner from the hospital. He always said it was just a *pied à terre* for the nights when he was on call, and I imagined a little room with a camp-bed and a scullery kitchen, a hotplate, you know, a sort of bedsit, but it was nothing like that. I had to wait for him on the step for a few hours before he came back. It was a miserable day, raining on and off, and I was damp and bad-tempered when he finally turned up and said, 'What are *you* doing here?'

'I should have known as soon as he opened the front door that this wasn't going to be a bedsit. It was one of those large, anonymous Bloomsbury houses near Lamb's Conduit Street, where the residents are rich enough to have installed a lift, and we got into it, and the doors closed. It was lined in some plastic material, pearl grey, very modern. We got to the third floor and there were two doors on either side of the hallway, and he turned to the right and I turned to the left. I have no idea why I was so certain it was the left-hand door, but I kept standing there, rooted to the spot, waiting for him to turn round and say, "Of *course* it's this flat," which was ridiculous but that's what I thought, and you can make of it what you will. And I'm sure you will.

'So, eventually, I turned round, and he'd already opened the door and inside you could see it was quite a palatial little set-up he'd got himself there, with *eau-de-Nil* walls, and all the sofas and armchairs were cream satin. There was a bunch of shop flowers in a vase on the sideboard. When we went into Sevenoaks I always used to wonder who bought flowers in a shop when the garden was full of them, but in his flat, I realised for the first time that it was people like Dad who buy cut flowers and for that reason I've never been able to stand them. I can't go into a florist. Every single flower standing on its amputated stem reminds me of him.

'We sat down and he made me a cup of coffee and he said, "To what do I owe the pleasure, Grace?"

'I told him, and I asked him to help me, and he said, "And who's the lover boy?"

'I had absolutely no intention of telling him – that was the last thing I wanted to do – but then I realised he wasn't going to go to his house and make a fuss, he was simply curious. He wanted to know about the boy who had fucked his daughter. He kept asking me questions about him, what he looked like, how tall he was, and then he asked me if I'd come.

'"Mind your own bloody business," I said.

'He just smiled and said, "Yes, I can see that was rather intrusive. But you know, you're a healthy young woman and you haven't inherited all your mother's gynaecological disorders, apparently. If you orgasm, it draws the semen up through the cervix and makes pregnancy more likely." Yes, I know *now* that that's rubbish, but this was my father telling me, so of course I assumed he was right even though he had absolutely nothing to do with gynaecology. He was paediatrician, a children's doctor.

'"Anyway," he went on, just sitting there in his black leather slip-on shoes – his town shoes Mum always called them, "what exactly is the form of help you're seeking?"

'I just couldn't help looking at how he was dressed. He'd get up after breakfast and put on his coat and hat and drive to the station in the Rover and I paid no attention because that was what happened every day, but I could see now he had a change of clothes. He had these *town* clothes, which he must have kept in the flat because he looked so different, slightly fashionable. At home he wore tweeds, but in London he had a suit which, now I think about it, was an Italian cut – it had narrow lapels – and he wore a narrow knitted navy tie, which was squared off at the bottom instead of coming to a point, and then I had this very precocious flash of understanding that these were the clothes a mistress bought for her lover.

'But all this was going on subliminally. I don't think I was aware of it at the time, at least not consciously.

'I said, "Can you help me get an abortion?"

'There was this terribly long silence. Was I supposed to think he was wrestling with his conscience? No, I emphatically do not believe he *was* conflicted. He never gave any evidence of that.

"'Hm," he said finally. "Hm. Well. I don't think I can risk that. No, I don't believe there's anyone I could ask. No."

'I was fighting myself. I was thinking, Don't cry don't cry don't cry. I could see my whole life disintegrating. I would be stuck at home with my mother for ever and I'd turn into a shadow.

"'No need for tears," he said. "All is not lost. I certainly can't ask anyone else to do it – I could get into very serious trouble. They might go to the police and inform on me, just for asking them. I could go to prison. But I don't like to see you in difficulties so I will do it myself."

'This had never entered my head. I tried to think of where I could go, but the only people I knew were the ones I went to school with, and James, whom I hadn't even told. There was no one. I was stuck, like those insects which pierce their food while it's still living and keep it in a kind of larder, alive. I sat there looking at him. I couldn't speak. You know that sensation when your tongue feels like it's been frozen, and it's huge and wooden and cold in your mouth and it won't move? No? Well, that's how it was. I couldn't say anything.

'And then *he* said, "Of course, you'd have to keep your mouth shut. You can't tell anyone. Do you understand that?"

'I just nodded. What choice did I have?

'He gave me a five-pound note and told me to come back a couple of hours later and he'd have everything ready. There had to be certain preparations. I took the money and I wandered through Bloomsbury. There was the British Museum – I could have gone in there, I suppose, it would have been educational, but I didn't. I just wandered around and I saw some people my own age talking on a street corner. I couldn't hear what they were saying but I knew that I now felt like a different species from them, I was cut off. I don't know what he thought I would do with the five pounds because I couldn't eat anything.

'I went into a phone box and began to ring James, but then I thought, What am I going to say? He didn't even know I was pregnant. What was the point? The only person in the whole world who knew was my father. I walked past the hospital and saw the children coming and going, the poor sick kids and their parents for whom my dad was a hero, a saver of lives. And to me he was this man who had complete power over me.

'The foetus was a tiny little thing, just a curled-up comma, I was only ten weeks, but I was skinny and my stomach had started to stick out slightly. I turned sideways and looked at myself in the plate-glass window of a shop. I could quite clearly see that little bump. If I could have stopped it there, if it had moved neither backwards nor forwards, I could have accepted it, but it was going to grow and grow like some parasitic organism inside me. It would suck out my soul if I let it. No, I didn't feel any maternal instincts. Whatever hormones are supposed to kick in, they didn't. Later they did, but not then. I mean years later, long after all of this. When I was in Paris the first time.

'When I went back, he said "Everything's ready. You can take your clothes off in the bedroom."

'The walls were covered with modern art, representational, no abstracts, and after I'd looked at them for a few minutes I understood that they were all nudes, life studies. I opened the wardrobe and I saw his London clothes, his suede brogues and all his suits with narrow lapels and narrow trousers. It seemed my father was quite a dandy. And there was a woman's perfume coming from a corner of the wardrobe, so I pushed past all the suits and there were *her* clothes, a couple of dresses, a skirt, a cashmere sweater. Down below there was a pair of stilettos and I saw these notches on the wooden floors where someone had been walking in heels.

'He called out to me to strip down to my bra and knickers,

which I did but I found his dressing-gown hanging on a hook behind the door so I put it on. I came out into the sitting room and everything looked the same, though he had said he had made preparations, whatever they were. 'Where am I supposed to go?' I said.

'"We're not doing it in here," he said. "Go into the kitchen."

'I looked at the kitchen table and wondered why a towel was laid out and a cushion from the sofa at one end, and then I realised that this was where I was supposed to be, I was supposed to lie down on his blue Formica kitchen table. This was his surgery.

'He came in. "Hop on," he said.

'I was still in the dressing-gown. "You can keep that on, if you like," he said, "but your knickers will have to come off. Here, I'll help you."

'And then he pulled down my knickers and he just looked at me for a while. "Very nice," he said.

'I started crying. No one would blame me, but it didn't make anything any better. In fact, I think he enjoyed seeing me vulnerable. No, I have no idea what was going on his head – and that's the point. You could drive yourself crazy trying to work out what other people think, which is why I don't. I take them at face value now. I've wasted enough of my life on my father and what was going through his twisted mind.

'And then he said, "Blunt end up."

'I had no idea what he meant. So I just lay there, not moving, and he took his rubber hand and pushed it under my pelvis and raised me.

'There's a total blank about the next half-hour. I'd have to have very deep hypnosis to recover it, and I don't want to. All I remember is the kitchen clock ticking, and people walking past in the street, all those tapping high heels, and the smack of expensive leather soles on concrete, and the lift ascending and descending and then the sound of the pedal bin opening and something being dropped inside and then it closing. I was in bed, waking up, and I could hear the sound of voices in the sitting room, and a woman saying, "Where's the lighter, Philip? I'm gasping for a cigarette." And then a click. "Thanks, darling."

'Once, the door opened and I could see her looking at me. She seemed quite ordinary, not the glamorous black widow I'd imagined. But apart from that, I can't recollect anything about her. Except that her name was Jean – I heard him call her that. And her hair was done up in a French pleat, which was fashionable at the time.

'Around ten o'clock I got up. She was gone. I felt weak and terrible.

'My father was sitting on the cream sofa in embroidered carpet slippers, watching television. The sound was turned very low. I think he was watching the news. He switched it off when I came in.

'"Chin up," he said. "It all went splendidly. You can go home tomorrow morning. You'll be fine. I've rung your mother and told her you missed your train and are spending the night here. She's expecting you tomorrow. Try to eat a soft-boiled egg when you can."

'I went back into the bedroom. He spent the night on the sofa. The next day when I got up he was gone. He'd already left for the hospital. He'd left me another five-pound note on the kitchen table with a note saying I could take a taxi to Victoria if I wanted. I still had the money he'd given me the previous day. I left the second five pounds where it was.

'On the train going home to Sevenoaks the rain was coming down in weary patches. It couldn't make its mind up what it wanted to do. I thought, When I leave home I will *never* live in London. He wanted me to go to art school – he thought I was very talented. He said I should go to the Royal College and study painting, but I said, "No, I'm going to Oxford". If he said "black", I'd say "white." That was the only reason I went to university. I won't entertain the idea that he might have been right. No, not even now, forty years later.'

# Going Home

After Stephen's mother died at the end of the 9/11 year, his father was alone for a long time until he was befriended by a widow called Mrs McLean, who had recently moved across the street. Stephen knew his father couldn't boil water. He was a magnet for what Andrea called the hot-dinner brigade, elderly widows and divorcees who lustred their charms with pot roasts and pies.

Even at the age of ninety, Si remained physically much the same man he had been in his thirties: short, wiry and still with surprising strength in his hairy white forearms; his stamina astonished his children. Yes, he had gone a little deaf and had an expensive hearing aid Stephen had bought for him, but his body seemed immune to most of the usual ailments that afflicted old age. No high blood pressure, no cancer, no heart condition, no peeing blood, no diabetes; maybe some arthritis in his knees but otherwise an indestructible force whom Stephen, the hypochondriac, sometimes feared would outlive his own son. There was no reason at all why he shouldn't hit one hundred; a shame he had no birth certificate to prove it. His date of birth was a notional set of numbers based on what the child, arriving in America in the twenties, speaking no English, had supplied to the relevant authorities. He might be younger or older than he really was, according to what long-forgotten lie he had glibly provided for the interpreter.

The widow began inviting him to dinner. She was a good cook and she prepared steak, with mashed potatoes and some indeterminate greens. Afterwards, there was always a slice of cake. It was a satisfactory arrangement for both of them.

Following the meal, they retired to two armchairs to watch television. There were no books in her living room, but a long shelf by the TV held a library of movies on videotape and so it was, in May 2005, that she turned to Si Newman with disbelief and said, 'What? You never saw Schindler's List?'

Mrs McLean had seen the movie three times already, and she wasn't even Jewish. She went out and bought a bottle of Scotch to fortify him for the ordeal. She positioned a box of Kleenex on the coffee-table, because she knew she would cry in the scene with the girl in the red coat, and again near the end when they light the Sabbath candles. By the time she reached the end credits she would be sobbing, and she was Scots Presbyterian who had never left California, so what might it mean to the old man from the floor above who came originally from Poland where all this had actually happened?

'Not bad,' he said, when it finished. 'Did you notice the fur Schindler's wife was wearing? I used to look after furs like that.'

'It didn't upset you?'

'Upset me? Why? It's just a movie. They're actors, movie stars. They go home to servants. I saw that Neeson on the street once. Good-looking feller.'

'But what about the end, the people they made the picture about? You understand that was the real people the actors played?'

'Of course I understood. I wonder how much they paid them. I hope they made a lot of money out of it.'

After this, Mrs McLean stopped preparing meals for Si Newman. He was an insensitive man, a horrible man.

Since he had arrived in America Si had left the state a few times to visit Las Vegas with his wife to see a big show, paid for by the Cuban cousins, trips to Boston and Phoenix to see his daughters and the momentous journey back to New York to see off his son on the SS *United States*. After his mother had died, it was understood that every year Stephen would make the trip home to check up on his dad. A couple of years before, Stephen had bought his father a cheap laptop and signed him up for a Hotmail account so they could converse by email. His dad had always been a dutiful if infrequent letter-writer, who would not pick up the phone to dial London on account of the expense.

Emails from his father arrived in Stephen's inbox in the mornings, written in California in the evening, after extensive use of the spellcheck, which made them more comprehensible, though certain words changed meaning altogether under the spellcheck's suggestions. But at home one evening in the early spring, when the clocks had gone forward and the days were growing later, Stephen was surprised to find an email from his old man. His father never knew what to put in the subject line. It wasn't mandatory to fill it out with anything at all, Stephen had pointed out, but his father regarded the demands of email as he would a form from the IRS.

So on the subject line was the word 'Trip'.

The night the widow had asked him to watch *Schindler's List*, he had dreamed of his parents. In his dream he could see his mother, with the braids pinned around her head, the cameo brooch at the neck of her blouse, in the kitchen pulling bread from the iron door of the oven, and his father yanking the bridle of a horse in his shirtsleeves, the smell of shit on his boots.

He walked through the house on light feet and no one could see him. He climbed the stairs to the bedroom where his older sister was combing her hair in front of the mirror and singing a Polish song. *Gittel!* he cried out in his sleep, and when he awoke he touched his papery cheeks and eyes, surprised that no tears had fallen.

Drinking his coffee, looking out at the dry grass on the lawns, he asked himself where he was, and was frightened for a moment that the blank cloud of forgetfulness had suddenly descended on him, as it had on others he knew from the fur depository who nodded in old people's homes; he understood that the small town was still there on the plain by the Narew river.

The traffic-lights along the street, changing colour from moment to moment, the high blue Californian sky, the automobiles parked by the kerb, the sound of hip-hop coming from a pair of cruising neighbourhood kids, this whole American morning was no more real than Lomza, with its heavy skies, looking down on the winding river.

To: Darwin6749@yahoo.co.uk
From: SNewman89006@hotmail.com
Subject: Trip
Dear Sun
I just saw that movie Chandlers List. You seen it? Not bad! I saw Poland again and it got me thinking of my mother and father. And my sister Gutter. I want to go and see what became of my home town Lima. I want to go to Europe. Can you fix this trip for me?
    Your loving father

Reading his father's email, Stephen was struck by the reversal of their situations. He was always thinking that one day he would go home to America, while here was his father, announcing at the age of ninety that his heart's desire was to return to Europe. Stephen had grown up in a silence. His mother and her brothers spoke of Cuba, of the island of their childhood, and the women selling fabric in the stores on Muralla Street. Havana was a city anyone would feel nostalgic for, but that ugly place in the middle of Europe had aroused no feeling or spoken memories in his old man. He remained mute on the subject of the past. For the first time Stephen learned he had an aunt Gutter. Weird name.

Andrea, who was always the instigator of any project that resulted in a change in the direction of his life, said, when he showed her the email, 'Maybe you could get some funding to make a documentary about it.'

But this proved, rarely, to be one of her unsuccessful ideas. No one was interested in the story of an old American Jew returning with his son to Poland. Jews, Stephen understood, after several meetings, were out of fashion. No one was interested in them any more and the Holocaust, he learned, had 'been done to death'. A few years ago everyone had been raving about a wonderful new novel he had to read – 'Simone says it's the first book she's read about the Holocaust that isn't upsetting,' Ivan said. This was what they wanted, these days, so Stephen organised the trip for just the two of them, father and son.

'I came from Warsaw and to Warsaw I go back,' his father said, when Stephen suggested that he fly from LA to London, rest for a few days and then make the much shorter flight to Poland. 'But this time I get on a plane and I'm right there.'

'Okay,' Stephen said. It was a stupidly expensive plan, the way Si wanted to do it, but he didn't have the heart to argue with his dad about cost.

In early July Stephen flew to Warsaw and waited anxiously for his father to emerge from Customs. Two hours in Poland, most of it spent at the car-rental desk, had induced in him a primitive angst about the place where everything came from, and which there was no good reason to go back to. Eventually his father appeared, on the arm of a young woman in Lot Air uniform, who smilingly presented him to his son. 'Your father speaks excellent Polish,' she said.

'What?' Stephen said. 'I didn't know you spoke Polish.'

'Just a little. I remember a few things.'

They drove east from Warsaw. A river ran through the landscape and on either side there were fields of wheat. The crops undulated in the summer breezes; the landscape looked as if it would not harm a fly.

His father sat chewing a wad of gum, which he had brought with him from Los Angeles. Over here, he had heard, everyone was crazy about American chewing gum. It was practically a currency and could be used to get you out of trouble.

'Yeah,' said Stephen, 'if you were a GI in 1945.'

His father occasionally turned his head to look at some unmemorable feature of the passing road.

'Do you recognise anything, Dad?'

'Yes, the same place. Very boring, isn't it? It reminds me of the prairies, where I was only once and once was enough.'

'Andrea and the kids weren't impressed with the Midwest, either. What did your father do exactly?'

'He worked for a miller. He was a farmhand, mainly in charge of the horses.'

'That doesn't sound like a very Jewish profession.'

'He didn't have a profession. No one had a profession. He had a job, like I did. *You* have a profession.'

Stephen had not yet told his father he had taken redundancy and early retirement. Andrea had forced him into it: it was either that or go into therapy for his depression. Ivan, who had accepted a huge redundancy settlement to go away and do nothing for the rest of his life, came round one evening and said, 'Stephen, you know what you are? You're a form of obsolete

technology, like eight-track or the cassette tape. Accept it.' Now
the two retired men sat all day in the conservatory drinking
coffee and planning businesses they might set up, all of them
foolish.

'Did you like horses when you were growing up? Did you get to
ride them?'

'Ride the horses? Are you nuts? These were horses to pull
carts, horses with hair round their ankles – I mean their hoofs.
No one rode them.'

They drove in silence for another forty minutes. Stephen
thought if he had to look at another ear of wheat he would hallucinate with the monotony. Eventually they arrived at an
uninspiring town, clean and orderly, with a marketplace in the
centre selling electrical goods and cheap shoes.

'My God, is this it?' Stephen said. 'This is where you were
born?'

'Just over there,' said his father, pointing with his finger.

'Where?'

'You see the pizza parlour? Our house was round the corner.'

'Do you want to go there first or to the hotel?'

'To the hotel.'

'You must be knocked out.'

'No, I slept the whole way over. I took two glasses of vodka
and when I woke up we were over France. Lot is an excellent air-
line. They took very good care of me. I'm fresh as a button, but
I want to see what kind of hotel they have here.'

It was nothing much. Most of the guests had business with the
brewery, or the company that made wooden doors. 'Don't buy
anything from the market,' the receptionist told them, when
she gave them their keys. 'The vendors come from Belarus and
they are dishonest. Anyway, you can buy much better things in
Vilnius.'

'Not bad,' Stephen's father said, when they had opened the

doors of their adjoining rooms. 'It doesn't need to put up the President of the United States or Julia Roberts.'

'Julia Roberts?'

'She's a big star.'

'I know. So why would she come here?'

'She wouldn't need to. This is what I'm saying.'

They went out straight after inspecting their rooms. There was nothing to stay in them for. In the square a troupe of Latvian folk dancers had arrived in their bus. The men wore mustard-coloured pantaloons tucked into soft leather boots, white shirts and red bows tied round their necks while the women were in skirts of rainbow stripes and embroidered waistcoats.

'What the hell is this?' said Stephen.

'The peasants. They always like to dance.'

'Weren't your family peasants?'

'No! What are you talking about? Of course we weren't peasants.'

'But you said your father looked after horses.'

'That's nothing to do with it. A peasant is a completely different thing.'

'Okay.'

They walked along the street under mild, milky, innocent skies past a small supermarket and various shops selling goods marked in euros. They might as well have been in rural France, Stephen thought. Or Ireland. His father turned into a street of old houses. 'This was where the Jews lived,' Si said. The houses were more substantial than Stephen had been expecting; he had imagined some kind of hut.

The apricot-coloured house lay behind a ramshackle wooden fence painted green. Steps and a green front door and a small enclosed porch with a pointed wooden roof. It had an air of poverty and dereliction. In London, properties like this would be worth a fortune; in the Polish town everyone had built themselves white stuccoed chalets with steep red roofs and a car port.

Stephen watched his father staring at the house. He waited for him to speak. He did not expect him to cry. 'Which was your bedroom?' he finally said.

'You think I had my own bedroom? I shared with my two cousins!'

'I didn't know that.'

'A lot of people lived in this house, not just us. The whole *mishpochah* lived here.'

'Who?'

'Relations. Uncles, aunts, my grandfather.'

'What was he like?'

'Very religious and smelt of fish.'

'Did you get on with your neighbours – I mean, the Polish ones?'

'Yes, we got on fine. No problems. Okay, sometimes there were problems. They were good Catholic boys and they said we killed their Jesus. They should have been grateful to us. If we hadn't killed him, he couldn't have died for their sins and they would all go straight to hell.'

'That's very true.'

His father nodded. 'Stupid people.'

'Do you want to go inside?' asked Stephen. 'Should we knock?'

'No. What for? I'm not going to find my mother in there.'

'Okay. What do you want to do now?'

'We'll just walk around.'

Stephen was waiting for his father to unburden himself of a past he had been silent about for nearly eighty years. He expected to learn about the mother, the father, the sister; he expected to have to face up to the horror of what had happened to them. He had already looked this up on the Internet: Treblinka, or a mass grave in the forest. But his father walked slowly along the pavements, remarking on how the town had spread out from its old square, stretching away into suburbs over what had once been farmland.

'What I always thought,' he finally said, 'a nothing place.'

'Do you feel any attachments? Do any memories return to you?'

His father shook his head. 'I had a mother and a father. I had a sister. You know who took them from me? Not the Poles. It was those immigration men at Ellis Island. They're the bastards. If it wasn't for them we would have all made it to America. The Poles always do what you expect of them – you should always fear the worst – but of the Americans we had high hopes. We believed in justice and freedom. All they gave us was a cross in chalk on our backs. They were the ones who crucified my mother and father and my sister.'

Stephen had never heard his father say a word against America. He had always assumed he was a patriot, a supporter of all of America's wars and a Republican voter because that was how his San Diego in-laws voted. 'And you have sustained this anger all these years?'

'What anger? Who said I was angry?'

'You sounded angry.'

His father shrugged. 'I lived my life among movie stars and their minks, what's to be angry with America about?'

Stephen saw him drooping with fatigue. 'Let's go back to the hotel and rest,' he said.

'Okay.'

His father did not get up for dinner. When Stephen rang his room, he answered, in a blurred voice, 'I'm okay, but I want to sleep.'

Stephen ate alone in the dining room. He had never felt so depressed in his life, as if his own father had abandoned him to this alien world of Poles whose language he did not know, and all of them, to him, had the eyes of the descendants of murderers, which was unfair. They were all in it together now, members of the European Union. After dinner he watched Sky News on television, amazed to find a TV channel he understood. Hey, he thought. London is going to host the Olympics.

The following morning his father rose early and had already finished breakfast when Stephen got down to the dining room.

'Today,' he said, 'I'll show you the mills where they made the flour and then we'll go to Warsaw. All my life my father told me it was the finest city in the world, and I never saw it. Warsaw! Now *this* is going to be something.'

# July

Warsaw, which Stephen's father insisted on pronouncing Vashar, was a flat disappointment and his father did not want to stay a third night. 'I don't know what I expected,' he told his son, 'but this is a big nothing. You might as well be in Culver City.'

But it was difficult to leave and get home.

London seemed marked and different to Stephen in the taxi coming from the airport. For the first time, he felt a sickening sense of imminent danger, that the nut jobs inside his computer had jumped right out of it, at first in monochrome, pale and printy, then wavering for a moment until they became flesh-and-blood young men with backpacks, walking purposefully into the Underground stations. His father was seeing something different: brick houses for the first time, and roads built long ago to bear horses and carriages, double-decker red buses – he cried out at the sight of them, 'Do they ever fall over with the people inside them?'

And Stephen said, 'Listen, there were bombs two days ago, underground. Do you understand?'

His father nodded. 'Terrorists. Like the ones who hit New

York. Not them, of course, they're all dead, but the brains behind the operation.'

'It's not a spy movie, Dad.'

They pulled up at the house. Stephen ran up the steps and Andrea opened the door. Si said, '*This* is what I thought I would see in Vashar.'

'Everyone is okay, everyone is accounted for,' Andrea said. 'I was with a client, Max and Cheryl were still having breakfast and Marianne says she was asleep. Ivan and Simone were at home, and no one else we know was anywhere near it.'

Si had not seen his daughter-in-law for several years. She was no longer the girl with the radiant expression in the rabbit-fur jacket, sitting by the window, and her once-red hair was blonde. He didn't know why women did this, but they all did, in his experience. All the dark-haired girls of his youth were now light-headed, even the Cuban sisters-in-law. Women had a great deal to lose from age. Some of them wrinkled and some of them sagged, and his daughter-in-law was the kind who sagged: dewlaps hung from her jaw. Unlike the movie stars she had not had anything done to her face – she didn't have the frozen-rabbit look he associated with the motion pictures. Still, he thought, she was never a beautiful girl or even a very pretty one, but she was a nice woman then and she was a nice woman now. A sympathetic face. His son had chosen well. And one thing that was different about her was that she had a lovely smile. That he saw at once. She had finally fixed her teeth.

She took his hand and led him up the stairs to his room. It was a long time since anyone had touched him. Mrs McLean had hoped to hold his hand when he wept in *Schindler's List* but he hadn't wept. Andrea's hand was soft with a scented cream. Passing the bathroom he saw an old lady sitting on a low chest in the hall, wearing a green robe. Maybe it's an hallucination, he thought. They used to have old people living here. I guess it's her ghost. The idea did not perturb him. Between the two worlds there were occasionally passages, wormholes you could slip in and out of and speak to the dead. He had never found his mother and father or his sister Gittel, but his wife came and went, usually on Sunday afternoons when he sat with a magazine on his lap in the empty house, thinking of the times when they used to go to the beach, and he turned to kiss her, out in public. Or the first time they met, just before the war, when someone from work brought her on a blind date, and he was knocked out by her sultry beauty, with a fresh flower pinned to her hair.

'What's she doing here?' Stephen said, when his father was resting in his room.

'She's come to stay.'

'*What*? For how long?'

'She's homeless. She doesn't have anywhere else to go.'

'Why does she have to stay with us?'

'Because we have a big house. We have more than enough room.'

'Ivan and Simone have a bigger house – let her stay there.'

'She barely knows Simone. It's not appropriate, and she doesn't have any real relationship with Ivan, as she does with me.'

'He said no, didn't he?'

'Well, yes, but —'

'She's not staying under my roof with my father here.'

'Your father is only with us for a week or two.'

'So? How long does she plan to stay?'

'I don't know.'

'Get rid of her, Andrea.'

'I can't and I won't. She's as much family to me as your father is. There are things I've never told you about Grace because I knew you'd be cross.'

'What things?'

'When her father died he left her some money. He had a flat in London and some art. That was what she got from him. She gave most of it away to her causes, but some she gave to Marianne. That was what she used to replace her camera when she was in Bosnia – a lot of her equipment came from Grace. It's expensive and she was always able to keep up to date.'

'This was her guilty conscience?'

'I don't think it was. I believe, if she's telling the truth, and she usually does tell the truth, that she wanted Marianne to have the freedom she had had herself, to travel.'

That his own daughter been able to go to war zones, those terrible places, because of a subsidy paid by Grace, made him feel demented. And now Grace had run though all her money and had slunk home to England. He supposed she could find no more boyfriends. They were all coming up to sixty, or he was; the girls, as he still thought of Andrea and Grace, were both a little younger, and Grace looked a wreck, years older than his wife, who was the same age.

Ivan confirmed what Andrea had told him: Simone had said absolutely not. She had never forgiven her for her terrible remark to Marianne the day of the twentieth-anniversary lunch party. If she could say that to the daughter of her best friend, what foul rudeness might she come out with when Simone and Ivan had guests?

'She has nowhere else to go,' Andrea said. 'If she doesn't stay here, what do you think will happen to her?'

'Cuba?'

'Don't be silly. One of my conditions is that she has to have a course of therapy. It's time we got to the bottom of all her problems to clear out the accumulated junk.'

'And she agreed?'

'Eventually.'

'Good luck.'

It was just the four of them at dinner, Si struggling with risotto, hunting out some evidence of meat in the dish. (I won't make that again, Andrea thought.) His tastes ran to meals with separate ingredients laid out clearly on the plate in quadrants: a protein, a starch, a vegetable and a slice of bread. Grace came down looking worse than Stephen had ever seen her. She made no comment on the food she was served, eating almost nothing.

'It's amazing how quickly everything has got back to normal,' Andrea said. 'Most of the tube lines are running and Oxford Street was full of shoppers today, according to the news.'

If she says London had it coming, Stephen thought, she's out. But Grace merely remarked, 'It will be interesting to find out where they came from.'

'Who?'

'The rebels.'

'For crying out loud, they are terrorists.'

'And what do you know about them?' she said scornfully.

'I read up.'

'I had several boyfriends from North Africa, sweet young guys. They see the world startlingly differently from the view in Islington.'

Bile rose in Stephen's throat. 'How can you sit there and complacently come out with this nonsense? Real people are dead. Don't you get it?'

'Baudrillard might plausibly disagree, but the real people include the rebels themselves.'

'The *terrorists*.'

'If it comforts you to call them that, then let's call them the terrorists. They made a literally superhuman sacrifice to achieve justice by embracing their victims and removing themselves from the ongoing struggle. Can't you see the complexity?'

'No.'

'Well, it won't work,' Andrea said. 'I mean, how could it? What do they think is going to happen as a result of those bombs? London is far too large to bring to its knees. I had clients all day Thursday and Friday and they talked about the same problems and anxieties as they had on Wednesday – adultery, eating disorders – the commitment-phobes, the lonely and the sad. The bombs made no difference to their sorrows. These things don't touch us. The terrorists are narcissists. Their influence is far less than they believe.'

Stephen's father was struggling to hear the conversation. Two of the voices, English-accented, were unfamiliar and his slight deafness could not always register what they said. He knew they were talking about the terrorists, but the ghost-woman, who was not a ghost but a friend of Andrea's, had a mouth that went up and down like the opening and closing of a pair of shears and *gornisht mit gornisht* came out. Nothing, salted and sweetened with nothing.

'Can we talk about something else?' said Stephen. 'We have, after all, just got back from Poland.'

'How did you feel about returning, after all this time?' Andrea said, laying a hand on Si's arm in the sleeve of a pale blue sweat-shirt, a garment he had begun wearing after his retirement. 'Was it traumatic, or a happy experience?'

'I saw my house. It was still there after all this time, but not in good condition. The Poles haven't looked after it.'

'And did you find out what happened to your parents and sister?'

'I don't need to go to Poland to find that out.'

'Was it not upsetting, being in the town of your childhood, walking the streets you walked when you were with your mother and father?' To Andrea, Si's case was fascinating. What childhood could have induced such life-affecting trauma as his?

'I don't get upset. Life is too short for tears. And what should I be upset for? I lost my wife. That was a tragedy – I thought I would go first, but these tragedies are normal. We live with them. I have nothing to complain about.'

'Warsaw was disappointing,' Stephen said. 'We'd planned to spend longer, but there didn't seem to be anything much to see.'

'My parents were from the sticks,' said Si. 'I realise that now. To them, Vashar was Paris and Rome. Maybe before the war it was beautiful, but now . . . a really ugly place with a horrible monument to Stalin. And no beach. That's the thing I forget about Vashar. I couldn't stand that.'

They ate ice cream, and went into the sitting room to watch the ten o'clock news on TV.

'We start tomorrow,' Andrea said to Grace. 'Please be in my office at eleven a.m.'

The day finally ended, the sun setting on the garden and the trees, the geraniums gradually losing their colour, turning black in the twilight. Cats passed and re-passed across the lawn, hunting mice in the shadows. It was only two weeks since the solstice, and summer seemed still the normal condition they would always be in.

# Sunday Lunch

Max knew. He was the only one she had ever confided in about having a married lover.

'It's him, isn't it?' he said, looking at the photograph on her living-room wall of the field-hospital triptych.

'Yes, that's him.'

Seeing Janek interviewed from his hospital bed on the news, Max got into his car and drove across London to his sister's flat. She had always justified her situation to him; she would batter him with words. But looking at her now, sitting on the white sofa, the desolation of her face looking out onto the street, he wished he had not been so malleable. He was the younger child, the little brother, and he had not manned-up to the situation. He had been too placid. He should have forced her to understand that she was making for herself a grave of her life. He should have said, he should have said, and he hadn't. Now she was going to make a shrine of the mantelpiece with Janek's picture above it. She was going to turn the flat into a mausoleum.

He didn't know anything about sorrow: he had not yet felt it. He fell in love aged twenty-two and the girl he had chosen had loved him back. He learned sign language to talk to her with his dextrous hands; he practised words of love with his fingers. Cheryl was an accountant. She spent all day with her fascinating numbers and in the evening she went out dancing, tap and modern ballet, and he met her at a wedding where he pulled scarlet ribbon after scarlet ribbon from her high-heeled shoes, bending down at her feet. All the happiness their parents had wished for their children had come to him, in compensation for what they thought of as his late start in life but which he considered a gift. The reward of silence, dark, mysterious, profound. He heard things Cheryl did not, birdsong, wind in the trees, waves, and he tried to make hand-words for her to express them.

And here was his sister, his noisy, confident sister, saying, 'I feel like I'm in a black hole. I'm buried alive. Am I going to have to spend the rest of my life in solitary confinement?'

They were expected for Sunday lunch in Islington to see their grandfather and listen to their father tell them of their origins, of the small town on the plain with a river running through it in Poland. The idea was that they would find out who they were, but Max knew *exactly* who he was. His passport was just a travel document.

Max did not get on with his father; he had no opinion of his grandfather. He was oppressed by loud voices and his father shouted. 'He doesn't shout,' said his mother. 'He just enunciates clearly. *He* says the British mumble and swallow our words.' He saw his father's face bearing down on him with its nostril hairs, shouting, 'You gotta have an education!'

'We will both have to go,' he said to Marianne. 'I don't think there's any way we can get out of it, but I will try to do most of the talking.'

He sat down on the sofa next to her and held her in his arms. It was the first time he had ever done this. She felt all kinds of strange objects beneath his clothes – it was second nature to him to keep magic things about his person: a few cards nestled in the small of his back and coins dropped from the hem of his jeans.

'I tried to go to the hospital. I got into his room for a minute but he told me to go away. It was like I was one of the bombers – he was scared of me, scared Lucy would come back. She'd just stepped out to go to the bathroom and I'd snuck in when he was on his own and the nurses weren't guarding him, and he looked at me, his face stricken, and he said, "Marianne, you have to go." Why? Why was he so cruel to me? I don't understand.'

He held her tighter but she floated out of her body and through the open window. She felt like a balloon let loose from its moorings, with nowhere special to go.

Andrea had laid the table in the conservatory. Grace was already there, standing with a drink, looking out at the garden. She looked as old as time, Max thought. The fabulous cheekbones remained but the skin was mottled and brown spots were already on the backs of her hands. He noticed she swayed slightly, as if unable to keep her balance, but still she remained standing, on her feet. 'Hello, Max,' she said. 'Long time no see. Where's your wife?'

'At home.'

'Can't stand enforced family occasions, I suppose.'

'Only Mum and Marianne have sign language and neither of them is very good at it. It's quite boring for her having to wait for me to translate.'

'And then what you would translate would be inconsequential anyway.'

Max tended to agree but he couldn't see the point of Grace. She had not excited him as a child with her comings and goings, and he thought there was nothing romantic about her life. Her opinions, her experiences bored him. He wasn't interested in politics, the bombings were just random acts of sadism, incomprehensible; they were not worth the effort of investigating their cause. They did not matter.

Andrea came out into the conservatory. Stephen and Si were in the study, preparing a slide show on the laptop of the visit to Poland. 'He's very much on the ball,' she said. 'He doesn't remember what he doesn't want to remember, but that's just a tactic, I suppose.'

Grace did not care about the visit to Poland. She was thinking about herself, and what had befallen her, about the Algerian who had finally become so unpleasant that she had been forced out of her own flat: she paid the rent, the furniture was hers, the scraps of jewellery, the pictures on the walls, amassed over all the years she had had a base in Paris. He had driven her onto the streets with a knife, and she had spent two nights in a homeless hostel. She rang everyone she knew but no one would take her in. They were all fucks, total fucks, these people you thought were your friends. She despised them, the so-called artists, the so-called intellectuals.

She was a down-and-out, standing with a drink in her hand, looking out at a garden that suddenly appeared to resemble closely the garden her mother had made in Kent. Andrea had never had any hint of imagination: she just copied.

But Andrea was the final default position. She had taken Grace in. She had defied her husband. Because they had once lain down together on the college lawn, aged nineteen, and looked up at the sky and told each other all their secrets. And everything was innocent and their day was only just beginning. All would turn out well, and they would do great things. Very great things, or that was what Grace had thought of herself. Andrea had thought she had already achieved the limits of her greatness by being there, a student at Oxford. But I have done nothing, Grace thought, apart from exactly what I wanted to do.

Marianne arrived, white and silent.

What is wrong with her? thought Andrea. Something has happened.

Stephen set up his laptop and they sat round it, looking at the photographs of the market square, the Latvian folk dancers, the apricot-coloured house where Si had been born, the distant wheatfields, the cemetery, the plaque marking the fate of the Jewish population, the flour mills, the concrete hotel, the road back to Warsaw, the site of the ghetto, now interred under blocks of flats, the synagogue. They were bad photographs, indifferently shot on a cheap camera. Marianne observed that there were generally no people in them. Neither her father nor her grandfather were posed by any site of interest. The only inhabitants were passers-by who could not be removed from the shot. The pictures were evidence that they had been to Poland. At the airport they had bought a bottle of kosher vodka.

And what did any of it mean? Si Newman, displaced in time and space from his natural environment, the house in Los Angeles, sat watching as the pictures flickered, one to the next. 'That's right,' he said, nodding. 'That's what it looked like.'

Max, who had promised he would do the talking, had no idea what to say. His grandfather was remote, strange, a relic of his father's paternity. The two of them looked so alike, *were* so alike, he thought.

'Come and sit next to me, Marianne, darling,' said Si. 'It's been so long since I saw you.' He wished she had turned out pretty. The genes of her two paternal grandparents ran strongly in her, and they had not combined the way they had in her aunts, who had briefly blazed as beauties. There was something heavy about this girl. She carried a weight around in her soul. Something wrong.

She laid her lips on his cheek; he smelt of soap and fragments of the previous night's risotto. A line of startling teeth lay across his mouth, white and even and plastic.

He tried to think of something to say to her. She was a woman of the world, that he knew. 'So tell me, young lady, who do you think are the terrorists? I guess you met plenty of terrorists in your time?'

'Not really terrorists. They're usually dead by the time you find that out. But I met plenty of warlords.' The words in her mouth were formed of lead letters, like old-fashioned type.

'What's a warlord?'

'Someone with an armed militia.'

'Doesn't sound like a nice gentleman at all.'

'Not really, no.'

'But here in London. Warlords?'

'Do you mean are there warlords here?'

'No. I mean who do you think is responsible?'

'I don't think *responsibility* came into it.'

'I don't know what you mean.'

'Never mind, it's a play on words.'

'No one knows who planted the bombs, Grandpa,' said Max, leaning across the tablecloth. 'We have to wait and see.'

'It's probably al-Qaeda,' said Stephen.

Grace snorted. 'What *is* al-Qaeda? Does it really exist?'

'Here's the expert,' Si said. 'Marianne, what do you think?'

'Have you ever met anyone from al-Qaeda?' said Grace.

'I've met people who claimed to support them.' They had no idea how much she hated al-Qaeda now, never having previously given them much thought.

'See? This is a girl who knows what she's talking about.'

'I've met people who believe in God, but that doesn't mean he exists.'

'What are you talking about, Grace?' said Andrea.

'Al-Qaeda is a convenient free-floating concept that attaches itself to actions and ideas we don't like and to people who want to feel powerful, that there's something bigger than themselves which can challenge known reality.'

How long can you hold your breath before you fall unconscious and your breathing starts without you? Marianne thought. You cannot kill yourself this way by your own volition. And Max is no use – I didn't think he would be.

'Marianne? said Andrea.

'What?'

'Do you think what she says is true?'

'I don't know.'

'I thought I was going to get an education,' Si said. 'I thought the girl was going to explain everything.'

'Don't nag her,' said Andrea. 'She's not a politician. She just photographs what she sees.'

'Look,' said Stephen, 'let's not beat about the bush. These people are nihilists. They believe in nothing but some black hole of destiny.'

'I thought we had established that they believe in al-Qaeda,' said Grace.

'Which you just said is nothing. Doesn't exist.'

'To believe in something that doesn't exist isn't the point. The belief is the point.'

'You get this from the Algerian, don't you, who took everything you had?'

'If you can relax people you can produce an elephant,' Ralph had once told Max. But perhaps producing an elephant would relax them.

'When we've eaten,' he said, 'I thought I'd do a show.'

'But you never do a show for us,' said Andrea.

'Well, it's in honour of Grandpa.'

'That would be wonderful.'

'I saw David Blaine many times on TV,' said Si. 'The man is a genius. If you are half as good . . .'

'I'm not even a tenth as good, but I'll do my best to please you.'

After the show, he told them that Cheryl was pregnant. It seemed disrespectful to flout her wishes, that it was bad luck to say you were pregnant until the third month, but the sight of his father's face, as he said, 'So you're going to be a grandfather, Dad,' gave him a satisfaction he rarely felt in his dealings with Stephen.

And Marianne was forgotten, except by Grace, who saw that she, too, was trying to fly away from the table and out of the room, and out out out of there.

# Stopwatch

If Marianne lays her watch on the table and waits until the second hand reaches its highest point on the dial, and then, concentrating, carefully follows the steel rotating round until it almost reaches the quarter just before it gets to fifteen – then fourteen seconds passes fast. But she has to try it five or six times before she can focus her eyes to fix on the fourteenth second. Eventually she realises that the only way to do it is with the stop-watch timer on her mobile phone, and over the course of a morning she comes to develop some understanding of fourteen seconds.

If, she thinks, you were on a descending plane and the pilot announced that you would be landing in fourteen seconds, your brain would alert you to an event that was happening right now: the wheels would have hit the runway before you really registered the passage of time. But if you were an athlete, watching the retreating back of your opponent taking the final strides to the finishing tape, it would be another matter. The fourteen seconds would pass agonisingly slowly as you willed yourself to catch up (though it might depend on the duration of the event – how long does it take to run a mile, these days?). So time is not fixed, it's all relative, just as her father had explained to her. Time has its own agenda and operates in its own interests.

Sitting at the kitchen table, waiting for fourteen seconds to pass, she is free to let her imagination roam. For as long as she can remember, her father has been a hypochondriac, detecting in every symptom the announcement of a fatal illness. A headache could be a brain tumour; heartburn is obviously a heart attack. Pain is magnified by his fear of what exactly the pain may mean. Pain itself, as a pure experience, is something different from the anxiety attached to it. But Marianne is investigating pain alone, unaffected by emotions. Pain, say, for fourteen seconds.

So, sitting in the kitchen, she takes a pair of pliers and clamps her little finger in them. She tries to hold on for as long as she can, but she finds she is able to bear a metal ache with reasonable fortitude for fourteen seconds, so next she tries putting her finger in the flame of the gas grill and doesn't last even for three seconds before involuntarily pulling her hand away in a reflex reaction that someone experiencing real pain would be denied. But that was pain's point: it was a signal to let you know something was wrong. Her father had once told her about a girl born with no sense of pain: she was a mass of scar tissue.

But how does anyone know it *was* fourteen seconds? It might have been two hours, and this is intolerable because she cannot imagine that length of time. In two hours anything can happen.

# Shoes

Meeting his father from the plane in Warsaw, Stephen had been so anxious that Si would disembark alive, in good health and not mentally disturbed at the sudden realisation of what returning to Europe meant, that he had not noticed his father's shoes. Failed to take them in until father and son were walking through the square with the folk dancers, looking around at the video-rental shop and the mini market.

'Dad, what are you *wearing*?'

'These? They're all the rage.'

Orange plastic clogs with holes in them? And since when did his father wear anything that was all the rage?

'You should try them. It's like wearing slippers all day long. I never had such comfort.'

Later, in the lobby of the hotel, his father took off one shoe, picked it up in his hands, the dust of the Polish landscape still clinging to the sole and to his sock and extolled their many virtues, how they had been engineered, and how cheap and indestructible they were. A craze had taken hold in California for these shoes. The President had a pair.

Stephen thought, I must have been in Europe too long, because to me, they seem an abomination. Their ugliness astounded him. He always wore the same white leather Nikes: He bought five pairs at a time and kept them in their boxes until one pair was too soiled to wear any more, then moved on to the next. In his side of the wardrobe were his Nikes, one pair of tan leather boots for the winter and two pairs of leather shoes, Florsheim penny loafers he had bought in Saks on a visit home twelve years ago, and black lace-up shoes from a fancy shop that specialised in footwear for Englishmen, which had been a present from his wife.

Arriving home in London, he had said, 'Dad, did you bring any other shoes?'

'Of course. These are just for sitting on a plane when your feet swell, and for sightseeing. Don't worry, I won't embarrass you.'

His father had purchased a lime green nylon fanny-pack in which to keep his money, plane ticket and passport. He had a blue baseball cap to keep the sun out of his eyes. He was ready to be a tourist.

'You don't really need that thing round your waist. All it does is draw attention to where your money is.'

'But I'll be robbed.'

'No, you won't. Give your money to me – and, anyway, you don't need to spend anything. It's all my treat. I'm rich.'

He was not rich, not compared to the neighbours, but it was a word his father understood, and the many-floored house had so deeply impressed him, with its garden and Andrea's consulting rooms, that he believed his son to be a huge success, wealthy and contented and admired. His name appeared on the TV screen at the end of science documentaries on PBS and the Discovery Channel. My son, he told everyone he knew, is an important man.

So he surrendered the fanny-pack but not the orange plastic

shoes, which he insisted were so heaven-sent for old guys like himself, with corns and blisters and fallen arches and hammer toes and all the other ailments of the foot that took him to a monthly appointment with the podiatrist, that he would not take them off for any occasion except their evening meal. Out of respect to his daughter-in-law, who cooked. And even so, who could see them under the table? But he agreed to some formality.

They set out from Islington on the bus, because Si's first request was to travel on the top of a red double-decker. Seated at the front, Si felt as if he was in the cockpit of a plane, flying through the unfamiliar streets of a city not as vast as Los Angeles – but LA, he realised, was not a *city* like London was, just a conglomeration of suburbs. Warsaw was a city; London was greater and grander than Warsaw. London to his eyes was unbearably beautiful: its houses, its public buildings, its shops, its triumphal arches, palace gates, parks, the red road leading to the Queen's house, the snaking river and its bridges, some graceful, one a kind of drawbridge, the parliament and its clock, the boats on their way to Greenwich or the open sea or upstream to Teddington lock.

The stores with beautiful clothes in the windows, watches, couches, the street markets with fruit and other produce, and cheap clothes and shoes and CDs. The blue sky under a sun warm but not scorching, not a sun anyone would ever need to escape from, even in July. And all the gardens, the roses and other flowers he had no names for, and the beautiful trees heavy with leaves and bearing fruits you couldn't eat that made new trees, little things that grew from any piece of ground they found themselves in – all making an *effort*. To grow, to be, to become.

And all the people walking and talking on their cellphones, and dressed very differently from people in Los Angeles, something more formal, more in keeping with life in a city. Everyone amazed him: when he overheard them speak, their accents sounded like an orchestra tuning up at the beginning of a musical show, discordant, crying, weaving through the words, and himself in this crowd, the American who was born on this Continent. He had the right to be part of all this.

The fur shops were all closed. The addresses he had once known, the famous furriers, were long gone. Harrods did not sell furs any more or keep them in cold storage. The people in England liked their animals: they kept them close by in their houses and they preferred a dog or a cat to the sight of a woman in a mink. It was tragic, and he was a relic of a way of life that had died under him. In his own lifetime, his occupation had been made obsolete: by whom? Moral puritans, zealots, people with no appreciation of the finer things in life, like a lovely face under a sable hat. They threw paint at such women. Barbarians. The Hollywood stars were afraid of them; they were frightened of the mob, the spoilt babies.

Stephen took him across the river to the great wheel. They stepped into a capsule that rose without the sensation of movement into the sky until the panorama of the city was revealed to him, the hills in the distance, the river winding through its banks and, towards the west, Stephen said, Oxford. This is what it's like to be a bird, he thought, not the plane, where you were strapped into your seat and could only see clouds or darkness. He wished his wife could have been here with him. Tears in his eyes, remembering her in bed next to him, her light snores, the opulence of her skin, her black hair smelling of scented oil and the bathroom full of her secret potions, which were still in the cabinets. He could not throw her away.

The magnificence of London on a clear day. 'Thank you, son,' he said. 'Thank you very much.'

Stephen, towering over his diminished father, the gnome, bent down and kissed his head. His father, he realised, retained his feeling of the wonder of the world, he was still alive, not half dead. His generation was indestructible: they had passed through the worst of what the twentieth century had had to offer, born during the first fighting in Europe. You could step on a train at Warsaw station in the year of his father's birth and step out of it at a station a car's drive from the trenches. His parents and sister were dust in Europe. He had arrived in America with nothing, begun with nothing, and had made a modest something. But its modesty belied its tremendous success: a job, a marriage, a family and no one coming to any harm. It had all taken hard work and fortitude. I have grown up with a loving father, he thought, remembering suddenly the hard whack on the side of his head as his father, turning, saw his son twirling in Marilyn's mink. He smiled. It was done from love. All love and pride and hope.

High in the air, he pointed out to his father the sights of London. 'This is the parliament. This is Canary Wharf, which is offices. This is what they call the Gherkin. This is the South Bank, where they have theatres and films and concerts.' The two men stood together, the younger with his arm round the shoulders of the older one.

'I'm glad you thought up this plan,' Stephen said. 'It turned out well.'

'I always wanted to travel,' said his father. 'It never happened.'

'But you travelled from New York to California. At least you had that.'

'Yes, of course. I forgot.'

A few hours later, when Stephen suggested that they take a taxi home, Si said definitely not. It was now time to take the famous London Underground train. The bombs the previous week seemed not to faze him, 'That was *last* week,' he said. 'They're all dead now, the terrorists. They can't come back to hurt me.'

They were at Pimlico. Stephen took him through the gates with his ticket and they stepped onto the escalator.

'This has been a wonderful day, son,' Si said. 'What a city London is. What a place! Warsaw was *nothing* compared to this. If I live for another ninety years I don't think I'll have another day like this one.'

The moving stairs went down and down. As they reached the final stage of their journey, Si's plastic shoe caught in the side of the machinery and unable to extricate himself, he fell on his face, smashing his nose against the metal staircase, which dragged him along until it came to the final step. The screams of the passengers brought someone running, who turned off the engine, and Stephen's father lay there, blood all over his face, and either, Stephen thought, dead or unconscious.

# Guilt

In hospital, shocked, sedated, Si thought, Is this my time? Does it end in this place? He shared a room with three others but he couldn't see them: he was partitioned off behind screens. The doctors and nurses came and went and he heard his son talking to them in a high, quick, angry voice. I wanted to be buried next to my beloved, he thought. Our bones belong together. I'd like to be in a soil that has the sun warming it. I don't want to be in a place that's damp.

'You're not going to die, Dad,' Stephen said. 'You're going to be fine. Everything is going to be okay. Tell me if there is pain. I don't want you to feel a thing. Are you thirsty? Do you want me to give you a drink? I have a beaker here. I can hold it to your mouth. We're going to get you out of here in a few days and your schnozz will heal in time. Everything is going to be okay.'

Not that he believed this. He had interrogated the doctors about brain damage, internal injuries and anything else he could think of from the School of Hypochondriac Medicine. They had assured him they had run the usual tests. The *usual* tests? He had watched enough medical dramas to know that the usual tests were never enough: there was always a medical genius who had a brainwave and ran the test that no one else had thought of, which revealed the rare condition that was moving through the patient's body like a death ray, aiming at the most vulnerable organs. Stephen thought of illnesses as comic-book villains: you were Superman, your illness was Lex Luther. In the comics, Superman always won; in life Lex Luther always did, in the end.

But it was only a broken nose, gashes to the face and legs and bad bruising that ailed his father. The plastic clogs were in orange shreds, lodged in the machinery of the escalator. Stephen brought in new shoes, Nikes identical to his own, soft on his father's feet. He sat by the bed holding his hand, thinking back to his own childhood in Los Angeles, and how, if he had never left America, if he had never applied for that Rhodes scholarship, had risked the draft, or gone to Canada like everyone else he knew, and returned a few years later, he would have had his whole life with his parents instead of abandoning them for this country, which had nothing to do with them or their histories.

Si was thinking about how it was possible to live an entire life based on a falsification and wondering whether the accident on the escalator was a punishment to him for telling such lies to his wife and children. This idea was expressed in his mind more woozily, an inchoate floating thought, a slight nausea in the stomach, a sense of guilt and dread. It manifested itself, in a post-morphine hallucination, as a small animal with a snout that pushed its way through the fabric of the screens around his bed. The first shot had given him a sense of overwhelming peace and happiness, not just being free from pain but a release from all suffering into a woolly realm of bliss.

The second shot was not quite so good; the third was just a painkiller. And now he felt confused and occasionally frightened, burdened with an anxiety that the truth would fall out of his mouth by accident. This trip had been a terrible mistake. He had unleashed bad things into the world, not just to himself but the poor people on the subway trains who had died a couple of days before he arrived. You can never go back. He had said that to his wife many times, when she wept for Havana. 'That's all gone', he said, and she said, 'But it's okay for you. You have nothing to go back *to*.' He said nothing. Lies on lies.

He had lived for so long with his secret and now it exhausted him. There were people who built their lives on fabricated foundations and came to believe in them, forgetting the truth; they could look back on memories of what had never taken place. The stories they told themselves became their reality, but it was a trick Si had never learned. He *did* recollect the past, and it had informed everything he had done; all his decisions had been based on what had been.

He resolved that it was time to tell someone. He could not face his son. You want your children to look up to you. You do not want to see contempt in their faces. But the wife, she was a good soul, an understanding woman: she had a kind face and a kind heart. I'll tell her, he thought, and she can tell my boy. He'll take it better coming from her.

With this decision, he felt a weight lift from his chest: the iron box that lay inside it unlocked and its burden emptied. The box folded up to the size of a dime. He could throw that dime across the room. The little animals with their snouts departed back into the screens, their curled tails twirling as they went until there was nothing left of them but a tip. Then, *pfff*, they were gone.

He could hear the voices of the nurses, the moaning of someone in pain and the smell of half-eaten meals on trays.

'Dad,' Stephen said, 'they're going to do another couple of tests, just to make sure everything is completely fine.'

Si did not need more tests. He began to feel well. He could sense his blood circulating strongly and his breathing grow more peaceful. He touched his face: the skin was warm but not over-heated. His little pulses were beating in all the normal places. He looked at his hand. I need a manicure, he thought. His nails looked to him like horns.

# Canada

'It never happened like I said. Nobody got left behind in Europe. No one died. I mean, they must all be dead now. Maybe my sister Gittel – she called herself Gertrude when she came over and had her hair shingled like the movie stars – she could be alive still, ninety-five she would be, but the rest all gone. Gittel was a good girl, even with the movie-star hair, and I was the wild one, the wayward boy.

'We never came to America, we never went to Ellis Island. If anyone is left they're in Canada. We went to Montreal first and then my father found work through one of his landsmen in Manitoba – what a terrible place, oh, awful. The cold. The horrible cold. Your eyes froze over. I don't mean the lashes, I mean the water on your eyes. You couldn't shut them, you couldn't blink. When the blizzards came and you weren't safe indoors you'd die. You could die a dozen feet from your own front door because you couldn't *see* your front door. It got cold in Poland but this wasn't cold. It was razor blades in your face. The weather was everything. And the summer, flies. That's all I remember about the summer, and the other bugs that bite.

'My father told me we were going to Warsaw because I always wanted to see that place. But what a journey! I never knew it took a train and a ship and another train and another ship to get to Warsaw. It was a month. And then we got there and it wasn't Warsaw, it was a country called Canada and I had been kidded. "When are we going home to Lomza?" I asked him. "Well," he says, "we are never going home." We lived in a slum with all the other Jews – you never saw such a slum, with everyone on top of each other and the women who couldn't talk the language and we kids having to learn and do the talking for them. I knew French once. I forgot it all. It was hard times, 1925. There was no work my father could do in a city. He was a farm man, a man who looked after horses. He smelt of horse-shit. Even before the Depression we were poor and my father hated the city life. He only liked the fresh air so he heard he can get a job out in Manitoba and that's where we went. On another damned train.

'It was a little place in the middle of nowhere and all the company you had was the sky. The stars out there were tremendous. But I never learned the names of them, I was too busy being made into a labouring boy, like my father. *Clean the yard, Go fetch the oats*. I wanted something better. I didn't know what exactly, but I hated the life. Wolves came into the outskirts of town – you heard them howling, horrible, horrible beasts. I used to dream of killing them. This is why I was so happy when I got a job with the furs. It was my revenge on all those animals that tormented me, the dogs that barked and the wild things like the racoons. I was happy to tear their skin off. The wilderness is no place for men. We don't belong there. Maybe some men do, not me.

'I don't know if I said that I hated my father. Nothing to do with the horses or lying to me about going to Warsaw. I couldn't stand him, not because he was coarse but because he was a very big man and I was hardly growing. I was going to be short, every-one could see that, and every month he'd put me against the wall where he'd made a mark from last time, and he would measure me, and every month he would say, "Not grown. Still a rat." This is what he called me, the rat. "The rat doesn't need to eat, he only has the stomach of a rat. A rat doesn't mind going hungry." And he would laugh. My mother said nothing. Many years later I realised what was underneath it all. He was saying I was someone else's. I wasn't his boy. My mother pulled down her pants for another man. I don't know if that's true – it could be. Gittel was his. She looked like him, a big girl. You know, Marianne to me looks a lot like Gittel. I never saw it at first but when she came of age, then I saw. I mean when she started to grow in the chest.

'So I was seventeen, it was 1932, and one day . . . I had enough. I don't remember it very clearly. All the things that happened afterwards rushed towards me and the incident I have trouble recalling. My father said something. I picked up an iron bar and hit him across the head. He looked like I looked when I fell down the moving stairs and they took me to the hospital, blood all over his face and in his hair.

'What did he say that provoked me? One day we went into town to the movies. It was very rare that this happened, but Cagney had just released a picture called *Taxi!* and it was a big deal because in it he spoke Yiddish, so all the Jews wanted to see this movie. To hear an Irishman talk our language. His father was a boxer, you know, and he grew up above a saloon. I saw him many times on the street in Los Angeles.

'In this movie he says, "Come out and take it, you dirty, yellow-bellied rat, or I'll give it to you through the door!" This is where it comes from, that line they always associate with him, "You dirty rat." He never said that. He said, "You dirty, yellow-bellied rat". And that is what my father called me. And he was laughing. And I hit him round the head with an iron bar. No, I don't know where it came from. It was just there.

'And I ran. I ran out and down the street. I hid for a day and a night, which is hard to do in the prairies because there is no forest, not where we were, anyway. Just land, flat land. I hid out in a barn. And then I ran to the railroad track and waited for the freight train. I jumped the train and went on riding it until I reached the ocean and then I crossed the border and that is how I came to America. My name was never Newman, by the way, it was Wollman. I was Motty Wollman. In those days it was easy to get papers – things were more lax – so all of my life I have been an illegal immigrant, a wetback, just like Stephen here in England. Yet they still gave me a passport. They never caught me. I have always tried to be a good citizen, to pay my taxes and vote, because I never wanted anyone snooping around in my affairs.

'I headed south and found myself in Los Angeles, and I looked around and I loved it. It was warm, it was beautiful. You had the ocean and the beach and the palm trees. But the thing that impressed me very much was the idea that a man could get on a ship and sail away if he was in trouble. When I met my wife, her family had big connections with the sea, with the maritime union, and this is why I wanted Stephen to join the merchant marine, because then he would always have a lifeline. You need to be able to escape, like I did. In time you couldn't ride the rails any more. But the sea is always the sea.

'I don't know what happened to my father. Maybe I am a murderer. It's a long time ago and everyone is gone. Unless Gittel is still alive, but how would I find her? Get a private detective? What for? I had a long and happy life. My wife never cared that I was a small man. My children grew up tall. I never passed my little stature on to them. I loved my wife, she was beautiful, and I had a job where I worked with beautiful things worn by beautiful women.

'And yet you cannot help thinking that one day you will be

punished. By God, maybe, or whoever else is out there. It should be the devil who does the punishing. There is a day for atonement, and a book of life, and God is supposed to write down or cross out the names of everyone in it. You cry and you rend your garments. I believe that justice is only in this world, not the next one. I don't believe in another world.

'I told a story since I was seventeen. I said they all got left behind in Europe. I saw that movie, *Schindler's List*, and I thought that if the story was true, this is what happened to my mother and father and my sister, but it's not true. Not for them. They were safe in Canada, in a little town where only the winter was a murderer. And so I wanted to go home to Poland because that is the only time when what I told of the story is not a story. It happened. There was a Lomza, there was a mill, there was a yard and there was a house. I wanted Stephen to see it, because everything else is a lie. I gave my son lies and I don't feel good about that.

'You tell him, you tell him everything and explain it to him. You know the words. There must be words that can make this right.'

# Unwrapping

When Si or Motty, whatever his name was, was in his room watching television, still bandaged, Andrea sat in the garden with a cup of pale, lifeless, milkless tea, supposed to be good for the heart, and contemplated the geraniums. Sturdy flowers. She got them in red and they usually survived the winter, the stems growing woodier. July is a strange month in the garden. It is the height of summer but the best flowers have already bloomed, the roses gone, and what you are left with are the all-rounders, the Michaelmas daisies and the geraniums. Everything is growing fast: the leaves are engorged with rainwater and sun, the grass needs mowing every few days and the dandelion clocks are shedding their spores. On the pear tree hard green lumps are appearing.

What is she to do about her father-in-law and his story? Does she even believe it? It sounds embellished to her. And should she tell Stephen anything? Her business was client confidentiality: it was not her job to right wrongs. She had urged her father-in-law to sit down with his son and make his confession for himself and take the consequences, and if he could not take them, he should not tell. She saw that he wished to unburden his mind of a secret held inside for most of his life, and that it was only the imminence of death that was forcing it out of him.

Stephen – in the years when he sat with his veins being fed the invisible ink of the Internet, the conspiracy theories, the crackpots, the propagandists – had become what he had never been in the whole of their marriage: a Jew. When she had first met him in the garden in Jericho all those years ago, when she was twenty, she had never before met a Jew. Jews were mythical creatures: like unicorns and pixies, they existed in books. Dr Freud was a Jew, of course, and many of his disciples she had studied, but that was an abstraction. In the town in Cornwall, a couple of Jews had been evacuated during the war and had vanished back to the East End of London as soon as they were able. A story had gone round that when they had arrived and were billeted on neighbouring farms, they had been ordered to lower their trousers to examine their backsides for tails.

Stephen had told her about the Jewish father and Cuban mother, and being brought up in a home without religion – America was their religion, he said, and the movies. But in the Internet period he had suddenly become one hundred per cent Jew. He had tried, on a genealogy website, to trace his Newman ancestors and failed. He had sent off to examine the records at Yad Vashem in Jerusalem and come up with nothing. He had talked to his children about how it was possible to live and then vanish from the earth, to be turned into smoke. And now to find out that none of it was real – she didn't know how to break it to him. How can you wind back your whole life and discover that a thread running through it, a red thread, is also a false flag?

She had thought for years that she had been lucky with her parents. They had given her life and not much else, and demanded nothing. Unlike so many of her friends, they were not suffering from final illnesses that required train journeys, the up-ending of parental responsibilities, the child becoming the mother or father. There was no Alzheimer's, no old people's homes and, of course, no inheritance. There was no ongoing psycho-drama. They had cut her out of their lives and, though she had been hurt, she knew that in meeting Stephen when she had she had fallen on her feet.

Her father died of lung cancer. It went through him very fast, seven months from diagnosis to the grave; he was dead at the age of sixty-two. Her mother lived on in a little flat in Keswick, eventually with a man she called her boyfriend. Lionel. The two of them went on coach trips together, visiting stately homes. She felt that her mother had finally got what she wanted from life, walking behind a guide looking at antiques, marble fire-places, maids' quarters, butlers' pantries and Persian carpets. She gazed at family portraits and fancied herself beneath the pow-dered wigs, while Lionel counted the rooms and peered into the lavatories. Then Julia died of a stroke. She took to death even quicker than her late husband.

Lionel gave Andrea her father's war medals. He had had, he said, a good war.

'But he never talked about it,' Andrea said.

'Did he not? Well, you should look him up. He was a good egg.'

Her father an egg. She found the records of his regiment. He had been, as they say 'all over the shop'; she had had no idea. He had been at El Alamein, then run up the boot of Italy, crossing the Strait of Messina, driving back Mussolini's forces and taking Rome. He had once had spunk and spit, then lost it again. She supposed that the trauma of his experiences of battle had never been dealt with, there was no counselling, no treatment. His generation of servicemen just went home and were supposed to forget all about the past. They turned their backs against history, they who were formed by it, each little fingernail growing or not according to their diet in the thirties, whether they had enough vitamins and minerals or not.

Frank had gone back into the wine trade, then met and married her mother, and they had bought the semi-detached house on the edge of London with the rows of toby jugs in the hall, the stained-glass panels in the front door that led to a garden with stiff, military flowers like antirrhinums, the pulley in the kitchen from which Andrea's rabbit had once been hung by its ears, the ottoman in her bedroom and the crows on the fog-bound lawn. Frank doggedly pursued his inheritance and they went to Cornwall. Her family history was so meagre she had never taken any interest in it. All she had focused on was the idea of the family itself, that place where the child was nurtured and grew, and where its neuroses were laid down, like DNA strands. They had executed her rabbit, but she had forgiven them that long ago.

What was the point of telling Stephen and why should she have to take on the burden of it?

'Have you told him yet?' Si said.

'No, I haven't.'

'When will you tell him?'

'I don't know.'

Until now, Andrea thought everyone could benefit from the talking cure. For the first time, in the summer garden with her pale tea, Andrea began to doubt her own profession. What would Si/Motty do with the insights he could learn from the hours he would need to spend excavating his relationship with his own father? He was an old man. He was looking not for insight but forgiveness from his son. *Would* Stephen forgive him? She had no idea, and the realisation that she did not know, did not sufficiently understand her own husband to be able to predict his response, worried her.

There was always another day. Events moved on. Marianne was extremely withdrawn and consumed with an inexplicable sadness. Grace was demanding more and more of her attention in their sessions. Andrea had two patients under one roof. If she told Stephen his father's story she would have three.

Grace came out in her green embroidered kimono, her feet bare on the patio tiles. 'How long is the old man going to be here?' she said.

'I don't know. Stephen won't let him get on a plane until he's better.'

'Stephen is just like his father.'

'In what way?'

But Grace clamped shut her mouth and refused to say more. She did not know herself why she came out with such things. It was a long-established habit, and she defended each statement with her insistence that she never had to explain herself.

She did not care about the old man. She was beginning, for the first time in her life, to feel fear. The fear that the future is a steep descent to a dark lake and people on the shore will hold your head under. She tried to think of something else, such as how she might turn the curtains in her room into a dress and how Andrea would be bound to forgive her, because she would detect in the action some meaning to be analysed, but all she craved was a new dress. She wanted one very badly. She was worn out with being her, Grace. She hoped a new dress would uncover a facet of her own personality she had not yet detected. There is always something inside you to unwrap, she hoped.

# Indecision

Sometimes Marianne gets into her car and turns the key in the ignition and feels the engine warming, her foot thrumming against the accelerator, and she takes off the handbrake, propels the Honda out of its space a few metres from her flat, drives to the end of her road and becomes completely stuck at the traffic-lights.

Should she turn left or should she turn right? For in this decision is her fate. You have the illusion you are in control, that you decide where you are going, yet these tiny decisions affect everything. There was another route to the hospital. Janek could have taken a different line. He could have eaten less for breakfast, not had a second cup of coffee. He might have noticed an inky mark on what he had thought was a clean shirt and climbed the stairs to the bedroom to change it. He could have overslept; he might have woken from a nightmare at five in the morning and, unable to get back to sleep, gone into work early. An interesting article in the newspaper or a news report on the radio could have delayed his departure, sitting at the kitchen table instead of hurrying into the hall to get his jacket and taking off down the road to the station. Or his wife could have turned to him in bed and touched him and he touched her, and he could have said, 'I'll be late for work, but it doesn't matter.'

This thought is unbearable. But she would rather imagine him having morning sex with his wife than taking off at that precise moment, leaving the house in his summer jacket and open-collared shirt to reach the station at the particular second at which his own life converged with some young guys marching towards their destinations with backpacks, who themselves could have been delayed or got there early. And anything could have happened to make Janek not on the Underground train, and yet he was, he was.

So she is paralysed at the intersection. The lights turn green and cars angrily blare their horns behind her because she cannot decide if right or left means death or life. The randomness of Fate is killing her. Had she not had her car stolen on the road to Sarajevo she would never have met Janek. The meeting had seemed to her so fated, so outside coincidence that it was unimaginable that she could instead have been sitting opposite him on the tube, a stranger behind his newspaper, getting up and leaving while she still sat, watching the faces of the passengers. Just a middle-aged man with sandy hair and freckled hands. But what was fated about his stepping on the very train – and not just the very train but the very carriage where the murderer was waiting?

And then she pulls out, to the right, because if she does not she will have to get out of her car and abandon it at the traffic-lights, walking home. There is no one she can talk to apart from Max because although she has friends, and some of them know she has a married lover, she has always been too discreet ever to tell them who he is or how she met him, and to do so now would be a betrayal, because he never gave her permission. So Lucy goes on living with and caring for the false Janek, the loyal husband and family man, who is a compassionate person, an excellent doctor, a church-attending Catholic, and an active member of an organisation that brings medical help to those in need. And Marianne is left with the real Janek, the adulterer, who didn't tell his priest everything. The real Janek who does not lie in the hospital bed, corporeal, but exists only in the change of clothes in her wardrobe and the toothbrush in her bathroom.

Marianne was in hell. Her private grief was a public event. When she turned on the television there it was. When she opened a newspaper, there it was. Everyone was talking about it, analysing it, expressing opinions, and she heard that *London had it coming* because of Iraq, Afghanistan, Palestine, or that the moderates should speak out to show their loyalty to their country, if they really were moderate, and all this chatter-chatter-chatter was irrelevant to her agony.

She took up smoking again. She had learned to smoke in her teens when she began to lose weight. Simone had told her it suppressed the appetite, and in the past Ivan had worked on tobacco accounts. Janek had told her he would not sleep with her any more when the stink of old nicotine was on her clothes and in her hair, though she knew it was medical advice he was giving her. She chewed nicotine gum and gradually lost the habit. She started smoking again because, as far as she was concerned, the worst had already happened. She often forgot to fasten her seatbelt.

When she worked abroad, she was never interested in the political questions; other photographers were, she was not. She simply wanted to be in that place where she could find an unusual range of human expressions instead of the flat complacency of people who were miserable in all the usual, banal ways.

Now she gets in her car and drives across London. They're all in on it, she thinks, looking at the women in headscarves and the men in white knitted caps. Then, recognising the stupidity of that idea, stopped at the traffic-lights changing from green to red, and a young man waiting to cross the street, a backpack over his shoulders, she says aloud, in her private box, 'But maybe *you* were.'

# Mummy

'So I did what you told me and I took the train to Kent and the weird thing was how much it was the same. You know, it's thirty-five years since I made this journey but I saw the oast houses and the wheatfields and the rosebay willowherb growing on the railway embankments, and church spires, and I could remember the names of all the flowers and the trees. I saw a flight of rooks rising from a wood and the pale sliver of moon in the morning sky, and there it all was, the sweetness of England, putrid fucking England.

'My hands were shaking. I really had the shakes. Maybe it's the DTs but it's not like I drink much. Alcohol gives me a headache, these days, and even eating hurts my stomach. When I lived with the Algerian he had a job as a sous-chef in a hotel and he got really pissed off with me because he didn't want to come home to do more work in the kitchen and I hadn't prepared any food. He used to get up sometimes on his day off and make croissants from scratch and bring them to me in bed, and I just wasn't hungry and I'd turn my head away and he would slap me hard on the thigh beneath the covers and say, "Be nice."

'I got the bus from the station, the same bus, at the same stop, and it went along the same streets, and there was the house with its four chimneys, red brick and black beams, ugly, pretentious, expensive and too big for us. Do you remember the woods? Were they still there when you used to come to stay? There used to be woods where I played when I was a child. There were foxes, badgers, voles, and beautiful goldfinches in the winter, but there were no more woods now. They chopped them down and built over them. The house seemed very hemmed in to me.

'I really didn't want to go in. I think I would have just stood and looked at it for a while and then gone back to London, but all the way down on the train I was thinking about the hats, me making hats – hats with ears and hats with horns, hats with bells and hats with whistles, hats that came down over the face with eyeholes. There's a lot of potential in hats. They're quick to make and you can design them in your dreams, more or less, so I'd decided that, yes, I would be a milliner. And that meant going up to the attic to find the hats I made before I came up to Oxford. I never showed them to you. I spent the summer designing and making them, and I wanted to know if they were still there.

'And, of course, to prove you wrong. You know, you have spent far too long with an American, who believes that everything is a problem, and so has a solution, instead of being a situation, and that all it takes to be happy is a happy ending. Because he's still the same idiot he has always been when it comes to trouble. All Americans are, not just him. Apart from the ones who made the temporary gardens – they were different.

'Eventually I rang the bell and no one answered. The house was silent. I just heard birdsong. I don't know where they nest since the woods were got rid of. I went to the side of the house where the gate was open, as it was always open when I came home from school, and I walked past the kitchen door with the lavatory next to it for tradesmen, past the dustbins, odorous and strange, and as I looked down the long, sloping garden there was my mother, bent under a cotton hat, weeding.

'She looked terrible. Her face was marked with brown age spots and her hands were like birds' claws in leather gauntlets. She looked up at me, and then she bent down again because she was working along a flowerbed, cutting the heads off chickweed.

'When she had finished she leaned the hoe against a tree and walked inside through the french windows where tea-things were laid out on a white cloth. I followed her in. I had the letter in my hand in case she was gone in the head and hadn't remembered that I was coming and I held it out to her, I wasn't sure if she even recognised me. The letter signed "Yours sincerely, Mummy".

'She went into the kitchen and came back with a pot of tea, and still she had said nothing, not a word. Finally, she spoke. "It's Earl Grey. Philip didn't like it so I didn't buy it while he was alive. He liked common tea, very dark. I hope you don't share his taste."

'When I picked the cup up to drink it, it tasted slightly sour. I said, "Antonia, the milk's not right."

'It was as if using her first name was like pulling some old thing out of a trunk. I had never called her Antonia when I lived at home, but what was I supposed to call her now? She shook her head. "Call me Mummy," she said, but I couldn't. The word stuck in my throat like a crumb.

'And then she asked about you. She said, "Do you still see your friend Andrea?" I told her I was staying with you in London and she said she supposed you were married, so I replied that you were. And then she said the most extraordinary thing – talk about breaking the ice. She said, "She wanted a husband. I suspected she was after mine." Isn't that funny?

'And in all this time she had not asked a word about me. I felt like a long-lost cousin, not her own child. She finished her tea and said she'd put me in my old room and I could take my luggage up. Of course, I hadn't brought any luggage because I wasn't planning to stay the night. I thought if I got there mid-afternoon, she would stop gardening for a few hours, but that was a vain hope.

'She stood and put the tea-things on a tray, the sour milk, the cooling pot of Earl Grey, the plate of currant-speckled biscuits neither of us had touched, which looked like they belonged in the century before last, and she said, "There's still so much light. I have hours of work to do. If you can wait until nine I'll make supper. The television reception is acceptable. We can talk then. I suppose you've come to talk."

'So I had to leave then, or stay. And I knew you wouldn't let me come back here empty-handed – it was you who forced me into it. I walked up the stairs and stood on the landing looking at the rooms that radiated out from the central stairwell. The house was succumbing to mould and dust and cobwebs and grime and subsidence. It was awful. In my old bedroom almost everything had been cleared out. Nothing was left of my childhood but a single bed, a table with a vase of garden roses, and an empty wardrobe. The desk where I did my school homework had gone. Not a book or a toy or a picture had been kept. Only the green carpet remained, with burn-holes from the cigarettes I used to smoke while I was reading.

'Yes, it was the same room I came back to after the abortion. I remember lying under the bedcovers and counting up to a hundred, then back down again. It gave me something to do. I decided I would never see James again. He had done this to me. I hated him. He had been too shy and stupid to go to the chemist and buy a packet of rubber things, so I said I'd do it, I didn't mind, but the chemist wouldn't sell them to me. I came out empty-handed and he was standing there, his face burning with the shame of me. Then we went to the woods and did it, until a walker came along with his dog and disturbed us. James pulled out in a rush of sticky fluid. "It will be okay," he said. "I'm sure it will be fine."

'All I remember about him was that he had red hair like you and wanted to be an architect. His last name has gone completely. I haven't thought about him since I went up to Oxford. It's strange to think that if I'd had it, there would be a forty-year-old with red hair, or blonde hair like mine. What a fuck-up that kid would have been.

'All the other rooms in the house had been emptied – there were just stripped beds – and in my parents' room my mother had got rid of the double they'd slept in and replaced it with a single. I felt she had ruthlessly disposed of us. She had got what she wanted, the house and the garden, not its inhabitants.

'I looked in the wardrobe. It was full of the most terrible old clothes, nothing of my father's, just her pull-on trousers with elastic waists, cotton shirts with and without sleeves, and jumpers. The smell of soil was everywhere, and everything was stained with grass and sap and roots.

'I walked through all the other rooms that had waited for new babies that hadn't come, and they were all empty too. I remember grandparents sometimes coming to stay in those rooms. I remember a moustache, a breath-smell of boiled eggs, an old lady whose hair was piled on her head and held in place with tortoiseshell combs. Cousins sometimes came, older boys and babies. I used to look inside the babies' prams and unpin their nappies to see what was hidden there. The boys played cowboys and Indians in the woods and wouldn't let me join in, until my mother came out and told them they must play with me. They took me down to the leaf-floor, where there were rabbit holes and a badger's set, and tied me to a tree, and I just waited there stoically for hours until my mother came and untied the knots.

'She said I was a silly girl to let them do this to me and that next time I had to be more firm. While I was waiting for her, tied to the tree, I thought of the story of Caliban who was trapped inside a tree by a witch. I thought I would like to be deep inside the trunk, fused with the wood. When I grew up, I was going to be a tree.

'I went down to the kitchen, which was exactly the same as it was in my childhood. My father went to the Ideal Home Exhibition in 1955 and ordered a modern fitted kitchen, which cost a fortune. In the sixties he had covered its surfaces with strips of that plastic called Fablon, which was all the rage, but now it was torn and dirty and it curled at the edges.

'Only the drawing room had any signs of life – gardening magazines, library books, a basket of knitting and a pair of sheep-skin slippers laid out on the hearth. And through the windows I could see my mother at the end of the garden, by the compost heap.

'It was six o'clock by now and there was no sign that she was coming in so I turned on the television to watch the news. God, this shitty little country, this fly-blown rubbish tip, it's sinking into the sea, all right. *Goodbye*.

'I suppose I must have fallen asleep in my mother's armchair because when I woke up the sun was well down in the garden. There were long shadows and I could hear Antonia in the kitchen clanging pans so I got up and went to see if anything was being cooked.

'"I'm making rice," she said, "and there's some tomatoes from the garden."

'She put this miserable meal on a pair of plates and we ate it in silence.

'So finally, after we'd finished, she said, "Well, why have you come?"

'I've never put up with bullshit, so why did this witch tie my tongue? I was struggling, so I just came out with it. "What did you know about Daddy?" It was an overly large question, I realise, but that was what I said.

'She sat there with her hands on the table, and soil under her fingernails. I couldn't take my eyes off them. She must have seen that I was fixated on her hands, because she said, "When you're a gardener the earth settles in and stays. Some of the ladies use dark red polish when they go out socially and your father was always nagging me to do it, but I could never be bothered. If he wanted nail polish he could get that from his mistresses. As long as he kept them in town they could have all the warpaint they liked."

'I said, "Why did you put up with it?"

'Her blue eyes were staring at me in that walnut face. "But that is what gentlemen *do*. Everyone knows that."

'I said, "In an Edwardian novel, perhaps. What about your self-respect?"

'"Such modern words."

'She cleared the plates and put a bowl of raspberries on the table. There wasn't any cream or sugar.

'I said, "I met one of Daddy's mistresses."

'"Did you?"

'"Aren't you curious about her?"

'"Don't be silly. I was never curious about those tarts."

'"She wasn't a tart, she was more of a secretary."

'"It amounts to the same thing."

'"Don't be ridiculous."

'"Secretaries are always out to pinch other women's husbands. That's the reason they learn to type. Did you bump into them on the street in London? I assume he went about with them in public. He came home reeking of scent on his evening clothes."

'"No, it was in his flat."

'"Oh, the flat. Wasn't it an awful place? That hideous decoration, like a Harley Street waiting room. I always knew your father was common, but I didn't mind because I thought that sort of thing was unimportant. The war turned everything upside down for a while, but it didn't last. My mother always said he was a bad egg. A bad egg with elocution lessons. He'd been to a teacher, you see, who had taught him not to drop his aitches."

"'I had an abortion in that flat," I said.

'Her face was stained with raspberry juice. It ran into the cracks around her mouth. Her tongue was engorged and pink. She stood up abruptly and cleared the table, snatching the spoon from my fingers. She took the dishes into the kitchen and I could hear the sound of tapwater running. I waited for her to come back. Night had finally fallen on the garden and my reflection looked back at me in the glass of the french windows, a double image. I saw myself twice. So I stood up and drew the curtains.

'She came back into the room holding a tarnished silver coffee pot and demitasse cups and she put them down on the table and said, "Why didn't you give it to me?"

"'Give you what?"

"'The baby."

"'I didn't want to have a baby. I would have been expelled from school."

"'Education isn't everything. Has it done you any good, do you think?"

"'Of course it has." Which was a lie, but I wasn't going to tell her the truth.

'She said, "You knew I wanted babies. I wanted them so much it was an ache in my body. I couldn't sleep for it. Have you never felt that? Lying there tossing and turning because your bones are hurting with the need to have a child inside you?"

"'No."

"'Then you don't know you're alive. To make something grow, that's the thing!"

"'I'm not a machine, making children to replace the ones you couldn't have."

"'You're selfish."

"'Antonia, you're the most selfish person who has ever lived. When did you ever do anything for anyone? You weren't a mother to me, you were always in the fucking garden."

"'Don't be ridiculous. I loved you – I still do."

"'And how have you ever expressed it?"

"'How could I have expressed it? I haven't seen you since you were twenty-one. You went away. I still don't understand why."

"'Because of him, of course."

"'Who? The boy who got you pregnant?"

"'No, my father."

"'Did you have an argument?"

"'I wouldn't call it that.'"

"'Oh. I see now. Did *he* get rid of it?"

"'Yes."

"'He was such a cruel man. He knew how much I wanted another child."

"'Cruel to you? What about me?"

"'What do you mean?"

"'He performed an abortion on his own daughter."

"'Well, you should have gone elsewhere."

"'How could I? It was illegal."

"'Then you could have come home and had it, and we would have been happy."

"'What a stupid idea. I wouldn't have been happy."

"'And are you happy now?"

'And then I got up and slammed the door and went to my room. I was lying in bed, dreaming. I was dreaming I was a bird and then I was woken by birds, in the trees outside the window, and my hands were trembling, as if they wanted to turn themselves into wings.

'The sun was coming up over the garden and my mother knocked and entered with a cup of tea. "I thought you might like this," she said, "though I've no idea. You always slept in and had no breakfast."

'She sat on the edge of the bed and started talking. "I see now that you believe I have not been much of a mother to you. I'll try to explain. Your father promised me babies, lots of babies, and a life in the country away from town, which I always hated. Those ghastly debs' balls and the parties and the chinless wonders and the awful stiff frocks they made you wear. I was prepared to put up with his common ways because he liked sex and he was a doctor, a children's doctor – what could go wrong? Well, me. I couldn't make them live. I went on trying until my ovaries packed up when I was forty-two, I still thought there could be a baby up to the last moment."

'I said, "You refused to love the baby you actually had."

'"What do you mean? I adored you. But you were your father's daughter right from the beginning, a daddy's girl. You were in love with him."

'"In love? I hated him."

'"You had an odd way of showing it."

'"What do you mean?"

'"Do you remember when you were thirteen and you came down to breakfast in your dressing-gown and I told you that you were revealing yourself in the chest and you should cover your-self up? And Philip said, "Let's take a look at the mammary development," and you showed him."

'"But he was a doctor, a paediatrician, I thought . . ."

'"You had a cunt, dear. That's all he cared about. He didn't ever touch you, did he?"

'Of course he didn't touch me. I wish now that he had because then it would have all been over long ago, but I just stared at her and said, "No."

"'I thought not. He wouldn't bloody dare. I warned him. I'd have murdered him and chopped his head off and buried his body in the garden and his head in the woods. So he got his revenge by making you fall in love with him.'

'But I was never in love with him – you don't think I was, do you, Andrea? She said I was. She said, "Oh, Grace, you had a thwarted sexual attraction. It was an unrequited romance. And then you went to him when you were pregnant. You silly girl."

'I said, "Why did you stay with him if you knew what he was like?"

"'You don't understand marriage. You don't just leave when it doesn't suit you. I did have lunch with Mummy but she was crowing. "I told you," she said. "I warned you not to marry beneath you." So I was too proud to admit I'd made a mistake. And Mummy said, "All men have their mistresses. You just put up with it."

"'But if you had taken me away when I was younger, everything would have been different. My whole life."

"'Yes, I suppose that's right. But you see, he promised me he wouldn't touch you, and I thought that the not-touching was what mattered."

'She stood up and said, "Before you go, I just wanted to say that your things from Oxford are still in the attic in your trunk, your books and your clothes, if you want to take them. I cleared out the room but I didn't throw anything away."

"'Where is my childhood?"

"'What do you mean?"

"'I can't see a single picture, or an album."

"'Go into the attic. You'll find everything there."

"'I'm leaving as soon as I'm dressed. I'm going back to London. Where are my shoes?"

"'I cleaned them for you."

"'You cleaned my shoes? Why?"

'"Guests always have their shoes cleaned. I was taught that at home."

'I went up into the attic and found the boxes of old things. They didn't seem terribly interesting when I saw them now, along with golf clubs, Panama hats and a croquet set. No, it was definitely time to move on. It was pointless coming. I warned you it would be. I couldn't be bothered to look for the hats.

'I went down to the garden to say goodbye. She was doing something with the roses. I said, "By the way, where did you have Daddy buried?"

'"I had him cremated and put his ashes on the compost heap."

'Is this over now? Can I stop this relentless self-examination because it's driving me crazy. Have I earned my right to stay under your roof? I'm definitely thinking about making hats. I want to be a milliner, hats with ears and hats with horns. I could make hats in my sleep.'

# Dearest Marianne

I am so sorry that it has taken so long for me to get to a computer so I can email you. I wanted you to know that I am out of hospital at long last and back at home and Lucy is looking after me splendidly, with the help of a nurse who comes in every day. I'm in a chair now and the hope is that they'll be able to fit me with prosthetic legs quite soon. They have even brought round catalogues to show me the different options available – it's like choosing a new car!

I have set up this special email account so we can go on talking, but only if you wish. I do understand how bereft and isolated you must have felt, how shut out, but I am sure you can understand that there was no other option. Now is not the moment to tell Lucy that I have for so long lived another life, with you. So you must be strong, and you must do what I have always asked – find someone, get married, have children. You don't know what you are missing and, indeed, until the attack *I* didn't really understand that family is everything. It is everything.

I am quite hopeful for the future. I know I will live with pain, but pain can be managed, and fortunately I know what to ask for, and what doses. I will return to work in a few months, though not, of course, to what I did abroad. I don't even think I want to. Lying in the tunnel, waiting for someone to come, if someone was going to come, I realised that that other world had reached out its long arm and come to me. I once said to you that you can't stop genocide with a stethoscope. I no longer know why I tried. In the past few years, the only reason I went on going abroad, into the war zones, was you, to be with you. I loved you.

And I was punished for it.

I'm sorry, darling, I'm a Catholic and I cannot escape sin and guilt and punishment and forgiveness and redemption. Right now I'm lying here learning to forgive those misguided young boys who got on those trains. Why should I hate them? What is the point? No, I pray for God's love to enter the hearts of all those who hate.

Write to me some time, if you like, but, please, don't be under any illusions that what we had before will be again. As long as you understand that.

With tenderness

Janek

# Bell Code

Max was waiting for his baby to be born. He already knew they were going to have a son and that the son would not be deaf like his mother. He would grow up oppressed by noise, by traffic, drills, sirens, alarms, shouting. The cacophony of music would assault his ears with its electric-guitar chords and the screeching voices of opera and the horrible bang-bang of drums. But he would be able to hear applause.

Cheryl had drawn up a spreadsheet of the coming expenses and how they were to be met; it made sense for her to return to work as soon as she had had the baby. Max would get up in the night when he heard his son crying while she slept on beside him, unable to hear their child.

He knew what his father thought about this arrangement. He did not know how to deal with Cheryl, was too clumsy to learn to sign, and so much of his reality was about sitting at the kitchen table holding forth about an article he had read on the Internet, usually, these days, about Muslims.

Max's grandfather was still staying with Stephen and Andrea; it had been months. He seemed not to be in a hurry to go home and the bruises on his face were taking time to subside, not surprising in such an old guy. Grace was still there and she, too, showed no sign of leaving. To Max, who, he acknowledged, did not have a well-developed sense of humour, this ménage was incomprehensible. Cheryl saw the funny side of it, the mismatched household, Si sitting down to watch a TV soap and inviting Grace to join him, the pair of them in separate armchairs, the old man near the set with the volume turned up, crouched as if on all fours, his face illuminated by its high-definition glow, Grace bolt upright, incredulous. 'So who do you think is the father of this kid?' Si would say, for all soaps seemed to depend on disputed parent-hood.

And Grace would reply, 'The one with the face like a brick, of course.'

'You think so? If you ask me, it's the good-looking one.'

It was autumn. Cheryl grew and grew. She could no longer dance and took refuge in a new hobby, embroidery. He under-stood that he had married a self-improver while he had a single fixation: learning new magic tricks. He wished his bones could be replaced by an as-yet-uninvented substance that had rubber in it so he could bend his limbs in every direction.

Cheryl told him Marianne was approaching a crisis. Marianne had learned to sign and could communicate adequately but without nuance or expression. Throughout these rudimentary conversa-tions, Cheryl watched her sister-in-law's face. There was something terrible in there, she believed. A dark implosion was imminent. She sent Max to her flat to take her by surprise and find out what she was doing when she did not have on the mask of preparation.

Max rang the bell. There was no reply. She might be out and he had had a wasted journey across London, but he rang again. He thought he should initiate a bell code with her, so she would always know it was him. After some time, her voice emerged into the street from the intercom.

The flat felt like a grave. Her laptop was on the table: she seemed to have been writing an email.

She was very thin. Years ago she had started to eat only half of what was on her plate and she had lost her excess weight, but now she seemed to eat just a few mouthfuls. He had no idea when she had last been on a job, and when he asked her, she said she couldn't work, was living off her savings.

He knew she had a couple of pals she went around with, young women from college who, like her, had not found permanent relationships. Dawn and Isobel. Together they maintained a social life but she hadn't spoken of them for some time. It seemed strange to him that she had grown up into his introversion while he had widened his social circle through his wife and all the magicians he knew on the circuit. She had made a fateful choice there on the road, when she was ambushed and her car stolen, and Janek had turned up in the UN vehicle and she had followed him like a dog because she wanted to get into Srebrenica.

He could see what she was doing: she was going the same way as their father, living life on the Internet, and the first thing to do was to get her out of the house, turn the damned thing off. He had no use for computers – Cheryl dealt with all of that. Max liked solid objects to manipulate, not screens. And his sister was being drawn into the beige box, to Email Land.

He persuaded her to go for a walk. It was late September and the trees were heavy with wet leaves from the morning's shower, but the sun was still warm on the concrete, an Indian summer, and so many women and young girls, he noticed, dressed like gypsies in long cotton skirts. It must be the fashion. But Marianne was in her jeans, and only her T-shirt strained around her heavy chest. She's becoming very gaunt, he thought, and it doesn't suit her. There were spots around her chin – she should have grown out of that by now.

They set off down the street to the park, which was full of young mothers with their children in pushchairs or running along the paths or buying ice creams. He reminded her of their childhood holidays in Cornwall, on the beach watching the china-clay ships come in and out. She nodded. 'Yes,' she said. 'We had a lovely time.'

They walked on, remembering how it was on the sand, their parents watchfully looking after them, the sun fading below a cloud haze, sand in their pants and crabs scuttling in the rock pools, their hands held by grown-up hands as they paddled in the little waves. Then the long stroll back up the hill to their rented cottage, being dried with a towel and their mother saying, 'This was my childhood too,' and their father saying, 'I grew up near the ocean, but it was nothing like this. This is just a channel, not a real sea. The sea is *huge*, kids – you wait, you'll find out one day.'

Max was filled with nostalgia for his childhood. He had been happy before they had discovered his deafness and taken him to the hospital to fix it. Long ago, the world had been quiet and peaceful and he would stand in the surf watching a silent sea. He was going to have a son and the son would hear the loud waves, but they would go there: they would sit on the same sand and it would be his arm around his child's shoulders, kissing his wet warm skin.

Marianne is never going to have a child of her own, he thought. She will leave it too late. It will take her years to meet someone else. It's all up to me to get the next generation up and running.

'Marianne,' he said, 'unhappiness can't last for ever. In a year's time everything will seem different, I'm sure it will.' He said this to comfort her. Always she had been in charge: she was his big sister and he was the little shrimp she looked out for. What could he do for her, so bereft and alone?

She turned to look at him. They were sitting on a bench by a small ornamental lake, with ducks and rushes. 'Why do you say that? I'm not unhappy.'

'Of course you are.'

'No, I still have Janek.'

'How?'

'We write to each other – we exchange emails. He's doing terribly well. His rehabilitation is coming along quite quickly and I'm convinced that when he gets new legs he'll be able to go back to his old life.'

'Has he said that?'

'No, but he misses me. That he has said. So he'll do everything he can to arrange things so we can see each other again. I'm sure of it.'

'I don't see how that's possible.'

'Anything is possible. You're a magician – you of all people should know that.'

'I don't perform magic. It's just illusion.'

'Janek and I aren't an illusion.'

'How often do you email each other?'

'I write to him every day, sometimes more often.'

'And he replies every day?'

'No, he keeps me waiting. Oh, it's hard, the bloody, bloody waiting.'

He knew he had to say something. Cheryl would not forgive him if he did not. 'Come and stay with us for a while. When the baby's born Cheryl will need help. She won't hear him crying.'

'I can't do that. *Janek* needs me.'

'You can still email him from our place. Please, Marianne.'

'You're becoming just like Mum. You always want to take care of people.'

'Will you think about it?'

'Maybe.'

They got up and walked slowly back to the flat. Max thought it would be good for his sister to learn to change a baby's nappy and listen out for its cries in the night. It might be an education. It might plug her back into the world.

# Google Search

Stephen had become obsessed with Google. He was busy all day tracing people from his past. You could reach a hand back all the way to the sixties, to Oxford, and far beyond even that, to his high school in Los Angeles and the kids he had grown up with in his neighbourhood. The members of the anarchist commune, John Baines who was best man at his wedding, the reporters he had worked with on *New Scientist* back in the seventies . . . There were many tricks you could use to track them down and, of course, the women were harder to find than the men if they had changed their names when they got married, but he had a high success rate because he had time on his hands and he was dogged.

You meet someone in 1970 and they are just starting out on their lives: they have crazy thoughts about what they want to be – you sit up all night talking to someone who says they want to be a shaman, or move back to the land and talk to trees, or be the drummer in a rock band; you are looking into a future that hasn't happened and making plans, spinning fantasies that might come true. And here they were now, over sixty, and their entire careers, which hadn't even begun when you had those stoned conversations, had already ended. There were no shamans, no rock stars: the people he had known at Oxford and in London in the early seventies had become academics, lawyers, researchers, teachers, salesmen, computer programmers, or they were found living on far-flung islands, like the dealer from his old college (*his flashing eyes, his floating hair*) who had turned up as something called a rear commodore, running yacht races in the Caribbean.

And others had vanished without trace: not even the determination of Google could find them. They had left not a single mark. Stephen supposed they had died before the Internet. Perhaps they could be located in one of the squares of an Aids quilt.

He did not know why he needed to know. He did not understand the obsession with finding out the end of the story. Perhaps it was merely curiosity, the same inquisitiveness that had led him to watch his mother with what he thought of as her chocolate-cake chemistry experiments, and his own first chemistry set. It was something to do, he thought, with probing for the truth, for answers to the chaos of life and all its messy relationships. But he knew that a life was not mathematics: there was no line of numbers to add up and arrive at a correct figure. He wasn't like his wife, who tried to rescue the drowning: he felt no urge to help anyone. He was just trying to understand how it had all worked out for him and for his generation, the ones who were born young and were going to stay young for ever because that was their privilege. Surely their parents had fought the war for them to do just that. And they had been betrayed because, despite their squawking insistence, they *weren't* young any more.

They had bald heads, dyed hair, crêpy eyelids, lined foreheads, stiff knees, and those wars going on inside their blood between the Reds and Whites: all the cancers that would eventually kill them. *This is not right! This is not just!* Stephen thought. *We are kids!*

There was a photograph of a guy sitting on the grass outside Stephen's own college room. His hair was blond and poker straight; his name was Nick Woodford. This fact was lodged inside his brain, when he had forgotten so much. And looking at the picture he could see that Nick was a deeply unhappy man. Or boy, for he was just a kid – they all looked like children and had been only a few years away from childhood. What was it in Nick's face that seemed, as soon as he looked at it, to summon such dread and despair? Maybe he'd just had a difficult tutorial, or had had bad news. Or was there something fundamentally wrong with Nick? He showed the picture to Andrea, who didn't remember him at all, and said she had no idea. So he Googled him. And produced nothing. He might have been killed in a car crash a year or two later; he might have had a sex change and be living under the name of Nicola; he might have died of lung cancer in his early fifties; or he might be one of those people who simply have no life on the Internet and therefore do not, Stephen thought, really exist. So he stayed young, lucky bastard. The rest of us just have to stumble along as best we can.

In the rest of the house, which was supposed to have emptied out, his children had been replaced by an ageing boy and girl, both dependent on him: his father and Grace. Andrea said that Grace was not inactive, she was processing the time they had spent together in therapy, but all Stephen ever caught her doing was sitting with her hands held tightly under the seat of her chair, staring out of the window. 'That's the processing,' Andrea said, but to Stephen it looked like some kind of experiment with her own body. He didn't know what that was about and neither did Andrea. Nor were there any hats. That idea had died the usual death. She didn't eat much or cost much to keep, she made no demands on his time, but he still couldn't stand having her there. She gave him the creeps.

His father, too, seemed to have settled in for the duration. He

would get up every morning and set out slowly along the pavement for Upper Street where he climbed onto the top deck of a
red bus and gave himself panoramic tours of London. This, he
said, was his education and he could do the whole thing sitting
down. He did not want his son to accompany him. 'You've seen
it all already,' he said. 'Let me be a tourist.' They all met up for
dinner in the evening and Si told him where he had been, as far
west as Kew Gardens one day, where there were palms and other
familiar and pleasant sights that reminded him of home in
California – so he had everything he needed right here and why
should he go back? There was nothing to go back to, just the
widow and her videotapes, and his far-flung daughters and grandchildren, and flights to Boston and Phoenix once a year. It was
obvious that Andrea had said nothing yet to Stephen about the
secret he had told her. He was still waiting. He had this unfin-
ished business. Meanwhile, he was enjoying an extended
vacation.

In December Stephen became a grandfather. Which is more surprising – turning sixty, losing your hair to the attrition of old age,
having no more hope of ever fitting into your maroon and white
SS *United States* cabin-boy jacket, never being part of a Nobel
team or seeing your own son, whose life you have never quite felt
to be properly on track, holding *his* son in his arms? And knowing that it is *his* job to protect the child whose head is cradled in
his hand, not yours. That your advice is unwanted and the
mother of the baby does not hear when you cry, *'Watch out!'*
because she is catching her sleeve on a pan that someone has left
on the table, and if she takes it down, she might stumble, and if
she stumbles, the baby might fall.

But the greatest surprise of all is what has happened to
Marianne, who has moved in with Max and his young family and
is effectively working for them as a nanny for nothing. Marianne

gets up in the night when the baby cries; she's sharing little Daniel's room. She feeds him Cheryl's milk from a bottle when Cheryl's out at work; she changes his nappies and takes him for short walks around the block, well wrapped up in layers of blankets against the winter cold. Her sign language is improving and she and Cheryl close the bedroom door and have long conversations, which, of course, Max cannot overhear. All he knows is that his sister is confiding all her secrets to his wife, and this is a vast relief because Cheryl is the most sensible person he has ever met, with her hard, clear head for figures and her understanding of the obstacles of everyday life.

Stephen was even more amazed at the sight of Marianne holding his grandchild. He had no idea why she had abandoned her career to become an unpaid nanny. He had been proud of her, with all her travels into war zones, terrified but boasting. Andrea said, 'I don't know what's going on but Max says we shouldn't worry. He says everything's under control and it's only temporary, she'll be back in the swing of things soon.'

'Something has happened, it has to have done. He should tell us if he knows anything.'

'Don't interfere. It's their lives, not ours. Let them make their own mistakes.'

'Don't tell me you don't worry.'

'Of course I worry. But I'm not getting involved. You can be very hot-headed, Stephen. Just leave the kids alone.'

'That's what we said to our parents.'

'And we were right.'

Andrea in her late fifties, post-menopause: taking to ageing with even more difficulty than him, sitting in front of the mirror holding her mascara wand, her face a mask of beige cream, her mouth not yet painted. He preferred her in bed at night, when she had washed it all off and they tried painfully to make love. The pain was hers, inside her. He didn't understand why she didn't take HRT, the wonder drug, but she said it scared her. Eventually he talked her into it. It starts with the pill and it ends with HRT, she thought, a life bracketed by artificial hormones.

'I only wish there was a drug like this for us middle-aged guys,' said Stephen.

'You've got Viagra.'

'I don't *need* Viagra!'

'That's true, if you've had a good night's sleep.'

Stephen watched his grandson. He had sought detailed reassurances about his hearing and had been told that everything was fine. He spent an hour a day practising sign language with limited success. Cheryl said she could lip-read him fine but he could not really lip-read her. Max was a marvellous father: he had inherited his mother's capability and her way of just getting on with it. Stephen and Marianne were the neurotics. What is wrong with my daughter? he thought. All he could think of was a broken heart. Was she gay? But why would she hesitate to come out to her parents, who would be totally accepting, if that was what it took to make her happy? Nothing made sense to him, so he took refuge more and more on the Internet, which in turns frightened and excited him.

# A Place in Time

The final email from Janek told her he was closing the account. She went on writing to him but her letters had nowhere to go. She spoke of how her heart was breaking and that he had been so cruel to her. His wife could not love him with such devotion as she did: it was not possible.

The whole city had taken part in this great public event. There was common grieving for the dead of the terrorist atrocity. People who had never met Janek felt empathy for his condition, the doctor who had lost both his legs, and she, who had been in love with him, had to share her heartbreak with total strangers. And now even Janek himself had cut her out.

He said that her daily emails were not what he had expected; he said he had not planned to continue the relationship by other means – he only wanted to keep in touch with her while they both made new lives but he had come to realise that he had led her to believe they had a future when there was none. He had spoken to his priest, confessed the entire affair and had accepted penance. It was a goodbye of characteristic tenderness, but it was, he said, definitively goodbye.

Some things come to an end, my darling, both good and bad. The war in Bosnia is long over and people go about their lives as they used to. They are renting DVDs now, not videos, and they have the Internet, but that terrible place out of time is back in time. They go forward to the future. And this is what you must do. God's love will take care of you. It is the same thing as mine.

How she loathed God.

# The Narrow Park

A delayed spring, and Marianne takes the baby for a walk along the disused railway line that has been turned into a thin park that snakes through London, from north to south. Max and Cheryl live in an anonymous block of flats, three storeys high, named Cedar Court, though there are no cedars anywhere near. There are cedars a mile west in Highgate cemetery. It is, in London, a funeral tree, coniferous and evergreen. The most famous cedars are in Lebanon, where they adorn the national flag, and there Marianne has seen bombed cedars, their trunks blackened by fire.

Halfway down the street a gate is usually open and you can pass through it to the narrow park. After ten days of rain, the sky has given a great sigh and the clouds cleared. This happened when it was dark, and when Londoners awoke the next morning, it was to a different kind of light, blue, sharp, making short, clearly outlined shadows. The sky is threaded with filmy strands of high cloud. It's what everyone calls a beautiful day, and in London a beautiful day drives people out of doors, rushing for keys and shoes, because by afternoon it will have clouded over, and a thin, drizzling rain will begin to fall with the monotony that is accepted with the usual moaning.

Marianne pushes baby Daniel through the gate and finds the path thronged with walkers, joggers, women with pushchairs, like herself, and many dogs. Max told her he had once seen horses being ridden here, huge chestnut creatures with iron feet, and she is hoping she will come across this strange sight.

The trees are still without buds. There is no sign at all of spring, apart from some twigs with catkins hanging from them. Half-frozen pools of water are filled with last year's fallen leaves. Some tree-trunks are tightly embraced with ivy and other parasites. She is like her father: she doesn't really know the name of anything – the names of the trees don't interest her: she is a London girl and has never joined her mother out in the garden with her trays of seedlings and little sticks with Latin words on them.

The path is lined with other people's houses and gardens; she can see conservatories and lawns and drawn curtains. The grass is rimed with frost. A man is standing on a lawn smoking a cigarette, looking up at the canopy of bare trees in which birds' nests are clearly outlined. Not much birdsong at this time of year.

Occasionally the trees clear for a few steps and the city spreads out to the east, unfamiliar, moving towards the estuary and the Tilbury docks and the sea, and then the trees close in again and she is walking behind her nephew, occasionally looking down at him to see if he is okay, but the motion of the pushchair always sends him straight to sleep, a small face slumbering beneath a hat, dressed in a Babygro, a jumper and several blankets and the canopy up to protect him from the wind, which still has the winter's bite.

Marianne has settled into a dull, tenacious grief. She can no longer bear to hear about the events of 7 July. She doesn't care about the identities and motivation of the four young men who travelled to London and got on the trains and the bus and blew themselves up. She can't stand listening to her father droning on about Islamism, a word he's picked up from the Internet and which means, he says, not ordinary Muslims, of course not, but religion fused with political ideology to form a kind of Fascism. Shut up shut up shut up, she thinks.

Max keeps telling her that in a year the grief will have died down; she will taste the sweetness of life once more. How can she be unhappy when she looks at the face of his newly born child with all his features in the right place, the nose in the middle and eyes above, the mouth and adorable little ears on either side? A child who cries and gurgles and hears and is beginning to form smiles.

She's an excellent nanny, he says. It's because she's responsible and good with her hands, and because having to respond to the needs of someone entirely dependent on you and not lie in bed brooding on your fate is a challenge to which she has risen. But she doesn't want to be a nanny for the rest of her life. Nor, she realises, does she want her own children. She has thought about it enough.

When she met Janek she accepted that when he left Lucy, as he was *bound* to do (only her parents and Uncle Ivan being so unfashionable as to stick to the same spouses their whole lives), he would probably not want to start a new family: he was already in his forties. As time went on, she understood that Janek wasn't going to leave his wife for her, that *she* was that place outside time. He was always telling her that he felt guilty for stealing her child-bearing years, but she didn't care. She was a photo-journalist: what business did she have to give birth to small dependent creatures?

Now she no longer had the urge to travel abroad. She didn't care about wars; she didn't care about floods and earthquakes and refugees and extra-judicial killings and occupation and imperialism and child soldiers. She actually wanted to shut all that out, she realised. Over the years she had amassed a collection of photographs of waiters: waiters with oiled hair, wearing long, spotless white aprons, in grand Parisian restaurants, and waiters in grubby shirts, laying a few tables in a bombed building with a sign blown to smithereens and just enough crockery intact, because life has to carry on, eating has to carry on, everyone has to eat. There were almost enough for an exhibition, Max pointed out. He liked her collections of people types; she could do conjurors next – he could get her the necessary introductions, and why not start with him?

She sat down on a bench, Daniel still sleeping. It was true that these sudden rare sunny days in winter made you feel exultant, she thought. Something soared inside you, the spirit leaped.

More and more people were making their way onto the path. It felt like a national holiday. Some ran fast and some ran slowly; some walked arm in arm in good wool coats and patterned scarves, as though they were parading along a European boulevard, and others were dressed as if for sport, in tracksuit bottoms and fleeces, and they were talking or they were lost in their own thoughts. A trio of three urban youths with paint in their pockets.

And dogs.

All her life Marianne had been denied a dog. Her father had stamped on that desire. Dogs marched up and down and ran and chased their tails and fought with other dogs and mounted them and strained on leashes and were carried in their owners' arms, like babies, and came in a huge variety of shapes and sizes and colours.

After a while, she started to watch the dogs. The dogs came over to her and she held out her hand and they licked it. She smiled at them: the dogs seemed to smile back. They had large brown or black eyes, which stared into hers. She began to consider the dogs' faces and their expressions. It was important, she thought, not to anthropomorphise them. They weren't human; feelings like joy and interest and indecision were human traits. No, they evidently felt something else. They felt with their noses, black and wet. The whole urban path was a banquet of scents whereas all she could smell was bark, faintly, sludgy pools of decaying leaves and dog shit.

A dog with smooth, hazelnut-coloured fur walked towards her and stood looking at her, its tail wagging. No owners were in sight. Marianne looked back at the dog. It has a face, she thought. They all have *faces*. Not just the usual arrangement of features, the eyes, the nose, the upright wagging ears, the lipless mouths: it all came together in a face as full of expression as those of the waiters and warlords. The dog reminded her of an army officer in Bosnia she had once seen leaning against a wall lighting a cigarette. He had stared at her over his long nose and allowed her to take his picture, smoking. The same arrogance and curiosity.

Marianne and the dog were transfixed by each other. What is it thinking? she asked herself. The dog's black eyes appeared to understand everything. The two of them could probably communicate by some form of telepathy if she tried hard enough. She would tell him about Janek and her tragedy and it would wag its tail, knowingly.

Daniel slept on for a few more minutes until an acorn from the tree he was parked underneath snapped from its twig and hurtled down, sharply tapping his sleeping face. He awoke with a howl. The acorn had drawn blood on his cheek. The dog barked sharply and ran off. Marianne attended to the baby, picking him up and holding him in her arms, dabbing the spot of blood away with a wet sleeve. But she went on looking after the disappearing dog.

# Fur

Si tried to avoid seeing the pictures of dogs spread out on the dining-room table. How many more of them were coming? She kept putting another one down and he had to look at these terrible creatures.

He knew he had outstayed his welcome. He had been there for months, waiting every day for Andrea to tell his boy the big secret, but she wouldn't do it. If he wanted Stephen to know, he would have to tell him himself.

His son was a big shot with time on his hands. He didn't have to do a day's work and still he was wealthy, drove a very nice car and owned this beautiful house. He had everything. Why should his own father take from him his self-respect by revealing a secret Si believed to be sordid? Only Andrea, the good soul, could present it in a way that would soften the blow, and she wouldn't, no matter how long he waited.

He could not find the words. The ones that had come so easily to him when he was talking to Andrea, with her sympathetic face, dried in his mouth when he thought of sitting down with his son. 'Your old man might be a murderer and your grandfather was a brutal, sadistic old-timer. You have nothing to be proud of.

You come from trash, at least on my side.' No, he couldn't do it. Better to let the girl soften the blow.

Although she wasn't exactly a girl, but that was how she seemed to him next to the old lady who was not so old, in fact the same age as his daughter-in-law. She was still there in the house too. They had settled into a routine of watching TV together and, just like the first night, *gornisht mit gornisht* came out of her mouth. For one thing, she didn't know anything worth squat about Cuba, even though she had been there and he hadn't. She talked to him about that island and the guy with the beard his wife had detested.

'My late wife could never go back there,' he told her. 'You have no idea what a beautiful place it was in the old days before the war, when the big gamblers from New York used to take a plane down there to the casinos. The women had to leave their minks behind. It was warm every evening. She told me all about it – she used to watch them in the streets with their American clothes and their wealth.'

Grace had plenty to say in reply. Most of it he didn't understand, and the rest he didn't listen to. The communists were like this: they had stomachs full of words they spat out at you, but words were all they had. The capitalists had everything else, the houses and the cars and the lovely women and the factories. This had always been the side he had been on. Of course, he was a union man, but that was because the union fixed your pay, no other reason. The union took care of a man in ways the boss wouldn't, but that was as far as it went.

All winter he tracked down the remaining fur salerooms. It was a tragedy what had happened. Not a single woman he had seen in Stephen's neighbourhood wore a fur. He heard they still wore furs in Europe, but not here. In Italy, which had the most stunning women in the world, apart from Cuba, they kept their furs but in England a fur was a hated thing.

It was hard times for his old business. He heard stories of how the furriers kept going by paying peanuts for second-hand furs that no one else wanted and remodelling them for wealthy Eastern European women who passed through London. Did they know, he told them, that Yoko Ono had a whole room in her apartment for her furs? Or, at least, she used to; he didn't have any up-to-date information. The old men mourned past times, when you could walk along the street even in Los Angeles and every wealthy woman had her mink or an exotic like an ocelot, and women who couldn't afford anything better had a fox-fur collar on their cloth coat. During the war, in England, when times got very tough, the furriers had had to resort to cats. They laughed when they remembered this. The good times were the fifties when a mink stole was all the rage. Such a wonderful garment: a lady could wear a stunning strapless evening dress and the stole kept her shoulders warm. It was very practical, and why had it fallen out of fashion? A woman earned her fur coat, the gentleman in Mayfair said. When she was forty and her husband was starting to have affairs with chorus girls, then he had to give her a pricey fur as compensation.

Now they cut their wives off, divorced them for trophy wives, there was no honour left.

The pictures of the dogs kept coming. All kinds of dogs were passed across the table, all shapes and sizes and colours. Si tried to concentrate on their coats: some had lovely pelts in cream and honey and brown, and others had short, tight black fur, and the poodles were all curls. But her pictures showed you very little of their bodies, and nothing of their tails. These were dog portraits, close-ups. The faces of the dogs with their dark eyes looked up at him from the table. They had expressions – you could see that however much you wanted to deny it. She had caught the inner lives of dogs, Andrea said. It was an incredible thing to do and this was just her early experimental work. She was getting a grant to put on an exhibition; she had a commission from a magazine; everyone was crazy about her pictures – she already had requests to buy prints and it was obvious that some would go eventually for high sums. The soul of a dog, the spiritual essence of a supposedly dumb animal.

'Not so stupid after all, Stephen,' Andrea said.

But Stephen still couldn't stand dogs.

The dogs looked at Si and passed judgement. It was time for him to go home to Los Angeles. He couldn't live in a house where every day a new dog was going to accuse him of being an accomplice in murder of all its fellow creatures. The dogs seemed to imply he was a Nazi. To hell with dogs.

Later that afternoon he told Stephen he was going home. In the time they'd had together, father and son had developed an easy relationship, one that neither cared to investigate or analyse. His father, Stephen thought, was a man of his own time, a hard worker and provider. He had earned the right to be a tourist in London. He reminded him of the time he had tried on Marilyn Monroe's champagne mink and had been whacked round the head for it.

'I don't remember that at all,' Si said. 'When did this happen?'

'But I dined out on that story my whole life,' said Stephen. 'I thought you thought I was gay or something.'

'You – gay? It never entered my head.'

Stephen thought it was possible that he would not see his father again. He was so old, he might not survive until the summer when he planned a short visit to LA to check up on him. At the airport he held in his arms the fragile little man. 'I love you, Dad,' he said.

'You made a hell of a life for yourself here in England. I can't criticise a thing. Thank God you never went into the army.'

'I know. Isn't it strange how it all turned out? You came to America and I wound up back in Europe. I never meant to.'

'Call it Fate.'

Stephen let his father go through security and into the departure lounge. He had bought him a business-class ticket: he was going to be comfortable.

Across the Atlantic, darkness enclosed Si's mind and he died. Failing to rouse him with infibulators, the crew had no option but to cover him with a blanket and on he flew across the ocean, no longer susceptible to air pockets or turbulence or the terror of take-offs and landings, peace.

# Bed

The froggy day is always returning.

The crows are back. They are hopping towards the house and won't stop coming. Someone has left a back door open and they are inside, navigating the kitchen, walking on their scaly feet towards the stairs where she lies in bed waiting for them, and Stephen can do nothing to prevent their advance. He can't protect her. It drives him wild. And Andrea needs to protect Stephen from his own failure. It's out of his hands.

She must find the strength to counter them by the power of positive thinking, which doesn't kill crows – she hasn't been married to a scientist for thirty-seven years to believe that, but fear itself can make you ill.

Returning to the froggy day, Andrea understands for the first time that though she had analysed her childhood she had never returned to it with the affection of nostalgia. She had not been an unhappy child. There was so much in the past to comfort her.

She thought about the radio programmes she used to listen to on the walnut radiogram in the sitting room of the house in Barnet. 'Do you remember, Grace?' she said. The lady with the cut-glass voice who came on in the early afternoons, after the shipping forecast, with its mysterious place names and terrible weather. German Bight. She imagined a German with huge teeth. 'Are you sitting comfortably?' the lady asked. 'Then I'll begin.' And would tell a story about teddy bears.

The programme's name was *Listen with Mother*. Neither her mother nor Grace's was often there to listen with their daughters, so perhaps the woman in the radiogram was the surrogate mother. She was incredibly nice. You could not help but love her. Her name was Daphne Oxenford, the prettiest, most melodic name in the world, and the simple piano music tinkled with the words. Deep, deep comfort to remember Daphne Oxenford and find the theme tune on the Internet, listening in bed on Stephen's laptop under a snow white duvet with a cup of green tea by her bed, which her throat found difficult to swallow, though she must drink it, so parched was she.

When they moved to the hotel in Cornwall there was a television room housing a huge piece of equipment with a tiny grey flickering screen set inside a monstrous mahogany cabinet and concealed behind a set of doors. It was turned on at lunchtime for the benefit of any small children staying in the hotel. They were provided with a special sandwich meal and Andrea was permitted to watch with them. Inside the grey screen she saw a strange doll called Andy Pandy with strings coming from his arms, hands, feet and shoulders, which her dolls didn't have. There was a family of clothes pegs, and two rustic men made out of flower pots who also lived in flower pots in a garden with a large talking weed thrusting up between their adjacent homes. To the accompaniment of xylophone music, hand puppets called Rag, Tag and Bobtail, (a hedgehog, a mouse and a rabbit) moved around a *papier-mâché* set.

Grace was unable to share fully in this intense nostalgia for a fifties childhood. Her parents had not bought a television until

1960 and she had spent those years playing in the as-yet-unbuilt-over woods. She knew the names of birds and plants and wild animals, and they had had three cats, whose litters she had seen born and then found new homes. She had ridden horses and been driven out on Boxing Day into the countryside to watch the hunt. She had been half promised her own pony and had gone to gymkhanas. She and Andrea had both read the same horsy books, but Andrea had never put her foot in a stirrup: there was no time for her to be taken on any pursuits like this – her parents were always too busy. She had the sea instead, the rock pools, the scuttling crabs, her bucket and spade and her friendship with the (harmless) ice-cream-van man.

Andrea returned more and more frequently to the house on the edge of London before it turned into Hertfordshire, the stained-glass shields in the panels of the front door and the pools of coloured light that fell on the parquet hall floor, the brass stair rods that she used to count when she had learned counting, the cupboard where the electricity meter was kept and the red and black wires, her doll Elizabeth, whose empty body cavity she had filled with water. Out in the garden the coal hole, the marks on the grass where the air-raid shelter had been, the beds of upright flowers, tulips and antirrhinums, which was the hardest word in the world to spell, the privet hedge, the rockery. Her mother in the grey early-winter light sweeping the ashes from the grate and building a new fire from black, glittering, dusty coal, the immersion heater and the airing cupboard, where clothes that had been taken down from the overhead pulley in the kitchen were left until they were bone dry. Green caterpillars crawling across a leaf, cabbage white butterflies, the garage where her father's Humber was kept, and also the washday mangle through which her mother fed the wet clothes. And Nunny hanging by his two ears from pegs in the kitchen's steam while the kettle boiled, and outside the fog advancing and retreating and the crow on the lawn looking up at her as she stood balanced on the velvet cushion of the window-seat, and her ottoman with all her picture books and toys (except Nunny), safe inside it. And the wallpaper was a recurring pattern of more rabbits, eating nettles.

Marianne drove to Barnet and found the old house, photographed it and brought a print to her mother. 'It looks exactly the same,' Andrea said, examining it in hands whose fingernails Grace had painted, at Andrea's request. She had done them an aggressive pillar-box red. Her wedding ring shone gold above them. 'It's just as I remember, and even the garden has the same rose-bushes. Do you think they're the originals? Do roses last so long? What's their lifespan?' How strange, she had thought, that the garden roses in her childhood home would live longer than she would.

Whatever fears we are prey to in childhood, she thought, it's so easy to be happy when you're two years old, waking up every morning and the memories of the day before are wiped clean. Even little children who are cruelly treated still smile; happiness has to be beaten out of them. Of course, she acknowledged, it's in childhood that we are building our neuroses, and God forbid, if you *are* abused and neglected, something can go so badly wrong so early that it can never be put right. But, on the whole, childhood is the time of our greatest happiness. Even Grace conceded this, remembering herself on her mother's lap, her mother singing to her, and Andrea tried as best she could, through the meditation classes she had been taking, to recall and restore what it was like to be a small, loved child, through the successive and horrifying nausea of chemotherapy.

Going back deep into her own past for hours every day, watching old episodes of *Watch with Mother* on YouTube, she feels comforted. These programmes can sometimes be as good as a strong painkiller, though she is very much looking forward to morphine, which Stephen had described to her, having observed his father's sudden happiness in the hospital after the escalator fall. The pain is worse than she expected, but she resents it mainly for preventing her from putting everything in order. From the start the diagnosis wasn't good. Cervical cancer is hard to detect in its early stages and she had missed one smear test, being too busy with patients to turn up. Now the cancer is all through her – it is secondaries, it's in her lungs, she'll die. It's just as she'd always thought: that it would be Stephen, with his neurotic hypochondria, who would have nothing wrong with him. And she, the healthy one, would die young.

Not really young, but she feels young – that is, she has no idea what it feels like to be old.

Stephen had forced Grace to go to the doctor about her shaking hands. He said to Andrea, 'She's got Parkinson's.' She hadn't: it was hypoglycaemia, low blood sugar. She just had to eat at regular intervals. When she did, the tremors stopped and she gained weight. She looked better than she had in years, without the eyes in shrunken sockets, outlined with black, and the wrinkles of her face filled out a bit with the extra fat. But Stephen had not foreseen his wife's cervical cancer – no one had – until she finally told him about the pelvic pain. In fright he took her to the emergency room at the hospital and sat and waited until she came out, white as a sheet.

*Why her?* Why my wife? Stephen screamed. *She* didn't care about why: she cared about what was going to happen now, if she was actually strong enough for the chemo and the radiotherapy, and whether it would offer her enough hope to be worth it. She could accept her fate, have a few months with her family and go, but Stephen went mad. How could she *not* put her trust in science? Sure, it may not always deliver, but you had to try, you had to goddam try.

She tried.

Now, lying in bed with the laptop, watching *Andy Pandy*, her mother's pet name for her, she wishes she hadn't bothered, had devoted her remaining time in the world to closure. For she feels that when she leaves her children behind, as she is going to, they will be in a state that seems to her to be similar to the moment when, as a therapist, she would suggest to her patients that they could manage without her. This often produced tears, anger and panic in the patient.

But Marianne had had a wildly successful exhibition of dog portraits, timed to the publication of her coffee-table book. She was constantly in demand from private clients to take close-ups of their dogs' faces, which seem to reveal the soul and essence of their pet. She had no plans to travel abroad to cover any more wars and she was seeing a dog breeder, who came to the house with the smell of dog on him, which Stephen couldn't stand, but Marianne was happy. This is all that matters. And Andrea's grandchild Daniel is three years old and loves his grandma, and tries to climb upon her knee but she is too tired to lift him and hold him in her arms and plant kisses on him, so Max lifts him onto the bed so he can crawl all over her, and she feels only sorry that she will not see him at five or ten or fifteen.

Her kids will be fine. Stephen will meet someone and remarry within a couple of years, of that she's certain: he's the type who cannot stand to be without a wife; he is simply not cut out to be single and never has been. He hasn't been on his own since his junior year in high school and she expects that a year will be about as long as he will be able to take without going out to look for someone else. But Andrea does not care because she knows that she has had the best of him. Someone else can come along and deal with the old age that will fall upon him soon enough, which she knows only too well he is going to deal with very badly indeed. Ivan will fix him up – she has already told Ivan he has permission to do so. 'But not anyone too young, Ivan. And please, promise me, not Mary Bitch.'

On some days she is terribly bad-tempered and shouts at her husband. She wants him to leave her alone. She is in pain and he is clumsy when he turns her in bed.

There was no one alive but her, she thought, who knew about the crows on the lawn, unless others were looking from the window that morning out at the fog and saw a bird staring up at their house. So when I die, the memory dies and the past ceases to exist, though I told Stephen, but that's just a story to him, like the mink stole is for me. I only see it through his recollection. The fog was all over London. In the winter of 1951 there must have been many others who experienced that blanking, frozen whiteness. But how many *remembered* it? It was possible that she was the only one.

She knew she had been born the year after a terrible winter when the trains were frozen on their tracks and lights were turned out for hours, and her parents were still hungry with rationing. 'It was so bloody cold,' her mother had said. 'That was when we started to talk about Cornwall, because the climate was milder. It was the Riviera of England – of course, they don't tell you anything about the rain and the estuary flooding. The winter was worse than the war, in my opinion, apart from the bombs, of course. We were all starving and your hands were numb and you went to bed and did whatever you could to keep warm, if you were married, that is.'

So I was conceived in a dreadful winter, she realised. If the weather had been milder there would have been no me. But everything was a game of chance, like Stephen moving into the house next door and the don's fountain pen rolling towards his fume-hood and the torn-out page of the library book, the party in Highgate, the walk across the Heath and the limpid midsummer morning below Marx's tomb.

And some clerical drudge in the university who had assigned her the room next to Grace's in college, and forty years later they still knew each other. How to account for this? She didn't know. She had been tormented by friends, colleagues, patients telling her to go some non-medical route: homeopathy, crystals, the power of positive thinking, herbalism, meditation, a visit from a shaman who would exorcise the cancer demon. Seeing Andrea sitting on a bench in Highbury Fields, with her post-chemo bald head, wisps of white hair, a woman actually approached her, sat down and said, 'Cancer comes from repressed anger. If you could let out your feelings the cancer would be driven away.'

Telling Grace this when she came home, Grace offered to go out into the park and find her, so she would see what unrepressed feelings really looked like. 'The stupid, stupid cunt.'

Grace was prepared to bathe her, to lift her in and out of bed, to inflict medicines on her that she did not want to take. She did it dry-faced. Stephen could be in the middle of a simple task, like preparing a light meal, and would begin to sob and run from the room. His heart was already broken while his wife was still alive. Andrea couldn't stand this. Grace carried on as normal. She behaved as if she was merely doing her duty, as if she had been asked to load the dishwasher or take the rubbish out. Nothing had changed in her except that she was healthier and Andrea was dying. She never acknowledged that Andrea was on her last legs: she seemed to think that the sun rose and set as normal and tomorrow would be another day.

Stephen spent hours on the Internet researching cervical cancer, sending emails to medical centres in the US and Canada. He was certain that there was some new treatment that could cure his wife or delay her imminent death. He opened window after window trying to see through to light. You could not absolve yourself, he thought, of the duty to look for a medical miracle, because medicine was always advancing, it was pushing away at disease. He believed that Andrea could be cured if only he spent enough time online, and he preferred the Internet to carrying her to the bathroom and holding her upright as she sat, urinating. He disliked the smell of her diseased body; the sight of her bald scalp repelled him. These thoughts thrashed around in his mind like bloody fish, taking a pounding against the rocks.

Grace's creed was to *always say what I think, and if other people can't handle it, it's their problem.* She remembered when she had worked on the movie and the director had disagreed with her ideas. She barged into his hotel room to argue with him and found him lying in the bath. She had started laughing. 'What are you laughing about?' he screamed. She crooked her little finger. And went round bending that small finger to everyone she met: 'Like that.'

'But why would you *do* that?' Andrea had asked her. 'You must have known you'd be fired.' Grace said she couldn't help herself – and why not? It was true.

So now she said to Stephen, 'I don't know why you spend so much time with that machine. She's dying, face up to it.'

Maybe because she had grown up on the edge of a wood and seen dead animals out there, shrews mutilated by foxes, badgers with bloody claws, life wasn't a sanitary thing for her. Her mother had probably drowned the three cats' kittens in a bucket of water when she wasn't looking. Out in Latin America, babies died of hideous diseases; in New York ghosts with canes shuffled along the pavement to the Aids clinic. One of the women who had made a temporary garden had a tremendous goitre on her neck; it looked like a second head. If Andrea had to wear nappies at some point, she'd change them. Stephen was a sap, a baby – he always had been. He was to her exactly the same now as when she had first met him: one of those Americans who believe that there are problems with solutions, rather than situations that have their own internal life and momentum. His relentless optimism made her laugh. Didn't he know how ridiculous he was? She fed Andrea a soft-boiled egg with a spoon and Andrea opened her mouth like a baby bird.

Grace rebuffed Andrea's attempts to thank her, let alone give her a weak hug, or take her leave before it was too late, before she sank into a coma.

When she tried to remember Andrea standing outside her room, frozen, intimidated, having turned the handle of the wrong door, and Grace had seen her, in her terrible clothes and dreadful carroty hair, she could clearly recall her initial sensation of withering contempt, even disgust. At home in Sevenoaks, Grace had usually designed and made her own clothes and had arrived at Oxford with a trunk full of them. She knew she didn't look like anyone else. No one had hair as short as hers: they all wore it parted in the centre, curtains falling either side of her face. Her own was cropped like a man's. Grace had style: the girl in the hallway was not even a slave to fashion. She had never seen anyone so appallingly dressed.

Grace remembered that she had taken this at first as a sign of some kind of originality, not that Andrea came from the back of beyond: Grace's parameters only included the Home Counties; there was London and its commuter belt. But when she questioned her about where she was from and heard that she had grown up in a hotel (Grace's idea of pure freedom, having stayed in one or two in France), and learned that Andrea was, even better, effectively homeless, she felt jealousy for the first time.

'What will happen at Christmas?'

'I don't know. I expect something will turn up. I'm not worried. If I have to I could get a job as a chambermaid in a hotel – they always provide accommodation and it's bound to be busy at that time of year.'

Grace understood that she was dealing with someone who had an inner toughness that she herself had not, with all her exterior confidence, achieved. But why was the girl so intimidated by her? 'You look like a frightened rabbit. What's the matter with you?'

'I don't think I fit in.'

'Why would you *want* to fit in?'

Andrea considered this question in a new light. 'Now you put it like that, I'm not sure. I just don't want to feel that everyone knows what to do and say and I don't.'

'I can teach you that stuff.'

'Thank you. I'd appreciate it.'

'You need to throw out your clothes.'

'I can't afford any new ones.'

'You can borrow mine.'

'I'm too fat.'

'Then I'll make them for you.'

Grace now sat on the edge of Andrea's bed, stiff, silent, rocking her body. What she wanted to say was too difficult. It might come out that she regarded herself as a parasite and Andrea as the host. It was a way of interpreting it that Juan, in Ibiza, had pointed out.

'I knew the first time I met you,' she said, 'that someone like you would always be all right, that you'd get what you wanted, that you could take care of yourself. And if you could take care of yourself, then you could take care of me. You were that type.'

'But I was practically suicidal.'

'You always say that, but I don't think you were. You were tough. You always have been. You took what you wanted the minute you saw it.'

There had never been affection between them, they did not even kiss each other on the cheek after long absences – but Andrea knew that Grace had taught her to see; she had taught her to walk around with her eyes wide open. She had taught her colour, form, texture, light and shade, proportion. She was almost entirely her creature from that point of view.

Grace had, she once told her, a profound understanding of surfaces. While Andrea was too busy looking past them to the secrets, the things people couldn't say, what made them tick, Grace didn't care about any of that.

Her life was like scaffolding: it held her up from the outside.

The pain became very difficult. The nurses came and administered injections but there was always too much time between them. Stephen was permanently on the Internet now, looking up anaesthesia.

Andrea's nose seemed very large in her face – it had taken it over. It seemed to Grace to be her biggest feature. The children had been and gone; they were arriving every day to sit with their mother. Max performed little tricks for her on the covers of the bed. He could pull a billiard ball from behind her head. He could do things with the abandoned wigs in the wardrobe that made her laugh feebly. Marianne told her about Janek; she felt that this final unburdening would allow her mother to stop worrying about her. 'It's all over,' she said. 'I hardly think about him any more, and I'm happy now. We've adopted a new puppy and we thought you'd like to give it a name.'

I am back in a bedsit, Andrea thought. She lived in her bed and was helped to the toilet. Out of the windows the trees were losing their leaves and the sky had assumed a flat, grey aspect. She disliked this median season between autumn and winter. Stephen always hated it. The house next door had sold for nearly three million pounds, he said. She had always been right about everything. She had made them rich.

But she could not pay attention.

The room is growing smaller until it's just her hands on the sheet and the square of pain around them.

'Grace,' she said, lifting a weak hand to the pillow her head rested on.

Grace's strength was that she had no reverence for life. After a moment, she lifted the pillow and did what Andrea had asked.

Stephen was walking up the stairs. He stopped to straighten a picture. This is how they killed Jesse James, he thought. Shot in the back, straightening a picture. When all this is over I'm getting into drugs again. I don't care what they do to me. You need something for the kind of pain I have.

He opened the door of the bedroom and saw Grace kissing his wife's cheek and closing her eyes.

'Where has she gone?' he cried. 'Where is she?'

# The Bonfire

When Andrea had seen her last patient, had found new therapists for the ones who wanted to continue and severed those who were merely dependent on her, habituated to arriving every Friday morning merely to talk over their week, she asked Stephen to burn her notes.

She was at the stage of her illness when she had accepted that there would be no recovery. Her calmness astonished him. She was making meticulous preparations for her own death, while the thought of dying terrified him, of being summarily wiped out, reduced to zero. But she was what she always had been: competent and philosophical. She was exactly like this when they had moved to London, to the squat, and without telling anyone had navigated the complicated buses and gone to the Savoy Hotel and found herself a job. It was typical that she should approach death with pragmatism.

She told Grace that she did not want Stephen to be faced with the task of disposing of her clothes. 'Please do it for me. The next day would be best,' she had said. 'Don't let Stephen have to look at them in the wardrobe, and make sure you remove the shoes. They bear the imprint of the foot and are practically part of the body. And my makeup, don't leave anything. I don't want vestiges. I want to leave memories.'

She had died leaving behind order, in the moments that Stephen had lingered on the stair.

His job was to arrange the funeral, to get the death certificate, to mourn, to comfort his children and then be left struggling on alone, attempting to work out who he was now that he was a single man. This one task of clear-up, of destroying her files, seemed to him to be an odd request. Why didn't one of her therapist friends take it on? But she had insisted that he must do it.

He had rarely entered her consulting room, on the second floor. It was her space, painted in a shade of white that she said had the idea rather than the form of lilac in it (he hadn't understood a word of this). There was no couch: the patients did not talk lying down, like in the movies, but sat in a low chair separated from Andrea by a coffee-table with one object on it – a box of tissues to weep into. The whole place ran with a river of long-dried-up tears. It depressed him. She spent all day in here. All day. Wearing her expensive jeans and white T-shirts – my uniform, she said – and a cashmere cardigan in winter.

It was, to Stephen, a place of sobs and little joy. Had she ever cured anyone? he once asked her. 'I'm not a doctor,' she replied curtly. This made him wonder if the whole of her career was simply a long progression of partial failures. How did she measure success? What measurements could you use? Where were the studies and experiments that analysed whether a patient had recovered? But she refused to answer his dogged, pedantic queries. 'You don't understand,' she said to him. And he didn't, and lost interest.

She was paid very well; she had no shortage of clients even though she didn't have a particular specialisation, preferring to stay as a generalist dealing with whoever needed her and with whom she struck up an intimacy. She wasn't right for everyone, she told him. Some patients required pushing and others coaxing. She was a coaxer. Some preferred a male therapist, others a woman. It was like starting a relationship that could progress into a temporary marriage. Crazes came and went; eating disorders were a permanent source of income, then childhood sexual abuse and the brief fad for recovered memory. But, as far as he understood, the women and fewer men who rang the bell of the house in Canonbury did so because they were merely unhappy.

Well, now *he* was unhappy. He had not burned the notes when she asked him to. She wasn't dead yet, so why should he? In the back of his mind was a hope that somehow there could be a recovery, a reprieve. There were always new drugs, new clinical trials; the whole of his career had been focused on the notion of scientific progress.

'If you had lived a hundred years ago,' he once said, when she had rashly expressed the view that nothing ever really changes, that we were primally the same people as our cave-dwelling ancestors, with all the same instincts, 'your teeth would have rotted from your head by the time you were thirty. You might have died giving birth to Marianne. There was no penicillin when your own parents were kids, so you could have been killed by influenza. And think about the pain. In the past people put up with the most intolerable torture because they didn't have a simple aspirin, let alone ibuprofen. If you broke your arm, they'd amputate it, because they didn't know how to set bones. Without anaesthetic. The people in the past were fatalists, they believed that nothing could change, that God decided everything, they were powerless. We're *completely* different. Everything that goes on in our heads is hard-wired to understand that there is the option of change, and change is in our own hands, not some guy on a cloud.'

The horrors of nineteenth-century people, who lived without

showers or toothbrushes or tampons or electric light or central heating or airlines, made him weep now. For in a hundred years' time, his great-grandchildren would say, 'And in the olden days, when a woman got cervical cancer *she died!*' And a hundred years after that, cancer would be a disease from the history books, like bubonic plague. 'And they *irradiated* them. Shoved chemicals into their systems. It was as barbaric as leeches.'

So he would not burn her patient notes while she was alive because, although improbable, he could not discount the hope that medicine could save her. Two months after her death Stephen built a bonfire in the garden out of wooden boxes he found in the basement that were from before their time – they might have been from Ralph's parents' day – and the furniture from her consulting room, which he broke up with a rented chainsaw and carried outside. He was not a man who was good with his hands or had ever built a bookshelf. The feeling of power tools in his hands frightened him, it was usually Andrea who stood on the stepladder and made holes for rawlplugs.

The weight of the chainsaw, carving her blue sofa, felt good. Ergonomically his hands fitted the instrument; it seemed designed for him. He looked round the office. Apart from the armchair, what else could he cut up with it? Once he had started, he thought, he might take down the whole house, beginning with the bed she had died in. He could go completely crazy with that thing, and then wreak havoc on the streets. Sometimes he thought he might go to a firing range and learn to shoot a gun. He wanted the experience not just of hitting the target but the explosion in the barrel, the bullet in mid-air taking his heart out there with it – zoom.

When he had sliced the rug into spaghetti strips and carried it down to the garden, he opened the filing cabinets with the keys she had instructed him to find in her desk drawer.

The oldest files dated back to the seventies, after they came back from America and he was facing what he regarded as the end of his life, the finality of the voyage on the SS *United States*, the reverse emigration, marooned for ever on the shores of an old continent, the Statue of Liberty behind him, its frozen beacon lighting the paths of others into safe harbour, freedom.

He read a few files. People's problems are so trivial, he thought. They believe they have difficulties; they don't. Her earliest patients had been seen at a rented office she shared with three other recently qualified therapists, so he could not put any faces to the details of their quiet or noisy despair. He read her notes, made with a red biro in her neat handwriting with its careful loops: 'Worked to death. Needs a holiday.' 'Always in control. Always insists she's right. Heading for major breakdown.' 'Obsessive compulsive disorder. Will get him into trouble if he's not careful.' 'Sexual abuse? Or subconscious?' 'Raped on street. Developing general fear of men.' 'Possible schizophrenia, refer elsewhere.' 'Transference. Get rid.'

He put all of the seventies and all of the eighties into a cardboard box and carried it down to the garden, went back upstairs to collect the nineties. In some of the files he found cassette recordings – he remembered she had bought a tape-recorder so she could listen back to some of her more recalcitrant patients, make detailed notes and discuss them with her supervisor, a woman in Highgate with a page-boy haircut that had turned an even and becoming shade of grey as the years passed. She always wore grey, dove grey, steel grey – graphite, anthracite – and turned up at the funeral in white: the Far East's colour of mourning, she explained.

Andrea herself had gone to be ash in the fire of the crematorium.

The tape-recorder was on a shelf, obsolete technology. He had fixed her up with a device that transferred the voice files onto a laptop. After he retired it was his job, every week, to do the technical work of updating her files. He showed her how to listen back to them. After several tries she got it, but then she became ill and the patients were sent away.

He put a tape in the cassette deck. A moaning woman's voice was emitted, talking about her useless husband. There was no Andrea there at all, except for some brief, muffled, faraway questions and the sound of the tissue box being moved across the table.

Good God, he thought. She spent all her life listening to *this*! How could she stand it? The nineties went into a crate. He wasn't sure what to do with the tapes. It was probably illegal to burn them, releasing toxic fumes into the atmosphere, but where else could they go other than to a landfill site? He had no idea how long a cassette tape would take to corrode.

The final decade of Andrea's life, and of her career as a psychotherapist, was the one he was most eager to discard. She had been, without either of them knowing it, sick and growing sicker. It was patients and their trivial anxieties that had prevented her going for a routine screening. Which patient? he had asked her. But she said she couldn't remember. She knew she had cancelled the appointment because someone had rung with a crisis and she had simply forgotten to make a new one, had ignored the slips of paper that came from the doctor, reminding her to call. Some stupid bitch had sat there, droning on about her self-inflicted or imaginary misfortunes, while his wife was being bombarded with disease. If he'd known her name, he would have punched her.

But also in the 2000 files were Grace's notes. Andrea had instructed him to hand them over to Grace in person – 'That is, if she wants them. If not you can burn them with the rest, but it's up to her. And anything else you find.'

'What else *would* I find?' he had asked, puzzled.

After her father-in-law had died on the plane crossing the Atlantic, and Stephen had returned home to California to bury him in the plot alongside his mother, Andrea had thought that perhaps she should tell him Si's secret. She had discussed it with her supervisor. But what, Andrea asked, was the point? Then he would be left with a situation without resolution. The old man had not had the courage to face his son, and she believed it was best to leave him with the comfort of illusions. Stephen had admired his dad. Why should she take that away from him?

So the story was still there, in the files, and she was conscious that he might come across it, and then she too would be gone, unable to help him. She wrote her supervisor's phone number on the file, and a note: *Is briefed. Call if necessary.*

Stephen thumbed through the files, pausing briefly at one with his own initials, SN, and inside a tab that said, 'Si Newman'. The sheets of paper inside were the notes that Andrea had made during the session, and stapled to them was a more detailed account of what he had told her. He went to the laptop and ran through the sound files. There was one he had uploaded with the name SN.

Having mutilated and destroyed the sofa, he was obliged to sit on a metal upright chair in her office as he heard his father's voice telling a story to Andrea that neither of them had chosen to reveal to him. Listening to the account of the whacking of his grandfather, his father's confession that he might be a murderer and was, anyway, not what he seemed, that the stories of his lonely solitary journeys across America were only stories, fictions, lies, Stephen felt ... Well, what do I feel? he asked himself. *She* would have tried to drag this out of me. She'd be nagging away, *What do you feel, Stephen?* The truth was, nothing, numbness.

When a person loses sensation in a limb through paralysis and they touch it, it feels as if they are touching someone else's leg. He knew this because he had made a documentary about it. When he probed his emotions now it was as if he was observing, with dispassionate detachment, the rage and hurt and betrayal of a stranger.

Numbness, which was replaced by a spasm of irritation: how *dare* the old man visit on his own son these outrages? Didn't he have enough to do, grieving the loss of his beloved wife? And she had indeed turned out to be his beloved, no faking that. Sweet Andrea with the carroty hair, the green velvet dress, the large eyes, the parted lips, the stink of patchouli oil, the blood on the sheets, the love of his life. There had been no other, nor would there be. She had left him alone in perpetuity; he had to deal with that.

Yet he might never have come to England, not applied for a Rhodes scholarship, or been rejected, or never got into that stupid scheme of manufacturing tabs of acid and been discovered and sent down. Had he stayed in America he might have avoided the draft by doing his doctorate there and getting successive deferments. Who would he have been if he had stayed in the States? Not the husband of Andrea but of some unknown woman with different unknown children. And that wife would still be alive: he would not have chosen unwittingly a girl with a fatal flaw, a clock ticking inside her, down to her sixtieth birthday and then a black line drawn under.

He felt a spasm of longing for this other wife, the one he had never met and the children they had not had together. The sensation made him feel sick, dizzy with nausea. That she existed, somewhere in America, the girl he would have married had his father not sent him to sea, given him the taste for travel, sent him off on the SS *United States* and made him apply for the Rhodes scholarship when he graduated. He wondered whom she had married, his girl, and whether they were happy or if he had been a no-good bum who beat her or left her, or if she had been the one who had done the leaving. Had been a two-timing bitch or a career woman who would have left any husband long behind.

Once, they had talked about an alternative society. Now he understood there were only alternative realities. He thought about his parents, how little he really knew about them. They both came with a big story, of how they arrived in America, the two immigrants who started from scratch and built new lives as Americans. It was possible, this narrative told him, for anyone to be reborn, to commence a new identity. It said, *Believe in the future*, and he always had. That was their precious gift to him, his birthright.

He had been to Poland, seen the small town on the plain, but he had never thought to go to Cuba, partly because his mother had sworn she would not return until the man with the beard was gone and her island was restored to what she thought of as the sweetness of the old days. But she had been barely in her teens when she left: what would she have remembered?

I have spent my whole life trying to surge forward, he thought. I've tried to fulfil the destiny they gave me, to be a new son of America, and always failing because I was trapped in Europe.

Perhaps Andrea and Grace were both right, that America and the whole idea of rebirth was an illusion. His past in the Los Angeles suburbs seemed now no less mythical to him than his father's stories of his determined orphan journey across the continent. There were no more soda fountains, no one walked to school, no one wore a poodle skirt, like his sisters, or went to Saturday movies.

But what he really could not get over was the sudden realisation that, for all the arrogance of his own generation, born to be young and stay young for ever, their parents were simply far more interesting people than their children would ever be. Even Andrea's father, whom he had never met, was supposed to have had a war record, to have been a brave man, broken, Andrea guessed, by post-traumatic shock disorder.

And as for him, what had he ever done since he sailed the

oceans on the SS *United States*? Not much. Worked in a doughnut-shaped building accumulating a pension and amassing equity in a house in a now-fashionable part of town (though its desirability was waning: everyone, he was told, was moving on to Notting Hill). A couple of his documentaries had been up for industry awards, he had attended the dinner in black tie and waited for his name to be called out, prepared to bound to his feet and run to the stage with his speech in his jacket pocket, but it was always someone else's name. His early documentaries had been wiped – the tape was needed for something else – the rest were never likely to be re-transmitted, except maybe in far-flung parts of the world on cable stations, where you still found decades-old episodes of *I Love Lucy*, and *Friends* was broadcast in a never-ending loop.

Finally he found Grace's file, and the link to the sound file on the laptop. Was he supposed to read and listen to them? There had been no instructions to hand them over to her in a sealed envelope.

Down in the garden the bonfire was waiting. He had only to put a match to it and his wife's career would burn.

He sat down and began to read. A few pages in, he went into the house and rang Ivan.

Blonde curls long gone, like disappearing soap bubbles, Ivan the butterball in his Paul Smith shirts and Crockett & Jones shoes, was rich, contented, still happily married against all predictions that he would be on his second or third trophy bride by now, childless, residing in a mansion on the other side of Upper Street, whose vast rooms intimidated his old friends with their show-off modern furniture imported from Italy. But still the bumptious character of the days when they had sat in the Jericho garden, smoking grass.

Grace spoke of him as if he were a caricature of himself, but to

Stephen Ivan was always the same person. He sat unselfconsciously patting and kneading his stomach as he talked, as if he were proud of his corpulence. Ivan didn't go to the gym, didn't jog, didn't eat lean protein, didn't worry about aches and pains, showed Stephen the first articles about Viagra and said, 'Look what God has given us now!'

'Ivan,' Andrea said, 'has the gift of happiness.'

'Anyone rich can be happy if they feel like it,' Stephen said. 'I'd like to see Ivan struggle with a mortgage he can't afford.' But Ivan had investments; a guy in New York looked after them. The man was a genius, he said. His shares were always rising, though it was hard to get into his fund – you needed a personal recommendation.

'I don't understand how shares can always rise,' said Stephen.

'I don't either. They just do.'

Stephen had no head for finance. He wished he had a guy in New York.

The two men sat in the conservatory looking at the unlit bonfire, winter birds balanced on the fence. It was a cold, clear, bright day in March. Ivan had come from Belsize Park, where he had been having lunch with his father. The old man, in his nineties, was still in the same house Ivan had been brought up in, the house where once there had been an Arabian-nights party and Stephen had dressed up in a costume made by Andrea. He was still toddling off slowly down the road to Swiss Cottage and coming back again with a newspaper, solely for the exercise. He was working on his book, *Trials of the Century*, the century being the seventeenth, and the decade the forties, one of extreme anarchy and anti-establishment views suppressed by the coming bourgeois administration. 'My father loves the Levellers and the Diggers, all that crew,' Ivan said. Stephen had never heard of them. He would get a large obituary in the *Guardian* if he ever died, which Ivan thought improbable.

'My son is a snake-oil salesman,' he said of Ivan, and smiled with a row of hideous English teeth, a smile nonetheless of real affection for his boy, one of a small brood of brothers who had fanned out across London and the Home Counties, larger-than-life characters, blond men who had the class confidence Stephen had been studying for forty years.

Their fathers were very different, but Stephen said that one of the things they had in common was that they were good boys who loved their parents. They had not been abused or neglected; they had been taught how to be decent men.

Grace's notes were on the table in the conservatory.

'Poor Grace,' said Ivan. 'She was so beautiful. What's to become of her?'

'You don't have a theory? You usually have some bullshit explanation. What do your guys have to say about all this?'

'What guys?'

'Marcuse, Reich – were they the names?'

'Wow, I haven't thought about them for years.

'They *were* bullshit, though, weren't they?'

'Not necessarily. I told you, we were throwing out a great deal of stuff, we were thinking a lot of new thoughts, and it was just a matter of separating the gold from the dross.'

'But most of it was dross. What did we accomplish?'

'I don't know.'

'It seems to me now that our parents led far more significant lives than we did. That generation was more interesting. Wasn't your father in the war?'

'Yes. Intelligence. So was my mother, for that matter. Whatever she did was so hush-hush she never breathed a word of it. But, then, my mother was a masterpiece of restraint. I suppose she had to be, living all that time with him.'

'And what have *we* done that was so important?'

'Look, Stephen, you have to accept that we're all condemned

to live in our own times, our own little period of history. We've been terribly lucky. You wonder if the luck is bound to run out, but we've had it made. I don't know what we could have done to transform the world when it had already been transformed for us. The people who won the war and made the peace did that. It's a hard fact to swallow – for us, I mean, our generation.'

'No, that's not right. They just cleared away the junk and we were supposed to build on top of it. What about orgone? What about turning the whole world on? The ideas were nonsense from the beginning. We screwed it up because we had no idea what we were doing. We never thought it through.'

Ivan, he thought, was the kind of guy who would have made it whatever age he lived in: he had been born lucky. As for himself, he had given everything he had to the idea of progress, to science. He admitted everyone was healthier and probably wealthier but still, in his own life, the rocket had burned out, fallen to earth.

Something was wrong with the economy, he wasn't sure what. Max reported getting fewer corporate gigs. Only Marianne's dog pictures seemed immune from the mysterious downturn, or whatever it was. Maybe things would pick up by the summer. He hoped so.

Ivan was waiting for the moment to tell Stephen his news. He had been holding on since before Andrea's death. He didn't want him to think he was being abandoned by his oldest friend, left alone in the too-large house that Ivan had observed Stephen seemed to be in the process of ransacking. He had seen the chainsaw: he knew that Stephen was capable of taking down his whole life with it.

'Simone and I . . .' He looked at Stephen, whose face seemed to be growing blacker, his forehead kneaded with lines and knots, rage tightening his mouth. He's not even close to getting over her, he thought. I don't know if he can ever be fixed up with someone new. He's already had the love of his life.

'Yes? What are you and Simone up to now?' said Stephen, turning. 'What are your plans?'

'We're leaving London.'

'What?'

'We're moving to the Caribbean.'

'When did you decide this?' Numb and heavy, like a log, he could roll off the chair and fall senseless onto the grass.

'We have lots of money and no kids and we want to live in a beach house and learn to sail and walk around with no shoes and drink all day. We want to go to pleasurable rack and ruin. The guy in New York has made us so much money we can do it.'

'When are you going?'

'In the spring, I hope. We're putting the house up for sale and going out to Bequia next week to find somewhere to buy.'

Stephen had never heard of Bequia. Ivan explained its beauty and attractions. He was definitely going to buy a yacht of some kind, for racing. This was what retirement was supposed to be, an advertising-supplement existence, while Stephen remained in the strangling embrace of this *numbness*.

'You'll be welcome any time,' Ivan said. 'You can come and stay as long as you like, no time limits. We'll make sure we have a permanent guest room for your sole use. You might fall in love with the place, like we did, and stay there.'

'I have children,' Stephen said, 'and a grandchild. I'm not going anywhere.'

For he had already thought of returning to America – at last he was free to do so – but return to what? To a continent of strangers, apart from his rarely met sisters. How would he live, totally alone?

'Plenty of time to think about it,' Ivan said. 'We just wanted you to know.'

Grace came into the conservatory. It was the middle of the afternoon and she had already poured herself a drink.

'I have your file,' Stephen said. 'Do you want it?'

'No. You can put it on the fire, if you like. By the way, my mother has finally died.'

This was what she was like, abrupt and harsh.

'No tears, I suppose,' said Ivan.

'Of course not.'

'What's happening to the house?'

'Which house?'

'Hers. I suppose she left it to the Royal Horticultural Society?'

'No. She left it to me.'

'There's a surprise. So finally you're independent. You're not going to give the money away, are you?'

You'd better not, Stephen thought, elated at the idea that he was finally getting rid of her.

'I'm going to live there for a while.'

'You? In Sevenoaks?'

'I have an idea about something I want to do with the garden.'

She was going to bring the poor and the dispossessed, the homeless and the mentally ill, the crack addicts and the glue sniffers to live there and let them make temporary gardens. She was not stupid. She realised they would burn the place down in a week, fights would start, there would be stabbings, and eventually everyone would be arrested, including her. It was a concept of wanton destruction, but someone would be outside, planting and watering: there were always a few. She had met them in Harlem. They did exist.

She was stubbornly, suicidally true to her principles. Andrea would have tried to talk her out of it and would not have succeeded. She could sell the house and buy a nasty flat somewhere, a place to rot. She would rather go out in a conflagration. The fire would extend out to lick at her mother's rosebushes, her hedges and hollyhocks and hydrangeas. The earth must be blackened before anything real can grow from it. She had always known this; it was her reasoning. In the garden were the bones of her brothers and sisters, the products of all those miscarriages. Her mother had buried them beneath the roses. Grace's father's ashes were there, and soon her mother's would be too.

At peace, she took her notes from the table and placed them on the bonfire. 'You can set a match to this any time you like,' she said.

After she returned to the house, Ivan said, 'Oh dear.'

'Much good all those sessions with Andrea did,' said Stephen. 'She's nuttier than ever.'

'She's stayed true to the sixties, I suppose.'

'It's a shame the sixties didn't stay true to us.'

Ivan stood. 'We've got people coming for dinner later. Why don't you join us? Have a shower and scrub up. Put your suit on – it'll make you feel like a different person. We've got a couple coming who already own a house in Bequia. They're bringing some pictures. I think you'll like it there – you always were a man for a palm tree.'

Stephen nodded. 'I'll think about it.'

He was a shallow person, Ivan, but a loyal friend. Shallow people, he thought, can be very good at heart. And he has had perpetual good fortune – he always will, with his man in New York and his island and that gorgeous, well-chosen wife and her subtle nips and tucks.

It was growing very cold. The bright morning had clouded over and a faint, fine drizzle was coming down over the garden. If it turned to hard rain, there was no point lighting the bonfire. Still, he had no urge to return to the house. He went on sitting.

Half an hour later Grace came back out. 'I found these,' she said, holding the rabbit jacket Stephen's father had sent from America when he and Andrea had got married, and still in its box, the mink hat, never worn. 'You should burn them,' she said. 'Some poor animal died to make these things.'

She laid them on a chair and returned inside. He tried to muster up affection for her: she had been wonderful when Andrea was dying, far better than him at washing his wife's frail body, helping her to the bathroom. The two of them had some lifelong bond from which he had always been excluded. Watching her kissing Andrea's face, moments into death, he thought that her name now, for a fleeting instant, suited her. She had already closed his beloved's eyes.

The wind was biting. Spring was only a month away but icy winds had blown in from the east. Across the Continent they flew, from Russia, Ukraine, all the cold places.

He picked up the fur jacket and draped it over his knees. He used the mink hat as a muff to warm his hands.

After a few minutes he heard the front door slam. Grace seemed to have gone out. He didn't care where.

Max let himself in and walked though the house. He saw his father sitting in the garden. He's got so old since Mum died, he thought. He had always cringed at the idea of his father: a noisy, overbearing presence, too American, too opinionated, too talkative, too much. He had once said, 'My father is like everyone else's father, only more so.' Stephen, to him, had an overdose of vivacity. Now his father's face had taken on the early shape of old age, the dewlaps round his chin, the grizzled hair, the chicken neck. I should tell him I love him, Max thought. Someone's going to have to from now on.

Yet his father, like all parents do to their children, seemed to him to be a mystery, a person of secrets. They keep so much from you and tell you stories, and the stories are just tales, like legends. He still was not entirely convinced that his dear dad had once eaten *petits fours* in a cabin below the water-line with Bill Clinton.

He watched his father slip his arms into the rabbit-fur jacket and put the mink hat on his head.

The smell of Andrea, her old patchouli scent, was suddenly impregnating his own skin. Tears poured down his face.

I don't understand, Stephen thought. How does it come to this? We were supposed to be so special, we were going to change everything and it turns out we're just the same, apart from that oddball Grace. He worried about his kids: they were going forward into an uncertain future. The world was warming – he had checked out all the climate-change science and the icecaps were melting. Disaster was waiting. There were floods and earthquakes and tsunamis.

He suddenly felt a rushing of air and a weight on the top of his head. A bird had landed on him: it was surveying the garden from the vantage-point of the mink hat. He waited for it to depart. A bird, absurd.

The rain passed, the bonfire waited for the match.

# Acknowledgements

A number of people kindly answered my questions about various aspects of this novel. So my thanks go to: Judah Passow, who really did work as a college-student cabin boy on the SS *United States*; Carmichael Wallace, who explained about proteins, biochemistry, labs and how to get sent down from Oxford in the 1960s; Margaret Rustin from the Tavistock Centre, who very kindly met with me to discuss psychotherapy training in the 1970s; Nigel Pike, who did a bravura job of defending advertising and explaining the significance of soap powder; Melvyn Atwarg, who didn't explain how magic tricks are done but explained the general principles of how magicians fool us; and Pam Dix from Disaster Action, who volunteered some hours to outline the after-effects of disasters on the surviving relatives and friends. I deeply appreciate the time that H. D. Miller, native-born Californian, took to read the completed manuscript and point out such matters as the temperature of the Pacific and suburban living arrangements in 1950s Los Angeles.

Once again, Antony Beevor and Artemis Cooper provided writer's respite in Kent, and Conny and David Ellis fixed me up with a house in Fowey where Andrea's childhood gradually came into view.

My agent, Derek Johns, and my publishers, Lennie Goodings at Virago in Britain and Alexis Gargagliano at Scribner in the United States, have been great supporters of this book, and I am very lucky indeed to have such a dedicated and talented team around me.